MEN · ON · MEN
2
· BEST · NEW · GAY · FICTION ·

EDITED AND WITH AN INTRODUCTION BY

GEORGE STAMBOLIAN

A PLUME BOOK

PLUME
Published by the Penguin Group
Penguin Books USA Inc., 375 Hudson Street, New York, New York 10014, U.S.A.
Penguin Books Ltd, 27 Wrights Lane, London W8 5TZ, England
Penguin Books Australia Ltd, Ringwood, Victoria, Australia
Penguin Books Canada Ltd, 10 Alcorn Avenue, Toronto, Ontario, Canada, M4V 3B2
Penguin Books (N.Z.) Ltd, 182–190 Wairau Road, Auckland 10, New Zealand

Penguin Books Ltd, Registered Offices: Harmondsworth, Middlesex, England

Published by Plume, an imprint of New American Library, a division of Penguin Books
USA Inc. Published simultaneously in Canada by the New American Library of Canada
Limited, (now Penguin Books Canada Limited).

First Printing, November, 1988
12 11 10 9 8 7 6 5 4

ACKNOWLEDGMENTS

"Snapshot" by Allen Barnett. First published in *Christopher Street*. Copyright © 1986 by
Allen Barnett. Reprinted by permission of the author.

"Life Sucks, or Ernest Hemingway Never Slept Here" by Tim Barrus. Copyright ©
1988 by Tim Barrus. Published by permission of the author.

"Anything You Want" by Christopher Coe. Copyright © 1988 by Christopher Coe.
Published by permission of the author.

"The Boys in the Bars" by Christopher Davis. First published in *Christopher Street*.
Copyright © 1987 by Christopher Davis. Reprinted by permission of the author.

"Red Leaves" by Melvin Dixon. Copyright © 1988 by Melvin Dixon. Published by
permission of the author.

"The Age of Anxiety" by David B. Feinberg. First published in *Mandate*. Copyright ©
1986, 1988 by David B. Feinberg. Reprinted by permission of the author.

"Why People Get Cancer" by Anderson Ferrell. First published in *The Mississippi
Review*. Copyright © 1986 by Anderson Ferrell. Reprinted by permission of the author.

"Magic" by Gary Glickman. Copyright © 1988 by Gary Glickman. Published by
permission of the author.

"Nobody's Child" by David Groff. Copyright © 1988 by David Groff. Published by
permission of the author.

"Adult Art" by Allan Gurganus. Copyright © 1988 by Allan Gurganus. Published by
permission of the author.

"Once in Syracuse" by David Brendan Hopes. First published in *The James White
Review*. Copyright © 1986, 1988 by David Brendan Hopes. Reprinted by permission of
the author.

"Solidarity" by Albert Innaurato. Copyright © 1988 by Albert Innaurato. Published by
permission of the author.

"AYOR" by David Leavitt. Copyright © 1987 by David Leavitt. Published by
permission of the author.

The following page constitutes an extension of this copyright page.

5

HIGH PRAISE FOR *MEN ON MEN*

"THE SPECIAL PATHOS, THE AMBIGUOUS HOPELESSNESS, THE SURREALIST COURAGE AND WIT THAT EMANATE FROM THESE PAGES ARE UNIQUE TO THE GAY MALE AUTHOR TODAY. . . . He is a writer beleaguered and thus must be heeded."   —Ned Rorem

"A SUPERB SELECTION. . . . ALTOGETHER, THE BEST GAY FICTION AROUND."   *—Kirkus Reviews*

"*MEN ON MEN* IS ONE OF THOSE RARE BOOKS THAT HOLDS APPEAL FOR THE SEASONED FICTION WRITER as well as for someone who is just being introduced to the works of contemporary gay writers. It is for anyone who enjoys fiction that entertains, astonishes, illuminates, and lives."   *—San Francisco Sentinel*

"SOME OF THE BEST GAY FICTION, PAST, PRESENT AND FUTURE. . . . It's a treat to have it conveniently collected. And it's a treat to read. Hopefully the word will now spread about the riches of gay writing."
                                              —Martin Bauml Duberman

"A survey course of the very best gay fiction that is available today and one that deserves all the superlatives it is bound to receive."   *—Bay Area Reporter*

"A DAZZLING COLLECTION OF SOME OF THE BEST NEW FICTION I'VE READ IN YEARS . . . should be of interest to all readers who are interested in the contemporary world and in contemporary literature."   —Julia Markus

---

GEORGE STAMBOLIAN teaches at Wellesley College. He is the author of *Marcel Proust and the Creative Encounter*, *Male Fantasies/Gay Realities: Interviews with Ten Men*, and the editor of *Twentieth Century French Fiction*, *Homosexualities and French Literature*, and MEN ON MEN, available in a Plume edition. He contributes to *Christopher Street*, *The Advocate*, and *The New York Native*.

CONTENTS

INTRODUCTION

THIS NEW COLLECTION of gay fiction by contemporary American writers builds on the success enjoyed by the first volume of *Men on Men* since its publication in 1986. It also reflects the continuing vitality of a phenomenon described in my earlier introduction—the extraordinary renaissance in gay letters that has been taking place since the late 1970s.

Here are a few of the novels and story collections published in 1986 and 1987: Tim Barrus's *Anywhere, Anywhere*, Joseph Beam's black gay anthology *In the Life*, Christopher Bram's *Surprising Myself*, Christopher Coe's *I Look Divine*, Christopher Davis's *Joseph and the Old Man*, Larry Duplechan's *Blackbird*, Gary Glickman's *Years from Now*, David Leavitt's *The Lost Language of Cranes*, Armistead Maupin's *Significant Others*, Stephen McCauley's *The Object of My Affection*, Ethan Mordden's *Buddies*, David Plante's *The Catholic*, James Purdy's *The Candles of Your Eyes*, and George Whitmore's *Nebraska*. Already scheduled for publication in 1988 are: C. F. Borgman's *River Road*, Christopher Davis's *Valley of the Shadow*, David B. Feinberg's *Eighty-Sixed*, Robert Ferro's *Second Son*, and Edmund White's *The Beautiful Room Is Empty*.

These titles represent only a fraction of the hundreds of

books now appearing every year on all aspects of gay and lesbian life: poetry, drama, science fiction, mysteries; a variety of nonfiction works from biographies and books on AIDS to an impressive list of scholarly studies on art, literature, and history. After adding the growing number of lectures, films, and theatrical performances related to gay subjects, one can more correctly speak of a gay cultural and intellectual renaissance whose impact on American society is becoming increasingly evident.

I have included at the end of this book a list of reviews that regularly accept fiction and essays on gay topics. Although the list is selective, it does indicate that writers now have more outlets for their work. Also, while independent gay presses continue to publish important works of gay fiction, there has been a marked increase in the number of mainstream houses entering the field. American publishing, it seems, has finally recognized two related facts: that there are many fine writers treating gay subjects, and that an audience eager to read their work is now solidly in place. In a world where economic considerations are always crucial, gay fiction has become good business.

Few of these achievements would have been possible without the work of past writers who transformed the literary treatment of homosexuality, encouraged others to write, and developed a strong readership. Many are also reading gay fiction today because their interest in gay life has been aroused by the considerable attention AIDS and its social effects have received in the media. Certainly, there are ironies in this situation, among them the price paid by thousands of men whose talents have been lost to us all. Just as the first anthology was dedicated to a young writer, Richard Umans, so this collection honors the memory of an extraordinary editor, William Whitehead, who demonstrated the commercial viability of gay fiction by nurturing the art and careers of such writers as Robert Ferro, Doris Grumbach, Steven Simmons, and Edmund White.

Another source of encouragement for writers has been the quality of the criticism devoted to their work in the gay and mainstream press. Gay reviewers are less inclined than in the past to make judgments based on their own views of political correctness and have become more sensitive to artistic values, especially the way various stylistic devices question political assumptions and literary conventions. Mainstream reviewers are more aware of the fundamental issues of gay life and less likely to criticize a novel, either implicitly or explicitly, for being "too gay" and therefore alien to their own experience. Despite the greater attention individual works now receive in the mainstream press, however, most reviewers still tend to discuss them without any reference to their place within the broader context of contemporary gay fiction.

By neglecting the particular aspirations and achievements of gay fiction, critics risk distorting the meaning of a work and denying the writer an important part of his history. Literature does not exist in a cultural vacuum. It is born from specific social and historical conditions; it reflects those conditions, and directly affects the way our lives are perceived and transformed. The term "gay fiction" refers not only to an impressive body of work but to the liberation of a complex subject, and an entire community's right to the free use of its imagination.

Gay fiction as a term is nevertheless problematic, for although it is possible to speak of common themes, a shared tradition, and even of an elusive "gay sensibility," there is no literary school of gay fiction; each writer remains an individual with his own style and artistic interests, which may place him in the company of writers with similar interests who are not gay. My approach to this situation has been to employ a double tactic—to insist on the historical reality of gay fiction as a collective phenomenon but also to show, by the diversity of talents it has brought forth, that it cannot be reduced to a single restrictive category.

Several years ago at a forum in New York called "Is There a Gay Sensibility and Does It Have an Impact on Our Culture?" Jeff Weinstein brilliantly answered by saying, "No, there is no such thing as a gay sensibility, and yes, it has an enormous impact on our culture." More recently, Vito Russo has remarked that gay sensibility is not something only gay people express. It is, he said, "a natural conviction that difference exists but doesn't matter." These properly paradoxical statements illustrate concerns shared by all minorities—the refusal to be denied one's history and identity as a member of a community, and the equally adamant refusal to have one's individuality reduced to being nothing more than a reflection of that community. What is being sought is a balance between one's need for self-definition and a wariness of all definitions. What is being expressed is a protest against all forms of cultural isolation.

Among the inevitable dilemmas created by this situation is the way gay books are marketed. Although the existence of gay bookstores and sections on gay studies in mainstream stores has been very effective in bringing gay fiction to its primary audience, writers have always viewed this arrangement with ambivalence because it diminishes their chances of reaching a broader audience and implies that their work is of limited appeal. But this arrangement is changing. Many gay bookstores are now stocking nongay titles by their customers' favorite authors, whereas a number of recent books have been displayed on the regular shelves of mainstream stores primarily because they have been published by well-known houses and have received considerable publicity. These signs suggest that the boundary between gay fiction and mainstream fiction is becoming less distinct. They also point to more profound developments—the gradual assimilation of gay culture into American society, and the progressive transformation of American culture itself.

Almost everyone is aware of the changes that have occurred within the gay community in recent years: the weakening of urban ghettos; the decline in importance of bars, baths, and discos as focal institutions; the rise to greater prominence of other institutions such as political groups, community centers, health and charitable organizations. Although these changes have usually been attributed to the AIDS crisis, it would be more accurate to say that AIDS has accelerated changes that had already begun.

Gay culture of the 1970s was largely established by a generation which after decades of repression could celebrate its new consciousness and the very fact that it was creating a new culture on its own terms. This process continues, but much that was culturally new in the 1970s is now understandably seen as a *given* both by a younger generation and by many who were earlier engaged in gay life. We are also witnessing another familiar pattern of cultural change: After a revolutionary ingathering, a movement outward toward the rest of society is taking place. This movement is less the result of disillusionment caused by AIDS than a manifestation of confidence based on the fact that a certain psychological, social, and artistic ground has been secured against the continued onslaughts of antigay discrimination and violence.

These developments partly explain why some writers with established reputations in gay fiction are now venturing to treat other subjects, whereas writers previously known for their nongay work are turning to gay fiction for the first time. They also explain why many young writers today seem relatively less interested in exploring relations among men within an exclusively gay world than in examining the way their lives as gay men intersect with the lives of people within the dominant culture. Given this influx of so many new and diverse talents, it is not surprising that terms such as "gay fiction," and especially "gay writer," are far less restricted in meaning than was the case a few years ago. And now, nineteen years after Stonewall, the word "gay" itself carries connotations that encompass a reality of ever more varied social, moral, and artistic concerns.

Gay fiction, like gay life, has ceased to be a cultural curiosity of limited interest. For a growing number of readers the essential contribution of this fiction is that it addresses our common humanity often by revealing our common gayness—those problems shared by others but which gay people must confront with particular intensity. Readers know that at its best gay fiction offers a unique point of view for exposing the contradictions of our society and can be a highly effective instrument for examining our fears, desires, and ambitions, especially during this period of disruptive change. And writers know that it is only by cultivating their particularity as individuals and as members of a community—their difference—that they can hope to provide new insights, among them the delicate truth that differences do not matter.

Many of these thoughts were in my mind when I began editing this second collection of gay fiction. I decided from the beginning not to request stories from writers already represented in the first volume of *Men On Men* in order to give more opportunities to others who had been unable to contribute earlier or who had emerged during the past two years. Although a few writers I contacted had no new work to offer, my search was greatly facilitated by recommendations I received from past and present contributors. I eventually read three hundred stories by more than one hundred men, many of whom had just begun to treat gay themes. As in the past, I considered unpublished and published works, finding the latter in *Christopher Street, The James White Review, Mandate,* and in mainstream periodicals: *The Atlantic Monthly, The Mississippi Review,* and a journal of progressive Jewish thought called, delightfully, *Shmate.* Some of these previously published stories were significantly revised for this collection.

I am pleased that the stories I finally selected are by established and younger writers, that several were written by, or deal with members of racial, ethnic, and affectional minorities within the gay community, and that others are set in areas of the country, notably the South, that were not represented in the first anthology. However, these factors did not serve as criteria for my selection, which was based solely on judgments of literary quality. I looked for stories that offered original insights and were fully realized in terms of character, mode of narration, and style. This book is a collection of fictional perspectives on gay life; it is also a gathering of distinct voices, each drawing the reader into a particular mind and world.

Given the unrelieved horror of the epidemic, it is not surprising that several stories deal with AIDS, and particularly with the intense conflicts the disease has produced between love and fear, compassion and discrimination. These conflicts are familiar ones in gay fiction, and in many respects the stigma of AIDS can be seen as a new homosexuality reviving old fears and the old quest of the individual for a community to end his isolation.

In his story "The Boys in the Bars," Christopher Davis captures this situation by describing the disintegration of one community based on pleasure and its replacement by another community born from the revelation of inescapable truths. Davis in effect reinvents the coming-out story by transforming his protagonist's illness into an occasion for self-discovery and renewed friendship. Drawing on his experience of the theater, Albert Innaurato dramatizes, often with comic insight, the cruel prejudices AIDS has inflamed among straight *and* gay people. Yet here again the "solidarity" that is almost destroyed by fear is reaffirmed, at least for a few, by compassion in the face of death. Fear and the hunger for friendship are also the subjects of David B. Feinberg's story, appropriately entitled "The Age of Anxiety." Feinberg's special achievement is to combine the anxiety of AIDS with the paranoia of urban living and then to view this confusion from a comically absurdist perspective.

The specter of AIDS is present in other stories, including Tim Barrus's "Life Sucks," which contains a stinging indictment of gay indifference toward some victims of the disease. Although it is never mentioned, AIDS informs the cultural context of Anderson Ferrell's "Why People Get Cancer," a story that examines with remarkable precision the potent combination of right-wing religious fervor and antigay prejudice that has become so familiar in recent years. Cancer also haunts David Groff's "Nobody's Child," but here it is not the gay man but his straight woman friend who is ill and seeks help. Like Innaurato's "Solidarity," Groff's story eventually offers the possibility of creating a new family out of the devastation of death.

Gay people have often been keen observers of the family as an institution to which they belong by birth and the bonds of domestic love, but from which they are frequently excluded because of their difference. The family is the scene of the Oedipal drama of identity, the source for models of behavior whose influence can be at once powerful and oppressive, the place where the choices one makes have their most immediate effect. Many works of gay fiction address these issues and describe conflicts between sexual love and familial love, dreams of acceptance and fears of rejection. Sometimes it is the family itself that is rejected, together with its stifling traditions and hierarchical structure dominated by the power of the father. A recurring myth in contemporary gay fiction is the invention of a more democratic family based on a community of friends or "sons." Writers know, however, that social inventions are never easy and that the essential drama of the family for gay people still turns on difficult choices and painful transitions.

Richard McCann offers a fascinating version of this drama in "My Mother's Clothes" by describing a boy's games with images of the self provided by his father and especially his mother. McCann then shows how the innocence of childhood, and its freedom, are lost when images acquire names, become social categories and divisive identities. Conflicting images of behavior are also central to Christopher Coe's "Anything You Want," a story that is itself built on exquisite visual effects. Caught within a disintegrating family where material excess and psychological want exist simultaneously, Coe's young protagonist moves toward a decision that will affirm his own desires and individuality.

In Tim Barrus's "Life Sucks" the destruction of the family and social traditions is seen as part of a more pervasive transformation of our society caused by the upheavals of war, AIDS, and relentless modernization. With this perspective Barrus succeeds in linking the difficulties of gay life to two rich themes in

American fiction—the loss of social and moral innocence and the wandering search for a home. The gay man in Lev Raphael's "Dancing on Tishe B'Av," on the other hand, is torn between his adherence to a strong religious tradition and a love condemned by that same tradition. His dilemma tests both his faith and the limits of his family's understanding.

Two stories explore the ambivalent relations that often exist between gay sons and their fathers. The young man in Allen Barnett's "Snapshot" searches for a father he never knew in order to comprehend the origins of his solitude and the meaning of his desires. In Gary Glickman's "Magic," a son's memories of his father are so powerful they repeatedly impinge on the present; yet the love he seeks in other men, like the love he sought in his father, remains elusive, appearing then disappearing beyond his grasp. Although their approaches are different, both writers examine the complex relationship between filial and erotic love that is another recurrent motif in gay fiction.

An intriguing variation on this theme is present in James Purdy's "In This Corner . . . ," which relates an encounter between an older man and a young "son." Purdy's inimitable blend of realism and myth creates a haunting tale in which the ache of longing and the despair of solitude finally lead to an affirmation of love. The search for love returns in David Leavitt's psychologically uncompromising portrait of uneasy friendship and sexual dependency, "AYOR," which explores the wavering boundaries of gay life, their temptations, dangers, and sudden reversals. Initiation into gay life is also the central theme of David Brendan Hopes's lushly romantic "Once in Syracuse," but here one man's love for another is both aroused and threatened by differing visions of beauty and masculinity.

Joseph Pintauro's provocative story of prison life, "Jungle Dove," dramatizes a more disturbing form of initiation. Instead of the violence of passion described by Purdy and Hopes, Pintauro examines the violence of sexual power and fear that engulfs two men divided by racial tensions yet drawn together by their loss of freedom. Fear and intolerance also produce extremes of violence in "Red Leaves," Melvin Dixon's penetrating and strangely poetic account of a gang of youths whose need to prove their manhood drives them to murder a gay man. Allan Gurganus's beautifully detailed story, "Adult Art," on the other hand, is a celebration of desire that recognizes yet transcends sexual categories and reaffirms the value of tenderness. Gurganus describes the joys and mysteries of sex, the tactics of pleasure, and the strategies of the heart in ways that are delightfully fresh.

The pleasures of a very different sensibility can be found in James McCourt's recreation of life in the 1950s and 1960s, "I Go Back to the *Mais Oui*." McCourt takes us on a voyage through the past, including a visit to the Stonewall Inn on the night of the famous rebellion, and offers a dazzling collage of characters and events, art and opera. At once autobiography and history, his story's ultimate subject is its style—one that is certainly his own, but also unmistakably gay.

Many writers in this collection, like McCourt, capture the diverse settings of an evolving gay world from the dusky parks of Paris to a Gay Pride parade in New York City; but there are several stories in which a recognizable gay community is absent, or in which various manifestations of gay life are viewed from an unusual psychological distance. The narrator of Hopes's story, for example, is a formerly straight hustler who is both fascinated and repelled by the gay world he enters. Barrus's story is told by a divorced Vietnam veteran with children who progressively becomes an outsider to the life of Key West; and Innaurato's narrator describes himself as a fat, unattractive man—characteristics that enable him to criticize the often excessive premium the gay world places on physical beauty.

Still other stories turn around characters who are either sexually ambiguous or straight. Gurganus's protagonist is a married bisexual; Purdy's is a widower without a conscious sexual identity. Pintauro follows the thoughts of a straight man who fears rape and longs for his wife; and the central character of Raphael's story is a sister who never quite accepts her brother's gayness. Dixon and Ferrell use more radical points of view by telling their stories, respectively, through a gaybasher and a religious fanatic—characters who, instead of appearing as nameless monsters, reveal a more complex, and perhaps more frightening humanity.

In my introduction to the first volume of *Men on Men* I noted that gay fiction is an opportunity for gay people to see and judge themselves rather than being merely observed and judged by others. This is still true except that now a number of writers are using a gay perspective to examine the way others see us, thereby encouraging those others to do the same—to look at us and themselves in a new light. The territory of gay fiction is expanding, even to the point of examining straight sexual behavior as in the stories by Pintauro, Dixon, and Gurganus. This expansion with its shifts in focus does not represent an effort to return gay life to the margins of existence it occupied for so long, but the determination to explore the neglected margins of gay life itself, which often overlap equally neglected aspects of the straight world. Gay fiction is proving that it is capable of renewing itself. It is also demonstrating its ability to renew American literature.

The history of any culture is a history of change, and of struggle. Throughout its own history, American culture has been repeatedly enriched by artists from different regions of the country and from different minorities—Jews after World War II, then blacks and women. In an essay published in the November 1987 issue of *Esquire*, Frank Rich discusses the great influence gay people have had on American popular culture over the past two decades, but then concludes that the advent of AIDS has now put a stop to this process of "homosexualization." It is clear, however, that a new period of gay influence has already begun despite AIDS, and in some cases because of it. Gay fiction is providing access to language for an ever more diverse community and producing writers whose superb com-

MY MOTHER'S CLOTHES: THE SCHOOL OF BEAUTY AND SHAME

• RICHARD McCANN •

He is troubled by any image *of himself, suffers when he is named. He finds the perfection of a human relationship in this vacancy of the image: to abolish—in oneself, between oneself and others—adjectives; a relationship which adjectivizes is on the side of the image, on the side of domination, of death.*

—Roland Barthes, *Roland Barthes*

LIKE EVERY CORNER house in Carroll Knolls, the corner house on our block was turned backward on its lot, a quirk introduced by the developer of the subdivision, who, having run short of money, sought variety without additional expense. The turned-around houses, as we kids called them, were not popular, perhaps because they seemed too public, their casement bedroom windows cranking open onto sunstruck asphalt streets. In actuality, however, it was the rest of the houses that were public, their picture windows offering dioramic glimpses of early-American sofas and Mediterranean-style pole lamps whose mottled globes hung like iridescent melons from wrought-iron chains. In order not to be seen walking across the living room to the kitchen in our pajamas, we had to close the venetian blinds. The corner house on our block was secretive, as though it had turned its back on all of us, whether in superiority or in shame, refusing to acknowledge even its own unkempt yard of yellowing zoysia grass. After its initial occupants moved away, the corner house remained vacant for months.

The spring I was in sixth grade, it was sold. When I came down the block from school, I saw a moving van parked at its curb. "Careful with that!" a woman was shouting at a mover as he unloaded a tiered end table from the truck. He stared at her in silence. The veneer had already been splintered from the table's edge, as though someone had nervously picked at it while watching TV. Then another mover walked from the truck carrying a child's bicycle, a wire basket bolted over its thick rear tire, brightly colored plastic streamers dangling from its handlebars.

The woman looked at me. "What have you got there? In your hand."

I was holding a scallop shell spray-painted gold, with imitation pearls glued along its edges. Mrs. Eidus, the art teacher who visited our class each Friday, had showed me how to make it.

"A hatpin tray," I said. "It's for my mother."

"It's real pretty." She glanced up the street as though trying to guess which house I belonged to. "I'm Mrs. Tyree," she said, "and I've got a boy about your age. His daddy's bringing him tonight in the new Plymouth. I bet you haven't sat in a new Plymouth."

"We have a Ford." I studied her housedress, tiny blue and purple flowers imprinted on thin cotton, a line of white buttons as large as Necco Wafers marching toward its basted hemline. She was the kind of mother my mother laughed at for cutting recipes out of *Woman's Day*. Staring from our picture window, my mother would sometimes watch the neighborhood mothers drag their folding chairs into a circle on someone's lawn. "There they go," she'd say, "a regular meeting of the Daughters of the Eastern Star!" "They're hardly even *women*," she'd whisper to my father, "and their *clothes*." She'd criticize their appearance— their loud nylon scarves tied beneath their chins, their disintegrating figures stuffed into pedal pushers—until my father, worried that my brother, Davis, and I could hear, although laughing himself, would beg her, "Stop it, Maria, please stop; it isn't funny." But she wouldn't stop, not ever. "Not even thirty and they look like they belong to the DAR! They wear their pearls inside their bosoms in case the rope should break!" She was the oldest mother on the block but she was the most glamorous, sitting alone on the front lawn in her sleek kick-pleated skirts and cashmere sweaters, reading her thick paper-back novels, whose bindings had split. Her hair was lightly hennaed, so that when I saw her pillowcases piled atop the washer, they seemed dusted with powdery rouge. She had once lived in New York City.

After dinner, when it was dark, I joined the other children congregated beneath the streetlamp across from the turned-around house. Bucky Trueblood, an eighth-grader who had once twisted the stems off my brother's eyeglasses, was crouched in the center, describing his mother's naked body to us elementary school children gathered around him, our faces slightly up-turned, as though searching for a distant constellation, or for the bats that Bucky said would fly into our hair. I sat at the edge, one half of my body within the circle of light, the other half lost to darkness. When Bucky described his mother's nip-ples, which he'd glimpsed when she bent to kiss him good-night, everyone giggled; but when he described her genitals, which he'd seen by dropping his pencil on the floor and looking up her nightie while her feet were propped on a hassock as she watched TV, everyone huddled nervously together, as though listening to a ghost story that made them fear something dan-gerous in the nearby dark. "I don't believe you," someone said; "I'm telling you," Bucky said, *that's what it looks like.*"

I slowly moved outside the circle. Across the street a cream-colored Plymouth was parked at the curb. In a lighted bedroom window Mrs. Tyree was hanging café curtains. Behind the chain-link fence, within the low branches of a willow tree, the new child was standing in his yard. I could see his white T-shirt and the pale oval of his face, a face deprived of detail by darkness and distance. Behind him, at the open bedroom window, his mother slowly fiddled with a valance. Behind me the children sat spellbound beneath the light. Then Bucky jumped up and pointed in the new child's direction—"Hey, you, you want to hear something really *good*?"—and even before the others had a chance to spot him, he vanished as suddenly and completely as an imaginary playmate.

The next morning, as we waited at our bus stop, he loitered by the mailbox on the opposite corner, not crossing the street until the yellow school bus pulled up and flung open its door. Then he dashed aboard and sat down beside me. "I'm Denny," he said. Denny: a heavy, unbeautiful child, who, had his parents stayed in their native Kentucky, would have been a farm boy, but who in Carroll Knolls seemed to belong to no particular world at all, walking past the identical ranch houses in his overalls and Keds, his whitish-blond hair close-cropped all around except for the distinguishing, stigmatizing feature of a wave that crested perfectly just above his forehead, a wave that neither rose nor fell, a wave he trained with Hopalong Cassidy hair tonic, a wave he tended fussily, as though it were the only loveliness he allowed himself.

What in Carroll Knolls might have been described by someone not native to those parts—a visiting expert, say—as *beautiful*, capable of arousing terror and joy? The brick ramblers strung with multicolored Christmas lights? The occasional front-yard plaster Virgin entrapped within a chicken-wire grotto entwined with plastic roses? The spring Denny moved to Carroll Knolls, I begged my parents to take me to a nightclub, had begged so hard for months, in fact, that by summer they finally agreed to a Sunday matinee. Waiting in the back seat of our Country Squire, a red bow tie clipped to my collar, I watched our house float like a mirage behind the sprinkler's web of water. The front door opened, and a white dress fluttered within the mirage's ascending waves: slipping on her sunglasses, my mother emerged onto the concrete stoop, adjusted her shoulder strap, and teetered across the wet grass in new spectator shoes. Then my father stepped out and cut the sprinkler off. We drove—the warm breeze inside the car sweetened by my mother's Shalimar—past ranch houses tethered to yards by chain-link fences; past the Silver Spring Volunteer Fire Department and Carroll Knolls Elementary School; past the Polar Bear Soft-Serv stand, its white stucco siding shimmery with mirror shards; past a bulldozed red-clay field where a weathered billboard advertised IF YOU LIVED HERE YOU'D BE HOME BY NOW, until we arrived at the border—a line of cinder-block discount liquor stores, a traffic light—of Washington, D.C. The light turned red. We stopped. The breeze died and the Shalimar fell from the air. Exhaust fumes mixed with the smell of hot tar. A drunk man stumbled into the crosswalk, followed by an old woman shielding herself from the sun with an orange umbrella, and two teen-aged boys dribbling a basketball back and forth between them. My mother put down her sun visor. "Lock your door," she said.

Then the light changed, releasing us into another country. The station wagon sailed down boulevards of Chinese elms and flowering Bradford pears, through hot, dense streets where black families sat on wooden chairs at curbs, along old streetcar tracks that caused the tires to shimmy and the car to swerve, onto Pennsylvania Avenue, past the White House, encircled by its fence of iron spears, and down 14th Street, past the Treasury Building, until at last we reached the Neptune Room, a cocktail lounge in the basement of a shabbily elegant hotel.

Inside, the Neptune Room's walls were painted with garish mermaids reclining seductively on underwater rocks, and human frogmen who stared longingly through their diving helmets' glass masks at a loveliness they could not possess on dry earth. On stage, leaning against the baby grand piano, a *chanteuse* (as my mother called her) was singing of her grief, her wrists weighted with rhinestone bracelets, a single blue spotlight making her seem like one who lived, as did the mermaids, underwater.

I was transfixed. I clutched my Roy Rogers cocktail (the same as a Shirley Temple, but without the cheerful, girlish

grenadine) tight in my fist. In the middle of "The Man I Love"
I stood and struggled toward the stage.

I strayed into the spotlight's soft-blue underwater world.
Close up, from within the light, the singer was a boozy, plump
peroxide blonde in a tight black cocktail dress; but these indis-
cretions made her yet more lovely, for they showed what she
had lost, just as her songs seemed to carry her backward into
endless regret. When I got close to her, she extended one
hand—red nails, a huge glass ring—and seized one of mine.

"Why, what kind of little sailor have we got here?" she asked
the audience.

I stared through the border of blue light and into the room,
where I saw my parents gesturing, although whether they were
telling me to step closer to her microphone or to step farther
away, I could not tell. The whole club was staring.

"Maybe he knows a song!" a man shouted from the back.

"Sing with me," she whispered. "What can you sing?"

I wanted to lift her microphone from its stand and bow
deeply from the waist, as Judy Garland did on her weekly TV
show. But I could not. As she began to sing, I stood voiceless,
pressed against the protection of her black dress; or, more
accurately, I stood beside her, silently lip-synching to myself. I
do not recall what she sang, although I do recall a quick,
farcical ending in which she falsettoed, like Betty Boop, "Gimme
a Little Kiss, Will Ya, Huh?" and brushed my forehead with
pursed red lips.

That summer, humidity enveloping the landfill subdivision,
Denny, "the new kid," stood on the boundaries, while we
neighborhood boys played War, a game in which someone
stood on Stanley Allen's front porch and machine-gunned the
rest of us, who one by one clutched our bellies, coughed as if
choking on blood, and rolled in exquisite death throes down the
grassy hill. When Stanley's father came up the walk from work,
he ducked imaginary bullets. "Hi, Dad," Stanley would call,
rising from the dead to greet him. Then we began the game
again: whoever died best in the last round got to kill in the

next. Later, after dusk, we'd smear the wings of balsa planes with glue, ignite them, and send them flaming through the dark on kamikaze missions. Long after the streets were deserted, we children sprawled beneath the corner streetlamp, praying our mothers would not call us—"*Time to come in!*"—back to our oven-like houses; and then sometimes Bucky, hoping to scare the elementary school kids, would lead his solemn procession of junior high "hoods" down the block, their penises hanging from their unzipped trousers.

Denny and I began to play together, first in secret, then visiting each other's houses almost daily, and by the end of the summer I imagined him to be my best friend. Our friendship was sealed by our shared dread of junior high school. Davis, who had just finished seventh grade, brought back reports of corridors so long that one could get lost in them, of gangs who fought to control the lunchroom and the bathrooms. The only safe place seemed to be the Health Room, where a pretty nurse let you lie down on a cot behind a folding screen. Denny told me about a movie he'd seen in which the children, all girls, did not have to go to school at all but were taught at home by a beautiful governess, who, upon coming to their rooms each morning, threw open their shutters so that sunlight fell like bolts of satin across their beds, whispered their pet names while kissing them, and combed their long hair with a silver brush. "She never got mad," said Denny, beating his fingers up and down through the air as though striking a keyboard, "except once when some old man told the girls they could never play piano again."

With my father at work in the Pentagon and my mother off driving the two-tone Welcome Wagon Chevy to new subdivisions, Denny and I spent whole days in the gloom of my living room, the picture window's venetian blinds closed against an August sun so fierce that it bleached the design from the carpet. Dreaming of fabulous prizes—sets of matching Samsonite luggage, French Provincial bedroom suites, Corvettes, jet flights to Hawaii—we watched Jan Murray's *Treasure Hunt* and Bob Barker's *Truth or Consequences* (a name that seemed strangely threatening). We watched *The Loretta Young Show*, worshipping yet critiquing her elaborate gowns. When *The Early Show* came on, we watched old Bette Davis, Gene Tierney, and Joan Crawford movies—*Dark Victory*, *Leave Her to Heaven*, *A Woman's Face*. Hoping to become their pen pals, we wrote long letters to fading movie stars, who in turn sent us autographed photos we traded between ourselves. We searched the house for secrets, like contraceptives, Kotex, and my mother's hidden supply of Hershey bars. And finally, Denny and I, running to the front window every few minutes to make sure no one was coming unexpectedly up the sidewalk, inspected the secrets of my mother's dresser: her satin nightgowns and padded brassieres, folded atop pink drawer liners and scattered with loose sachet; her black mantilla, pressed inside a shroud of lilac tissue paper; her heart-shaped candy box, a flapper doll strapped to its lid with a ribbon, from which spilled galaxies of cocktail rings and cultured pearls. Small shrines to deeper intentions, private grottoes of yearning: her triangular cloisonné earrings, her brooch of enameled butterfly wings.

Because beauty's source was longing, it was infused with romantic sorrow; because beauty was defined as "feminine," and therefore as "other," it became hopelessly confused with my mother: Mother, who quickly sorted through new batches of photographs, throwing unflattering shots of herself directly into the fire before they could be seen. Mother, who dramatized herself, telling us and our playmates, "My name is Maria Dolores; in Spanish, that means 'Mother of Sorrows.'" Mother who had once wished to be a writer and who said, looking up briefly from whatever she was reading, "Books are my best friends." Mother, who read aloud from Whitman's *Leaves of Grass* and O'Neill's *Long Day's Journey Into Night* with a voice so grave I could not tell the difference between them. Mother, who lifted cut-glass vases and antique clocks from her obsessively dusted curio shelves to ask, "If this could talk, what story would it tell?"

And more, always more, for she was the only woman in our house, a "people-watcher," a "talker," a woman whose mysteries and moods seemed endless: Our Mother of the White Silk Gloves; Our Mother of the Veiled Hats; Our Mother of the Paper Lilacs; Our Mother of the Sighs and Heartaches; Our Mother of the Gorgeous Gypsy Earrings; Our Mother of the Late Movies and the Cigarettes; Our Mother whom I adored and who, in adoring, I ran from, knowing it "wrong" for a son to wish to be like his mother; Our Mother who wished to influence us, passing the best of herself along, yet who held the fear common to that era, the fear that by loving a son too intensely she would render him unfit—"Momma's boy," "tied to apron strings"—and who therefore alternately drew us close and sent us away, believing a son needed "male influence" in large doses, that female influence was pernicious except as a final finishing, like manners; Our Mother of the Mixed Messages; Our Mother of Sudden Attentiveness; Our Mother of Sudden Distances; Our Mother of Anger; Our Mother of Apology. The simplest objects of her life, objects scattered accidentally about the house, became my shrines to beauty, my grottoes of romantic sorrow: her Revlon lipstick tubes, "Cherries in the Snow"; her Art Nouveau atomizers on the blue mirror top of her vanity; her pastel silk scarves knotted to a wire hanger in her closet; her white handkerchiefs blotted with red mouths. Voiceless objects; silences. The world halved with a cleaver: "masculine," "feminine." In these ways was the plainest ordinary love made complicated and grotesque. And in these ways was beauty, already confused with the "feminine," also confused with shame, for all these longings were secret, and to control me all my brother had to do was to threaten to expose that Denny and I were dressing ourselves in my mother's clothes.

Denny chose my mother's drabbest outfits, as though he were ruled by the deepest of modesties, or by his family's austere Methodism: a pink wraparound skirt from which the color had been laundered, its hem almost to his ankles; a sleeveless white cotton blouse with a Peter Pan collar; a small straw summer clutch. But he seemed to challenge his own primness, as though he dared it with his "effects": an undershirt worn over his head to approximate cascading hair; gummed holepunch reinforcements pasted to his fingernails so that his hands, palms up, might look like a woman's—flimsy crescent moons waxing above his fingertips.

He dressed slowly, hesitantly, but once dressed, he was a manic Proteus metamorphosizing into contradictory, half-realized forms, throwing his "long hair" back and balling it violently into a French twist; tapping his paper nails on the glass-topped vanity as though he were an important woman kept waiting at a cosmetics counter; stabbing his nails into the air as though he were an angry teacher assigning an hour of detention; touching his temple as though he were a shy schoolgirl tucking back a wisp of stray hair; resting his fingertips on the rim of his glass of Kool-Aid as though he were an actress seated over an ornamental cocktail—a Pink Lady, say, or a Silver Slipper. Sometimes, in an orgy of jerky movement, his gestures overtaking him with greater and greater force, a dynamo of theatricality unleashed, he would hurl himself across the room like a mad girl having a fit, or like one possessed; or he would snatch the chenille spread from my parents' bed and drape it over his head to fashion for himself the long train of a bride. "Do you like it?" he'd ask anxiously, making me his mirror. "Does it look *real*?" He wanted, as did I, to become something he'd neither yet seen nor dreamed of, something he'd recognize the moment he saw it: himself. Yet he was constantly confounded, for no matter how much he adorned himself with scarves and jewelry, he could not understand that this was himself, as was also and at the same time the boy in overalls and Keds. He was split in two pieces—as who was not?—the blond wave cresting rigidly above his close-cropped hair.

"He makes me nervous," I heard my father tell my mother one night as I lay in bed. They were speaking about me. That morning I'd stood awkwardly on the front lawn—"Maybe you should go help your father," my mother had said—while he propped an extension ladder against the house, climbed up through the power lines he separated with his bare hands, and staggered across the pitched roof he was reshingling. When his hammer slid down the incline, catching on the gutter, I screamed, "You're falling!" Startled, he almost fell.

"He needs to spend more time with you," I heard my mother say.

I couldn't sleep. Out in the distance a mother was calling her child home. A screen door slammed. I heard cicadas, their chorus as steady and loud as the hum of a power line. *He needs to spend more time with you.* Didn't she know? Saturday mornings, when he stood in his rubber hip boots fishing off the shore of Triadelphia Reservoir, I was afraid of the slimy bottom and could not wade after him; for whatever reasons of his own—something as simple as shyness, perhaps—he could not come to get me. I sat in the parking lot drinking Tru-Ade and reading *Betty and Veronica*, wondering if Denny had walked alone to Wheaton Plaza, where the weekend manager of Port-o'-Call allowed us to Windex the illuminated glass shelves that held Lladro figurines, the porcelain ballerina's hands so realistic one could see tiny life and heart lines etched into her palms. *He needs to spend more time with you.* Was she planning to discontinue the long summer afternoons that she and I spent together when there were no new families for her to greet in her Welcome Wagon car? "I don't feel like being alone today," she'd say, inviting me to sit on their chenille bedspread and watch her model new clothes in her mirror. Behind her an oscillating fan fluttered nylons and scarves she'd heaped, discarded, on a chair. "Should I wear the red belt with this dress or the black one?" she'd ask, turning suddenly toward me and cinching her waist with her hands.

Afterward we would sit together at the rattan table on the screened-in porch, holding cocktail napkins around sweaty glasses of iced Russian tea and listening to big-band music on the Zenith.

"You look so pretty," I'd say. Sometimes she wore outfits I'd selected for her from her closet—pastel chiffon dresses, an apricot blouse with real mother-of-pearl buttons.

One afternoon she leaned over suddenly and shut off the radio. "You know you're going to leave me one day," she said. When I put my arms around her, smelling the dry carnation talc she wore in hot weather, she stood up and marched out of the room. When she returned, she was wearing Bermuda shorts and a plain cotton blouse. "Let's wait for your father on the stoop," she said.

Late that summer—the summer before he died—my father took me with him to Fort Benjamin Harrison, near Indianapolis, where, as a colonel in the U.S. Army Reserves, he did his annual tour of duty. On the propjet he drank bourbon and read newspapers while I made a souvenir packet for Denny: an airsickness bag, into which I placed the Chiclets given me by the stewardess to help pop my ears during take-off, and the laminated white card that showed the location of emergency exits. Fort Benjamin Harrison looked like Carroll Knolls: hundreds of acres of concrete and sun-scorched shrubbery inside a cyclone fence. Daytimes I waited for my father in the dining mess with the sons of other officers, drinking chocolate milk that came from a silver machine, and desultorily setting fires in ashtrays. When he came to collect me, I walked behind him—gold braid hung from his epaulets—while enlisted men saluted us and opened doors. At night, sitting in our BOQ room, he asked me questions about myself: "Are you looking forward to seventh grade?" "What do you think you'll want to be?" When these topics faltered—I stammered what I hoped were right answers—we watched TV, trying to pre-guess lines of dialogue on reruns of his favorite shows, *The Untouchables* and *Rawhide*. "That Della Street," he said as we watched *Perry Mason*, "is almost as pretty as your mother." On the last day, eager to make the trip memorable, he brought me a gift: a glassine envelope filled with punched IBM cards that told me my life story as his secretary had typed it into the office computer. Card One: *You live at 10406 Lillians Mill Court, Silver Spring, Maryland.* Card Two: *You are entering seventh grade.* Card Three: *Last year your teacher was Mrs. Dillard.* Card Four: *Your favorite color is blue.* Card Five: *You love the Kingston Trio.* Card

Six: *You love basketball and football*. Card Seven: *Your favorite sport is swimming*.

Whose son did these cards describe? The address was correct, as was the teacher's name and the favorite color; and he'd remembered that one morning during breakfast I'd put a dime in the jukebox and played the Kingston Trio's song about "the man who never returned." But whose fiction was the rest? Had I, who played no sport other than kickball and Kitty-Kitty-Kick-the-Can, lied to him when he asked me about myself? Had he not heard from my mother the outcome of the previous summer's swim lessons? At the swim club a young man in black trunks had taught us, as we held hands, to dunk ourselves in water, surface, and then go down. When he had told her to let go of me, I had thrashed across the surface, violently afraid I'd sink. But perhaps I had not lied to him; perhaps he merely did not wish to see. It was my job, I felt, to reassure him that I was the son he imagined me to be, perhaps because the role of reassurer gave me power. In any case, I thanked him for the computer cards. I thanked him the way a father thanks a child for a well-intentioned gift he'll never use—a set of handkerchiefs, say, on which the embroidered swirls construct a monogram of no particular initial, and which thus might be used by anyone.

As for me, when I dressed in my mother's clothes, I seldom moved at all: I held myself rigid before the mirror. The kind of beauty I'd seen practiced in movies and in fashion magazines was beauty attained by lacquered stasis, beauty attained by fixed poses—"ladylike stillness," the stillness of mannequins, the stillness of models "caught" in mid-gesture, the stillness of the passive moon around which active meteors orbited and burst. My costume was of the greatest solemnity: I dressed like the *chanteuse* in the Neptune Room, carefully shimmying my mother's black slip over my head so as not to stain it with Brylcreem, draping her black mantilla over my bare shoulders, clipping her rhinestone dangles to my ears. Had I at that time already seen the movie in which French women who had fraternized with German soldiers were made to shave their heads and walk through the streets, jeered by their fellow villagers? And if so, did I imagine myself to be one of the collaborators, or one of the villagers, taunting her from the curb? I ask because no matter how elaborate my costume, I made no effort to camouflage my crew cut or my male body.

How did I perceive myself in my mother's triple-mirrored vanity, its endless repetitions? I saw myself as doubled—both an image and he who studied it. I saw myself as beautiful, and guilty: the lipstick made my mouth seem the ripest rose, or a wound; the small rose on the black slip opened like my mother's heart disclosed, or like the Sacred Heart of Mary, aflame and pierced by arrows; the mantilla transformed me into a Mexican penitent or a Latin movie star, like Dolores Del Rio. The mirror was a silvery stream: on the far side, in a clearing, stood the woman who was icily immune from the boy's terror and contempt; on the close side, in the bedroom, stood the boy who feared and yet longed after her inviolability. (Perhaps, it occurs to me now, this doubleness is the source of drag queens' vulnerable ferocity.) Sometimes, when I saw that person in the mirror, I felt as though I had at last been lifted from that dull, locked room, with its mahogany bedroom suite and chalky blue walls. But other times, particularly when I saw Denny and me together, so that his reality shattered my fantasies, we seemed merely ludicrous and sadly comic, as though we were dressed in the garments of another species, like dogs in human clothes. I became aware of my spatulate hands, my scarred knees, my large feet; I became aware of the drooping, unfilled bodice of my slip. Like Denny, I could neither dispense with images nor take their flexibility as pleasure, for the idea of self I had learned and was learning still was that one was constructed by one's images—"*When boys cross their legs, they cross one ankle atop the knee*"—so that one finally sought the protection of believing in one's own image and, in believing in it as reality, condemned oneself to its poverty.

(That locked room. My mother's vanity; my father's highboy. If Denny and I, still in our costumes, had left that bedroom, its floor strewn with my mother's shoes and hand-bags, and gone through the darkened living room, out onto the sunstruck porch, down the sidewalk, and up the street, how would we have carried ourselves? Would we have walked boldly, chattering extravagantly back and forth between ourselves, like drag queens refusing to acknowledge the stares of contempt that are meant to halt them? Would we have walked humbly, with the calculated, impervious piety of the condemned walk-ing barefoot to the public scaffold? Would we have walked simply, as deeply accustomed to the normalcy of our own strangeness as Siamese twins? Or would we have walked gravely, a solemn procession, like Bucky Trueblood's gang, their man-hood hanging from their unzipped trousers?

(We were eleven years old. Why now, more than two de-cades later, do I wonder for the first time how we would have carried ourselves through a publicness we would have neither sought nor dared? I am six feet two inches tall; I weigh 198 pounds. Given my size, the question I am most often asked about my youth is "What football position did you play?" Overseas I am most commonly taken to be a German or a Swede. Right now, as I write this, I am wearing L. L. Bean khaki trousers, a LaCoste shirt, Weejuns: the anonymous Amer-ican costume, although partaking of certain signs of class and education, and, most recently, partaking also of certain signs of sexual orientation, this costume having become the standard garb of the urban American gay man. Why do I tell you these things? Am I trying—not subtly—to inform us of my "male-ness," to reassure us that I have "survived" without noticeable "complexes"? Or is this my urge, my constant urge, to compli-cate my portrait of myself to both of us, so that I might layer my selves like so many multicolored crinoline slips, each rus-tling as I walk? When the wind blows, lifting my skirt, I do not know which slip will be revealed.)

Sometimes, while Denny and I were dressing up, Davis would come home unexpectedly from the bowling alley, where

he'd been hanging out since entering junior high. At the bowling alley he was courting the protection of Bucky's gang.

"Let me in!" he'd demand, banging fiercely on the bedroom
door, behind which Denny and I were scurrying to wipe the
makeup off our faces with Kleenex.

"We're not doing anything," I'd protest, buying time.

"Let me in this minute or I'll tell!"

Once in the room, Davis would police the wreckage we'd
made, the emptied hatboxes, the scattered jewelry, the piled
skirts and blouses. "You'd better clean this up right now," he'd
warn. "You two make me *sick*."

Yet his scorn seemed modified by awe. When he helped us
rehang the clothes in the closet and replace the jewelry in the
candy box, a sullen accomplice destroying someone else's evidence, he sometimes handled the garments as though they were
infused with something of himself, although at the precise
moment when he seemed to find them loveliest, holding them
close, he would cast them down.

After our dress-up sessions Denny would leave the house
without good-byes. I was glad to see him go. We would not see
each other for days, unless we met by accident; we never
referred to what we'd done the last time we'd been together.
We met like those who have murdered are said to meet, each
tentatively and warily examining the other for signs of betrayal.
But whom had we murdered? The boys who walked into that
room? Or the women who briefly came to life within it?
Perhaps this metaphor has outlived its meaning. Perhaps our
shame derived not from our having killed but from our having
created.

In early September, as Denny and I entered seventh grade,
my father became ill. Over Labor Day weekend he was too
tired to go fishing. On Monday his skin had vaguely yellowed;
by Thursday he was severely jaundiced. On Friday he entered
the hospital, his liver rapidly failing; Sunday he was dead. He
died from acute hepatitis, possibly acquired while cleaning up
after our sick dog, the doctor said. He was buried at Arlington

National Cemetery, down the hill from the Tomb of the Unknown Soldier. After the twenty-one-gun salute, our mother pinned his colonel's insignia to our jacket lapels. I carried the flag from his coffin to the car. For two weeks I stayed home with my mother, helping her write thank-you notes on small white cards with black borders; one afternoon, as I was affixing postage to the square, plain envelopes, she looked at me across the dining room table. "You and Davis are all I have left," she said. She went into the kitchen and came back. "Tomorrow," she said, gathering up the note cards, "you'll have to go to school." Mornings I wandered the long corridors alone, separated from Denny by the fate of our last names, which had cast us into different homerooms and daily schedules. Lunchtimes we sat together in silence in the rear of the cafeteria. Afternoons, just before gym class, I went to the Health Room, where, lying on a cot, I'd imagine the Phys. Ed. coach calling my name from the class roll, and imagine my name, unclaimed, unanswered to, floating weightlessly away, like a balloon that one jumps to grab hold of but that is already out of reach. Then I'd hear the nurse dial the telephone. "He's sick again," she'd say. "Can you come pick him up?" At home I helped my mother empty my father's highboy. "No, we want to save that," she said when I folded his uniform into a huge brown bag that read GOODWILL INDUSTRIES; I wrapped it in a plastic dry-cleaner's bag and hung it in the hall closet.

After my father's death my relationship to my mother's things grew yet more complex, for as she retreated into her grief, she left behind only her mute objects as evidence of her life among us: objects that seemed as lonely and vulnerable as she was, objects that I longed to console, objects with which I longed to console myself—a tangled gold chain, thrown in frustration on the mantel; a wineglass, its rim stained with lipstick, left unwashed in the sink. Sometimes at night Davis and I heard her prop her pillow up against her bedroom wall, lean back heavily, and tune her radio to a call-in show: *"Nightcaps, what are you thinking at this late hour?"* Sunday evenings, in order to help her prepare for the next day's job hunt, I stood over her beneath the bare basement bulb, the same bulb that first illuminated my father's jaundice. I set her hair, slicking each wet strand with gel and rolling it, inventing gossip that seemed to draw us together, a beautician and his customer.

"You have such pretty hair," I'd say.

"At my age, don't you think I should cut it?" She was almost fifty.

"No, never."

That fall Denny and I were caught. One evening my mother noticed something out of place in her closet. (Perhaps now that she no longer shared it, she knew where every belt and scarf should have been.)

I was in my bedroom doing my French homework, dreaming of one day visiting Au Printemps, the store my teacher spoke of so excitedly as she played us the Edith Piaf records that she had brought back from France. In the mirror above my desk I saw my mother appear at my door.

"Get into the living room," she said. Her anger made her small, reflected body seem taut and dangerous.

In the living room Davis was watching TV with Uncle Joe, our father's brother, who sometimes came to take us fishing. Uncle Joe was lying in our father's La-Z-Boy recliner.

"There aren't going to be any secrets in this house," she said. "You've been in my closet. What were you doing there?"

"No, we weren't," I said. "We were watching TV all afternoon."

"*We?* Was Denny here with you? Don't you think I've heard about that? Were you and Denny going through my clothes? Were you wearing them?"

"No, Mom," I said.

"Don't lie!" She turned to Uncle Joe, who was staring at us. "Make him stop! He's lying to me!"

She slapped me. Although I was already taller than she, she slapped me over and over, slapped me across the room until I was backed against the TV. Davis was motionless, afraid. But Uncle Joe jumped up and stood between my mother and me, holding her until her rage turned to sobs. "I can't be both a mother and a father," she said to him. "I can't, I can't do it." I could not look at Uncle Joe, who, although he was protecting me, did not know I was lying.

She looked at me. "We'll discuss this later," she said. "Get out of my sight."

We never discussed it. Denny was outlawed. I believe, in fact, that it was I who suggested he never be allowed in our house again. I told my mother I hated him. I do not think I was lying when I said this. I truly hated him—hated him, I mean, for being me.

For two or three weeks Denny tried to speak with me at the bus stop, but whenever he approached, I busied myself with kids I barely knew. After a while Denny found a new best friend, Lee, a child despised by everyone, for Lee was "effeminate." His clothes were too fastidious; he often wore his cardigan over his shoulders, like an old woman feeling a chill. Sometimes, watching the street from our picture window, I'd see Lee walking toward Denny's house. "What a queer," I'd say to whoever might be listening. "He walks like a *girl*." Or sometimes, at the junior high school, I'd see him and Denny walking down the corridor, their shoulders pressed together as if they were telling each other secrets, or as if they were joined in mutual defense. Sometimes when I saw them, I turned quickly away, as though I'd forgotten something important in my locker. But when I felt brave enough to risk rejection, for I belonged to no group, I joined Bucky Trueblood's gang, sitting on the radiator in the main hall, and waited for Lee and Denny to pass us. As Lee and Denny got close, they stiffened and looked straight ahead.

"Faggots," I muttered.

I looked at Bucky, sitting in the middle of the radiator. As Lee and Denny passed, he leaned forward from the wall, accidentally disarranging the practiced severity of his clothes, his jeans puckering beneath his tooled belt, the breast pocket of his T-shirt drooping with the weight of a pack of Pall Malls. He whistled. Lee and Denny flinched. He whistled again. Then he leaned back, the hard lines of his body reasserting themselves, his left foot striking a steady beat on the tile floor with the silver V tap of his black loafer.

THE AGE OF ANXIETY

• DAVID B. FEINBERG •

I BLAME IT all on the existentialists. Before I heard of them compliments Madame Escoffier, third-year French, life proceeded as smoothly as the automatic door at the A&P. I would step on the rubber pad outside the supermarket, activating sensors causing the door to open automatically; I would enter and the door would close silently behind me. I would sleepwalk through life with as little thought as the electric eye on an elevator. I had such confidence! I operated under the assumption that no conscious intervention from me was really ever necessary. My life was a moving sidewalk, effortlessly transporting me from one destination to another.

But then in tenth grade Madame Escoffier had us read *The Stranger* by Albert Camus and nothing was ever the same. I realized that intention underlay every action. At gym class when Mister D would call attendance I would be overcome with fear. Suppose I didn't answer "here" when he called out "Eisenberg"? Suppose that at that moment I were unable to speak, temporarily struck mute? Suppose instead of responding in an appropriate manner I swore involuntarily? And what if I did not recognize my own name? What if I opened my mouth and a pigeon flew out?

Now, twenty years later, I stand at the 50th Street IND station. I hear the buzzer; the sign flashes "DOWNTOWN" in dot-matrix red bulbs; I stumble down the stairs. Although the train is not yet visible I know it will turn the corner in approximately one minute and thirty seconds. I can already feel the breeze in the tunnel. I see the bright lights approaching: the eyes of a snake. The train thunders closer, an unstoppable natural phenomenon, an act of God. I stand, transfixed, and wonder, will this be the time that the bright lights will hypnotize me into jumping? Will I spring out onto the tracks at the last possible moment, leaving no time for the conductor to pull the emergency switch? I walk backwards and cling to a steel girder, grasping it tightly, fearing that the rush of air may suck me onto the track, that the third rail live with 600 volts may erupt in an electrical explosion, shooting sparks on the platform. If I stood in front of the painted textured line that the Transit Authority has painted parallel to the tracks for the blind, some madman might push me onto the tracks after bounding down the stairs with an evil glint in his eye.

The train pulls in and stops. One door opens near me (the other is stuck) and I enter the car. The door closes. I know I have passed the point of danger. Now there is nothing to worry about except whether the man who is smoking a cigarette has a knife and whether the soda stain on the floor will make my shoes pick up the discarded *New York Post* with the latest AIDS HYSTERIA headline screaming at me and whether the sleeping man with urine stains on his pants is breathing or dead and whether the well-worn cards giving instructions on signing the alphabet the deaf-mute passes out have any contagious diseases and whether the teenage couple of alien ethnicity are laughing at me because they've seen my earring and whether the extremely obese woman who has sat next to me will allow me to exit at West Fourth Street.

Why I'm Upset

I'm upset for a variety of reasons, but mainly because my best friend and former lover Richard has just informed me that he is moving to San Francisco in two days. I'm on my way downtown to see him tonight for dinner and maybe to try to persuade him not to go. Richard had called me at work, around noon.

"Hi, BJ. Do you want a cat?"

"What cat?"

"Jessica." Jessica was Richard's eighteen-pound misanthropic cat. She had spent eight months at the Bide-A-Wee shelter on the East Side before Richard rescued her. People would coo "What a beautiful cat" and try to pick her up. After Jessica bit them, they'd decide on some cute kittens or an unhousebroken angora instead. Richard took one look at Jessica and fell for her. He sensed that she too had been abused. I loved to go over to Richard's and play with Jessica; it was always fun watching her squirm out of my arms. Richard called her The Weasel. "Jessssssssica," he would sibilate, "come over, sweetie, potato."

"Why would you want to get rid of Jessica? Are you sick of her or something?"

"No, I'm moving."

"You're WHAT?"

"I'm moving to San Francisco."

"What do you mean, you're moving to San Francisco?"

"I'm moving to San Francisco Friday and I wanted to know if you would take care of Jessica for me."

"You're moving to San Francisco in TWO DAYS? Richard, this is crazy. You don't just move to San Francisco in TWO DAYS!"

"I've had the tickets since Sunday. You know I've always been thinking of moving to San Francisco. I just can't take the heat anymore. Remember last summer, and the summer before, I said I couldn't take another August in New York City? I hate it here. I hate my job. I hate the subways. I hate the noise. I hate the crowds. I've been living in New York for eleven years and I think it's time to move on."

"But you never even been to San Francisco! You don't just MOVE to a place you've never even visited. You go on a vacation and then you come back. If you like it, you quit your job, give up your apartment, pack up your belongings and go. You make arrangements with your gym and your phone and your electric and your cat. You don't just leave on a week's notice."

"I had a feeling you would react this way. I should have known, you've never been supportive of my decisions."

"Have you told any other of your friends? Have you even told your therapist? I bet you haven't because you're afraid they'll talk you out of going. I think you're just trying to run away from all of your problems and moving to San Francisco won't help. I think—"

"I think this discussion has gone far enough and it's quite pointless to continue it. I called to ask if you wanted my cat. I guess you don't. I'll speak to you later when you're more rational. Good-bye, BJ."

Richard himself was no model of sanity. I had met him four years ago on the street. He had gone home to pee because at the time he had found that he was incapable of performing this bodily function anywhere other than home. Richard had a history of depression that went back ten years. He had an extensive support network of friends and acquaintances who would do nearly anything for him, and for a while he liked me the best because he knew that compassion didn't come easy to me and he saw me as a challenge.

I have a photograph of him on the wall, above the desk. Richard is at the beach, covered with baby oil, reading *The Magic Mountain*. The photo was taken from a skew angle; the camera near ground level, directed at Richard's torso and the clouds above. Consequently, his visible arm is massive, his chest gigantic (a pun on *The Magic Mountain*), and his head unnaturally small in comparison.

Richard went to the gym five times a week, which left two nights for me. He tended to be a creature of habit, settling into patterns quite easily. Before I met him he would have a cheeseburger and a protein shake for dinner every night. I taught him how to make chicken in a skillet. So he switched to chicken every night. There were periods where he would go to AA meetings for support, sometimes as many as three in a day. The year I met him he went through more therapists than I did boyfriends, which is to say quite a lot.

Why We Broke Up

We ended up breaking up because one day at Sheridan Square he pointed at my thickening waist and then at a display for starch blockers at the General Nutrition Center. "That's it," I said. "It's over."

We actually broke up because I was compulsive and he was addictive and our relationship had never been properly consummated because he refused to sleep over in my apartment because it was too noisy and threatening in Hell's Kitchen and too messy in the apartment and he lived in a single-room occupancy residence with a single bed so when I slept over it was on a foam mattress on the floor while he would sleep in the bed which was too tiny to fit both a Sheridan Square Health Club (Exercising and Reducing) Gym Queen who had used steroids a few years ago to gain friends and influence people and me, so the relationship could have been annulled properly had I been Catholic and had papal permission.

We actually broke up because after spending months anticipating the movie version of *Sophie's Choice* Richard made a date to see it with someone from one of his therapy groups who had been telling Richard how wonderful he was whereas I was long past the stage of praise unmitigated with sarcasm and cynicism and I was furious because I had tacitly assumed that we would see it together and my pettiness knows no bounds.

We actually broke up because I wanted more than two nights a week, maybe, and he expected me to be faithful on two nights a week, maybe, and he was interested in sadomasochism as a purely theatrical act of the imagination (he had joined Amnesty International a few years earlier just so he could read the documented accounts of torture in third world countries, complete with photographs and illustrative diagrams) and I was interested in achieving the type of popularity I had always dreamed of in high school but never imagined would be possibly by (a) going to the gym three or four times a week, (b) buying a pair of contact lenses, and (c) eliminating the word "NO" from my vocabulary.

We actually broke up because he would lose his erection fucking me if I moved too much and I was tired of playing Nicaraguan corpse to his freedom fighter.

We actually broke up because I wasn't supportive enough of him and he wasn't responsive enough to my needs and he claimed that I was making him feel guilty with my passive aggression and although I denied this on some level I knew that I was eating him alive.

We actually broke up in December of 1982 because Richard had persistently swollen lymph glands under his arms and in his groin and his doctor had diagnosed him as having lymphadenopathy and he told me that any diminution of his immune system was not contagious, that whatever virus he had been exposed to had long since left his system, after decimating his T cells, so he would pose no risk to me in regards with sex but that I must be absolutely faithful to him for fear of spreading something dire and this was just something that I could not do, TOTALLY, at that stage, with an unconsummated relationship.

So we broke up three years ago yet remained close friends. Two weeks after we broke up I was mugged on the PATH train coming back from a New Year's Eve dinner in Jersey City. Then Richard called me, telling me that his mother had died a few days ago, and could I come over? We were drawn together in a hostile world.

After he told me he was going to move, it felt as though I had just lost a limb. I thought that I was slowly disappearing, and that the next time I tried to look at myself in the mirror, there might not be anything there. I took two deep breaths and swallowed. I paused, and tried to calm myself. I thought slowly, deliberately: I . . . must . . . not . . . get . . . upset . . . It . . . is . . . im . . . per . . . a . . . tive . . . that . . . I . . . not . . .

get . . . up . . . set . . . How can you do this to me, Richard, after all I have done for you? How can you abandon me like this, so easily? And NOT WHEN I HAVE HERPES.

The Little Disturbances of Man

For the past several years, it seems that I have turned into a mass of symptoms and inchoate disease. As soon as one minor inconvenience leaves me, it seems another fills its place without a moment's loss. I tend to think of it as some cosmic law, like the conservation of matter and energy in the universe: the conservation of bacteria, microbes, viruses and disease. In moments of endearment, Richard would call me his walking petri dish.

I've had herpes for about five years, on the lower lip. It tends to recur when my defenses are down, when I am overtired, when my resources are low, when I am overdrawn at the bank, when another prospective boyfriend turns out to be living with his lover of ten years and I call by chance at the incorrect time, when I sit and wait for two hours at the dermatologist's reading about Arnold Schwarzenegger and Rock Hudson in *People* magazine and after being tortured with WRFM's mellow music I'm admitted and he scrapes off some tiny warts from my chin ("We won't need any anesthetic for this," he says, beaming beneath his headlight, a strap-on light I expect coal miners use) and I rush home afterwards to get stood up for dinner by a friend named Paul who lives down the block whom I haven't seen for about a year who had called me last week saying that he had been diagnosed with AIDS so how can I possibly be mad at him, or when I sit and wait in expectation of Mister Right to open the door and come into the steam room at the health club and sit across from me and start stroking his dick all the while not letting his eyes leave mine and an hour later, having lost ten pounds in water I manage to pry myself off the bench with the last ounce of strength I have and go back to the office from the gym and eat a tuna salad sandwich in a pita pocket that leaks through the bag because it has too much tahini dressing and sweat through another shirt because my glands have not decided to stop, or when the local from 14th Street turns express one stop before mine and I have to take a local back downtown and it's midnight and it's August and the subway is at least twenty degrees warmer than surface and I decide that even though I am dead tired because I only got four hours' sleep the night before it will be quicker just to walk home from 72nd Street, or when my phone is out of service for an extended period of time (e.g., more than fifteen minutes) or invariably after I have sex with the person who had initially given me herpes.

Unnatural Acts, Nonstandard Positions

Herpes is just a minor indisposition, a major irritation; certainly not worthy of a cover in *Time* magazine, compared to Madonna, I mean. Hardly cause for alarm. The anal warts are, however, a major source of grief and humiliation. Every two or three weeks I am in a nonstandard position on the doctor's padded table; not lying, not sitting. I can only describe it as follows: imagine that I am wearing suspenders, and a crane has caught them with its hook at the seat of my pants and has lifted me by the ass a foot off the table. My elbows dig in tight to the padding; my hands are clasped behind my head as if I were a hostage in a bank robbery. My shirt is sweated through; my pants are now down to my ankles, my underwear not far behind. Doctor Rotorooter tells amusing jokes (about, for example, why warts are not burned off electrically when they occur in this area; should the patient fart, he might spark an explosion) and he applies the acid with the utmost of care and delicacy. How I appreciate the bedside manner. I close my eyes and think of more pleasant things: favorite dentists and root canal work. Doctor R doesn't have a particularly busy practice. He waits for flu season the way that some people wait for Barney's annual warehouse sale. After I button up and sit on the most extreme edge of the chair in order to minimize contact, I write him a check and listen to him talking about the anxieties that accompany closing the deal for his co-op in the Village. On the memo section of the check I write "real estate: extortion."

Aside from herpes and warts, there's a host of minor dermatological disasters, including psoriasis, impetigo, dermatitis, seborrhea and dandruff, virtually anything you would care to name that requires sixty dollars for a five-minute visit with a skeletal dermatologist who seems to be spending an inordinate amount of time in Peru and always seems to have a case of the sniffles. All this is minor.

Except now I am worried that my lymph glands are slightly swollen at the neck. Is this because of the herpes, or did they cause this outbreak? Questions of teleology concern me deeply. Was it the chicken or the egg? How did the first sheep catch the clap, if not from an errant farm boy? Everything, of course, has a reasonable explanation in the end. The recent unexplained weight loss of four or five pounds became an equally mysterious weight gain the next day. This, due to a faulty scale. The purplish bruise on the arm is terrifying until it is realized that that particular arm had been burned on the frying pan during an unsuccessful attempt at chicken Marengo. Again, the temperature reading of 105.5, which caused severe hysteria (shallow breathing, profuse perspiration, and a host of other allied symptoms) last Sunday, turned out to be the thermometer's only reading. Unlike the stopped clock which is at least accurate twice a day, the broken thermometer has no value whatsoever. And on it goes. The sweating at night: is this pathological or just because of the August humidity?

Nonetheless my neck aches and it is 95 degrees outside with 200 percent humidity and the office is littered with shrink-wrap covers of the well-bred kitchen gourmet fruit squares, a testament to my willful exertions (they are nigh impossible to remove) and Dr Pepper empties (even my empty calories are directed toward quasi-medicinal sources) and once again I seem to be without prospective boyfriends and the thought of reading through ten pages of fine print personals in search of more prospective boyfriends in the *New York Native* is not at all appealing and going to a bar would be too depressing and going to the baths is of course out of the question and now my head starts to hurt which could be dehydration from the endless series of carbonated beverages I flood my system with or else could be from the minor case of the runs I've had off and on for weeks or months or years and might even be from the herpes which also seems to affect my sinuses and I don't even know why I should be THINKING about prospective boyfriends considering the state I'm in, I should probably be eating more saltpeter in my diet but the equations are just too complicated or maybe too direct and simple for me to comprehend. Sex equals death. Libido equals Thanatos. They used to be flip sides of the coin, didn't they?

I've been convinced that I was dying about three times in the past three years. My head was pounding, I was at the gym and I noticed a swelling at the side of my neck. I did my fifty pushups mechanically, thinking, "This is it. The final curtain. The big sleep. The deep six." How gladly I paid Doctor Rosen (fee due in advance; no checks or credit cards, please) to tell me that the swelling I was feeling was a subcutaneous pimple, a gathering of pus not even a cyst. Sad for me, I never believed in an afterlife. If I ever come back chances are it will be as a strand of worry beads.

I used to think that VD could be eradicated if everyone on the planet abstained from sex for fourteen days and anyone with symptoms was treated. This includes sheep. You would only have to wait for the period of transmission or detection. As precautionary measure, all sexual contacts of those infected would also be treated. And, just to be safe, all contacts of those contacts. With AIDS, we merely have to extend this fourteen-day period to eight or ten years. This might even do something for the population explosion as a side-effect.

Love for Lydia

Well, I'm in my office, in shock, after Richard's phone call. Ten minutes later Lydia Magnussen, deranged Southern Belle, called me on her WATS line at work.

"BEEJAY! It's Lydia!"

"Oh, uh, hi."

"What's wrong BEEJAY? You don't seem OVERWHELM-INGLY OVERJOYED to hear from me."

"Uh, I'm a little low. Richard just called and said he was moving to San Francisco in two days."

"Worrying about RICHARD again. I told you that Bernard or Edward would have been much more suitable for you YEARS ago, but DID you LISTEN? Well, I'm REALLY sorry, but I can't say that I didn't WARN you. It must be my SEVENTH sense." Lydia had met Richard on the street in passing a few years ago, and after we broke up, she told me I should have been lovers with Bernard or Edward, two hopelessly charming and irresponsible English boys. One worked at Lloyd's of London as window dressing; he was devastatingly attractive and utterly bored by the business. The other sold used cars and defrauded credit cards for a living. They would pop in at odd intervals and just as randomly pop out. Lydia is a hopeless Anglophile: anything said with a proper English accent, brack-eted by "rathers" and "quites" was smashing in her estimation. I must admit my spine does get goose bumps when I hear an English man being abusive to his boots or companions. Lydia had visited Bernard and his family for two weeks a few years ago. Bernard was a bit resentful that she always seemed to disappear into the ladies' room when the bill for lunch arrived, but his parents were quite impressed with her, to the point of wanting to adopt her as a daughter-in-law (Bernard was most distressed at the position in which that would place him). I stopped speaking to Edward when the mail that I had said he could have sent to my address turned out to be bills from American Express and I subsequently received several extremely rude telephone calls from credit officials.

"Gee, I'm sorry," said Lydia. "Do you want me to send you my recipe for breakfast biscuits, like the ones I made the last time you visited me in Raleigh? God, it seems like it was AGES ago. I remember exactly what you said that morning. You said that those were the best biscuits you had ever eaten in your entire life, you said that you PREFERRED those biscuits to Arlene's buttermilk donuts in Santa Monica and I know you weren't just FLATTERING me, I could tell that was the TRUTH, and those donuts used to be your FAVORITE breakfast in the ENTIRE WORLD, although I've heard a great deal of positive things about the blueberry muffins they serve at the Ritz Carlton in Boston. I remember what I was wearing. I was wearing that extremely tacky T-shirt that you gave me when I visited LA that said 'I'm with stupid,' remember, I made you buy us matching TACKY T's? Well, would that make you feel any better if I sent you the recipe for those shortening biscuits?"

I gurgled some reply and listened to Lydia rattle on about the wedding plans (this was her third; for some odd reason or coincidence the husbands were always named Michael; now whenever she meets a man named Michael she gets this odd glint in her eyes, whether or not she is currently between spouses) the utter dearth of high culture in the Low South, the latest Victorian novel she had reread, and other minutiae of *la vie quotidienne*. I muttered a threat that when the reverend (she always prefers to have a religious ceremony) got up to the question that ends with "or forever hold your peace," I would shout, "But the bride has syphilis and the groom is a homosexual and the wedding cake isn't chocolate," or confess my undying love for the best man and she said so long as I record it for posterity on videotape that's fine with her.

She wished me good luck and cheer up and she hung up.

I spent the rest of the afternoon under the desk doing the *New York Times* crossword puzzle. Somehow I dragged myself through the rest of the working day. I made seventeen promises I knew I could not or would not fulfill to associates and strangers and bosses and underlings, my legions of serfs (five or six of them, I'm never quite sure: this is one of the keys to my success at the job past my level of incompetency), typed up a few meaningless memos and went home to check the mail and lie down.

Be It Ever so Humble

The apartment in a moment of whimsy and miscalculated aesthetics is painted two shades of blue: morose and inconsolable. There is no television in the apartment. This, less of a moral stance than a snobbish and elitist affectation, enacted when I realized that more households have television than indoor plumbing. Presently the management has chosen to upgrade the apartment with an intriguing avant-garde design concept: exposed plumbing. There was a leak in the wall. After ripping up a significant portion of the bathroom wall, the super, evidently pleased with the effect he had created, chose to leave the wall in this seemingly unfinished state.

The ceiling hasn't collapsed, so I am grateful. Each day I come home and the ceiling is still there I am thankful, remembering the day four years ago when this was not the case. The phone is working, another one of the modern conveniences I do not take for granted. I seem to lose phone service about once every three months. Most recently, after the hurricane, my phone has undergone a curious metamorphosis. On pulse I got nada, but when I switched to tone I heard a tiny voice exhorting me to give my soul to Jesus. It was "The Voice of Prophecy," a syndicated radio show. In some bizarre fashion my telephone had transformed itself into a radio receiver. I call Richard and arrange to meet him for dinner.

I look through the mail. Two bills (VISA and *Mother Jones*), six appeals (Cesar Chavez Farm Workers, Planned Parenthood —I'm already doing my part—Common Cause, League of Women Voters, Gray Panthers, National Gay Task Force, and a raffle for the Gay Men's Health Crisis), and something from Publishers Clearinghouse.

I look up. This is one of those apartments that is too cheap to ever leave. I don't understand where all of the money goes. I mean, pornographic magazines, theater tickets, eating out, long-distance phone calls, Godiva chocolates, and hardcover novels can't account for it all, can it? I debate on whether to play an album before going down to see Richard. I am pathologically polite at times—too polite to turn off a record before it's finished for fear of offending the artists. I look at the floor: a sock or two, my dressy shoes, some dirty sneakers, the telephone book, the phone, a book, a magazine (*Mother Jones*), a shopping bag from D'Agostinos, a pornographic magazine, a bill from

VISA, an invitation to a Halloween party, some souvenirs from a trip to the Far East. On the couch is underwear, a *New York Native*, a *Playbill*, a small black telephone book, a pair of shorts, a pen, a folder of things to do in New York for visitors, and a sweater. On the desk is a watch, a pair of scissors, a sushi handkerchief, a clock, a lamp that doesn't work, a typewriter, a glass at the edge of the desk, waiting to be knocked over. I go to the bathroom to brush my teeth and see: a dirty mirror losing some of its reflectivity covering a medicine case overflowing with pills and ointments, Band-Aids, adhesive tape, eye drops, a package of Good News blue plastic razors (unopened), dental floss, a rusted pair of scissors for trimming the mustache, shaving cream, nail clippers, mouthwash, a bottle of Eau Sauvage cologne, toothpaste, and my six or seven "guest" toothbrushes.

Back in my bedroom, I see the bulletin board with: theater tickets, postage rates, a postcard from the board of elections indicating the electoral district, along with a small photograph of a man doing situps in profile advertising a brand of polyesterless clothing. Under the paper are subway tokens and quarters and dimes. Where are the keys? I change from school clothes to play clothes, find something appropriate to read so the train won't get stuck in a tunnel, and leave.

Driven to Tears

I go past the oppressive sign flashing GET RIGHT WITH GOD on one side and SIN WILL FIND YOU OUT on the other, and then the Adonis (Flagship Male Theater of the Nation) and go down to the subway. By the token booth, there is a little sign: Courtesy is contagious, let's start an epidemic. I imagine that everywhere people's faces are being replaced by life-size have-a-nice-day yellow smile buttons, like in *Rhinoceros* where all the characters turned into rhinoceroses. I catch the train uneventfully at 50th Street. I get off at West Fourth Street and cross to the uptown exit because it always smells of piss on the downtown Seventh Street exit. I have to call from the corner. I pace back and forth from phone booth to phone booth. A Puerto Rican woman about forty is speaking Spanish rapidly into the working phone; the other has its coin drop stopped. Richard tells me he will be down in a minute.

Jessica is in the window, looking out, in the planter. She ignores me. Richard and I sit down. I cannot look him in the eye. "Well," I say in a quiet even voice, so small it amazes me that it is coming from my mouth. "I hope you know what you're doing. It's rough moving to a totally new place without friends."

"I've thought this through," says Richard in his oddly sane voice. "I know it will be difficult at first, but it's time for a change."

"Are you doing anything about the TV set?" It was rented from Granada TV rentals.

"That's not that important. William downstairs will look after things. If things don't work out, I can always come back. You know, nothing is irrevocable."

"What about your mail? Are you going to have it forwarded?"

"It's just bills. No. I want to start from scratch. BJ, you're not being totally honest with me now. I want you to look me in the eye and tell me how you FEEL."

Why are you doing this to me? I think. Why are you trying to drive me to tears? You know how I feel. Do you want me to beg you to stay? Will that make any difference? If it does, does it only prove that you are incapable of making decisions on your own? Are you trying to humiliate me? Why are you doing this to me?

There are a thousand and one reasons why you shouldn't go. I want to be calm, rational. I don't want to start crying. The last time I cried was at a phone booth after another prospective boyfriend jilted me because he was disease conscious and I had just gotten another herpes outbreak because I was so upset when I came home to discover the apartment in utter disarray, they had installed new windows and not bothered to clean up afterwards and somehow managed to cut my phone wire in the process and of course it was on a Friday so I wouldn't get repair service over until Monday, I was buying the *New York Daily News* and saving the quarters for phone calls so I could call people and get their machines from the phone booth around the corner and I had called up Lloyd to tell him that we could have dinner that night but we couldn't fool around because my face had broken out and he had said well maybe we shouldn't be seeing each other anymore because he was unable to give me what I wanted which was to be boyfriends because that required a time commitment he couldn't really afford because he had this new job that he had to work sixty hours a week and he was learning the piano and in therapy and working out at the gym and he really didn't have time for a relationship and I knew that his job was more important than me and the times that I slept over at his apartment he forgot to set the alarm clock to get me to work on time because subconsciously he wanted the extra hour of sleep and of course he wouldn't sleep at my apartment so this said to me in effect that he was more important than my job which I suppose totally negated my existence when you put the two together and I kept on getting these little illnesses and he was spooked, he had had several friends die of AIDS so maybe it would be the best thing to not see each other anymore, and I paused, and I kept my voice calm and even and said "Sure" and then he said those same six words that Richard said, "But how do you really feel?" and I don't think I will ever forgive him for making me break down in tears at a phone booth in public, I mean he was crying too after a while but at least he was home in his apartment, the spineless bastard, the least he could have done was break up face-to-face, and here my phone was out of order and I had gone out of my way to please, I had even bought a bottle of Rose's Lime Juice for his infernal vodka gimlets, which I decided to mail to him, although there was the question of whether I should shatter the bottle before sending it or rely on the United States Postal Service to do my dirty work for me. Three years ago Richard and I had broke up in the very same apartment, leaving me with the ignoble task of returning home by SUBWAY, and here I am again, I sobbed to Richard.

"I worry about you all of the time."

"You wouldn't know it from that exterior."

JUNGLE DOVE

• JOSEPH PINTAURO •

REMY LOMBARDI HAD two paperbacks in his pocket when he was released from the prison infirmary: *Dear Theo*, the letters of Vincent Van Gogh, and *Halfway to Heaven*, a book about Carthusian monks. Remy's eyes were swollen and bloodshot from the beatings the night before. He was led to a small room where he waited in a chair as his guard, Diaz, dipped a buttered roll into a Styrofoam cup.

For Remy, it was sweet to be in a soundless place. His head had become a bell, reverberating with sharp echoes: men shouting, steel doors clanging, keys jangling, but this room was soundproof and the walls were covered with a dark green vinyl which soothed his eyes.

Diaz's sparse hair was spun into a black, acrylic-looking cloud, which floated over his balding head. His mustache was so thick it stuck out horizontally. He caught dripping coffee and melted butter with oversized lips. Little explosions would occur in his mouth when his gold teeth caught the glare of the overhead light. The man ate with pinky finger up, shined shoes apart, yet he attacked his roll like a shark. Remy closed his eyes to enjoy the silence, but Diaz, resenting it, spoke out.

"Know why you're getting this here cell change, Lombardi?"

Remy shrugged, keeping his eyes down.

"You're going to a two-man cell, the honeymoon suite." Diaz laughed. "You lucked out, man." Remy focused on the coffee droplets on the floor. Diaz erased them with his shoe. "A pretty man is no good in prison. We gotta keep your dago ass safe, man." Remy tried to reunite with the silence. "But you gotta help yourself. You get what I'm tryin' to say to you? You gotta make your cellmate a soulmate is what I'm trying to say. You cooperate with him," Diaz laughed, mockingly, "and your ass won't be public pussy no more."

"Nobody got me yet."

"Guards don't always break things up that are happenin', you know. Sometimes they like a good show." Diaz smiled. "You don't get lucky every time around here, you know."

The door opened and a tall crew-cutted guard entered the room. His name tag read "Washburn." He had the face of an Olympic swimmer, red-eyed, tired, waterlogged. Dark skin surrounded the man's eyes, giving him a pandalike countenance, but the tips of his yellow hair caught light and glowed. He wore the sad expression of the condemned angels in the fresco at Our Lady of Pompeii Church near Remy's apartment in Greenwich Village. It was obvious that Diaz didn't like this man.

"Are you Lombardi?"

"Yeah," Diaz answered for Remy, throwing his cup toward the basket. "Let's go, dago. Up to top ramp." Washburn eyed Remy with sorrowful curiosity.

"Hold it a second here." The guard took a yellow paper from his shirt pocket. "This guy originates in this building? Right, Diaz?"

"That's right." Diaz let his impatience show.

"What's the sense transferring him just to another ramp when the same bastards who jumped him are still in this building?"

Diaz's face flushed.

"He's going to a different *cell* . . ." Diaz answered, picking his teeth.

"How's a different cell gonna protect him?" Washburn's eyelid fluttered. "On top of it you got him bunkin' with Coco here."

"Oh cut out this shit, man," Diaz spit out.

"You tryin' to tell me the warden *approved* of this?"

"That's correct," Diaz said, now growing pale. "Check out the signature."

"What's happening here?" Remy asked softly.

"This is so full of shit," Washburn said, dashing the paper against his thigh. Remy's mouth had become dry.

"I'm jus' gonna get another guard to assist me then," Diaz said, reaching for the doorknob.

"Oh fuck you, Diaz." Washburn stopped him.

"*Fuck yourself, man*. I don't like you mouthin' off in front of my prisoner, that's number one, man. Two, this dago's in deep shit wherever we put him so you gonna assist me or do I call the warden?"

Washburn blinked then grabbed Remy's arm with a trembling hand. Diaz pulled the door open and the three men marched softly down the corridor, past the noisy cafeteria. One inmate on the breakfast line, knowing the situation, let go a sexy whistle. When Remy, Diaz, and Washburn started up the stairwell, other inmates made kiss sounds.

"Tonight's the Night," one inmate sang out. Others made it a chorus. "Tooooonaaaahts da naaaaaht," they sang. Remy's eyes darted to Washburn for help.

"You know why you were jumped last night?" Washburn whispered.

"No."

"The donut incident. You hear about it?"

"What donut incident?"

"Some wise guys in an Italian neighborhood jumped a carload of blacks who stopped to buy donuts on their way home from work. One was killed. So there's revenge attacks going on in prisons all over."

"But I had nothing to do with it."

"They're just looking for dago virgins."

"So what does this mean? Where you taking me?"

"Don't listen to that creep. Shut up Washburn, okay?" Diaz spoke gently to Remy. "You know what they call this tier we're takin' you to? Heaven. We're makin' you safe, man. What can I tell you? Trust me."

"Don't," Washburn whispered.

The three climbed to the top tier, so high, Remy was afraid to look down.

"Good-bye and take care of yourself," Washburn said, unlocking the walkway gate. "Things could be worse." He winked at Remy. "Really."

Diaz pushed Remy onto the narrow ramp that ran for a hundred yards alongside open cells. Washburn locked the gate behind them.

"Walk in front," Diaz ordered. Remy walked dizzily, fearful of looking down. But if any place in the prison could be called heaven, this was certainly it. The master gate was open and all cells were empty, beds made. It was warmer up there. "Walk to the end," Diaz ordered. Privacy was the main feature of the cells on that level. They all seemed to float on air looking out to a chasm of light, then to the blue, cement-block wall opposite. Fancy bedspreads, radios, and rugs were in the cells. When they reached the end of the ramp, Diaz pointed.

"Top bunk."

Remy's new cell was partially constructed of old black stone. One wall was concave. Obviously, the new wing was joined to the old building at that point. The stone wall was clearly the interior of an old tower because Remy could make out marks along the wall where a stone staircase had been. The cell had ceiling bars to prevent anyone from scaling the stone wall. Beyond the ceiling bars, some ninety feet up, were lighthouse windows that shone with an exciting burst of light. Looking up soothed Remy's eyes. The light at the top of the tower was unlike anything he had seen in that prison. It cascaded downward into a cloudlike asparagus fern which hung from the ceiling bars. A guitar lay on the bed, and a tape deck was set up with small speakers attached to the wall. A philodendron plant inside a bamboo bird cage was climbing up through the ceiling bars, falling back over and over, giving the cell a partial roof of leaves. The strange light unshackled his nerves. If his eyes were birds, Remy thought, he'd set them loose to fly up, out the tower windows, across the East River, home to Greenwich Village and Little Italy.

"Why am I being put here?"

"How come you got to jail in the first place?" Diaz smirked.

"I'm clean."

"Innocence don't mean shit here."

"Aren't you afraid I'll hang myself from these ceiling bars?"

"Hang yourself. If your cellmate don't like you, your ass is back in the bullpen anyway. You heard those guys on the breakfast line." Diaz stepped out to the walkway. "We got a good morgue, man. Only you can't breathe in them refrigerators. It sucks."

Diaz pulled the master gate, which rolled quietly, then he turned, walking away, softly whistling. Remy listened, staring up at the cloudlike fern till the clamor of footsteps died on the rampway. Then he lay back on the bunk and blinked at the light. The cell was as quiet as a church. The light at the top of the tower was changing, as if clouds were passing the sun. "God please, lift me up with your almighty hand and put me back in your good world. Why'd you let this happen to me? You want me to hate you? Don't force me to hate you." He felt tears coming. He wiped his eyes and mouth with his shirtsleeves and the brightness of Coney Island appeared in his mind, the sand, the ocean and sky, and behind the horizon, the peachy light of heaven. He remembered a priest at Power Memorial High School describing how those who commit suicide are turned into birds in the ninth circle of hell with their feet frozen in ice, and the constant batting of their wings to free themselves only makes the ice colder and this is their eternal punishment. He thought of Maria Goretti who was attacked and raped but who forgave her attacker before she died, and was beatified, canonized and given a Saint's place in heaven.

Remy belonged to the Dominic Savio Club in grade school. He wondered what happened to his lapel pin. He didn't want to become angry with the saints. He uttered a short prayer to St. Theresa Little Flower:

"Save me from this shit."

A loud buzzer rang, the master gate rolled open and hundreds of footsteps began tramping up the steel stairs, drumming on the ramps of each tier. The sound became lighter as the inmates dropped into their cells, softer and softer, until it was just the shuffle of two feet before him.

A light-skinned black man stood looking down at Remy. His hair was all finger waves like old Cab Calloway and his eyes were green. His beard was red and kinky.

"I'm Coco. This is my cell. Here's your breakfast." He spoke with a New York City accent.

The black man kept to his bunk the rest of the day, moving his long body only when necessary, his eyes avoiding Remy completely. There was a slow grace to his movements, which appeared to be a learned discipline, a way of undermining the confinement.

At dinner in the mess hall, the two sat together. No one dared to speak to Coco. He ate as if alone, like a king in a private chamber. For the first time Remy felt the pleasure of having no one looking at him. The inmates neither stared, nor winked, nor grinned as usual. Remy ate calmly, not even tasting what he put in his mouth, just savoring the dignity.

That night the tower windows glowed with the moon. Coco lay on his bunk, his elbow in his pillow, a magazine before him. The black man held a position of repose, but his catlike muscles rippled and his eyes jiggled at high speeds, catching movement before it started. In that light his eyes were the color of a dark sea. They nailed Remy's, and the man smiled. A cold terror went through Remy. The smile was too sudden, purposeful, and Remy turned away, refusing to trust it.

Even past lights out, Remy hadn't moved. He remained leaning against the bars with his back to the walkway, letting the strange blue light wash down his face. He planned to fall asleep standing up. He would never go near that bunk and Coco. Only when Coco threw aside his magazine and fell back yawning, Remy closed his eyes. Minutes passed, of silence, except for their breathing. Remy liked the breathing sounds, their cadences. Then Remy's nostrils caught the strong odors of almond and black cherry. Coco, still in his bunk, was screwing the cover off a white jar that glowed like a communion host.

"You want a hit?" Coco asked.

"Hit of what?"

"Cold cream." The black man laughed appealingly, rubbing some into his temples. "It's laced with Ecstasy." The black man spoke in a throaty whisper.

"No thanks."

"It works, man."

"I get off on quiet."

"That helps you sleep, but Ecstasy takes you to paradise."

"That where you'd like to put me?"

"You think I want you dead?"

"Not before you rip my ass open."

"Hey, man, I don't hold no grudges against you."

Remy kept his eyes on the windows. Coco touched a black finger to the glowing white cream. "It's got DMSO," he whispered.

"What's DMSO?"

"Makes the skin absorb. Ecstasy through the skin man. It's fuckin' cool."

Remy faked a yawn.

Coco rose and slowly came toward Remy, standing before him. He reached down for Remy's hand, very carefully taking it. When Remy tried to pull away, Coco viced him strong.

"Easy, man." With one black finger, he rubbed the cream into the center of Remy's palm, stroking hard to the underside of his wrist. Remy pressed the back of his head into the bars as Coco's bony fingers rose touching Remy's temples. "You never used a drug this way." Coco's eyes in the blue light were satanic.

"Where's Diaz?" Remy hoped for the guard's shadow.

"Off duty."

"Who's on?"

"Lambert."

"Aren't you taking chances with that shit?"

"They're all on my payroll." The black man smiled wide. "We gonna be friends?"

"Don't make me laugh."

"You ain't even had the decency to tell me your name."

"You know my name," Remy said with hurt. "You had me put in here. You wanna crucify my ass."

Coco smiled, looked down and in a shy voice said: "No such thing, man. I jus' wanted to get near the dick that makes love to the woman with the black feathers and the perfume. What's that chick's name?"

"My *wife*," Remy answered, startled that Coco had seen her. Valetta's only visit had infuriated him. She'd dressed in a retro black suit and coat, carrying an oversized black fur muff and wearing a fifties hat covered with blue-black feathers that curled under her chin. It was a gag for Remy's benefit, but he hated it. Valetta wrote an apology, promising she'd dress plainer if he let her return, but he forbade her.

"That woman made me forget I was in jail, man. She made me breathe easy that woman did."

"She's pregnant," Remy said spitefully.

"She happy about it? That's all that counts, is a woman happy."

"What's she got to do with Diaz sticking me in here?"

"I can still smell that woman in these stones."

"Oh yeah?"

"But I don't smell her on you. You stink too much of yourself."

The black man turned, walked back to his bunk and started to undress. "I'll tell Diaz to put another guy in here, but when they hear about it downstairs your pretty ass is Yankee Stadium again."

Naked, Coco slipped under a blanket, curling his knees up to the wall, but his long, bony spine stayed uncovered and the sight of it repulsed Remy, who was still standing, his thighs hard as marble, not softening until sounds of sleep came out of Coco.

Remy dropped his shoulders and threw back his head in relief letting his eyes loosen, letting them rise upward, like birds softly flying toward the window's shining whiteness. He closed his lids, imagining the birds breaking through the glass, flying toward the silver moon above a planet of tiny lights: the lights of the Manhattan Bridge, the millions of skyscraper window lights, aircraft: helicopters, seaplanes, all blinking mutely, lights floating, lights dancing, zigzagging, lights streaking, neon ribbons, white, green, red, yellow. His birds flew southwest toward the Chrysler Building, around its needle in a great semicircle to Fifth Avenue, then downtown to Greenwich Village over the great arch of Washington Square Park. Downward they dipped, across the fountain; then zooming up and banking west toward Sheridan Square, over Christopher Street, over the Lion's Head Bar, across Seventh Avenue, up over the big billboard and Smiler's Deli, they hovered, and descended silently to the gardens behind Grove Street, narrowing into the airshaft of an old house, to an open window on the first floor, lighting on the sill, several white birds at a time, each entering, pushing others in, until the room was filled with hundreds of birds where Valetta slept, in the ruby aura of votive candles. She opened her eyes for a moment, sensing Remy's presence. She saw nothing, closed her eyes, then imagined his whisper:

Valetta! Valetta!

Remy's own voice woke him. He felt the coldness of death washing over him. Only a woman's body could save a man from this coldness. He wanted Valetta's arms wrapped around his head. He wished his grandmother were alive, even his mother would do. He clung to the thought of women. He pictured Valetta bathing her feet in a stainless steel tub, lifting her full thighs, not hiding anything from him. He knew his seed was alive in Valetta. Maybe a son. If he died, a son would be himself again. If he had known this was going to happen to him, he would have bred with a thousand women. He feared every trace of his existence would be lost in the world.

His heart was clanging against his chest bones like an iron tongue inside a bell. *Oh, yes, there was something in that cold cream.* He looked up, mentally paraphrasing one of Van Gogh's sentences. "Dying young is like flying to the stars. Dying old is making the trip on foot."

Remy whispered to the stars. *"If I'm going to die in this cell, take me now, take me fast."*

"How was you framed?" Coco's voice flew out of the shadow under the bunk. He turned waiting for Remy to answer. The black man's groggy green eyes seemed sincere. Remy stood there wondering if in some unpredictable way, telling Coco the truth might help him:

"An old lady was snuffed on the top floor where we live in Greenwich Village, you know? She kept this big bird, this cockatoo . . ."

"Yeah?"

"My wife'd cook extra for the old lady, but we ate out that night, so she sends me up to the woman with this doggie bag. I go in and the woman's in her big chair like she's asleep. I didn't know that her head was bashed in . . ."

"Shit."

"I hear this flapping down the airshaft in her bathroom as if her bird flew down there. I go in and I knock over a glass. I cut myself . . ."

"Poor motherfucker." Coco yawned.

"Am I boring you, man? Don't ask me to talk then yawn."

Coco's yawn froze. He eyed Remy with distrust, turned his back to Remy and pulled a blanket up to his shoulders.

"You'll fall dead if you don't lay down and sleep, man."

"I never sleep."

"Never huh?"

"I'll die standing here."

Next day, after lunch, Diaz pulled Remy aside.

"You don't give him some ass, dago, you're a dead-meat dude. I'm warnin' ya."

"Fuck you. We're getting along . . ."

"Naaaa. Naaaa. He wants a replacement. You don't put out tonight, man, you're back on the meat rack."

At dinner that night Remy was too depressed to eat. After lights out, something flew out of the bunk shadow and hit Remy in the chest. It clattered to the floor. Remy picked it up. It was a little plastic cylinder.

"What *is* this?"

"Lip ice. Strawberry flavor, man. Makes you forget your troubles."

Remy uncapped the cylinder, screwing out the sweet-smelling pink tip. An unexpected self-loathing, self-destructive urge, a feeling of both mischief and surrender overtook him. Imagining clowns, he traced a line of strawberry grease over his top lip, then his lower. In a moment his temples were swelling. He replaced the plastic cap and threw it toward the double moons of Coco's eyes shining in the bunk shadow. Coco caught the cylinder, opened it, and used it himself, watching Remy closely.

"Why do you want to hurt me?" Remy said suddenly.

"Who's gonna hurt you?"

"I don't wanna go back to the bull pen, man. Please."

"I like you, Lombardi. What're ya talkin'?"

"Fuckin' bullshit, man. You want an Italian in here because of the donut thing. I'm your revenge."

"No, no. No revenge. But you're right. I need a piece of meat in here. That's all. Plain and simple. I paid for you, man."

"Fuckin' insanity."

"Don't get nasty."

"I'm a man like you. I ain't some *dude*'s pussy."

"I ain't your protection either," Coco said softly. "You stand there all day and night like a piece of stone. I don't need a statue in here. I need a warm body."

"I can whack off with you," Remy ventured. "I'll talk dirty. We jack off."

"Like Boy Scouts?" Coco laughed. "Look, ma friend. I need *skin*, you know? I could have a ton of porno shit sent in here. I don't need to dirty talk. Skin, man. Shit, I could be havin' a good time with somebody else. Shit, man."

"What did you think I was gonna do for you?"

"Whatever I asked for, man. I thought you'd wanna save your life."

"I'm not afraid to die."

"Good. We'll get Diaz to get me someone else."

"Advise me what to do."

"Don't lower yourself, man."

Remy pointed at Coco. "This is a trick to get up my ass."

"Go to sleep, Lombardi."

"All because of a fuckin' donut."

"You're full of shit, man. I ain't no activist."

"This is a revenge move."

"Go to sleep."

"I'll talk *dirty* and jerk *off* with you," Remy pleaded. Coco stared, his eyes blinked tentatively.

"Okay, tell me 'bout your ole lady."

"Her name's Valetta . . . she's an actress . . ."

"Her body."

"Okay. She's thin . . ."

"Her pussy."

"Okay, man. Take it easy . . ." Remy heard the swooshing of the sheet under Coco's hand.

"Let your dick out," Coco ordered in a whisper.

"Lemme finish what I'm sayin'."

"*Don't push me, dago.*" Coco's voice rang out. "*Take the goddamn thing out.*" Remy unbuttoned his top button and zipped down his fly. "Go ahead, Lombardi. Jerk it."

Remy's body wasn't interested. He could only pretend to be masturbating.

"What you thinkin' of?" Coco asked shakily.

"Her."

"Who?"

"My ole lady."

"Talk about her pussy."

Remy wanted to attack the man—to tear his throat out like a dog. Instead he swallowed hard. "She's a normal woman."

"You got her legs up in the air?"

"What the hell you talking about?"

"Go along with me."

"Yeah, I got her legs up," Remy said, feeling ridiculous.

"Now, stick it up her. *Stick* it in there, you hear? You got it in?"

"Yeah . . ."

"All the way up?"

"Hold it a minute."

"Push, goddamnit. All the way now."

"Yeah." Remy was sweating, "I'm in."

"Now pump, man. You hear? Pump your fuckin' heart out." The sheets over Coco's hand sang like a hurricane. "Pump, dago. Pump your ass off. Now . . . get out. Get *out*," Coco screamed.

"Outta what?"

"Outta *her* and lemme in there quick!"

"Okay. I'm out."

"I'm in. Oh, yeah. Oh, yeah . . ." Coco moaned, "Oh sweet pussy. Sweet . . . pussssssyy. Uhhh, huuggg. Ooooff."

The odor of semen rose in the cell. Remy could hear snickers far off. No sign of Diaz on the ramp. Remy buttoned up, feeling safer, feeling ashamed. Coco lit a cigarette and sat on the edge of his bunk with both feet on the floor. Slowly, he let his face fall into his hands. When he looked back up at Remy, the black man seemed to have been crying.

"You get crazy in here. You understand? It just builds up and you're ashamed," Coco said.

"It's okay."

"I never cheated on my wife with another woman, forget about a man. Then I hit prisons. A man needs to fuck somethin'. Shit this ain't no good, Lombardi. I gotta get rid of you."

"Fucking nightmare."

"I need somebody else in here."

"I don't know about this shit."

"Guys who on the outside'd kill some motherfucker for puttin' a hand on their shoulder, in here, they're expert cocksuckers. Prison does things to people. Diaz'll get one of them in here to blow you and show you. This guy Duane. He's a pro, man. He'll put you in heaven with his mouth."

"Duane? What's in it for him?" Remy asked.

"He's queer. Jus' loves sucking cock and he ain't ashamed of it. I respect the guy. When it's over, Diaz brings the cocksucker back."

"What's your wife's name?" Remy took the black man by surprise.

"Whattya changing the subject?"

"No. Just curious."

"Bonita's her name," Coco said suspiciously.

"Bonita? She Italian?" Remy smiled deliberately. Coco looked surprised, then let go a laugh that lasted long enough to bring moans from nearby cells. Diaz's shadow crept up the ramp and then retreated.

"Hell, Bonita's black as they come. Blue-black. She shines like an African princess, like coal. Her hair's short and her eyes are like some Egyptian. Bonita's black." Coco yawned, grabbed the blanket and turned to the wall. "Don't worry, Lombardi. You're safe for tonight. Sleep on your bunk, man. Nobody's gonna mess with you tonight."

Next morning Remy received a letter from Valetta, saying that their landlord had come to the door reminding her that they were behind in rent. This worried Remy because in a few weeks the landlord would have legal power to evict her.

That night, after lights out, Diaz came down the ramp and whispered something to Coco. When he left Coco threw himself angrily on his bunk.

"No Duane tonight." Remy waited for Coco to cool, then spoke:

"Tell me more about Bonita."

Coco swallowed two pills, then staring up past the philodendron, he started speaking, taking on the voice of a storyteller. A smile creased his face and he made Remy laugh, explaining how Bonita stashes twenty thousand dollars into one carton of Lucky Strikes:

"See, she irons the bills flat with a steam iron, then she rolls 'em so tight that she fits two bills inside one roll of paper. She seals the packs with cellophane and a hot curling iron and she puts that red pull-tab, just like real. She's got cigarette cartons stashed in safe deposit boxes in the Chase Manhattan Bank. That's how Diaz is gonna retire in Arizona, on Lucky Strike payola."

"You feed him too much, you lose your inside man."

Coco laughed. "Everybody is for hire when it comes to Lucky Strikes."

"How'd you wind up in here?" Remy asked.

"Why you interested?"

"Maybe I was . . . hoping you weren't a criminal, and I'd have a chance here."

Coco laughed. "You are full of shit. Of course I'm a criminal," Coco said with distrust. "Now you spoiled my story . . ."

"Sorry."

"Well . . ." Coco talked on, about how he and Bonita started a mail order business out of an old building in Queens. The Aloe-Aloha Skin Saver Corporation. It was set up to launder coke money, but the crazy business made a profit. He said they sold the business for one point five million. He said he was in jail on a trumped-up manslaughter charge and was spending record time waiting for trial. He claimed the Feds were piling up delays as punishment for his drug dealing because the manslaughter evidence didn't really exist.

Remy laughed in spite of himself when Coco described how Bonita refused to dump a couple of keys of drugs down a toilet bowl and used her mother's pestal and mortar to grin them up, then her mother's blender, mixing the drug with Aloe-Aloha skin products. She mashed Ecstasy and coke into the fruit-flavored lip ice, then reconstituted it into containers and refrigerated them. He told Remy he used one as a suppository, and that Bonita's mother's old freezer in St. Albans was stockpiled with loaded cosmetics.

In turn, Remy told the true story of how a hot diamond was stashed in zeppole dough during the Feast of San Gennaro, and how the pastry was sold for twenty-five cents to a nun who said she broke her tooth and swallowed it, but soon after the convent got a new furnace and a new roof. Remy told of the social clubs in Little Italy, little empty shops where men play cards and sell soda and kids play jukeboxes and dance on the streets, and how before SoHo got ruined, he worked there as a mechanic on mafia limos. He spoke of his grandmother's grape arbor in her backyard behind the Neopolitan record store and how, when she died, he moved six blocks across Seventh Avenue, into the uppity world of West Greenwich Village where he met Valetta.

Coco told Remy how as a kid, he ran away from Alabama to Harlem when his mother died, and lived with his aunt, and how he witnessed the murder of Malcolm X and put a finger into Malcolm's blood, then touched it to his tongue. He described Bonita as a beauty, a French woman with high morals. He said he was ashamed of his green eyes because some people thought he had white in him.

The men talked nervously, in whispers, till three A.M., putting forth one little story after another, like little gifts that they could unwrap. Still, not until Coco was snoring did Remy climb into his bunk and lay there, gazing at the moonlit windows, glad to be awake, floating above the black man, imagining those Harlem brownstones and the old black ladies leaning on pillows as they looked out their windows, and beautiful black girls humming the blues from fire escapes. Coco slept, but Remy stayed awake till the light of dawn appeared at the windows at the top of the tower. He lay there interpreting sounds, isolating faraway noises, turning them into something else. Cars on the highway became the swish of a woman's stockings as she crossed her legs. Guards running the stairs became high heels drumming on steel stairways. He imagined Valetta in the building, wandering past cells in her black coat, carrying her big black fur muff.

* * *

But the next day, Coco acted as if he despised Remy. The black man's actions confused Remy. Remy could only assume that Coco felt manipulated by the friendly talk and decided to become hostile again. Still there was no transfer to any other cell and after lights out Remy managed to speak up.

"Hey, Coco? What about this Duane?" Coco didn't answer. He just took a pill, jumped into his bunk and went to sleep.

Remy used the toilet as quietly as possible. He brushed his teeth, wiping his mouth and hands with a little towel, then read for an hour, but when he looked up, Coco was sitting up in his bunk, masturbating openly, unashamedly pinning Remy's eyes. Remy walked self-consciously to the gate bars, glancing over the walkway. Diaz's shadow wasn't on the ramp. All kinds of things went through Remy's mind of what could happen. He figured that Coco's actions were a dangerous sign, a test or an ultimatum, but he knew he couldn't bring himself to perform anything sexual with the black man. He couldn't even imagine the words to speak of it with Coco.

"Turn around, Lombardi," Coco said softly. "Look here."

"I thought you said Duane . . ." Remy looked down.

"The biggest joke in prison is a man holding out when he ain't got a nickel's worth of leverage. You just look silly, man. You think you can win soft-soapin' me? Why should I let you do that, man? You dagos would kill a black man for buying a donut. Why should I let you play the fuckin' stag when you ain't got a pot to piss in, turkey? You're just a jail bum, struttin' in rags on my turf. You don't own *shit*. You're my property. I bought you, Lombardi."

"C'mon, brother, you don't mean that stuff," Remy said softly.

"Don't brother me."

"What did I have to do with the donut murder? Shit, I never even got a traffic ticket and I'm in here takin' shit from you."

"My black brother never got a traffic ticket. He was bustin' his hump to feed his kids and he stopped for a lousy donut."

"I'm innocent. I don't go by color."

"I ain't payin' Diaz so you can keep your pride. You tell yourself I'm a crazy nigger . . ."

"No . . ."

"You look down on me, but you gonna feel this yourself . . ."

"I don't look down on you. I listen to you breathe."

"Don't give me no bull*shit*," Coco shouted.

"*I listen to you*," Remy topped his shout, then quieted. "I watch over you when you sleep. I'm grateful to be in here with you. I know the score. I just can't give you warm skin, man. Don't you see you're killin' me? You want me to turn queer? I'm trying to be a friend, you want me to be a piece of meat. Don't you believe in God?"

The black man looked at Remy embarrassed, but not hiding it. He leaned forward.

"You turn to meat or die."

"Duane is out now?"

"He'll be my cellmate tomorrow."

"C'mon, man, you been away from Bonita too long," Remy said.

Coco sprang up and came face-to-face with him, grabbing him by the shirt, bringing his mouth close.

"*I know I been away from Bonita.*"

Remy ignored Coco's intense breath and tried to eyeball the man with strength of his own. Suddenly Valetta's letter came to mind, eviction in two weeks, and that thought became a stepping stone. He wasn't sure he wanted to take the step, but he summoned up a daring that made the skin on his arms tingle.

"I'll make you a deal," he said pushing Coco back uncertainly.

"What's the deal?"

"Send one pack of Luckies to Valetta, and we got us a deal. Take it or leave it." Remy shocked himself. Coco's mouth shaped itself into a hurt little smile.

"And what do I get?"

"You can go down on me."

Coco's face turned dark red. His eyes peered deep into Remy's. "There's a little hustlin' whore in you, isn't there, Lombardi?" Remy swallowed, as if he had opened a door on hell.

"I ain't got long to live in here. They'll find me hanging. But my old lady—she's having a kid and we need the rent." Remy found himself crying without understanding why. "We need the rent," he kept repeating. "We need the rent." The black man understood what he was seeing somehow. He went back to his bunk, the gears of his mind obviously spinning, his eyes stalking. "If you weren't in this cell with me, you'd be gettin' your cheeks crowbarred apart by a dozen crazy inmates a night. You know that?"

"I do."

"I already bought your ass from Diaz and you want me to send money to your old lady?"

"If I had money, I'd have Diaz in here kickin' your ass all over this cell. If I had money I'd be buyin' my body back from you." Remy let tears show.

"It's not just your body, Lombardi."

Remy swallowed. "What the hell *do* you want from me? *Out* with it."

The green eyes disappeared under their lids. In a deep and shameful voice the black man said: "I need to balance the pain. You know? The pain my brothers feel. I need to balance the pain so that wisdom can return to the world." Remy blinked, trying to understand, hoping the statement meant something good. Then Coco opened a box under his bunk and took out two packs of Lucky Strikes. He placed them in a padded envelope, then grabbed a marker.

"Write:" Coco demanded, handing Remy the envelope and the marker. " 'Do not smoke. This is money. Slice open the cigarettes.' Now, put her name and address on the envelope." When Remy finished, Coco grabbed the envelope, sealed it and gave out a loud whistle, throwing the envelope out between the bars. It fell on the ramp. Diaz appeared and took the envelope. "I want a post office receipt. I want a delivery receipt for this." As if it were routine Diaz walked away with the small package. Coco faced Remy once again. "My part is done. Now pay up."

A sharp pain hit Remy in the stomach. Sweat was coming on. He thought: "This is an ulcer or a heart attack, this pain in my chest." He pushed Coco away gently, just a few inches, in order to put his hand into his shirt, to touch his chest where the awful pain was. Beads of water streamed down Remy's forehead. He felt drips running down the line of his belly hair. He pressed a finger over his left breast. These pains always went away in a minute, he reminded himself. He forced thoughts of Van Gogh, of dying and going to the stars, but that all seemed ridiculous now. He belched the pain away. The next wave of feeling was shame. He couldn't hold back the tears. He was afraid of Coco; he was afraid of sodomy and AIDS and he was afraid of wanting to kill himself.

Coco unbuttoned the top of Remy's pants. Remy blinked away sweat as he looked up. How had he lost himself? His life was over now whether he lived or died. No matter how good the lawyer was, no matter how clear his frame-up, it was already too late. The worst had already happened. The bad luck was staring him in the face, biting his face, chewing on him, consuming him. He was a criminal, though he committed no crime. And beyond the screwed-up judicial system, beyond crazed and angry Coco, beyond the poor black carpenter who'd been killed, beyond Valetta and the dead old woman and her crazy killer freely roaming the streets, there existed one stubborn truth: that Remy was just the unluckiest sonofabitch ever to be born on the face of the fucking earth. He cursed God and his grandmother's saints. He cursed Our Lady of Pompeii and Saint Theresa Little Flower. But he cursed Valetta more bitterly for sending him up those creaky stairs with that old woman's dinner.

Coco, with trembling hands, was pulling down Remy's zipper. Long fingers hooked into his belt loops, pulling down trousers and underwear in one motion, over thighs, past his knees. Diaz's shadow reappeared, stopped, and froze where it was.

"Don't ask me for no help," Remy said. "I can't help you, man."

"Don't worry, baby," Coco said with a strange smile. Suddenly, there was Diaz outside the cell and he had another man with him.

"Hey! *Duaaane!*" Coco's voice sailed. Remy reached for his trousers. "Keep your pants where they are. Get Duane in here," Coco ordered.

The master gate rolled quietly as Diaz pushed the man into the cell. Duane was taller than Coco, a pale, white man of about forty-five with pale eyes like Remy's grandmother's, gas-flame blue, fiery blue, eyes that darted nervously between Remy and Coco. His white shirt was fluorescent, as if it had absorbed light elsewhere.

"Go down on him." Coco pushed Duane toward Remy.

The man had very large hands and a craggy, wise face like the face of a bishop or a monk. His tall crew cut was pure white, fine as feathers, fanning out, catching the blue light from above and glowing over black eyebrows. The man's eyes offered sympathy as they descended, going down lower and lower until the crop of white hair was below Remy's waist. When Duane's large hands grabbed on to Remy's thighs, Remy threw back his head and sent his eyes up to the blue light, to the God beyond the God who betrayed him, unable to forgive, hating the world and all the creatures in it for failing him. Coco pushed in closer, offering Remy the strawberry lip ice, but Remy turned away from it, gripping the bars behind his back with both hands, trying to imagine it all being over, not just the moment, but the year, the next thousand years, when the other side of the stars would be discovered, the other side of life, the other side of death.

The moment Duane's mouth contacted Remy's penis, a shock of pain went through his groin and a weakness in the legs started coming over him. There was a moment of dizziness and then the sensation became erotic and Remy lifted on his toes. The feeling in his body was a momentary power of some sort, an assurance, not from his mind, but from his body's own hidden wisdom. He wasn't sure of what to compare it to. He didn't want to accept it for what it was. So he summoned up Valetta washing her feet again, lifting her legs so high that he could see under them, opening for him a little wider, wider still, and he let his body yield in a sort of kiss. Then suddenly he was aware only of Duane's mouth working. He blinked, unbelieving, up at the blue light, grateful for an unexpected assurance which seemed to come from beyond them all, grinding gently with it, while his thighs were swelling in Duane's hands. And then he groaned fearfully, as if his very life were about to leak out. His skin tightened, as if touched by ice, followed by that sensation he never understood, the silent eruption inside, the release, the weakness in the knees, the illusion that his parts were flying outward in all directions, as if pins had fallen from his joints, arms coming off, legs floating away, his head rising up like a balloon, so high he had to reach and grab it by the hair and pull it back down to his shoulders, to hold it down there, *hold it* . . . safe. And that's where his hands wound up, screwing his head back on, holding his forehead, running his hands through his hair.

Remy opened his eyes to Coco's strange smile.

"I've had enough. Get rid of this guy," Remy panted. No one moved. Duane stood up glancing expectantly toward Coco.

Suddenly Coco's fist crashed blindingly into Remy's face.

"Ohhh. Ohhhhh . . ." Remy groaned.

"Christ, what're ya doin?" Duane protested.

"Ugh. Uggghh." Remy heard his own groans as if they were coming from someone else. His nose and eyes, glowed in one massive pain. He tasted blood in his mouth. Stunned, Remy felt his body being turned so that he was looking through the bars now, face-to-face with Diaz who reached in and pulled Remy's arms through the bars, handcuffing them above the elbow. Before he could utter another sound, a six-inch elastic bandage was stretched over Remy's mouth and nose, making it impossible to breath. Diaz tore the bandage to below his nostrils, and Remy gratefully sucked in air. As his knees and ankles were being strapped to the bars, Coco's fingers pushed drug-soaked cotton up one of Remy's nostrils. As he sucked air through one free nostril, his heart began to clang, the veins of his head to swell. He was losing vision, barely aware of a cold hand slapping grease between his buttocks. He felt the penetration of a thumb, then the thumb pulled out. Coco's hands gripped the bars at either side of him and unbelieving, Remy felt the pressure of a cock between his ass cheeks, finding his rectum, then sliding inside. Remy's muscles were powerless to prevent the invasion. Coco entered him with sharp, cruel speed, upward as far as he could go. Remy screamed with the sudden pain but the sound reentered his lungs, hurting his chest. Coco savagely grabbed at pleasure, panting into Remy's ear: "When you go back to your people, tell them this is what happens. And I don't just mean you dagos. I mean the white man, the white man all over the world. Tell 'em you got this because you're white. . . . White. White. White. That's right. Open that ass. Open it. Here I come, baby. Here I come . . ."

Diaz was looking into Remy's eyes, smiling. "Trust me," he whispered, making kiss lips.

Coco removed himself from Remy's body with suddenness, then walked to the toilet. There was a moment of silence then the noise of his pissing echoed across the ramp. "Help yourself, Duane," Coco said. "Have your fun with him."

Remy felt Duane's hands wiping sweat from his forehead.

"Take off the cuffs, Diaz," Duane ordered in a whisper. When Remy's knees and arms were free he fell backward into Duane's arms. Duane's lips touched Remy's ear. "Easy, son. Easy now." Duane's breath smelled like tree bark. The man stuck a small pill in Remy's fist. "Take this. You'll sleep." In a matter of seconds, Diaz and Duane were gone.

The pain in Remy's body was overshadowed by the pain of his mind. All civilization was slipping, being sucked into its own asshole. All history, Christ, all the art, the Woody Allen movies, TV evangelists, Power Memorial, his life, all was fake, all shallow, all waste, all sucked out through a tiny donut hole in his mind. He was worse than dead. Who he was, was gone. What little was left, he was afraid of. There could be no funeral, no mourning, for no one would notice the death except himself.

Coco stared with stunned, moist eyes from out the shadow of his bunk, until he fell asleep. Remy stood frozen against the bars for an hour before discovering Duane's pill in his hand. He gratefully swallowed the thing and climbed into the top bunk where he fell asleep numbly, without hope and without fear, unable to forget the scent of Duane's whispers.

That night Remy dreamed he was hosing down the grape arbor behind his grandmother's record store on Sullivan Street, where wide cheesecloth lay across the arbor beams to protect the fruit from soot. Stained purple and rose, the cheesecloth lifted like long translucent curtains frightening the pigeons upward through tiers of clotheslines, until the birds burst into a clean sky. A soprano sang Puccini's "Un bel di" from one of the upper windows. Her voice wavered down through the clotheslines. There were flies where the beer had spilled the night before when the grape crushers had celebrated, playing poker and smoking DeNobili cigars. Remy zapped the flies with the hose, making rainbows, letting the icy wetness spray back into his face. The sun snaked down through pink and orange sheets and towels, turning the yard into a bowl of color. Dahlia and zinnia plants were still in bloom in his grandmother's beds, tired after a long summer, so he put a finger over the nozzle, baptizing the plants with a fine spray. Then the cellar door sprang open and the odor of wooden barrels rushed into the yard. Saint Francis of Assisi climbed out, with birds and rats clinging to his frock. The saint brushed himself off and a swallow fluttered out of his sleeve, zooming up into the flapping clothes, and the saint laughed in an effeminate voice.

"Summer is over, isn't it?"

"Yes," Remy answered politely, not looking into his eyes. But the odor of the cellar was growing too intense to ignore. Remy looked down, into the dark mouth of the cellar, and suddenly: "Salvatore . . . *Salvatore*," his grandmother's voice called out from the depths. Salvatore was Remy's real name. He twisted the hoze nozzle, dropped it and stepped cautiously down the cellar steps, squinting in the darkness.

"*Veni ca*. Com'ere," a woman's voice called in dialect from within. He walked blindly toward the voice.

"Gran'ma?" Feeling his way around the pumping oil burner, he reached the steps to the sub-cellar where the wine was kept. On his way down a hand touched his face, as fragile as a moth wing. He reached to it. He knew it was his grandmother. He knew by the smell of her apron. He kissed her palm.

"*Che sucese?*" he asked in a friendly whisper. What's up?

"*Beve,*" she said. Drink. He felt a glass touch his lips. He tasted. It was her wine.

"*Buono?*" the old woman asked.

"*Si. Saporito.*"

"*Allora, beve ancora.*" Again, she poured.

"*No. Basta.*" He pulled the glass back, but she kept pouring, spilling wine on his shirt, trousers, and his shoes.

"Geez, Grandma." He was annoyed with her.

"*Per ou nir.*" For the black man, she said. He longed to see her face.

"*Veni ca,*" he said, urging her into the light, but she refused to let him see her.

"*Vattene.*" Get out of here. She pushed his hand and the full glass softly. "*Per ou nir,*" she said, turning, going deeper into the darkness. He turned toward the light of the cellar door, went to it and climbed out, balancing the glass of wine. Saint Francis was gone.

He placed the overflowing glass on the wet table, sat on the wet chair and looked up. The clothes were gone. He sniffed the air. It was a warmer, cloudier day. The flowers weren't zinnias and dahlias; they were exhausted cosmos and petunias gone to seed. It was September but of another year, a different September.

IN THIS CORNER . . .

• JAMES PURDY •

WHEN HE WAS 42, Hayes's second wife, like his first, died unexpectedly. She had left instructions that there were to be no special services for her, that she should be cremated and her ashes scattered over the water. The farewell note did not say what water, and her husband one late evening threw the ashes into the river near the docks in Brooklyn. Once they had been disposed of he felt a loosening of tension such as he had not experienced since boyhood. This was followed by a kind of exaltation so pronounced he was nonplused. He breathed deeply and looked out over the dark river on which a small tugboat with green and orange lights was gliding in perfect silence.

A few moments later he found himself whistling.

When he got to his flat near Middagh Street, he opened the seldom-used store room which contained his archery set and his punching bag. He got his boxing gloves out, and punched the bag until he was tired. That night he slept with the deep unconsciousness he had experienced as a soldier on furlough.

It was beginning to get nippy, for they were in late September, and yet he went to his Wall Street job without bothering to put on his jacket or tie.

For some time now, whenever he got off at the Bowling Green subway stop, he had been noticing a young man, almost a boy, holding up a stack of missionary tracts. Today, on a sudden impulse, Hayes bought up all the tracts the boy had for sale. The vendor did not seem too pleased at this unusual generosity, but managed a husky thanks.

The next time he got off at his subway stop, he looked immediately for the young man with the tracts, but when he went up to him, the boy turned away abruptly and began talking with a vendor of Italian ices. Hayes did not feel nervy enough to buy any more tracts.

There was an unexpected killing frost, which was supposed to have set some kind of record, and the next day, shivering from the change in weather, Hayes, as he came from underground, caught sight of the boy with the tracts sitting on a little folding chair. He had no tracts in his hands, and was wearing only a thin summer shirt, very light trousers, and worn canvas shoes without socks.

As he was late for work, he hurried on, but that evening as he left work he observed the young man still sitting on the folding chair.

"Hello," Hayes called out. "Where's your tracts?"

The boy's lips moved fitfully, and then after considerable effort, he got out the words: "I'm not with the missionary society any more," and his eyes moved down to the pavement.

Hayes walked on toward the subway entrance without having been able to make any rejoinder to the boy's explanation. Then all at once before descending he stopped and looked back. The boy had followed Hayes with his eyes. The expression on his face was of such sad eloquence Hayes retraced his steps, but could think of nothing to say. Studying the boy's features he could not miss the evidence that the boy had been crying.

"Supposin' we go over there and get something to eat," Hayes suggested, pointing to a well-known chop house.

"Suits me, but I don't have a dime to my name."

They sat in the back part of the restaurant, which was nearly deserted at this hour owing to the fact that most of their clientele were luncheon patrons.

"What looks good to you?" Hayes went on, shifting his weight in the roomy booth, and watching the boy study the elaborate pages of the menu.

"Oh, why don't you choose for me?" the boy finally said, and handed over the bill of fare to his host.

"We'll have the deluxe steak platter," Hayes told the waiter.

"So that's that." Hayes smiled awkwardly as they waited for their order. The boy flushed under his deep tan, and brushed a lock of his straw-colored hair from his eyes.

When the deluxe steak platters were set before them, the young man kept his knife and fork raised over the still sizzling Porterhouse, as if unsure how to begin. Then after the first hesitant motions, he was eating almost ferociously, his tongue and jaw moving spasmodically.

When the boy had finished, Hayes inquired: "Wouldn't you like my portion?"

"You don't want it?" the boy wondered blankly, looking down at the untasted steak.

"I had a very hearty lunch today," Hayes explained. He pushed his platter toward the boy. "Please don't let it go to waste."

"You're sure?"

Hayes nodded weakly.

"Well, then, if you say so." The boy grinned and began on the second platter. He ate it with even more relish.

"I love to see a young guy with a good appetite," Hayes congratulated him when he had finished.

"How about some dessert? Their pies are all baked here on the premises, you know."

The boy shook his head and put his right hand over his stomach.

"By the way, what is your name?" Hayes wondered bashfully.

"Clark," the boy raised his voice. "Clark Vail."

"And mine is Hayes." The older man stood up and extended his hand, and Clark followed suit. Their handclasp resembled somehow that of two contending athletes before the fray.

"Where do you live now that you're not with the missionary society?" Hayes wondered after they had finished their coffee.

Clark gave a start. "To tell the truth, nowhere." At a long look from Hayes, Clark lowered his eyes and said, "I've been sleeping . . . out."

"Out?" Hayes spoke with something like affront.

A kind of warmth was coming over Hayes. He felt little pearls of perspiration on his upper lip. He wanted to take out his handkerchief and dry himself but somehow he felt any movement at that moment would spoil what he wanted to say. Finally, he forced out:

"Clark, you are more than welcome to stay the night at my place. It's not too far."

Clark made no answer, and his mouth came open, then closed tightly.

"If you are sleeping out, I mean," Hayes went on. "I insist you come where you'll have a roof over your head."

They both rose at the same moment, as in a business meeting where a project had been approved.

Owing to the clatter and noise on the subway they did not speak again until they had got out at their stop.

"I live near the river," Hayes told the younger man.

"You have boxing gloves," Clark cried, picking the gloves up admiringly when they were inside his apartment. "Were you a boxer?"

"Amateur." Hayes colored. "Golden Gloves," he added almost inaudibly.

"I was in the CYO bouts a few times," Clark volunteered.

They both laughed embarrassedly.

"This is a big place you have here," Clark said wonderingly. "And you look out over the water and all the skyscrapers!"

"Excuse me if I take off my shoes," Hayes said. "They pinch."

"You have big feet like me." The boy looked at his friend's feet. He relaxed a bit.

"Want to try my shoes on for a fit?" Hayes joked.

Clark went over to the chair near where Hayes was seated, and picked up one of the shoes.

"Go on, try it on."

Finding the shoe more comfortable, Clark smiled broadly for the first time.

"Try the other while you're at it, Clark."

Clark obeyed.

·"Walk around now to see if they feel all right."

Clark walked around the room in Hayes's shoes. He looked as carefree and joyful as a boy who is walking on stilts.

"They're yours, Clark," Hayes told him. When the young man acted perturbed, Hayes walked over to a partly closed door, and opened it fully to reveal inside a whole closetful of shoes.

"Look at my collection," Hayes quipped. "Two dozen pairs of shoes, and every one pinches!"

Clark laughed. "These do fit," he said, looking down at his feet. "But I don't think I should have such expensive shoes."

"Well if you don't, I do." Hayes's voice had a kind of edge in it. At that moment, their eyes met. Hayes's right hand raised, and then fell heavily against his thigh.

"I'm glad you chose to come here tonight," he managed to say. He had meant to say *come home*, but instead changed it to *here*.

Hayes rose very slowly then like a man coming out of a deep slumber and walked in his stocking feet over to where Clark, seated in a big armchair, was looking at his new shoes.

Hayes put his hand briefly on the boy's yellow hair. "I know I need a haircut." Clark looked up trustfully at his friend.

"I like your hair just this length," Hayes told him.

Clark's lips trembled, and his eyes closed briefly.

"You should never have to sleep . . . out," Hayes managed to say. His hand moved from the boy's hair to his cheek. To his relief, the boy took his hand and pressed it.

"I have only the one bed, Clark. Come on and look."

They walked over to the next room where a four-poster faced them.

"Big enough for four people," Clark's voice came out rather loud.

"Could you stand to share it? Be frank now. If not, I can always sleep on the davenport."

"Sure, share," Clark agreed.

Hayes strode over to a big chiffonier and pulled out from one of the drawers a pair of pajamas.

"Here, Clark, you can put these on. Whenever you want to turn in, that is."

"To tell the truth, that bed looks good to me." Clark sat down on a small stool and took off his new shoes. He yawned widely.

There was a long silence.

"Do you want to change in the bathroom?" Hayes wondered when the boy sat motionless holding his pajamas.

"No, no." Clark rose from where he was sitting, and then as if at a command seated himself again.

"It's just that . . ."

"What?" Hayes prompted him, a kind of urgency in his tone.

"It's the *change* in everything, all around me. From being out there!" Hayes saw with acute uneasiness that there were tears in his friend's eyes.

"Talk about *change*," Hayes began huskily. "Your coming here has changed a lot."

As if this speech of Hayes were a signal, very quickly Clark undressed, and even more quickly stepped into the fresh pajamas which gave off a faint smell of dried lavender.

"Remember, though, if you would be more comfortable alone." Hayes reminded him of his offer to go sleep on the davenport.

Hayes's eyes rested on the boy's pajamas, which had several buttons missing, revealing the white skin of his belly.

"Don't you worry, Hayes," the boy told him. "I'm so dead tired I could lie down in a bed with a whole platoon."

Hayes began taking off his own clothes. He deposited his shirt, undershirt, and trousers on a little chest.

"I can see you was a boxer, all right," Clark noted. "You're pretty husky still."

Hayes smiled, and went to the bed and pulled back the comforter and the sheets under it. Then he helped himself in on the right side of the bed.

"Would you mind if I prayed before I get in?" Clark wondered.

Hayes was so taken by surprise he did not reply for a moment. Then he nodded emphatically.

Clark knelt down on the left side of the bed, and raised his two hands clasped together. Hayes could only hear a few words, like *I thank thee O Father for thy kindness and thy care.*

When they were both under the covers, Hayes extinguished the little lamp on the stand beside the bed.

They could hear the boat whistles as clearly as if they were standing on the docks, and they could see out the windows the thousands of lights from the skyscrapers from across the water.

To his sharp disbelief, Hayes felt the younger man take his left hand in his right, and the boy brought it then against his heart and held it there.

"Clark," Hayes heard his own voice coming from it seemed over water.

The boy in answer pressed his friend's hand tighter.

Hardly knowing what he was doing, as when in the morning he would sometimes rise still numbed with slumber, Hayes turned his head toward the boy and kissed him lightly on the lips. Clark held his hand even tighter, painfully tighter. He felt the young man's soft sweet spittle as he kissed him all over his face, and then lowered his lips and kissed his throat, and pressed against his Adam's apple.

Hayes had the feeling the last twenty-five years of his life had been erased, that he had been returned to the Vermont countryside where he had grown up, that he had never been married, had never worked in a broker's office, and ridden dirty ear-piercing subways or had rented a flat in a huge impersonal building designed for multi-millionaires.

He helped Clark off with his pajamas and turned a kind of famished countenance against the boy's bare chest, and to his lower body.

"Yes, oh yes," the boy cried under the avalanche of caresses.

In the morning, Hayes realized he had overslept. It was nearly nine o'clock by his wristwatch, and he would never be able to get to the office in time. The place where Clark had slept beside him was vacant, so that he assumed the young man was in the bathroom. He waited, then, hearing nothing, he walked down the hall. The door to the bath was open, the room vacant. The apartment, he knew, was also vacant, vacant of the one he had loved so deliriously.

"Clark?"

Hayes felt a kind of stab in his abdomen, as if a practiced fist had hit him with full force.

After such a night when he had felt such unexpected complete happiness, and when he had felt sure the young man, despite the great difference in their ages, had returned his love—how could Clark then have left him? A rush of even greater anguish hit him when he saw that the shoes he had given Clark were resting under the chair near the closet.

He knew then Clark had left him for good, left him, that is, for dead.

He did not bother to shave or wash before going to work. Several of the secretaries looked at him wonderingly. They probably thought he had been out on a tear. His boss, an elderly man who favored Hayes, was, as usual, out of the office on a trip somewhere.

He finally made no attempt to keep his mind on his work, but stared out at the vast gray canyons of buildings facing him from the windows. Each time he signed some letter or memorandum for a secretary, he would mutter to himself that at five o'clock he would begin his search for Clark.

"And if I don't find him," he said aloud to himself, "what will I do then?"

One thing he saw was certain: if he did not find him, he could not live.

The sudden unforeseen upheaval in his life was just as difficult to understand as if he had fallen under a subway train and lost his arms and legs. He went over the implausibility, the impossibility even of it all, a 42-year-old man, married twice, had taken a young man home, and never having loved any man before, had fallen somehow ecstatically in love, had confessed his love, as had the young man, and then after this happiness, it had all been taken from him. He had been ushered to the gates of some unreachable paradise, and waking had found himself in an empty hell.

His search went on day and night. Often he did not go to work at all, and he did not even bother to call his employer. He quit shaving and soon sported a rather attractive beard.

He looked crazily and brazenly into the face of every young man who crossed his path, hoping it would be Clark. He wore out one pair of shoes after another. He no longer was aware that his shoes pinched, and taking off a pair at night he saw with indifference that his feet were not only afflicted with new calluses and corns, but that his toes were bleeding from so much walking. Had he seen his toes had been severed, it could not have meant less to him.

"Clark, Clark," he would cry at night. He could still smell the boy's hair against the adjoining pillow.

One night while walking late on the promenade, two men approached him and asked him something. Hayes was so lost in his own misery he paid no attention to them. The next moment he was aware they were ripping off his jacket, and robbing him. After taking all he had they beat him with what seemed to be brass knuckles and then knocked him to the pavement.

He lay there for a long time. He felt his jaw aching horribly, and he noticed that he had lost a tooth. The physical pain he found more bearable than his loss of Clark.

He knew then that he would kill himself, but he did not know what means to choose: the wheels of the subway, jumping from his building, or swallowing countless pain-killing pills.

The elderly widows of his building were very much alarmed by the change in "young Mr. Hayes," as they called him. They blamed it on the death of his wife.

The mugging he had received left several deep gashes on his forehead and cheek which did not heal. He did not want to go to a doctor, but whenever he touched the wounded places, they would open and a thin trickle of blood would run down his face. He spitefully welcomed this purely physical anguish. It made his losing Clark at least momentarily less excruciating.

The loss of Clark was equaled only by his failure to understand why the boy had deserted him. What had he done wrong to drive him away when they had felt such great happiness in one another's arms?

In late November a heavy wet snow began falling. Hayes went out only in a light windbreaker, and no hat. He walked to the end of the promenade and then as he was about to turn and go further north down the steep hill on Columbia Heights, he slipped and fell. The sudden sharp blow to his head and face opened his still unhealed cuts and abrasions.

He lay as if lifeless with the snow quickly covering his face and hair. A few persons began stopping and looking down at him. Soon others began to gather.

A policeman got out of a squad car and hurried over to where he lay. When he saw the policeman, Hayes rose on one elbow, and made every effort to get up.

The cop kept asking him if he was going to be all right, or if he thought he should go to the emergency room of a hospital.

Hayes managed somehow to get on his feet, and, shaking off the accumulation of snow, assured the policeman and the onlookers that he was all right. But his eye fell on someone in the crowd the sight of whom almost caused him to fall to the pavement again. There, watching him with a kind of lunatic fear, was Clark.

Hayes moved quickly away from the last of the onlookers and sat down on one of the benches thick with snow. He was as a matter of fact not certain Clark had really been there staring at him. He decided that he had sustained a slight concussion and it had made him imagine Clark's presence. He held his face in his hands, and felt the wet snow descending on his mouth and throat.

Presently he was aware someone was standing close over him. He removed his hands from his face. It was Clark, no mistake.

All at once a great anger took over, and he rose and cried: "Well, what's your excuse?"

When Clark did not respond, he moved close to him, and taking a swipe with his right hand he hit the boy a fierce blow knocking him to the pavement.

Standing over him, Hayes muttered again, *"What's your excuse?"*

Then he must have blacked out, for when he came to himself he was again seated on the wet snow-covered bench, and Clark was standing over him, saying, "Can I sit beside you, Hayes?"

"What ever for?"

"Please."

"Well," Hayes snarled, "to quote the way you talk, *suit yourself.*"

Clark sat down beside him, but Hayes moved vengefully away from him.

"The reason I left, Hayes," the boy began, "the reason has nothing to do with you, understand. It's only what's missing in me . . . I wanted to stay—stay forever," he gulped and could not go on.

But Hayes's anger was only getting more intense.

"That's a lot of bull, if I ever heard any," the older man roared. "You missionary people are all alike, aren't you. All nuts. You should all be locked up from meddling with the rest of the human race."

"I'm not a missionary person, as you call it. I never was, Hayes. They took me in, true, but I couldn't believe in what they believed. I couldn't believe in their kind of love, that is."

"Love," Hayes spat out. "Look at me when you say that. See what it did to me . . ."

Hayes stopped all at once. He could see that Clark's own mouth and jaw were bleeding, evidently from Hayes's blow.

"I have done lots of soul-searching," the boy was going on as if talking to himself. "But the reason, Hayes, I left, you ain't heard, and maybe you won't believe me. See," he almost shouted, "I left because I felt such great happiness with you was . . . well, more than I could bear. I thought my heart would break.

And I feared it couldn't last. That something would spoil it. When I first left you I thought I'd come back at once, of course, once I got myself together. But a kind of paralysis took over. The night with you was the happiest of my life. And you were the best thing ever. I couldn't take such happiness after the life I have led. I couldn't believe it was real for me."

"Bull, bull," Hayes cried. He rose, the anger flashing out of his eyes, but as he moved toward the street where he lived he fell headlong and hurt himself on the paving stones. He was too weak to rise, too weak also to resist Clark picking him up.

"Hayes, listen to me . . . you've got to let me help you home."

Hayes swore under his breath. Then, as if remembering Clark had been a missionary, he used all the foul language and curses he could recall from his army days.

Impervious to all the insults and abuse, Clark helped him home, holding him under his arms. Hayes tried a last time to shake him off at the front entrance, but Clark insisted on coming up to his apartment with him.

Hayes fell almost unconscious on his bed.

"If you could only believe me," Clark kept saying. He began taking off Hayes's wet clothing. Then he went into the kitchen and heated some water, and put it in a basin he found under the sink.

He began wiping Hayes's face of dirt and blood and snow. When he had finished these ablutions he took off Hayes's shoes and socks. He drew back for a moment at the sight of his naked feet, for they looked as if they had been run over, and at his touch the toes streamed with blood. He wiped them gently, bathing them again and again though Hayes winced and even cried out from the discomfort.

All at once Hayes raised up for he felt Clark kissing his feet.

"No, no," Hayes cried. "Don't humiliate me all over again."

"Let me stay," Clark begged him. "Hayes, let me stay with you."

"No," Hayes growled. "I don't want you."

Hayes could feel the boy's lips on his bare feet.

"You need someone," Clark beseeched him.

"Not you, not you."

Clark covered his friend's feet, and came up to the bed and lay down beside him. He refused to budge from this position, and then slowly without further remonstrance from Hayes he put his head over Hayes's heart, and kissed him softly.

At these kisses, Hayes began weeping violently. Almost like an athlete who has been told he must give up his place to another younger, more promising candidate, he yielded then any attempt to dispute Clark's claim.

Clark removed all of his own clothing now, and held Hayes to him in an almost punishing embrace. Still weeping, indeed almost more violently, Hayes nonetheless began to return Clark's kisses.

Then slowly began a repetition of their first evening of lovemaking, with perhaps even more ardor, and this time Hayes's cries could be heard beyond their own room, perhaps clear to the river and the boats.

"And tomorrow, I suppose, when I wake up, you'll have cleared out again," Hayes said, running his fingers through the boy's hair.

"No, Hayes," Clark said with a bitter contriteness. "I think you know now wild horses couldn't drag me from your side. Even if you was to tell me to leave you, I'd stay this time."

"And do you swear to it on that stack of tracts you used to peddle?" Hayes asked him.

"I'll swear to it on my own love of you," the boy confessed. . . . "Cross my heart, Hayes, cross my heart."

SOLIDARITY

• ALBERT INNAURATO •

EARLY IN THE AIDS epidemic, my friend and I decided to march in the Gay Parade. We wanted to take some kind of stand and show our solidarity. He had been christened La Golgotha, and I, Sandy, by our mutual friend Leatherette, a giver of names if there had ever been one in Western history. We'd often talk about this issue of solidarity—among gay men, fat people, opera queens. Was solidarity possible for us? Was it possible for anyone?

AIDS had begun to haunt us, although rather theoretically. We didn't know anyone who had the disease, but we understood the symbolic value of AIDS in a country become rabidly right wing. The arch bigot, Patrick Buchanan, had been vomiting forth the most vicious calumnies about homosexuals in the *New York Post* and elsewhere, using AIDS and his much vaunted Catholicism as his excuse. La Golgotha and I were both ex-Catholics. La Golgotha was Irish-American as was Buchanan, and loathed what he stood for. I am Italian-American but am a renegade from the simpleminded idiocy blasphemers such as Buchanan insist on calling Catholicism or Christianity.

We were both fat and in our mid-thirties. Neither of us had sneakers or jeans, helpful one would think for the long march.

La Golgotha summed up our opinions about fashion neatly: "There are certain kinds of clothes fat people oughtn't to wear."

Both of us tended to affect shapeless, seasonless pants, usually wrinkled and sometimes linty. Comment in our circle was that La Golgotha was color blind rather than flamboyant, for he was given to multihued checks and stripes which rarely matched. Whatever he spent, La Golgotha's toggery tended to the scrubby. Once, upon seeing La Golgotha in spanking new threads, Leatherette, dowager regnant of our circle of queens, had crowed (it was at the ballet, Moreshita was making a doomed Samurai attempt at the Black Swan with the agonized Ivan Nagy): "Oh, she's gone cycling out to Sears of Queens once again for a panty raid!"

Leatherette was fonder of ballet than opera, La Golgotha adored both, I tended to suffer the dance, being too stupid to follow the steps and too cowardly about my French to battle over this or that dancer's fouettés or jetés. In any case, Leatherette and La Golgotha were the divas of a mafia that specialized in getting themselves and a select corps of fellow gallery girls into cultural events for free.

"There isn't a passageway, a back alley, a hidden entrance to any theater, opera house or concert hall that I don't know about," Leatherette would claim, "and there isn't a Security Guard of color I haven't sucked off in one of them." Since Leatherette had studied to become a Jesuit, and then gotten his doctorate in Logic, I believed him.

But I suppose my point about our clothes is, I had discovered Brooks Brothers, and tended to look fleshy but neat. La Golgotha, recently hired after a long stint of unemployment, had economized on clothes for too long to feel comfortable spending money on them, and had a certain naive pride in being an outcast. That one looks somehow distinguished is a reverse narcissism one finds in many lonely, ugly people. Smirks and snubs become one's badges and scars.

I had felt much the same myself in the old days, and had also flaunted what was unsuitable, even grotesque about myself. But then I had a brief period of promise on the concert circuit as a pianist and learned that La Golgotha and I had shared a provincial delusion. As my promise evaporated and I had to struggle harder for ever less remunerative engagements, I realized the habit of not fitting in has serious and concrete disadvantages in the real world. It is only desperation and anonymity which allow the fantasy that abasement is transcendence.

There came the night before the march. I have to admit, I was nervous. There'd been rumors, even promises, of violence. Some from the hate-filled orthodox Catholics, incited by Buchanan, others from the police, furious that there would be a section of marchers calling themselves "gay cops." According to the *New York Times*, there was going to be unprecedented mass media coverage of the march. This was the first year AIDS had seemed a major enough story to make the march more than a freak show. There would even be a section of marchers openly admitting to having AIDS.

I wasn't able to sleep and forbore taking the heavy dose of Nembutal my shrink of those days was recommending. Instead, I paced; I pondered practicing. I watched television: WTBS had an all night program running all the Flash Gordon serials. I watched out of the corner of my eye as I read for the seventh time Giovanni Battista Meneghini's memoir about his wife, Maria Callas. Her death, six years before, had signaled the end of a portion of my own life.

False dawn, then the real thing; I glanced out my barred window at the brilliant sunshine. I patted the piano and went through the ritual of rebuking myself for not practicing. I set about preparing coffee, trying to find a comforting daydream to distract myself during the millennium it would take my Chemex to drip. Nothing came, so I went to the Chinese bakery on the corner for donuts.

It was a beautiful day. I wonder if there have been many like it in New York since. When I used to run away from Philadelphia to the Old Met, a precocious queen of fifteen, it seemed to me the weather was often like this. Autumn might be colder, spring more volatile, but there was, in those days, the same sweet city promise. The sun would be there in a clear blue sky, a friend almost, and what a breeze there would be! A current— complex (smells of coffee, baking, bus exhaust, last night's perfumes) yet simple in its easy optimism. I remembered that endless promise with a pang. I was surprised that it seemed to spring up in me still, automatically, easily.

I got just the donuts I wanted and, on the way back, inhaled a fresh jelly donut, praising God for creating sugar and this weather.

Going into my building, I passed our super. He was holding his two year old, a baby so large its diapers could well have been sold for weapons once the dung dried. The first time I saw the super, I told La Golgotha we were guilty of hubris about our weight. The super would have sunk the *Andrea Doria* just by sitting down heavily, say on a gilded toilet. It was all he could do to squeeze through my apartment door.

"What are you doing up so early?" the super declaimed, truly a loss to Wagner. "Oh, that's right, the fag march! Well, have a nice day." He had smiled when he said it; but he had also put his mega hands around his infant son's gigantic ears. Perhaps this was plebeian humor; but I think it was resentment too. At that time he must have regarded all the gay men in the neighborhood as likely to live better and longer than obese married men like him.

Coffee, Callas, donuts, a shower. Drying my bulk, I surveyed the little garden, bright and fragrant outside my barred windows. I would have preferred staying home, but no, I had promised La Golgotha. We were meeting for breakfast before the march, at La Pincushionova's coffee shop.

I rode the subway uptown. It was packed with mostly young gay men going to the march. They got off at Columbus Circle. I stayed on to Lincoln Center. As I stood waiting for the doors to open, a middle-aged woman smiled at me.

"It's their day," she said, "the sickos! And now they're spreading this disease. It's God's punishment on them."

I leaned over her: "How do you know that?"

"Pat Buchanan makes the case. Can't you read?"

I climbed the steps to the street slowly. That I hadn't slept, or taken my Nembutal, weighed on me all of a sudden. There were mists in my head; and when I gained the street, the day had turned muggy. I strode across Broadway and walked to La Pincushionova's. The place was surprisingly crowded with people breakfasting before the march. Entering, I heard: "Here is Sandy." My hand was taken, and my interlocutor continued: "Sandy, I have been betrayed, one of my girls (pronounced gurrels) has betrayed me."

"It was I, Miss Brodie," I answered, twisting vowels and trilling consonants, in our version of a Scottish accent.

"Who do you think it was, Sandy? Can it have been Marrrry MacGrrrregor?"

"Marrrry's dead in Spain, Miss Brodie."

"You're so gloomy, Sandy. My gurrels are the crème de la crème. Give me a gurrel at an impressionable age, and I'll turn her into a boy. Look at the Scottish army. They're all my gurrels. Who do you think betrayed me, Sandy?"

"It was I, Miss Brodie!"

"You're so self-centered, Sandy. I like that in a man. Pity you aren't one, like Mussolini. Are you?" My dialogist paused and sighed melodramatically: "Carrumpet?" Then, he reared back in operatic shock and horror, and cried: "Sandy, it was you!"

La Golgotha and La Pincushionova clapped madly as they always did when Leatherette and I did one of our routines. Leatherette tossed his head, accepting their applause regally, and sipped his bourbon.

Leatherette and I had met at the broadway production of *The Prime of Miss Jean Brodie*. I was at Juilliard. He was at Columbia in Logic. I started sneaking into Broadway theaters when there was nothing at the Met. I much preferred opera to concerts and recitals. I would, in fact, have loved being a singer or conductor, but I had no voice, and my classes in conducting were a shambles. So I was stuck with the piano.

I liked plays, too, and had no shame about sneaking in. For a time I thought I was the only person doing it. Then I started seeing a small man with a tiny line of thin brown hair over his upper lip, invariably carrying a huge leather bag slung over his shoulder. I saw him at various performances, darting for empty seats as the lights went down. And I saw him on matinee days, scurrying around for stubs and used programs, as I did. And I saw him watching, as I watched, for the best moment to use those programs and stubs to go in—usually while the oldest or dimmest-looking ticket taker was at his or her busiest. Every once in a while somebody would get caught, but neither he nor I ever did.

Finally there came the evening when we went out for coffee. "I usually go to the baths, but it's my time of month and I'm tender there," he said. With him was a fat young man with an oddly shaped face, who walked his bicycle as he accompanied us, chaining it when we arrived at a dingy hole-in-the-wall. We were greeted by a young woman who sat us in the booth of honor, the only one where there was enough room between the table and the back of the seats for someone with a big stomach to fit comfortably.

I said to the little man, "Excuse my being a cliché, but it makes me uncomfortable that I don't know anyone's name."

"Well," he began, "I'm called Leatherette, and this is La Golgotha of Queens, works at Alexander's and rides a bicycle. I dub you Sandy, and this is La Pincushionova." He pointed at the young woman who had admitted us. "She owns the place."

"I'm the ugliest genital female alive in America," Pincushionova said, and it might well have been true. "I don't mean deformed, I don't mean scarred or burned, I don't mean Mongoloid or handicapped, I mean ugly. Simply and impurely ugly. What do you think?"

"Do you think you're uglier than any of us?" I asked her.

"Yes, for genital females are always more harshly judged than nongenital females, let alone males, genital or not. I emphasize female, born with the appropriate genitalia."

"I don't believe you, Pincushionova," crowed Leatherette.

"Have faith, friend."

"I had faith, but a bishop I know sucked it out of me when I was thirteen."

"Then look and lament!" With that, she stood on the seat, lifted her dress and pulled down her panties. Leatherette and La Golgotha screamed and averted their eyes, shrieking with laughter. The other people in the coffee shop whistled and applauded. Her vagina was shaved, but normal looking, and rather large, though perhaps that was the absence of hair.

"You don't mind confronting the reality principle," she said to me. "Swing?"

"No, sorry."

"Only for yourself; I bet you pine for the young and the hung, and you'll only have them when you can buy them. I wager you'll die without ever having a good spontaneous fuck."

"Give her time, give her time, Pincushionova," Leatherette yelled, patting me, "she's got years before menopause, and there are plenty of spontaneous fuckers in Manhattan."

"And now, may I take your orders?" Pincushionova asked, pulling up her panties. "It's on the house!"

A few weeks later, I saw Pincushionova at the opera and we stole seats in the first row of the orchestra, right behind the conductor's podium. Using her program as a funnel, she blew air into his hair, getting him to turn around repeatedly. We were evicted, but not before we were hysterical.

Then came the dreary Sunday afternoon when I was to make my New York recital debut. I had won a prominent competition. The sponsors warned me not to expect an audience. It had never occurred to me to tell my fellow sneakers-in about my playing. Information about daylight hours was rarely exchanged, and one had to guess and glean at occupations, aspirations, private concerns. In any case, I never took my playing all that seriously. It had come easily to me, and I had known approbation early. Curtis, in Philadelphia, had admitted me when I was fifteen, getting me out of high school. Then, I'd been given a scholarship to Juilliard. I had a knack for playing with power and velocity, and rarely needed to practice. I had exceptional memory and there were occasions when, for some mysterious reason, I became possessed by someone else, a thin, darkly handsome, demonic virtuoso, who colored the keys with mystical fervor. But the only music I really adored was opera. The only time I applied myself musically was in reading scores of my favorite operas.

At my debut, I walked out onto the stage depressed, only to be given a big ovation by a respectable-sized audience. About half were the result of La Pincushionova's lining up people and either finding comps for them, or sneaking them in. This enthusiastic response impressed the sponsors, and perhaps, even the *Times* reviewer, with the result that a career of sorts began for me.

La Pincushionova was born Inga Pincus. Her nickname came, of course, from Leatherette. Inga had wanted to be a ballerina, and had taken classes from the time she was eight or so. This despite her bow legs, flat feet and truly hideous face. She was much brighter than any of her classmates. Even when I knew her, she was amazing at spotting and remembering complex combinations. But, in every other respect, she was hopeless. She had resigned herself at sixteen to stock market speculations, and in her late teens made a respectable fortune by investing a small legacy left her by her blind grandfather.

After that, she traveled for a while. She loved sex, and took the opportunity of sleeping with every genital male who was willing. Apparently, they were legion. There were many heterosexual men who found her atrocious looks aphrodisiacal. They were men of all ages and kinds: married and single; some celebrities, a few cripples. But, while La Pincushionova loved sex with heterosexual men, she loathed them otherwise. And when she decided to have a child, she determined the father would be a gay man, preferably an artist. Here she ran into the great wall that separates straight and gay. For the gay men she wanted often disdained her—not because they were phobic or disliked women—but because, almost always, they were obsessed with looks, and with the status beautiful lovers bestow. But La Pincushionova loved a challenge, and eventually, she found a beautiful artist of genuine talent, and seduced him. He had moved on, no one knew where; La Pincushionova successfully bore his child. She bought the hole in the wall, mostly as a hangout for her friends, and here she was, encouraging Leatherette and me in our craziness, utterly in her element.

"Do more Jean Brodie!" Pincushionova cried.

"I've got to tip; I have to be in the vanguard of white women at the parade!" Leatherette chugged back the rest of his bourbon and started out. Pincushionova was carrying her son, who against all the odds was a pretty baby. She held him up as Leatherette turned to leave. "Spawn of Pincushionova!" He screamed, making a cross with his fingers, but the two year old gurgled and squealed at him, and he, suddenly and rather surreptitiously, kissed it. Then, hastily looking around, and ostentatiously wiping his lips, he called: "Be gay, be girlish, be Christian." And flew out.

Pincushionova took our orders, then busied herself with her other customers. I looked over at La Golgotha and saw he was wearing a blue-and-green striped sweater, despite the heat.

"Don't ask," he began. "I felt fat this morning, and wanted to hide it. There'll be all these cute guys in the parade today, and I don't want them to see my worst side. I know it's hard to miss it, so I wore this sweater."

"But, La Golgotha, if one fell for you and you went home together, you'd have to undress, wouldn't you?"

"Of course not. I'd do him and he'd go home."

"But somebody's who's only looking for a blow job isn't going to care how you look."

"Oh yeah? When was your last free trick?"

"You'll give yourself heat stroke. And then where will you be?"

"In the hospital with a cute intern?"

I dug into my waffles and ice cream, and he said: "Do you think I should get my face remade? At work they have this great insurance plan. And it covers all sorts of things. And my boss was telling me that her sister looked just like me, and went in and had these operations. You see, they break your jaw . . . can I have some of your vanilla ice cream for my pie?" I nodded. He slipped some off my plate, and continued. "Then they reset it; they're able to do all sorts of things. They can cut out extra bone, for example, then can shave your adam's apple. Then they can peel away the extra gum and give you braces so your teeth'll come into line. I think I'd have to have three or four operations, but they'd be cheap."

"Now, La Golgotha, you really don't look that bad. In fact, you're aging better than anybody I know."

"But I hate my face. I look just like Joan Sutherland, and you know I can't stand her."

"Do you think we would have liked Maria?" I asked him as he gobbled his Boston cream pie. We had had this conversation often in the years since La Callas's death, but we, or at least I, found a strange comfort in repeating it. "I was re-reading her husband's book last night. We would have understood her, don't you think?"

"You think she would have understood us?" This was his usual response, but today, smacking his lips after his last bite of pie, he went further. "I think she hated fags."

"She was surrounded by them!"

"She needed them. Who else had time for her and liked soap operas, westerns, and ice cream, as much as she did? But that doesn't mean she liked them. The only people she liked were rich old straight men who were uncircumcised. We don't know anybody like that. We better get going."

We rose to leave. He still had his sweater on. I shook my head. La Pincushionova rushed over to kiss and wish us well. "I'm going to take a taxi down to the Village later this afternoon. I'll see you then."

La Golgotha leaned over and absently kissed her son, muttering: "Spawn of Pincushionova!" We walked down to Columbus Circle to join the parade.

We had hoped to meet up with our friends, and maybe march with them, but, of course, the scene was one of utter chaos when we arrived, and we saw no one we knew.

"I'm feeling kind of nervous," I said to La Golgotha.

"So am I. I just hope I don't get made fun of too much today."

"But that's not supposed to happen . . . is it?"

"It's not supposed to happen in real life, but it does all the time. People throw garbage at me or scream remarks when I'm riding my bicycle. They giggle at me at work. Last week, when we went to that movie, those queens on line in front of us were laughing at us for being fat and interested in them. Why do you think this will be any different?"

"Well, let's hope for genuine solidarity. Shall we start here?"

"Might as well," he said. We joined a group of marchers.

The march started, and we ambled along, but there was something strange about the group of men around us. They seemed to be eyeing Golgotha and me. I felt, more than saw, their discomfort. They were all very blond, very built, in tight T-shirts, some artfully torn. They all wore shorts, with shining white socks and expensive-looking, rather baroque sneakers that had been painted an ugly shade of purple. I caught Golgotha's eye, he had been staring at these men. I could tell he was simultaneously in heaven and in hell.

Finally, the slightly older man who was heading this section jogged back to us. "I beg your pardon," he panted aerobically, "but what the fuck do you two think you are doing?"

"Marching?" I answered hopefully.

"We are the Lavender Sons of Body Beautiful section. You and your pet are giving us a bad aura. You mind shoving off?"

"Well . . . ," I began but he cut me off with a loud snort.

"No well about it, honey. We take obesity as a personal insult. And just look at your shoes! Where did you get them? On sale at the Buster Brown's in Bangladesh? Our athletic shoes are the foundation of our solidarity, that's why we broke our asses last night, painting them lavender! See? SEE?!" He began kicking up his feet in rhythm, higher and higher, obviously with the idea of pounding his lavender sneakers into my head. "Now, get the hell out of here before we cripple you!"

I grabbed La Golgotha without a word and hustled him to the section in front.

"They were so beautiful," he sighed. "I knew it was too good to last."

"They were dumb jocks; and jocks are jocks, gay or not. In fact, jocks are all the same sex. And that's impotent from exhaustion!"

"That makes me feel better," he said wistfully, looking back over his shoulder and tripping.

"I'd like to see them all crucified!" I spat.

"Oh, yes," he breathed longingly.

We marched for a time, getting closer to Saint Patrick's Cathedral, where we had been told we could expect a counter-demonstration.

It still didn't feel right to me. I said to Golgotha: "I feel strange here."

"So do I," he said, uneasily.

We were about to move on, when a woman marched up beside us. "We appreciate your support," she said, "but me and my sisters have been talking about you two pigs, and look, men are men are men, gay or not. You get me? So move out!"

"But," I said to her, "we're just looking for a place to march."

"So you're not supporters?! Then die, you pricks. On the double!"

"Come on, Golgotha," I yelled, and we ran as fast as we could, nearly knocking over a baby policeman, who had evidently been instructed to obstruct the parade.

"Hey, watch it, you fat fags!" he screamed.

From our newest phalanx, we looked back and saw the banner of the group we had been marching with. It was being waved proudly aloft in front of their group. We hadn't seen it since we had approached from the back. It read: Third World Lesbian Sado-Masochists.

I called La Golgotha's attention to the banner. "No wonder they didn't like us," he said. "We're not third world."

We were in a ragtag section, it seemed. Those around us looked tired and sick. Many were holding on to one another. I knew we had stumbled into the section of those suffering from AIDS. I was about to turn to Golgotha when I saw someone I knew. My heart sank. I stared, hoping it wasn't he.

He saw me looking at him and smiled. His teeth were broken

and discolored. He approached Golgotha and me and marched in step with us. "Yes, it's me," he said. "I could see you wondering. It's obvious you don't have it yet. You should move out of here, you and your friend."

La Golgotha was looking at us; he knew who I was talking to.

"This is—"

"I know," Golgotha said. "I have some of your records. I like them."

"Thanks. There won't be any more. I don't have the energy, now. Oh, they're stopping us again. You should move on," he said to me, "or some fool will think you have it." He coughed, then continued, "You still have a career don't you?"

"Not really," I replied. "I thought you still did."

"I started losing engagements as soon as it got around. Then, when I didn't think I'd get through March, I had to cancel everything. In April, for the first time, I started losing my memory, then my coordination. I can't practice, even. I miss it so much. Don't you?"

"Oh, no. I was never happy concertizing. I was never as successful as you, not with the cognoscenti. Anyway, I hated to practice . . ."

He smiled, then self-consciously covered his mouth. They let us start up again. "I remember," he said with a laugh, coughing, "I remember how you hated to practice, and you never fooled Maestro. You could fool everybody else, but he'd catch the smallest mistake and go crazy. He thought you had a great talent."

"Oh, come on," I said, "a knack, maybe."

"No, a talent. I can admit it, now. That's why we all hated you. You were fat and mean and arrogant, we just disliked you for that, but it was the combination of laziness and talent we hated."

Another marcher came up behind him and hugged him. He eyed Golgotha and me suspiciously, but my friend kept on talking to me. "You remember . . . ?"

We both laughed. I did indeed remember. We had met at

Curtis, in Philadelphia. He was a few years older than I, and brilliant. His musicianship had everyone at Curtis in awe. And he was openly gay, the first I had ever met. I knew about myself and had dirty fantasies, but hid behind my bulk and clumsiness. I was a desperately shy and hopelessly unengaging sixteen year old, utterly without friends. He was always nice to me, though. And there was something—I hate to use the word—liberating about his attitude. I was so tired of provincial Italian-American judgments. Not only about sexuality, that was the least of it, but about everything. I didn't know how to breathe, and he showed me how. I was also desperately, madly horny, and he sensed that too.

One day he saw me in the lobby, flopping around. "How do you expect to make a career when you act like that? You know what you need? You need to get laid!"

"How?"

"What do you mean, how?"

"I live at home. I don't have any money for a hotel."

"What do you think the practice rooms are for?"

"The practice rooms?"

"You never practice in them, God knows, but you have the same access to them we all do. You can lock the door, use them all night. No one ever monitors them. You could sign up a room, sneak a trick in through the back way, lock the door behind you, and fuck like bunnies as long as you wanted."

"You think so?"

"I know so. What's your problem? You have to be pubescent. You can't have pimples without pubic hair, can you?"

"But where would I meet somebody? And who would be interested in me? I'm so . . . well, you know."

"Oh, I see. Well, that's a tough one. But maybe . . ."

At that point, Maestro came back, grunted at the two of us, and we followed him into his studio, but I kept looking at my friend during the lesson. Eventually, he arranged for me to meet a twenty-year-old hustler. He paid (the rates were low in those days, at least in Philadelphia) in exchange for my taking him to a small family restaurant in South Philly to which only locals had easy access. As it happened, I was a local celebrity, and we got a sumptuous meal for nothing.

I'll always be grateful to him. The hustler was Lochinvarlike. I was terrified he would act like the boys in gym class. In the century before I was able to leave high school and study piano all day, I had become very experienced with, but not inured to their taunts. But no, we locked the door of practice room thirty, and he seduced me. I can imagine the horror of the Pat Buchanans of this world at my initiation, but my friend, rather than leading me to hell, showed me a bit of heaven. I was full of self-hatred, of course. What fat child isn't? And don't mention guilt—scratch an ex-Catholic! And it was worse to love classical music. And far worse to be slightly effeminate and hopeless in every ritual of the straight world. And then to be a performer, why, even when they applauded, I felt a freak. By stage managing a sexual experience that was neither painful nor ugly, that was completely free of the clumsy fumbling of guilt-ridden adolescents, he taught me that there was nothing sinister about a little pleasure.

The next day, I seemed to be glowing; even Maestro noticed. My friend asked me how it had gone.

"It was wonderful. But something worries me."

"What's that?"

"Well, it was paid for."

"So?"

"But that's supposed to be . . . well . . ."

"Look at it this way, isn't it better to shop than to burn?"

Eventually, though we were rivals, we went out for evenings together. I met people. I wasn't so alone. And I saw what life was among humans. It was ugly and complex, suddenly beautiful, then infuriating, and always to be treasured and grasped, not fled from as my parents and their parents had fled, into the malnourished safety of platitude. Heavy loneliness and sullen rage, my boon companions since consciousness set in, disappeared for a time. My playing improved, became freer. Even Maestro thought so. And my friend opened me to music. The piano works of Boulez, Messiaen, Stockhausen, Crumb, forced me to think, to confront the whole idea of sense in sound through one player's touch in ways I could never have imagined. I'll never forget his rebuking me for thinking the Debussy études boring as well as unplayable, by sitting down and playing them as though they were effortlessly spun poetry. He opened my ears. As a result, I manhandled Schumann and Chopin less, and found colors in Schubert, and solutions to Beethoven that were mine and interesting. What little success I had, I owed to him.

And here he was, dying.

"Oh dear, oh dear," he said, "we're in for it, now."

We were at the Cathedral. There were many people there, carrying signs, raising rosaries. Mounted police waited in front of the Cathedral itself. As we passed the center doors, catcalls and furious insults rang out. I saw many Catholics with pictures of Pat Buchanan in one hand, and holy medals held aloft in the other, as though they were weapons. Was Pat their idea of Jesus, I wondered? If so, could we hope for an imminent crucifixion?

My friend was shaken by this demonstration. At one point he stumbled. I took one arm, his friend took the other, and we held him up. He weighed next to nothing. Suddenly, a furious man with a huge potbelly and a purplish face was right beside me. He began screaming, pointing at my friend.

"Look at the perverts," he screamed, "look at them, parading this carcass through our streets." This man pushed closer to my friend, and spat on him. "He's like a rat. It's like they're carrying a rat through the streets during the bubonic plague!"

La Golgotha ran at him and kicked him heavily with his big black shoes. Then he ran back to me. "Let's run for it," he panted. We raced away, carrying my friend to the front of the line where we were surrounded by other AIDS victims and their friends.

I looked back over my shoulder and saw the potbelly rolling on the ground, in agony, grabbing at his shins and yelling. Police were swarming around him. They weren't paying any attention to us Despite his bulk, La Golgotha had moved very quickly indeed.

"Thanks," said my friend to La Golgotha, who blushed. "It's nothing," he said, "but I was raised in Queens where they're all like that. I've always wanted to kick one. I hope I crippled him."

Suddenly the Marshal of the AIDS section was beside us. He was staring at La Golgotha as we marched. "Are you crazy?" he cried. "You could have created an incident. We're better off as martyrs! Are you too dumb to understand that?" He looked us over coldly. "You two don't have AIDS. This section is just for AIDS victims and one friend each. Move out, go on, move out!" He pressured us out of the line, barely giving me time to nod good-bye to my friend.

"Martyrs?" La Golgotha huffed. "What did he mean, martyrs?" I pointed to a man with a long beard and yarmulke who seemed to be having convulsions of condemnation, egged on by similarly attired but younger fans. "Didn't they learn anything from the Holocaust?" La Golgotha said, and he ostentatiously made the sign of the cross in the direction of the furious rebbe. His entire group cried out as one and averted their eyes. La Golgotha beamed, proud of himself.

We marched on downtown. The heat began to bother me—that, and the many Diet Pepsi's I had drunk.

"God, I'm uncomfortable. La Golgotha, is there a place to pee?"

"Corinne and Joe's," he answered, "they're right up there, I bet."

He pointed to our right. We started scanning the many people who had come out onto fire escapes, roofs, or who were hanging out of the big windows of loft buildings. Golgotha and I saw Corinne at the same instant and waved. She waved back and screamed at us, waving a glass of something in a beckoning manner.

"She's asking us up," said La Golgotha.

"I've always hated her," I said.

"She may be hateful, but she's got a bathroom and something to drink," said La Golgotha, the survivor.

We entered a newly remodeled and very handsome loft building. The "in" buzzer was already ringing. We got on the former freight elevator, which, after a noisy climb, opened on a vast airy space, one of Joe and Corinne's three apartments, the one they lived in. The others were vacant; they were warehousing them.

Corinne greeted La Golgotha effusively, throwing her long arms around his neck and elaborately putting her cheek to his; first, right side, then, left side, then, front. Since she was tall and thin, with a long sharp face, she looked like a long-legged bird fishing in Golgotha's face.

Joe, her husband of record, smiled at me. He gave the brown maid some orders, then approached. He was a weak-looking man, too thin, too tall, pigeon-toed, and with facial hair insufficiently thick to justify the mustache he continually fussed with. He shook my hand. Corinne contented herself with a curt nod in my direction. Joe gave both La Golgotha and me glasses of wine. I used the gothic bathroom. On my walk back to the party, I took my time looking at the amazing number of toys Corinne and Joe had assembled from their world tours. I eventually found them in their living chamber, more or less large enough for an orchestra. I slipped on the wood floor, spilling some wine. Corinne and her guests were hanging out the huge windows, looking at the parade, so they didn't see me. She had her arms around La Golgotha and was playing with his hair, as though he were an enormous creature purloined from some strange foreign wood, and smuggled into this country. They were drinking Roederer Cristal poured from transparent bottles and eating strawberries.

"I can't imagine marching," one of the friends said. "What if one were seen?"

"Especially by a client," drawled someone else.

"Oh, heaven forfend!" a third gurgled, slurping up her wine.

"Sex is all well and good," a fashionable young man ventured, "but to turn oneself into a freak? I don't understand it. Give me a guilty secret over a political statement any time."

"It's a big parade, today," Corinne said pensively. "I hope it doesn't depress the market. We've been slaving to attract the best types to Manhattan, and while this is a hoot in its way, part of the local color, so to speak, I wouldn't want anyone watching this on TV to get the wrong idea."

"What idea?" I asked her.

"Oh, any idiot can see that," she snapped. "The idea that Manhattan is full of diseased and irresponsible children, sure to be drags on the city services, unable to pay rent, unwilling to vacate when they get sick. Would you locate your business here if you thought that? Would you warehouse an apartment building if those might be your tenants? Would you buy one of our apartments if those were your neighbors?"

"Oh God, Corinne, you're scaring me," whined one of her lady friends. "I was enjoying the parade."

Joe, who had been dangling dangerously from the window, gleefully shrilled: "Oh, look . . . !" He pointed to a group of men dressed as nuns, cavorting outrageously. La Golgotha squealed in delight. Corinne petted him. "I hope that doesn't turn off too many Catholics," she sighed.

From the safety of the big windows, the group cheered the flamboyant "nuns" below. When their next-door neighbors booed, those in Corinne's window rebuked them with much hilarity.

Why did I feel a sudden anger at this well-heeled and harmless group? They meant no offense; some were even kind. They were all barely in their thirties and had the easy manners and docility of that generation. They were probably all reasonably tolerant of eccentricity. But they were consumers, totally and solely consumers. They loved to dine on the tasty lives of others, happy to see anything exciting: wonderful or nightmarish. They adored it when others suffered, took risks, cried out in agony, died, or lived, succumbed to or escaped from the worst luck, so long as they could shut it all off as they did their TVs.

"I think we should go," I said to La Golgotha.

"I'd rather stay," he whined.

"All right," I said, "see you later."

"You seem more than usually off-putting," Corinne said to me. "Did you look in the mirror this morning?"

"Sandy's upset because one of his friends from his career is in the AIDS group," said La Golgotha, a trace complacently.

"A pity," responded Corinne. "What upset you?"

"What do you mean, what upset me?"

"Well, I've never known you to be overly concerned about anybody else, unless it was a concert pianist getting better reviews than you. It can't be concern for your friend, it must be concern for yourself. He opened his asshole to the world; you've done the same thing, haven't you? So it follows you're afraid you'll get it."

I wanted to call her the most vicious names, but stopped myself. I guess I was afraid of looking foolish, or getting too upset, which would have meant she had won. And perhaps there was some truth in what she had said. Maybe some of my concern about my friend was guilt over my own past. Scratch an ex-Catholic . . .

"Well," Corinne continued, smacking her lips after a deep draft of bubbly, "grow up. Life is a bag. One bag closes, another opens. The gay thing, the open thing, that was the seventies bag. It was like a big veal dinner at Lutece. It's great while you're there. But the next day it's just shit running down the wall. And it's terrible to learn while you're squatting there, you couldn't really afford it. If you're still alive, it's time to move on, change, invest, build. Now, I've been nice enough to explain myself, so get out of my loft."

"Uuuuhh!" squealed La Golgotha, delight having regressed him to kindergarten.

It was late afternoon when I emerged from the building. The parade had passed. I decided to amble downtown and hear the speeches. As usual, I tried to calm myself by reviewing opera records in my head.

The Village was packed with every kind of gay person.

There were teenaged boys, queeny or tough; squadrons of lesbians, some boyish, some voluptuous. I saw a herd of nuns; either that or the girls dressed that way had found very authentic looking costumes. I saw many old men, some in what had to be uncomfortably tight and hot leather. There was a mood of celebration. There were thousands of balloons around. Dope sellers of all kinds hawked their wares. Giddy drunks made spectacles of themselves. And I saw many middle-aged, stout couples, taking pictures.

I stopped at Washington Square Park and sat down on a bench. I had often cruised there in my early days in New York. It was shady, even dark. I sneezed a lot, a sure sign evening was near. I saw a bunch of cops mounted on big horses. I heard my name, not Sandy, but my real name and saw Earl, a boy I knew.

He was probably fifteen—a hustler around the Village bars. I'd talked to him a few times, and we'd flirted about getting together, but I was nervous about his age. He was handsome, very all-American looking. He seemed bright, despite what was probably heavy use of any drug he could find. I guessed he was a suburban gay kid, unable or unwilling to hide, or chased away by his parents.

"Hey, man! Let's take a walk. All these pigs on horses freak me."

I smiled, and we walked out of the park. He looked unwell and seemed nervous. "What's the matter? You look hungry."

He laughed. "Nothing, man. Look, see you . . ." I didn't know whether to leave or not.

I was about to walk away when he sat down on the ground.

"Earl?" I asked. "What's going on? Are you stoned or what?" I saw he was crying. He shook his head. I wanted to run. The cars, backed up around the park, were honking their horns. Several joggers, one wearing handcuffs and ankle chains, ran by, looking at us curiously. Earl coughed. I bent down, creating quite an obstacle on the sidewalk.

"I'm scared," he whimpered, so softly I barely heard.

"Why?" I asked. But I knew why. As I squatted close to

him, I saw a large, jagged, violet mark on his throat. Instinctively, I recognized it. I realized what his thinness meant, and I saw there was something dreadful in his eyes.

"I don't . . ." He was whispering, and I had to lean closer to hear. "I don't know what to do, man . . ." He bent over and threw up. I saw there were small sores around his mouth, and there was blood in his vomit. I was afraid to touch him.

A mounted cop rode up on the sidewalk. "What is it? An overdose?"

I ignored him. I've got to touch him, I thought to myself. I can't run away. I forced my hand to Earl's back. He was heaving so much my arm shook. I felt nauseous, terrified.

"You want to answer my question? And you better have a good one, because that punk is underage."

His horse pissed, a powerful flood of water, noisy and wild, that steamed inches away from Earl. I took Earl's hand and saw another mark on his forearm, bigger, darker than the one on his throat.

"Look, you fat asshole, I ain't gonna ask you again!"

"What do you mean, you aren't going to ask again?" I was roaring, loud enough to stop the implacable joggers who had been moving around the cop on the horse, Earl, and me. "I'm a taxpayer in this city and what does that get me? Pissed on by some turkey, mounted on his mother?!"

"You faggot!" He reared back on his horse and pulled his stick out.

A figure emerged from the small crowd, grabbed my arm forcefully, and spoke to me with the utmost urgency: "Senator, what are you doing here? Oh dear, what if somebody recognized you? Oh, officer, thank God, you're helping the Senator. He wanted to observe this demonstration for the Agency, and . . . who is this? Who is this boy, Senator? It's not your son, Teddy? Oh my God, Teddy! Wasn't he supposed to be at Groton, still? This can't get into the press! Can we trust you, officer?"

Leatherette had appeared from nowhere and simply taken over. The cop was just as shocked as I. Leatherette talked so fast and with such authority that both the cop and I pricked up our ears as dogs do when their masters speak.

"Wha . . . ? I mean, Wha . . . ?" was all the cop could manage.

Leatherette plunged on fervently: "This would be a disaster for the Catholics in this country, if it got out . . ."

"The Catholics?"

"You're Irish, of course?" asked Leatherette sweetly.

"Of course, but—"

"I knew it; we're probably cousins. Here, buy some candles for Senator D'Amato here." Leatherette, with stagey discretion, pointed at me. "He's half Irish . . ." Leatherette was reaching a twenty-dollar bill up over the saddle. The cop looked at him, at it, at me, at Earl, back at the bill. There was an endless instant. I saw Leatherette getting arrested for trying to bribe one of New York's Finest. I saw myself getting arrested for cradling a fifteen year old on the street, and thanks to Leatherette, for impersonating a Republican Senator. But there was something frying in the officer's brain pan. I saw from the way his pimples were twitching, he was young enough not to be absolutely certain about what Leatherette was trying to do.

Suddenly his walkie-talkie squawked to life. "All right," he said, "get that asshole and his chicken off the street!" He backed up his horse. "Get the hell out of here," he screamed at the joggers, who all started running again. He turned his horse very rapidly, then suddenly swept the twenty out of Leatherette's hands.

"Thank you, officer, thank you!" cried Leatherette. "And if anybody asks you about all this, just say the twenty's Pat Buchanan's contribution to the Force!"

This really impressed the cop. "Is that you, Pat?"

"Oh shit, I gave myself away!"

"I'm with you all the way, Pat, even to the White House!" His walkie-talkie sputtered again. He was clearly unwilling just to ride off. "Gee, Pat, you don't look like your pictures."

"Thank God! I mean I wouldn't want these fruits to recognize me, they might lynch me!"

"You just give a holler, if there's a problem, Pat, we're here!" The cop patted his revolver. For the first time, Leatherette looked nervous. He turned to me. "Senator, we've got to get you off the street! And then we'll write our report about all these sick fags!"

"Right on, Pat!" cried the baby cop, who got his horse to rear up as though he were the Lone Ranger and galloped down the street.

Leatherette collapsed beside me. "Thank the Sucking Cherubim they have to fail tests to get on the Force!" he cried. "And thank the Creator of All Anal Warts that you Italian girls all look the same. Sandy, what in the name of Mary, Mother of Drag Queens, are you doing on the sidewalk with a child?"

"He's sick, Leatherette."

"Well, at least let's get him in the park and behind some bushes."

A gigantic figure entirely in leather, with golden spurs, strode over to us. It was our friend, Doctor Ignacio Micheluzzi.

Leatherette saw him, and called out: "Oh, Rose Hips Medicatrix, thank God! This child is sick, and Sandy's playing the Lady with the Lamp, not one of her best roles."

"Let's get him onto a park bench," said Rose Hips. "Is that his vomit?"

"Yes," I said.

"Let me look at him before we move him." He bent over Earl. The sidewalk was now impassable. Pedestrians saw a leather-clad giant, a fat man, and a small man with a huge leather bag, bending over a prostrate teenager.

Rose Hips had changed from being frighteningly flamboyant to acting utterly professional. I knew him vaguely from standing room at the opera. Although we all loved operatic sopranos, especially fat ones, Rose Hips was the maddest Caballé Queen I have ever met. He had attained heaven alive by becoming part of the team treating her during one of her innumerable health crises some years before. Since he was the only one of her doctors who loved opera, and spoke Spanish, she had discovered his home phone number, called him, gotten his answering machine, and sung all of "Vissi d'arte" as a way of saying thank you. Rose Hips walked on air for years afterward.

He and Leatherette had met while temporarily sharing a sling at The Mineshaft. They had amused each other so much, they had committed the gravest faux pas in that dark dungeon of tough anonymous sex—giggling uncontrollably at their would-be "masters." They had been thrown out and had avenged themselves by shrieking opera arias outside the place for hours until the police came and embarrassed the tough and punitive leather queens inside.

"What's your name?" Rose Hips asked Earl.

"Earl." His voice was high and slight. Rose Hips took a deep breath.

"Well, I'm Doctor Micheluzzi, but my real name is Rose Hips Medicatrix. Do you know what all that means?" Rose bent over Earl, looking at him intently. I saw his eyes go immediately to the mark on his throat, then, to that on his forearm.

"Aren't rose hips, vitamin C?" asked Earl.

"Yes, a great curative. Like me. Sometimes." Rose Hips looked into Earl's mouth, took his pulse. "Have you been to the doctor, Earl?"

"No."

"I understand. I hate doctors, too. That's why I became one, to get my own back, and teach the Surgeon General how to fuck!" Earl laughed a little. "But Earl, I think we have to get you to a hospital . . ."

"No!" Earl cried out, "then my folks'll find out . . ."

Leatherette and I exchanged a look, guessing that Earl's folks had thrown him out.

"Earl, listen to me . . ." began Rose Hips, but Earl was starting to get up. This was difficult for him but he worked at it fiercely. Rose Hips held on to him. Another crowd had gathered. A cab screamed to the curb, and La Pincushionova leaped out. She was dressed in a long unflattering gown, with her makeup misapplied and smudged. Earl gasped when he saw her. She probably looked like Death to him. He weakened and lay back down. Rose Hips caught and held him.

"Did you bribe that cop, Leatherette?" demanded La Pincushionova. "I saw it a block away, and tried to get your attention but the traffic just wouldn't move!"

"She make me honk," complained the cab driver, an Iranian, leaning out of the passenger side of his cab, and screaming, "I could have got the citation!"

"Oh, shut up, you crybaby!" she screamed back, then turned to Rose Hips and pointed to Earl, "Is he sick?" When Rose Hips nodded, she asked, "Where can we take him?"

"They'll do me a favor at Saint Vincent's."

"No!" cried Earl.

"He's afraid," Rose Hips said to La Pincushionova. "His parents . . ."

"Should we try for an ambulance, or can we use the cab?"

"Ambulance crews have been refusing to take cases like this . . . ," said Rose Hips. La Pincushionova's eyes widened. Rose Hips continued, "In any case, we should try to get him there as fast as we can."

"That's the cab!"

"He sick, he sick, you no use my cab. He sick."

La Pincushionova drew herself up and said menacingly: "If you give us any trouble, my husband here," she grabbed Rose Hips, "will grind his golden spurs into your face!" La Pincushionova grabbed the door handle, making it clear she wouldn't let go if the cabbie tried to drive off. The cabbie looked Rose Hips over. He was at least six three, and very muscular. "But," said La Pincushionova seductively, "if you take the kid, I'll double the fare."

"Hurry, make hurry," snapped the cab driver, looking nervously in his rearview mirror.

It was evening now. The lights of oncoming cars cast an eerie glow over us. Earl tried to get up again. "Please, I'm sorry, I can't go to a hospital." He sobbed, and then, losing his strength, vomited again. There was a terrible smell about him. Leatherette and I started away from him, instinctively. La Pincushionova took Earl's head in her hands firmly and held it as he threw up. The cabbie moaned something in Parsi. La Pincushionova glanced at him to shut up. Rose Hips got up and opened the back door of the cab.

La Pincushionova spoke firmly to Earl: "Look, my parents hate me too. They disowned me, you know, when I was about your age." Calmly, she took Kleenex from her purse and started wiping his face. "We're outcasts, you and me, and they like it best when we suffer like you're suffering now. They want you to think there's nobody for you." He had stopped heaving. She rested his head on her breast and stroked him. Rose Hips gestured at her to hurry. She turned all her attention on Earl. She was a small woman but seemed hard and firm as a rock. "But you aren't alone. You have friends here. We'll help you. I'm sure we can, between us. And you'll feel a lot better than you're feeling now, cleaner and safer. Even if that's the best we can do, that's a lot. Nobody's going to scare you or make fun of you while we're here. Now, come on, let us lift you into the cab. You hold on to me and squeeze when you need to, okay?"

"Okay."

We got him into the cab's backseat. There was only room for Earl and La Pincushionova. Rose Hips got into the front. The cabbie started to honk his horn again and soon they sped off. The people who had been watching the show walked away, many shaking their heads disapprovingly. Leatherette turned to me: "A trick?"

"No. I've only spoken to him a few times. I guess I'll go over to Saint Vincent's and see what I can do."

"I want to go to the rally. Call me later if you need to."

"Thanks."

He started down the street and I crossed to walk to the hospital. Suddenly, I heard: "Girl! Hey, girl?!" It was Leatherette, screaming at me, and literally stopping traffic. "Just remember, girl, you owe me a twenty!"

*   *   *

Earl died eventually, of course. My pianist friend also died, though he held on much longer than I would have thought possible. We never spoke again.

La Pincushionova also died. Sometime after the march, those violet marks spread over her legs. This was just before the HIV test, so we hoped against hope it was some eccentric manifestation of inner oddity. But it was AIDS.

La Golgotha, Leatherette, the failing Pincushionova and I went to Leonie Rysanek's Gala at the Met. We sneaked in for old time's sake, and we shared a joint right before it started. "Does anyone die tonight?" she asked, inhaling very cautiously, and repressing a cough.

"No," I answered, "it's just act two of *Parsifal*, and act one of *Walküre*."

"What a pity! Leonie's so good at death scenes." She exhaled, which triggered a noisy spasm—the wages of dope.

She asked me to stand with her in the Dress Circle where her coughing would disturb people less.

Leatherette was with one of his security guards, who was trying to get culture; they stole seats in the Orchestra. La Golgotha, who loved La Rysanek so much he sometimes confused himself with her, was sitting as close as possible, in ecstasy.

La Pincushionova got through the second act of *Parsifal* despite her cough. During the first act of *Walküre* the cough was replaced by a horrible wheezing.

I was concerned for her: "La Pincushionova, I think we should leave."

"No not until the end."

The last third of the act came. Sieglinde emerged from the bedroom, having given her life-denying husband a sleeping potion. She told Siegmund about the sword hidden high in the ash tree by a one-eyed stranger (their father, the orchestra let us know). The doors of the hut flew open and spring flooded the room. Sieglinde—La Rysanek in full cry—had screamed in alarm. And my, how Leonie could scream! But Siegmund told her it was only the spring summoned by their burgeoning love.

La Pincushionova was leaning her face into the wall behind the Dress Circle. I suppose the wood was cool. Sieglinde burst into her aria: "You are the Spring," the song one sings to the young god who against all the odds has brought love into one's dead life. La Pincushionova slid down the wall as the music mounted in ecstasy. I bent over her, then ran for the house manager, who called an ambulance. Perhaps it was fortunate she never awoke from her coma and died peacefully enough a week later.

I have to laugh remembering La Pincushionova. I look out through the bars into my garden. Her son plays there. He answers to two names: Ingo, when he's been good, and "Spawn of Pincushionova," which Leatherette is apt to thunder, when he's been bad.

Leatherette is his guardian, it looks as though an adoption will go through. No one came forth to claim him when his mother died. In fact no living relative of La Pincushionova wanted to acknowledge ever having known her. "Ingo might as well join the holy unwanted," Leatherette had said, and surprisingly, the foster care people have helped him with every step of the process. When my gargantuan super won the lottery and moved to Westchester with his family, Leatherette moved into his apartment. With Ingo, he needed more space, and more lockable doors. Luckily, my landlady decided we could share the super from next door if we paid more rent.

As for me, I no longer perform. I teach. I'm quite a success at it. One of my first pupils, an epicene ephebe of Oriental extraction, has gone on to win numerous competitions. That has resulted in my having a full schedule of naive hopefuls. I do my best to teach them reality but they scoff. They think it was really a lack of talent that sank me, and after all, maybe it was. I had nothing to do with my star pupil's success, certainly. I couldn't bear to hear him massacre Schubert and Mozart, his specialties on the contest circuit, so we read through *Norma* and *Carmen*, two of many favorite operas, playing my favorite parts over and over, transposed up, transposed down, in thirds, in octaves, à la Liszt, à la Schoenberg, à la Chopin, in variation form, with divine simplicity. He tells everyone it helped, but maybe this is evidence of the sense of humor I kept expecting to emerge but never saw manifested in our long lessons.

Leatherette leaves Ingo with me when he is out sneaking into things, or when he is practicing his version of safe sex—videotaping security guards as they strip in his apartment.

I used to fear children, but I don't mind Ingo. He's much like his mother: He's turning into an ugly little boy; he loves the ballet. He'd much rather watch Leatherette's pirated ballet videos than "Miami Vice." He was born HIV positive, but seven years have passed and he is still asymptomatic. Since Ingo's health has been good, Rose Hips, who recently went skiing with Caballé (he said seeing her toboggan slowly down the beginner's hill, her hippopotomic bulk swathed in tons of multicolored furs, singing Castillian folk songs, was as close to the beatific vision as he expects to get), is optimistic.

Neither Leatherette nor I have taken the HIV test. We don't speak of what it would mean should one of us get the disease. I shouldn't exaggerate my closeness to Leatherette. He's an elusive spirit for all his camping. I'm alone, I suppose. There isn't much of a circle anymore at the opera. There hasn't been much worth going to recently.

Though I don't know how much longer I'll survive, I have some survivor guilt. I'd like to reach out to La Pincushionova, my pianist friend, Earl, and the many others and tell them . . . what? Could I have been a better friend to them knowing I'd live a little longer? And would that have made a difference to them, given they were to die? But after all, I tell myself, people die, consciousness ceases, and that's it. La Pincushionova, and the others, have done nothing different from millions of other humans who died young from inexplicable and cruel diseases. I suppose I've learned the only true solidarity humans have is with death.

Ingo flings himself around the yard, yelling *Swan Lake* at the top of his lungs. At least he's imitating the male lead; it would be sad to have another failed ballerina in that family. He sees me looking at him through the bars and suddenly bows elaborately, as he has seen the Bolshoi dancers do in one of Leatherette's tapes. I clap for him. He leaps to one side, gathers up some roses (the landlady, who tends the garden, will go crazy; luckily she likes and forgives Ingo), and presents himself with them. He accepts them, miming shocked modesty, then, tears flowing, enfolds them with the tenderest vulnerability, and slowly collapses to the ground, as though to a crowd of raving ballet queens screaming themselves hoarse.

"Bravo, Pincushionov," I cry, applauding, "bravo!"

He slams into my apartment, grabs a Diet Pepsi and a Sara Lee mini snack, and runs to the VCR to check some of his moves against the dancers on tape.

Somehow I don't want to accept that our only solidarity is with death. Scratch an ex-Catholic . . . But what can a spinster piano teacher make of it all? Is it that everything is nothing—America, and TV, and opera, and nuclear weapons, and technology, and advanced degrees, and Star Wars (movie and defense initiative), and the musical establishment, and gayness, and beauty, and Madonna (the icon and the Icon), and obesity, and ugliness, and secret longings—is all pointless, because death, smiling and insolent and mysterious death smothers everything? Maybe it's true, as the dying Pincushionova suggested to me, that some million years ago, alien beings, for a lark, infected a she-ape with a communicable disease called consciousness, and altered her DNA so she could pass it on to her progeny, and laughed and laughed as she went around fornicating. Because they knew the only cure for that terrible disease would be death; and in time, that would be seen as the most dreaded cure in human history.

Luckily, I am rescued from this unprofitable line of thought by a phone call from La Golgotha. He's looking for Leatherette. We get off the phone quickly. Fate was kind to La Golgotha. One rainy night while riding his bicycle he got run over by a garbage truck. His face was all mashed up and had to be redone. The trauma killed his appetite. Within a year, he was transformed into an ordinary-looking man with muscles. Corinne was so happy about this, she hired him to run her burgeoning real estate business which has made her a multimillionaire. One can see her on cable around the country, a mannish frau in radiant health, promising you too can get rich, just by sending her a large sum of money.

In the hospital, La Golgotha tested negative for HIV virus. Leatherette told me he had known all along. For, despite all his queenly grandeur, La Golgotha has had exactly one sexual experience, after which he was so upset he needed shock therapy. His breakdown was due to the terrible guilt nurtured in a sensitive soul by a Catholic education. That's why Leatherette gave him the name: Golgotha.

I suppose I should feel happy for La Golgotha, but I no longer feel comfortable with him. Though I'll love Maria Callas until I die, I preferred him when he looked like Joan Sutherland.

DANCING ON TISHE B'AV

• LEV RAPHAEL •

BRENDA WAS ALREADY used to the men across the chest-high wooden mehitzah separating the men and women, saying they needed one more "person" to make the minyan of ten, while she and sometimes as many as four other women might be there. Like now, suspended in summer boredom, their conversation as heavy with heat as the sluggish flies whispering past in the small gray-walled shul on the musty Jewish Center's ground floor. Sometimes they all waited half an hour before continuing with services, for a man, any man, to be tenth. It amused her that even the dimmest specimens counted when she didn't; shabby unshowered men who shouted rather than sang and read Hebrew as if each line were a heat-wavering horizon; yawning men whose great round gasps for air seemed their profoundest prayers; men who sneeringly hissed game scores (and had to be hushed) to show how immune they were to the ark, to anything sacred and Jewish.

Sometimes, on the other side, her brother Nat corrected them and said, "Man. You mean another *man*." And she smiled at his embarrassment for her.

Though raised Conservative, she had come to like the Orthodox service. Here the purpose was prayer, not socializing, showing off Judaic knowledge, filling the shul, or even getting away from the kids for a morning. People sometimes joked, but the service itself was serious. At the faculty dominated shuls in their university town, the persistent chitchat and laughter were like the desperate assertion of rationality and control in the face of what was mysterious—as if to let go, to be silent and feel, would be an admission of nakedness and shame.

"Too many Ph.D.'s," was Nat's comment, and she, a graduate student in history, had felt accused. A junior, Nat had been attending the Orthodox services for two years, and his commitment was as fierce and sullen as the clutch of a baby's hand on a stolen toy.

Nat went out now to practice his Torah portion in another room. Thin, with the twitching walk of a jerky marionette and that pale and narrow slack-mouthed face, he seemed a genetic rebuke to their handsome family, a warning that all gifts were uncertain. As a boy he'd been aloof, watchful, building castles out of blocks and books, pretending to be powerful, a knight. He never cried, never apologized. Spanking him was pointless, scolding absurd. The little mean eyes just shut inside, his face grew stupid and closed.

"*Red tsu a vant!*" their father would shout in Yiddish: "Talk to a wall!"—uneasily admiring the stubborn ugly boy. The stocky pharmacist would peer down at Nat, hands clenched, as if wishing they were equals and could fight.

Nat was sullen and silent until he went into theater in high school, stunning Brenda with his intensity as Tom in *The Glass Menagerie*. He had felt, to her, more maimed by life than the girl playing Laura. Onstage, his walk, his thin face were larger, more compelling; his *authority* was beautiful. It was the same here at State the few times he did a show.

What did their parents think?

Their mother said, "He takes makeup very well, it doesn't look like him."

His father, when he didn't fall asleep in the darkened auditorium, smirked, "Sure—*here* he can act—so what? Try Broadway!"

They were just as supportive of Nat's move to Orthodoxy,

his father shaking his head: "What I gave him isn't enough—he has to go to *fremde menshen*, strangers, to be a Jew." And their mother wondered if Nat would be allowed to touch any woman he wasn't married to, and was he going to Israel to throw stones at cars that drove on Saturday?

How much this affected Nat, Brenda didn't know. He had always refused to acknowledge successes as well as failures, lived, she thought, in stubborn exile, unreachable, untouched.

Nat had learned to tie his shoes too early, was too neat and alphabetical in his approach to life. It was as if saying "First things first" and making points in conversation by clutching successive fingers could order and control the world. He read Torah in a dry triumphant chant as if the letters piled around him in tribute. He was a vegetarian and drank only mineral water and herb teas. He ran seven miles a day, even in the winter. He loved men.

She had known this, known something, for too long. When she was sixteen and Nat eleven she found a folder in his pile of *Life*, *Car & Driver* and *Reader's Digest*, crammed with pages sliced from magazines, all ads. They were men, whose exquisite eyes and hands and hair, whose tough hard bodies shot one hopeless accusation after another: "You are not beautiful—you never will be." Nat had distilled this terrible poison from harmless magazines.

It was that year Brenda found an open notebook on his desk in which he'd written out pages of new names for himself, first and last, a parade of loathing.

And worse, because she was worried, she saw too much. She noticed that her mother's closet door would often be closed when her mother—who always left it open—was out for an afternoon and Nat alone. It was their stale family joke, her mother and closets, cabinets, drawers.

"Yes," her father would growl. "Let everything in the breadbox see what's happening in the kitchen they shouldn't feel lonely."

At first she thought that Nat was just snooping in that rich confusion, as she had done years before. But then, allowing herself no vision of what she suspected, Brenda set little traps for him: a purse hung just so, a dress belt folded under. And she learned that Nat did something with Mom's clothes—put them on, pretended he was beautiful, like her? What did plucking earrings from the shiny madness in her mother's jewel box *mean* to him?

Before these discoveries, Nat had been annoying to her, or unimportant, or sometimes, unexpectedly cute. Suddenly, he was dangerous, unknown. In the next years she'd wait for Nat's oddities to burst from the neutral box of his silence like trick paper snakes, but he was only more sullen, blighting family dinners like the suspicion of a pitiless disease. Her father gave up cursing and her mother shrugged, as if Nat were a strange country she'd never been able to find on a globe. When her mother did talk about Nat, she had the brisk bored sound of a librarian stating facts that anyone could check.

"He doesn't have wet dreams," her mother announced, folding laundry in the basement.

Brenda, nineteen then, tried to think of something adequate to her surprise.

"I've checked his sheets, Bren."

And when Nat was in high school: "Why doesn't he date more? I think he's afraid of sex. Your father said he blushed when they talked about condoms."

"Wait till eleven," a man on the other side was saying now. "We always wait."

"Forget it." That was Nat. "I called this week and no one's in town." He listed all his calls.

She knew that Nat was right; the Orthodox minyan drew on a very small group of Jews, strangers rarely joined them.

The women behind her stirred the pages of their prayerbooks as if scanning merchandise in a dull catalog. They were mostly the bleak girlfriends of men who ran the minyan, wearing artless, dowdy plain clothes and talking after services about movies or food. She imagined they would welcome marriage and the children who would release them from regular attendance. She thought of them as The Widows because though in their mid-twenties they already seemed isolated, like the survivors of a historic loss.

Around her, the heat, spread by a weak ceiling fan, settled like a film of soot or car exhaust; her light dress, sandals, and short hair didn't help her feel cool.

"Brenda, you look very nice today."

Clark, the law student who looked like Al Pacino and thought he was Bruce Springsteen hung over the mehitzah. From Bloomfield Hills, he always talked to her with the smugness she remembered in adolescent cliques, as if his good looks and hers bound them in undeniable complicity.

Before she could say anything, Nat was back at the door, bleating, *"Gut shabbos!"*

At the chipped bookcase with the prayerbooks and Bibles, stood a tall tanned man who looked thirty to her, blue-eyed, with thick close-trimmed mustache and beard that seemed very black above the tan summer suit and white shirt. He slipped a prayer shawl from the wooden stand, covered his head with it as he said the blessing, and found a seat up near the front of the men's side, shaking hands, nodding. After finding out the man's Hebrew name, Nat marched up to the lectern.

It was a blessing to be the tenth man, she thought, as services continued with unexpected excitement. They sang and chanted like forty people, not fourteen. When there wasn't a minyan and the Torah stayed in its plainly curtained ark, she felt a fierce longing to see it borne around the shul to be touched with prayerbooks, prayer shawl fringes, or kissed like a bride as some of the men did.

When the stranger, *Moshe Leib ben Shimon haCohen*, Mark, was called to the Torah for the first blessing, he loomed over the lectern like a dark memorial in a way that dried her throat; his back seemed broad and forbidding. But his voice was sweet, smooth, rising and falling with the self-indulgent sadness of a Russian folk song. He sight read the first portion without a mistake. They were all impressed.

Nat, always well-prepared, read badly today. He made mistakes even she could catch and it was painful watching him struggle with easy words. The silver pointer in his hand usually paced serenely along each squarish path of Hebrew, but now it was as listless as an uninspired divining rod. She looked away from him, from her Bible. Nat would probably tell people after services that he was tired and because he never read poorly no one would doubt him.

She hoped.

What did people say about him? Could they tell?

"He should date more"—his mother's verdict. Mrs. Stern was often mentioning friends' daughters to Nat at holiday dinners as if genially passing a liqueur, but to Brenda she had recently said:

"Is he gay?"

"No!"

"You're sure—"

"Mom."

Her father said nothing directly or indirectly to Brenda; if it concerned him that Nat hardly dated, he probably classed that with Nat's habitual stubbornness. Besides, she imagined her father sneering, "With that *punim*, that face, who would want him?"

For Brenda Nat was Coronado discovering the Seven Cities of El Dorado everywhere—in the pumping bare thighs of bikers on campus, the ripe curves of jeans-tight asses, the heavy twin arcs of runners' chests under cool molding cotton—flash after flash of heaven-sent gold in hundreds of men around town. But he was a Coronado without armor, without guides, troops, provisions, maps, or even a commission. He had only his hunger.

She never spoke about this with Nat, never asked about dates or parties, had no idea what his life was like. Nat lived in his dorm and she in her apartment in town with the huge ecstatically landscaped campus between them like the florid alibi for a crime. They lunched sometimes, she phoned him, they met at services and occasionally drove home to Southfield together, but she seldom mentioned that her brother was "up at school." She was afraid for him.

She was ashamed.

In her freshman year at Madison, on her coed floor, there had been a lovely dark-haired boy named Tom who did up his single room with Japanese fans, silk scarves, and other gentle souvenirs of summers abroad. Cool, quiet, musical, literate, he was the eye of a storm: doors banged, voices hushed and growled, or cracked with laughter, and the jocks on their floor simmered like guard dogs on maddening chains. One morning a camping ax was found buried in Tom's door, the handle chalked, for clarity, "Faggot Die." Tom moved off campus, and that was what she feared—violence in the night, a scandal.

Having drifted away during the Torah reading she didn't reenter the service, but stood and sat with everyone and prayed aloud mechanically as if she were in an educational filmstrip, each action large and stiff. Mark, the stranger, had asked to do the last part of the service, and his Hebrew was fluent in the thick summer air.

On the way out after the last hymn, Mark wished her *Shabbat Shalom*.

"You read well," she said as they milled at the table set with kiddush wine and cakes in the little social hall.

And then Nat was there, grinning, his pale face splattered with excitement. After blessing the wine, Nat pulled Mark aside to talk about the next week's Torah portion.

Helen, Clark's cousin, bore down on Brenda. With her thin ugly legs, heavy shifting hips and rear she resembled to Brenda a pack mule struggling up a hill.

"*Gut Shabbos*," Helen murmured, round face doleful, as if she were passing on unpleasant gossip. "Isn't he terrific?"

"Mark?"

"Uh-huh. What a *spa*."

"Spa . . ."

"Sure, he works out—look at his chest, those shoulders. Yum."

Brenda watched them, Mark with the cool, one-dimensional

beauty of a brass rubbing, Nat grasping him with a sickly smile. She ate a dry piece of pound cake.

There were at least a thousand Jewish students on campus but hardly any came to the Orthodox minyan, which was a mix of graduate students, one or two shabby faculty members, and several University staffers. Mark's arrival was exciting, she knew, because he could take much of the burden of running services from Clark and Nat and the others who sometimes felt like prisoners of their obligations. An assistant to the Registrar, Mark spoke little about himself, but seemed to have for Nat the impact of an analyst whose silence and concern at last permit an entrance to oneself. Nat talked about his acting, his Russian and French classes, his desire to enter the Foreign Service, about everything, like a child dragging pretty treasures from pockets, under the bed, from drawers, to entertain, attract, possess a fascinating friend.

Brenda saw in Nat, for the first time, a resemblance to their mother. Generally their mother was like an antiques dealer displaying a find—herself—with chic reverence. She was slim, wide-eyed, fashionable even in a bathrobe, especially in a bathrobe whose rough folds set her off like a pretty girl's plain companion. But sometimes her mother emerged from this haze of self-absorption to talk to strangers or her children's "little friends" with merciless charm. She asked them endless unimportant questions until they found themselves like flood victims forced onto the roof of their self-possession, praying for the waters to subside.

Brenda saw Nat talking like this to Mark one Sunday afternoon, two weeks after that first Shabbat, at a restaurant in town, saw him through the wide front window, face twisted and alive, fingers plucking at a sugar packet. Mark sat deeply back from him, sky-blue tennis shirt open at a dense-haired throat, heavy fine arms crossed, a smile, some kind of smile nestled in the mustache and the beard. Mark was not just passively beautiful, she realized as she hurried on to buy her *Times* at the chain bookstore down the block, not a man to merely watch, admire, but warm, receptive, inviting. It was the lush curves of shoulders, chest, the gleaming hair and beard, the hard-lined nose and high cheekbones, the paintable mouth.

Not her type at all, too dramatic, too intense. The men she dated were at most "cute," and their ideas about third world debt or Euro-Communism gave them more color than the way they walked or dressed or *were*.

"They don't scare you," Nat had concluded, and it was too obvious for her to deny.

Mark and Nat started running together at the high school track near her apartment, like a boy and his puppy that was eager to show off how fast it moved. Mark's legs were hairy and dark, strong admonitions to the pale, weak.

They'd stop at her place afterwards for water, to towel off, talking about the weather and their wind, old injuries. Mark spoke even then as if emerging from a past that wasn't his but something he had learned, borrowed details of a spy. He sat on the floor, back against her gray-green sofa bed, legs out, relaxed, holding the tumbler to his face and neck. Nat looked wild and flustered, as if he couldn't decide whether to yell or leap or cry.

In July, when the whole state settled into a heat wave that seemed as inexorable as lava sweeping down a barren slope, Nat made an announcement to her one Friday afternoon.

"Mark has the use of a place on the Lake, near Saugatuck, and he invited me to go next Saturday night after Shabbat and spend a day or two at the beach." Nat's face was so surly that she saw him as a boy again, daring their parents with his refusal to eat beans, or wash his hair, or turn from the television.

"Does he know you're in love with him?"

Nat gave her a liar's grin, stalling. "What?"

She looked down at her cool plate of deviled eggs, potato salad, tabbouli, as if the food were an exhibit in a museum case, proof of customs stranger than one's own.

"What?"

She felt guilty now, tight-eyed. "If he's not gay he's being very cruel."

Watching Nat lean away as if the sprigged tablecloth were dangerous somehow, she understood how strong soft people really were—they could retreat across vast plains of silence, disappear.

"I wrote him a poem," Nat brought out heavily, a pauper facing his last, most precious coin. And when he turned away she jerked up from her chair to crouch by her brother, hold him and ease the ugliness of tears.

Mark called after Nat was gone, to invite himself over that evening. From Nat she'd learned that he and Mark had spent many nights together since the first Shabbat in June, at Mark's apartment in a nearby town.

Mark wore white jeans, Top-Siders, and a white Lacoste shirt as if to show her he was normal, American, no threat. But sitting in her small, crammed living room he looked like a model posed in an unlikely spot to throw his beauty into high relief.

They drank coffee.

"I was married," Mark offered. "Nat didn't say? In New Haven. We split up two years ago, I moved to Philadelphia, then here." He nodded like an old man in a rocker whose every motion confirms a memory.

"Children?"

"We couldn't."

She wished, in the quiet, for a clock that chimed, a noisy refrigerator, dogs outside, something to ease the tension in her neck and hands. She imagined her parents there, Dad scornful, incensed, Mom peering at Mark with distaste, curious, purring, "But he's handsome, don't you think?" Closing her eyes, Brenda saw the ax saying "Faggot Die" like the afterimage of a too-bright bulb.

Nat had pursued Mark, she knew, so there was no blame for her to spatter on the canvas of his silence.

"What about AIDS?" she asked.

"I've been tested, I'm okay. And Nat was a virgin."

"What about people seeing you at the lake, or in town?"

"It's not a secret for me being gay."

"But Nat's only twenty-one." She rose to bring the coffee pot to them. "It could destroy him."

Mark shrugged.

She asked about the house on Lake Michigan two hours away and Mark described the drive there, the beach. While he spoke, a thought crossed her mind with brazen clarity: even though she felt warmer to Nat after his crying, she didn't love him, still, and feared what people would say about *her* more than what might happen to Nat. I'm like Mom, she thought. Cold.

The "weekend" was fabulous, Nat raved, returning with color, some new clothes, and a haircut that made him subtly more attractive.

"He wants to take me to Paris next year!" Nat crowed.

"On *his* salary?"

"He has friends there."

Friends, she thought.

At services Nat sat next to Mark, the fringes of their prayer shawls touching, perhaps, beneath their chairs. Nat had coolly talked about Mark's divorce to most people there, had reported it with enough vagueness and somber gaps to make it seem a tragedy of some kind, a wound too open to discuss. "That's why he came to Michigan," Nat would conclude, delighted with his subterfuge. He could've been a child pretending there were dragons in the dark that only *he* could slay.

"Mark doesn't like my talking like that," Nat smirked.

Did she? Did she like any of it? When she wasn't plowing through the book list for her first comprehensive in September, she wondered what she felt. Mark was apparently kind to Nat, and luckily not one of those bitchy homosexuals whose standards were as vigilant and high as satellites, but he was real, and puzzling.

"What do you see in Nat?" she asked one noon in town where she'd come across Mark waiting to cross a street to campus. He frowned and she felt exposed, her lack of understanding, her contempt as clear to him as diamonds on blue velvet.

"He's very sad," Mark said. "I like to make him smile."

She remembered Nat years ago, little, ill, awash in bed-clothes, small eyes tight with disapproval as their mother brought tea, sat on the edge of the bed holding the saucer in one hand, bringing the cup to his lips and back in a steady hypnotic beat, meanwhile telling him a complicated silly story to get him to smile.

Mark and Nat started spending less time with her after she asked Mark that question, as if she, a bumbling parent, had mortified a group of teens by trying to be sincere. Mark was busy helping Nat prepare for Tishe B'Av, the Ninth of Av fast, teaching him *Lamentations*. She didn't like the fast or memorializing the Temple's destruction, which reading Josephus's *Jewish Wars* had made more awful to her. The slaughter, the terrible thirst, starvation, and ruin were all too real for her, too historic, harbingers of camps and numbered arms. At least Mark and Nat, leading the services, would have something to do to keep them from falling into the past—or so she felt.

Her parents were even less sympathetic to Tishe B'Av—they liked the more decorative holidays, like Passover and Chanukah, and suffered through the High Holy Days as if paying stiffly for their pleasure later in the year.

A week or so before Tishe B'Av, Helen's grocery cart pulled up next to hers at one of the mammoth vegetable counters in the town's largest market.

"Is your brother a fag?" Helen shot, and the two women feeling tomatoes nearby glared up at them. "Because I saw him coming out of Bangles downtown last Saturday night and, honey, he was drunk. And Mark too—*what* a waste."

Rigid, Brenda imagined a dump truck dropping tons of potatoes on Helen, sealing her forever.

Helen grinned, looking like a grotesque carnival target. With more strength than she knew was in her legs and arms, Brenda moved her cart away and down the aisle, then left as if the metal burned, and hurried out to her car. Getting in, she thought of flight, retreat—no one would ever find her, hear from her again. But starting the Chevette seemed to drain the panic through her hand into the key and she drove out along the Interstate to Mark's apartment complex ten minutes away.

"You moron! Why'd you go there!"

"I wanted to dance," he said, sitting down, untouched by her distress. "So did Nat. I love dancing with him. He's beautiful then, the way he moves, his *eyes*—"

Brenda flushed. She had only seen Nat dance at wedding receptions, and then he had seemed to her stiff, embarrassed, dancing only because he had to.

"I *hate* it, I hate thinking about the two of you together. I don't understand what it means."

"Do you have to?"

"Don't be so cool."

"I'm thirty-five," he said. "What should I be?"

She felt inflamed by her father's angry pounding voice, but didn't know the words to destroy Mark.

"Well," Mark said, "how about a drink?"

"Yes," she said. "I will."

He joined her on the beige, pillow-backed sofa that was as neutral and expensive-looking as everything there—prints, cushions, lamps.

"You know it doesn't bother Nat, somehow," Mark began. "But for years I thought God would get me, like Aaron's sons, when they offer up 'strange fire' and get zapped. My best friend all through school, from way back, was gay too—in college he told his rabbi about us and got sent to Israel."

"Did it help?"

"Well, he got married."

"Was he like Nat?"

"No one's like Nat."

She asked for another drink.

Nat showed up just then and she tried to tell him about Helen. He said he didn't care and they went off to the best Szechuan restaurant in the county for a lavish dinner. Later they drank at a bar like witnesses of an accident, desperate to blur the vision of that crash, the blood and smoke. Nat wouldn't discuss what'd happened; each time she tried to bring it up, he looked away.

Two days later, Brenda came to Shabbat services late, right before the Torah reading and everyone was up, jabbering, flushed. Clark stood at the lectern, his back to the ark, as pale as Nat and Mark who faced him from the narrow aisle between the men's chairs and the mehitzah.

"Get out," Clark was saying. "I won't let you touch that Torah. My grandfather donated it."

"You're crazy," Mark said.

"You're *sick*."

Brenda wavered at the door, disgusted by the ugly atmosphere of children squashing worms to make them writhe, exploding frogs with firecrackers.

"Come on," Mark said, slipping off his prayer shawl, jamming it into the gold-embroidered blue velvet bag. Mark smiled relief when he saw her, squeezed her hand. White-faced, Nat followed out to Mark's Volvo and they drove, no one speaking, to his apartment as if speeding on the road could strip away that scene.

Upstairs, Mark dumped his blazer on a chair, wrenched off his tie to sit with an arm around Nat, who was still pale and silent. Mark said, "I didn't think it would happen. They need us, it's our minyan too."

"Technically," Brenda said, "it's not *my* minyan," but no one smiled.

"We'll move," Nat finally said. "We'll go to New *York*."

Mark smoothed Nat's stringy hair with such gentleness that Brenda felt unexpectedly released. Their closeness warmed her like a Vermeer, rich with circumstantial life.

Tishe B'Av was the next night and they made plans to attend at one of the faculty shuls. Leaving, she surprised herself by kissing both of them.

Nat didn't call her that night and she hardly slept, awash with a sort of amazement that the children they had been had grown to see such ugliness. She longed in her restless bed for escape, for some wild romantic lover, a Czech perhaps, a refugee musician who'd fled in '68, whose loss was larger than her own, a nation's freedom instead of a woman's pride. He would have an accent, she decided sleepily, imagining herself in a sleek black dress, and have a mustache a bit like Mark's. . . .

Mark was alone when he came over Sunday evening.

"Nat isn't coming. He went out."

"OUT?"

"Bangles. To get drunk. To dance. He's furious." Mark smoothed down his gray silk tie, looking much too calm.

"He's dancing on Tishe B'Av?" She sat at the dinette table, more confused now than ever.

Mark pressed his hands to the back of his neck, massaging, stretching. "He had this dream last night, that he was swimming far from shore and there were sharks. He woke us both up. Shouting. He couldn't get away."

Brenda could feel her dress sticking to her back despite the air-conditioning. "What if he sleeps with someone? He'll get herpes, he'll get AIDS!"

Mark eyed her steadily. "Maybe he'll just dance."

She followed Mark out to his car, and on the drive to the faculty shul, Brenda knew she was feeling the wrong things. She should be understanding, compassionate now, not think that Nat was doing something ugly and vindictive, desecrating the fast day that *he* believed was solemn and holy. She should be *happy* for him, happy that he knew who he was, what he wanted, could feel his feelings, had found Mark—all of that.

She could hear her father snapping out the contemptuous Yiddish phrase for when two things had absolutely no connection: *Abi geret.* Says *who?*

As they pulled into the temple parking lot, Mark asked, "You okay?"

She wasn't.

What she wanted now was to slip out of the past months as if they were only a rented hot and gaudy costume she could return at last.

What she wanted more than anything on this burning night of Tishe B'Av was to forget.

SNAPSHOT

• ALLEN BARNETT •

THERE IS SOMETHING I do not like about old photographs—snapshots, I should say—the kind that one's grandmother keeps in a box on a closet shelf, or in old albums that crack as the black pages are turned, spilling more photos than are held in place. I don't like the way the people in these photographs speak in a tense which is theirs alone, or their unquestioning faith in the present tense. Now, the smiling person seems to say (Should I sit on the couch or the coffee table? Should I hold the baby? Should I hold my knee? Yes! Now!), this is me at my best. I do not like the way these old pictures fail the trust that is placed in them. I do not like how easily we are betrayed, and more, how easily we betray ourselves.

When I was seven my mother showed me a snapshot of a young soldier standing at ease in front of a building made of corrugated iron. The photographer and his Brownie were too far away from the subject—the soldier's face was nothing but a squint against the sun.

"This is your real father," my mother told me. "Dale is not your Daddy, honey, and never was. You don't have to love him." On the back of the snapshot was printed Kodak 1954.

"That boy will grow up hating you and him both," my

grandmother said with her face in the bulge of the screen door, referring to the man in the photo. She was a woman with black and white convictions, and a mouth that seemed weighted at the corners, especially when she smiled.

"He will hate me more if he finds out for himself," my mother replied, implying that I would hate her, either/or.

My grandmother stepped back into the house and my mother went in after her. "Illegitimate," I heard my grandmother say. I did not know what the word meant, but I knew its reference was to me, for it was always said to imply that I hadn't been sufficiently punished for something, or that I was spoiled and in some way responsible for my mother's state of affairs, which had never been much good.

I went to sit on the curb to get away from this adult conversation and its implications, which made me feel self-conscious and imperiled. We lived in what my mother called a subdivision, in a crackerbox house on a slab of cement. If you fell on the floor and cracked your head it could be heard out on the street. Up and down May Street the houses were identical to ours, distinguished only by the upkeep of the lawn, or the color of the stamped-sheet, tar-paper shingles that covered each house.

It was early summer and the curb was filled with drifts of shiny black cinders that had been spread there over the winter. Hiding on the other side of the house across the street was a teen-aged girl staring up into the eyes of her boyfriend. Her mother came to the screen door often, looking up and down the street for her daughter to come in and set the table. It was five-thirty and time to eat; her dad and everyone else's dad was home from the factory, but she remained in the bed of petunias, flowers which have always reminded me of girls who wear too much make-up and cheap fabrics because they don't know any better.

A group of children rode by on their bicycles and a grief rose up in me like the kind of nausea that overwhelms without any kind of warning, and which I struggled—unsuccessfully—to keep down. It was also that hour of the day when the petunias smelled like the lady's counter at the shopping center Walgreen's, and unseen clouds of their scent hovered at the level of my face, dizzying as a kitchen filled with cigarette smoke and adult laughter.

"Honey, why are you crying?" my mother asked with enough self-blame in her voice to hurt both of us. I was not a particularly sensitive child, and I seldom wept. My mother's shadow was stretching long and thin into the street. I wanted to tell her, "For no reason, for no reason at all," the way she would answer when I walked in on her and found her crying into a ball of tissue for no apparent reason. But something urgent was beating at the base of my skull, You, you, you.

"I don't know how to ride a bicycle," I said.

She sat down next to me on the curb. She put her head down and covered her face with one hand. Her shoulders trembled. I stopped crying then.

Unoriginal as this may sound, it occurred to me as we sat on the curb of a street of identical houses that there were probably a good dozen other moon-faced kids hiding on the side of the house from their mothers in this sub-division alone, that there could be as many other seven-year-olds who could not ride a bicycle or swim, sitting with dusty sneakers in the cinders beside their beautiful young mothers, who were themselves sitting there crying at the pain and failure of everything they had done.

This little scene repeated itself over and over in my head as if we sat between two mirrors, nothing at all unique about us, and felt like the solution that, once found, turns a puzzle into a used toy. If it was not completely comforting, this vision, it did give the world a kind of balance, or at least tipped the scales in my favor, and I wouldn't have to think about myself so much. There is a school of thought that says children know more than they let on, but I am willing to concede that I knew nothing at all.

My mother divorced Dale, married again a year later, and her second husband adopted me when I was thirteen. At the arrival of my new birth certificate in the mail, my mother said, "No one will ever be able to prove that he isn't your real father," as if this would be a point of pride or contention, I wasn't sure. Anyone looking at us could tell that we were not related. He looked like a prince from a picture book. We didn't love one another, but we could talk out of a mutual, if casual, curiosity. When I turned seventeen they bought me a used Volkswagen.

Teaching me how to use the clutch, alone on a country road, he said, "I've always wanted to ask—do you ever miss your real father?"

Inside the dim light of the car, the headlights just grazing freshly plowed fields, I imagined we could be the subject of a magazine ad. "His first car. There are things you've never talked about. Aren't you glad it's a Volkswagen?"

"How could I miss someone I never knew?"

"Do you want to know him?"

"I don't even know his name."

"Don't you ever want to tell him about yourself?" he asked with uncharacteristic concern. "Don't you think he wants to know? He is your father."

"No, really. I don't think of him as my father." I told him the truth and I told him what I thought he wanted to hear.

"Turn around."

"What?"

"Just turn around at this farm."

I drove us home and he jumped out of the car even before it came to a stop.

I didn't think about this evening until six years later when he and my mother were divorcing. He had already moved to Denver and I was packing to move to Thunderbird, Arizona, to get my M.B.A.

"Do you think you'll ever see him again?" my mother asked.

"I will not go looking for him, if that's what you mean."

"You were always a mother's boy," she said. "That's probably my fault."

"The adoption wasn't my idea," I told her. "You just wanted you and me to have the same name."

"Is that so bad?" she asked.

"The only time he wanted to know what I thought about anything was the night I got the Volkswagen. He asked me if I ever wanted to know my real father."

"I remember that night," she said. "He got drunk and cried himself to sleep."

"Him drunk? Really?" He and my mother drank only on Christmas and New Year's Eve. A bottle of gin lasted them three years.

"He had a daughter, you know. From a previous marriage. His wife got custody of the little girl and then skipped state. She never wrote, never called, and he didn't have the money to go looking for them. The last he heard, his wife had married well and her second husband adopted the kid. He still carries a snapshot of her in his wallet. I think that's the saddest thing."

Sentimentality in my mother always surprised me for she had had many illusions shattered at an early age. She stood and walked away from me in a graceful but masculine manner. Her pose at the sink reminded me of her recent husband, an attitude he would take when he was talking about plans for the house or lecturing me about Vietnam and duty to one's country. It occurred to me that he was legally still my father despite the divorce, and I wondered if there would ever be an incident in which I would be called back into his life. Was I responsible for him in case of accident or old age? Would someone call me if he died without a will? I wondered if there wasn't an expiration date on relationships like these.

I considered the color-coordinated kitchen, the pot holders hanging from the refrigerator by hidden magnets, all the evidence that the two of them had worked hard enough to ascend tentatively into the middle-class. I was going after an M.B.A. to make that ascendancy all the more secure. If anyone would have asked me what I wanted from life, I would have replied quality. I wanted to be able to assume my right to things.

My mother asked, "Don't you ever want to know the circumstances of your birth?"

I went to the kitchen door. "No," I said, telling her the truth because I didn't know what she wanted to hear. "You make it sound as if there were criminal activity involved."

"In some states there would have been," she said, and picked at something caught in her teeth with a matchbook cover.

Out the door I looked across the back yard. It ended at a high-voltage tower, beyond which there had once been a cornfield, which was beautiful; then soybeans, which were not; then one year nothing was planted. Weeds grew in the fertile ground as high as a woman's head. There was nothing in the field then. It was supposed to be a park, but it was only an ugly spread of short, stubby, hard grass. I was just about to walk out the door to get away from my mother's gaze for a moment when she said, "I don't want you to blame me."

"As a matter of fact," I said, "I have always blamed myself." Then I broke into a sudden and foolish laughter.

"That's ridiculous."

"Nevertheless."

"You can't take responsibility for your own birth."

"Nevertheless," I repeated, still laughing. It was preposterous and absolutely true, and the recognition of this fact made me feel light-headed and released, like a balloon detached from a child's hand. My mother had more to say, but I wasn't helping her. I was comfortable, isolated, floating away.

But when I arrived in Arizona the next day, I opened a suitcase and found three old letters and a snapshot of my mother. On the back of the snapshot was written, "Lorraine to Joe. October 1954. Union City, Tenn." My mother's hair in the photo was very long, bleached blonde and parted down the side like Veronica Lake's. She was braced on the arm of a large sofa, legs crossed like a man's, smiling directly at the person for whom the snapshot was obviously intended. It was easy to imagine even from the black-and-white picture that the color of her lips was bright red. Her bravura was touching—fifteen years old and pregnant with me.

The three envelopes were postmarked from Fort Leonard Wood, Missouri, an army base, dated the September and October of the year before I was born, and sent to Union City, Tennessee. They were from a Private Joseph James.

"Joe wanted to marry me," she said. "It was his mother who made him join the army. I took the bus from Michigan to Tennessee so we could be together. I didn't tell anyone where I was going, either. There was a bar in Union City where my dad used to sing before he married your grandmother. They gave me a job because they thought I was your Aunt Esther. The picture I gave you was taken in the little apartment they gave me right above the bar."

I felt leaden, weighted, stilled: the feeling you get when a blanket that has been tossed over you descends, then is tucked up to your chin. I had only called to tell her I had arrived safely in Thunderbird. She wanted to tell me everything, and everything she wanted to tell me required my wanting to know. She must have felt that she had no claim on me as a mother if she could not tell me the truth I was supposed to desire. For my part, it was like being the object of longing by someone who loves you too much and wants to tell you everything in hope that that will make you love them more. Under this pressure, I was the one to acquiesce, and I asked the requisite questions, but only like an uninvolved stage manager rehearsing an actress who has trouble with her lines.

"Why didn't you marry Joe in Tennessee?"

"Because people figured out where I was and his mother sent him a letter telling him he couldn't marry me until he was out of the army. You would have been almost four years old by then. Joe wrote to tell me what she said, and I got so mad I tore the letter up, and wrote back to tell him not to worry about marrying me. I told him I was already married. And I signed the letter Mrs. Ernest Wray."

"Who was that?"

"He was a very nice old man who bought my bus ticket back to Michigan and sent you a blue blanket when you were born. I went to work at the Victory Grill, the truckstop where I met Dale."

"And why'd you marry him?"

"He was kind to me, bought me cigarettes, and didn't mind that I already had a baby. What choices did I have?"

I had by this time only a vague memory of the man she married instead of my real father; the thickness of his hair, the shape of his nose, the kind of clothes he wore. We saw him only when he was moving us from one place to another, dark basement apartments in marginal neighborhoods, or those war-built housing developments in factory towns that spread during the baby boom like measles among school children. Dale had been one of the first of the successful truckdrivers in the years when highways were replacing the railroads, but my mother and I were dependent upon bags of groceries from neighbors, upon landlords who would wait for their rent check while Dale was on the road for weeks at a time. So my memory of him was like an allergy you don't get until you are older, and suddenly your head fills up, your eyes burn, or skin breaks out in reaction to something you've been eating all your life.

"Why did you give me these letters?" I asked her.

"In case you wanted to go looking for Joe he couldn't deny who you are."

"These are your letters," I said to her, meaning I did not want them.

The tone of her voice bottomed out. "But I saved them for you!"

"Where is he now?" I asked, for she must have wanted me to, although it seemed as if I knew all this already without knowing how. It's hard to remember.

"He moved back to Michigan after the Korean War and got married. I was going to give you his letters on your sixteenth birthday, but you never seemed much interested, and it was about that time when Esther called to tell me—she used to tell me whenever she saw him—that Joe's two little girls had been found molested and murdered in a vineyard behind their house. They couldn't have been more than ten or eleven years old. No one ever found out who did it, not even a clue. Esther sent me the clippings from the papers, even the Detroit ones. I saved all of them for you too, just in case you ever wanted them."

There was a long pause, then she asked, "Are you mad at me for not telling you sooner?"

"No, Mom," I murmured. "How could I be mad?"

"Do you ever think about writing him? You have a right to, you know," he said, his hand on my stomach, envious of how tightly my body held to its youth. He was a man old enough to be my father.

"A right to?" I repeated. "No, really, I never thought of it as something I was entitled to do. Other people find the idea of reaching him more intriguing than I do."

"If you were my son I would want to hear from you," he said.

"If I were your son? Me, you mean? Not someone else?"

He placed one leg through both of mine and pulled me up close to him, back to chest, and said, "When we're in bed together like this I like to imagine that you are."

We had met when he was looking for someone to take care of his cats while he was in Miami conducting a Broadway-bound musical, and while I was looking for an apartment. I was in New York where I had been hired at an advertising agency. I did well from the start and got the campaign for a toothpaste I had been using all my life. His show closed before I found a place of my own. Although our living arrangement was meant to be only temporary, this confession allowed me to think that he wanted me to stay.

Also, his life opened up to accommodate mine, as if such a space had been held in reserve for me. It never occurred to me at the time that that space may have had an occupant before me, and I had slipped into it like a possessionless tenant into a furnished room. He would be cooking when I came home from work. We would have a drink while I set the table and listened to the news. Before the weather changed, I built a redwood deck for the terrace of this penthouse apartment, and we ate out there till November. After dinner, he would work some more at the piano, and I did the dishes and read business magazines. Later I would join him at the piano, where we played a game

we had stumbled upon by accident. Once he had been orches-
trating a song for a nightclub act. The music seemed familiar to
me, and after he finished the verse, I suddenly opened my
mouth and essayed the chorus in my uncertain tenor. I found
myself singing the lyrics to "All the Things You Are" without
even knowing its title.

"How does someone your age know the words to that old
song?" he asked.

"I don't know," I said. "Maybe my mother liked it."

"You have a nice voice," he said. "It's small but sweet. Like
Blossom Dearie."

"Who's that?" I asked, turning away to look out the window,
over the terrace, at the skyline of Manhattan.

"You're blushing," he said.

"I've never blushed in my life," I said. At that moment,
everything felt exact and right and comfortable, the way you
might have felt in gradeschool when your teacher told you to
put away your books and to fold your hands on the desk
because she was going to tell you a story.

"So much the better," he said. Then, turning everything into
a game, he asked, "Do you know this one by Kern?" When he
began the verse of yet another song, I sang the chorus.

Sometimes I watched him shave—naked and framed by the
doorway and the length of the hall—in the same attitude that I
might consider a painting, and I experienced that same kind of
rewarding detachment. With his classical proportions, his was
the kind of body that art teachers find for their students to
sketch, not muscular but manly. From the bathroom he would
walk down the hall and smile at me. Space seemed sentient,
and measured by the way he filled it. Watching him like this
once, I knew that there was nothing more serious than the
desire of one man for another, and that what we don't understand we underestimate.

I came up behind him in the bedroom. He was examining his
own body in the mirror behind the closet door. I put my hands
on his waist. He looked at me in the mirror.

"That's fat," he said. "If I didn't have it I'd be perfect."

"If you didn't have it," I said, "you'd be my age."

He laughed abruptly at that, and as abruptly, he stopped. "You're good," he said, "very good. And you don't know how good you are."

Later that night we were looking at pictures that he kept in a box. There was a studio portrait of a beautiful woman, his mother, and from her expression one could easily assume that she had chosen the autumnal backdrop herself from the photographer's selections. In front of it she posed dark and dolorous, looking over her shoulder at the photographer as if to say that she had never been happy on this earth and doubted if any of us were meant to be.

"It's such a wonderful photograph to keep in a box," I said to him. "Anyone else would have it framed and sitting on the piano."

"I've considered it," he said, "but I don't think my mother ever liked me much." Then something in his face gave way. He cocked his head away from me. His chest dropped slightly and I saw him swallow. When he looked at me again it was as if to see how I had tricked him into saying that and then in another moment, as if to look in a mirror to see what lines betrayed his age.

I knelt in front of him and put my head in his lap. We were both wearing bathrobes and I could feel the warmth of him against the skin of my lips.

"How I care for you," I said. This did not say what I wanted to say, but love was not a word we used between us. Even so, I willed some impulse in him to reach out and touch my head. This did not happen.

Then one night he rolled away from me in bed. I could not sleep after that and went into the other room. Flipping through a guidebook to Rome, where we were to have gone together, I heard him stir in his sleep, I heard his sigh of resolution, then his bare feet on the parquet. Next he was facing me on the couch.

"Here's a place where the Italians line up to have their shoes shined," I said. His eyebrows raised and dropped. I said, "You probably want me to move out."

He nodded. "There's no hurry," he said, smiling like a psychoanalyst.

"I could move into a hotel tomorrow."

"That wouldn't be nice for you."

"It wouldn't be for long."

"I don't want you to hate me," he said.

"If anything, I'll hate myself."

He seemed to understand that. "Will you look for an apartment in this area?"

"I know all the shopkeepers."

"Then you'll stay in the neighborhood."

"If I can find an apartment."

He considered that for a moment, was satisfied, then placed his palms on his thighs, nodded, and went back to bed.

I remained in the mission-style rocker that he had bought for a song in graduate school, wondering if there were such bargains still to be had, and where I might find one for myself. There were the dark-stained parquet floors, the brass pen trays, the Weller vases, the Italian sofa, the oil painting that had increased in value a hundred times since its purchase. In the hallway there were autographs of great composers, in his bedroom a portrait of him by a now famous painter of the New York School. The kitchen was well-shelved, well-stocked, machined: copper pans, sponge-glazed bowls, Mexican tiles, bean pot, an urn of spoons and spatulas, a counter's length of cookbooks. All of it bought in the pursuit of that balance between the domestic and the sensual, and all of it a strong statement to me that I had nothing to do with the exclusive moment that any of it was purchased, the meaning it had without me, what happened before me and was happening—still. I had failed to endure, maybe not domestic, maybe not sensual enough. And even the apartment building had history: movies had been made here that showed up in revival houses; Steiglitz had done studies on the stairwell.

It was occurring to me, like a sensation that has not yet turned to pain, that detachment from all this would not be without its own kind of terror. I poured myself some of the expensive cognac that he had introduced me to but I had bought, and lit one of the cigars he had encouraged me to smoke. Then I sat down with his box of photographs. One of his cats jumped onto the couch then and tried to climb into the box. I knocked her down somewhat too violently. She stood sideways considering my behavior, then arched her back and hissed, bolting away. The half-feral cat with the extra toes looked down on me from the bookshelf, and blinked, watching everything over the inside membrane of its eyelids.

I soon found what I was looking for: an 8½-by-11 glossy of him when he would have been about ten years older than I was at that very moment. He was holding a saxophone in one hand, an instrument he did not play, and a cigarette in the other, although he never smoked. The cigarette smoke rose in a straight column in front of his black T-shirt. There was nothing on his face but a show of anger, part of the pose, I assumed, and predictions of how his face was going to age, predictions that came true. But I found myself pulled to him, drawn to him by the gravity of the photograph, the weight of its sensuality. With equal force I felt the sheer shove of time between the moment that the photograph had been taken and the moment that I was seeing it. From that moment on I would be looking at him from some distance, over an enormous gap that my heart leapt to cross, beat after beat, but could never, not to save my life.

I had never known this side of desire, this longing for health one recalls from childhood illnesses that modern medicine has all but eradicated, those dark miasmic fevers and the pain we asked our mothers to explain. Only out of this fever the question is one we know better than to ask, "Why can't you love me?"

I put the box of photographs on the shelf where I had found it, and read a while longer, knowing that would be an excuse to fall asleep in the chair.

*　　*　　*

Not long before I moved out, I saw him leaving our apartment building with someone closer to my age than to his. They were leaning close together, as if listening to a mutually loved passage of music.

On the mail tray inside the apartment, there was a note to me. It said that he was spending the night and the next day in Atlantic City and would I please give Gershwin, the half-feral cat, the homeopathic medicine he himself had prescribed for it.

Next to the pewter dish was a carton of slides. The date stamped on them told me they were about five years old. Naturally, I slid the carton open and held the slides to the light. He was in a variety of standard poses in each of them, except that he was naked, and smiling as if for a passport photo that would assure the customs man—"I am normal, let me into your country." This, I thought, is a man afraid of death and even more so of aging. I had to wonder: What mixture of vanity and urgency had prompted these photos? Had he shown them to anyone? Who was the photographer? Do they remain on intimate terms? Is there something I should be doing that I am not? I felt as if I were looking for clues on the white-edges of these transparencies, as they are called, where there were none. I was looking for ways to reach this man, and I had never been one to consider motive before.

It was very warm for May. The subways were already absorbing the heat, and the passengers looked, or did not look at one another, as if blaming themselves for this spring-less year. I needed a shower before I could go out again in search of an apartment.

As I had seen him do, I watched myself in the large round oceanliner mirror through his transparent shower curtain. An older man at my office gym had suggested that were it not for my moustache, my hairy chest, I would have the body of a sixteen-year-old athlete. The man I lived with had smiled at this, obviously having the same thought himself, but suggested nothing. With his shaving brush I lathered my entire torso, and with the straight-edge razor he taught me to use, I shaved my chest from breastplate to navel, watching the anticipated result in the huge and elegant mirror.

Looking very much indeed like a sixteen-year-old athlete, I felt a sudden tender generosity toward the world and myself, unfocused, neither self-centered nor self-exempting. Sun angled into the bathroom window and made the room and my body shimmer. I put his old silk bathrobe on. Then I went to the oversized dictionary where I kept my father's letters.

Each had a three-cent stamp on it. I blew into the end that my mother had torn open and shook the letter out of the envelope. With it fell a picture-booth snapshot face down to the desk. On it was written, "Hi, honey. What do you think of me now?" I turned the picture over. There was a soldier, and he had my eyes, my ears. Our cheekbones were the same height, our noses were identical, his smile was more certain but similar. The snapshot was blurry around the soldier's hat and temples, but there was fine detail and surprising depth in the open collar and the shadow on his neck.

The letter I read was written in pencil on unlined paper. I held the snapshot in one hand and read, "Honey, I look at your picture every night. Your eyes seem to dance and sparkle, and your sweet lips seem to keep saying I love you. Sweetheart, there isn't a morning that goes by that I don't think of you when I wake up. Your voice seems to go through my dreams as clear and as sweet as the stars in the sky and the sweet smell of flowers here on camp. I seem to be able to reach out and touch you, then you come to me and place your arms around my neck and I go almost wild with love for you. Darling, I laid in bed last night and thought of how we acted the last time I was with you. I can almost feel your arms around me and it makes me feel like coming to you right now. I get so involved thinking about you that the night flies by. I could never prove my love to you, honey, it's just beyond words.

"There's a beautiful moon out tonight, honey, just like the one we used to park under. It seems to look at me and smile. It says to me, Don't you worry, Joe, she's thinking of you and she loves you as much as you love her. You'll be with her soon and speak the words of love that are being stored in your lonesome heart. Oh, darling, how can a guy like me deserve your love, you're so wonderful in every way. I love all the things you are, Lorraine. I love you more than words or actions could ever explain. My love for you will never die, Lorraine, it will never die. We'll always be together, won't we?"

The next day I went to the New York Public Library on 42nd Street. I didn't know what I was looking for until I found it. On one shelf in the large reading room was a row of telephone books for the entire country. In the book for Northeast Michigan, I found my father's address in the city where I was born. I went back to my office and wrote him what I thought was a wonderful letter. There was nothing incriminating in it at all. I told him what I thought he wanted to hear: that I was a success at what I wanted to be doing, that I expected nothing from him, and that if he didn't want to write me back I would understand.

The same evening when I got home there was something from my mother on the mail tray in the hall.

"Is that a birthday card?"

I looked up. He was sitting at the kitchen counter watching television while he ate. I was made hopeful by two things: he remembered that my birthday was at the end of the week, and this was the first time he had spoken to me first in two weeks.

"No," I said to him after I'd opened the envelope. "It's something I have to sign to make me executor of her estate when she dies."

We both smiled at the irony of thinking it had been a birthday card. I thought that my mouth felt like his, that my smile had taken on the shape of his.

"That shouldn't be too much to handle," he said.

"No," I said, and managed to laugh. "It won't be at that, although she writes that she just sold her half of the house to my—her ex-husband for fifteen thousand."

"What's she going to do with the money?"

"Buy a car, for one thing."

"That's the problem with these bourgeois," he said. "They get a little money and they spend it."

I paused. "Did you win in Atlantic City?"

"No," he said.

There was another pause while we watched television a moment and he served himself another helping. Then I said, "I wrote my real father a letter today. I thought I'd tell you."

"Why would you do a thing like that?" he asked.

I watched the fork raise from the plate to his mouth, thankful that he was not looking at me. "You said—"

"I beg your pardon."

"You said that if I—" I tried again, but instead, "It didn't seem an inappropriate thing to do."

"You might have waited until you had a place of your own," he said. Since all my mail did come addressed to him, another man, this might have been a consideration.

"I don't suspect that it will matter in the end," I said.

"What's that?"

I signed the card that would make me executor of my mother's estate in the event of her death, and took it out in the hall to the mailchute. One moment more, my ear against the slot, I listened to the card fall sixteen floors—foosh, foosh, the way a doctor described the murmur of my seven-year-old heart, which would heal by itself. I recalled a conversation that I had once with a friend when she lost her sole remaining parent.

"I've always wanted to ask," I began. "Is it at all liberating?"

She looked at me with wide astonished eyes and grabbed my wrist. "Yes," she said. "Yes."

Each time I walked into my new apartment, I had to orient myself anew, for I had a picture in my head of how it should all eventually look, and I would be slightly awed, somewhat pained to see that the wood floors had not been bleached, the harlequin pattern laid in the kitchen, the right sofa purchased, or any of the blueprints of my imagination realized yet. I was longing for things out of proportion, the way a Piranesi etching dwarfs human beings in the foreshortened area before a ruin.

Yet if I longed for things with a spurious scale, one that made everything seem huge and distant in the short forefront of desire, I do not think this kind of longing unique to me, but as common to my generation as a popular song. But to want and want and want, and not to know that you're wanting, means that you're never sure of anything. It means that you do not know how vulnerable you are, how open to attack. It means that you don't know how great the space of your longing is until there is a specific object to fill it.

The man I had lived with finally called me a month after I had moved out to tell me that Gershwin the cat had died of diabetes in an animal hospital.

He said, "I thought you would want to know since you were the only person he ever liked immediately. In fact, I called to ask you to join me at the hospital, but you weren't home. The doctor had given him a 200-to-1 chance against survival, and said that it would be less expensive to put Gershwin to sleep, but I said we had to take the chance. Cost was no consideration."

"How much did it cost?"

"Three hundred dollars. We did what we could, though." He began to cry a little into the phone. He apologized for himself, and then he began to sob. I was certain I knew what he was thinking: had he taken the cat to the vet a month ago, the cat would have lived. I suspected that if he were still crying now three days after its death, he had been blaming himself all along. I even hoped that this was the case.

"I just got back from burying him in the country where I found him ten years ago. On the way home I wrote a eulogy for the poor thing, which I was going to deliver to you by hand. Maybe I could come over now."

I did not want him to see my apartment until it was finished. What's more, there were a couple of things I had left in his apartment in the hope that I would be able to collect them and see him again, but I never had the courage to go back uninvited. And I had also convinced myself that had he wanted to see me he would have called. "Do I have any mail there?"

"Yes, lots," he said, more cheerful now. He began to read me the return addresses, none of it at all important until, "And here's one from your father! Shall I bring it with me?"

"No, no," I cried out. "I'll be right there. Wait for me."

I knew I could get to him faster than he would to me, for there were twenty short blocks between us which I could run without effort. I rushed out the door without my keys, ignoring the phone as it began to ring again. A saxophone teacher who lived in my building was giving a music lesson. His student yearned to play with the urbane detachment of the teacher, but whether it was breathing, or phrasing, or whatever determines these things, I do not know; he played feelingly. And whatever his intention, it was the way he played the song that I heard the lyrics as I ran, "Time and again I longed for adventure, something to make my heart beat the faster. What did I long for, I never, never knew."

It was that time of the year when the sun appears to set down the center of Manhattan streets. It was that hour of the evening when the dusk light makes the surface of things important. Everything seemed suddenly proportionate and complete. I felt as if I were running back in the face of time to meet a stranger to some part of myself.

The apartment door was open when I got there. I walked in and saw him sitting on the edge of the bed with the receiver of the telephone in his hand. When he smiled at me it was with the smile of one mourner to another.

"You're out of breath," he said.

"I ran."

"You look good," he said, and embraced me. Once his face was on my shoulder he began to cry again. He cried so hard that I had to lower him to the floor. The bottom of his sweatshirt did not cover his stomach, and I could not decide if that was because he had put on weight or if the shirt had always been too small. I sat on the edge of the bed and tried not to look at him. Something about the way he wept told me that he did not blame himself for the cat's death after all, for having diagnosed its illness as one he had suffered himself, for having prescribed it the same homeopathic medicine he had prescribed for himself. A kind of dread came over me, maybe phobic, maybe instinctual, as if I should be prepared to bolt, and which suddenly forced me to wonder: Why hadn't I ever noticed this air of failure about him before? Were all men like him? Was I?

"You have something for me?"

He reached behind for the envelope I could see in his back pocket, and handed it to me with a grateful smile. It was the eulogy for the cat, which he then waited for me to read. His beautiful handwriting only made the contents more mawkish, made it easy to imagine him covering the Upper West Side giving individually written copies to the doormen of buildings where his friends lived, the envelopes marked By Hand.

"I'm touched," I said. He had managed to remember me in the cat's eulogy, as if it were a will. "It's lovely." He nodded, smiled again, and looked down at the floor.

I paused with due respect. Then, "The letter from my father?"

"Oh, that," he said. He didn't move. "I tried to call you. I was only joking."

I leaned forward, as if to urge someone on in a bank line. "What's that?"

His tragic smile disappeared. "I'm sorry," he said. "I didn't think that you'd run all the way down here for that. You said he never meant anything to you." Then he smiled again.

I didn't bolt. Walking out of the apartment I considered the value of what I was leaving behind: a Mexican knit sweater, a picture of me in the same sweater, half obscured in shadow and dark glasses, and a hat. I went into the hall and held the call button down, hoping that the elevator man would think there was an emergency, although the arrow above the door indicated that the opposite was true.

"I am sorry," he said in the doorway. "Really, I had no idea. Maybe someday you'll even blame yourself," he said hopefully, meaning that someday I might forgive him.

Someday, yes, I thought, but there was no hurry. I started running down the white marble stairs. The walls were wainscoted with the same marble, although polished and not so worn, and the frosted windows made the light in the stairwell gauzy. I swung from one flight to the next around the banisters at each landing. On one of the landings below me there was a model in a winter coat, and a photographer with a shiny umbrella on a tripod. He had turned his camera on my descent. I could hear the accusation of his shutter release. He thought he was so lucky. But I was running too fast to stop, and I was certain that if I ran hard enough, fast enough, and in the right direction, I would find myself back in the raw heart of time, that point of detachment, and be beat out again, with nothing at all behind me.

ANYTHING YOU WANT

• CHRISTOPHER COE •

THE DAY OF his father's wedding, when the boy came down in the morning, he was ready to out-perform himself in the water. Most days, he swam thirty lengths, six sets of five, but earlier in the morning, the boy had made up his mind that before he would visit his mother in the hospital on his way to the church, before he would stand up for his father, he would swim six sets of ten.

His grandmother was out by the pool when the boy came down. She was in her wheelchair, putting on lipstick, giving herself a crooked mouth. A smoking cigarette was burning the smoked ones in the small glass ashtray that the old woman had set on the wheelchair's arm. In the glass in her hand, the hand that she did not need for the lipstick, his grandmother clutched what the boy was sure was a bullshot.

"It's morning," he said. "I mean, pardon me, but isn't this still morning?"

The old woman made a show of looking up, of squinting at the sky to read the time of day. "So far," she said. "So far it's been morning all day. Your point is?"

The boy said, "Only that it's approximately ten o'clock in the morning last time I looked, and you've been told you can't smoke, Angel Pie, and how much vodka have you got there in that glass?"

"Skip it," the grandmother said. "Just drop dead right now."

"But Angel Pie," the boy said.

"It's not every day," the grandmother said, "that we have a night like last night."

The boy said, "That's a stunning reason to be killing yourself at ten o'clock in the morning."

The old woman went once more around with her lipstick, widening her mouth. She was the boy's mother's mother. The boy was hoping that his extra swimming would make him tired for his visit to his mother. Lately, for about a year, the water had been kept warm, even hot enough to give off steam on all days but the hottest, and most days his swim made the boy feel languid.

"It's a perfect reason," the grandmother said. "Such a stunt." She screwed the lipstick down, snapped it shut.

The boy frowned at the grandmother. "All right," he said, "keep the drink, but give me the ciggie. You can't smoke, Angel Pie."

"Look," the grandmother said, "I'm an old lady. I can do anything I want."

The boy shrugged. He hung his robe over the back of a garden chair and went toward the pool. At the edge, he turned somewhat theatrically to his grandmother.

"Let's all do stunts," he said. "You can smoke those ciggies and drink those drinks, and I'll go down to the bottom of the pool and think of reasons not to come up."

Then the boy stepped into the shallow end and began his sets of ten.

The water was heated for the women. The grandmother complained of a shoulder that she had broken years ago, and the heat was also good, the old woman said, calming for the boy's mother.

His grandmother claimed that the steam was her secret for the jade trees that grew around the pool. The boy never said what he knew to be the truth, that the jade trees had thrived around the pool long before the old woman had come to live in the house, long before the pool began to steam. He did not remind the old woman that the jade trees had thrived around the pool through the years that the water was kept cold for his father, who liked to start each day with an invigorating plunge.

His father was a man who pursued invigoration.

The boy did not. He did not take to water with a swimmer's form or rhythm. Every day, he swam where his form showed least, not on the surface but under it, brushing along the pool's floor with strokes that made no sound as he swam from end to end. The women floated themselves, in dark glasses, drifting on their backs. The boy swam where the women could not float.

Since his father left and his grandmother came, every morning, the heated water made him feel slow, and most nights, when he looked out the large dining room window, he could see the steam rising in the garden that was lit up every night, through every dinner with the women, and in the glass itself he could see his mother from behind, her hair worn up, steam rising over the back of her head, surrounding her in her new place at the head of the table.

Upstairs, the boy was standing in his mother's three-sided mirror when he heard his grandmother wheel herself into the elevator downstairs. He heard the elevator, and next, the inner and outer doors, sliding, banging, and then the faster, high-pitched sound of the old woman's wheelchair, its motor bringing her around the stairwell, until she stopped at the open door of his mother's room.

He saw her from three sides, surrounding him. He saw that she had freshened her drink.

He was dressed for his father's wedding, rubbing his mother's vitamin E cream under his eyes.

"How do I look?" he asked.

The grandmother stayed in the doorway. She said nothing.

The boy said, "I should look better."

The grandmother wheeled herself into the room, toward the mother's desk. She took a cigarette from a cutglass cigarette box and lit it with a matching lighter that was set on the desk. She took an envelope from a stack of mail that had been waiting for the mother, opened it, took out what was in it, and with the cigarette in her mouth she folded the envelope into a shape for catching ash.

She flicked ash into the shape she had made.

"By the phone," the boy said. "Mother keeps an ashtray by the phone."

The grandmother said, "I know that your mother keeps an ashtray by the phone. It may interest you to know that I happen to know where things are in this house."

"You didn't answer me," the boy said.

"I didn't answer you *what*?"

"You didn't answer me how I look," the boy said.

The grandmother blew smoke at the ceiling.

The boy said, "I don't like it either, but I have got to do this thing today for Daddy."

"Call in sick," the grandmother said. "Pretend it's school."

In profile, the boy sucked in his stomach where it did not stick out. He rubbed more vitamin E cream under his eyes. He was using his mother's vitamin E cream because his mother had stolen and used up the anti-aging cream that the boy had sent away for the week he turned sixteen.

She had also stolen his skin-tightening cream and his three new eyelid creams.

As he had read to do, the boy rubbed the cream into his face in upward, outward strokes.

"I don't know about you," the grandmother said, "but usually, most of us put our faces on *before* we get dressed. We do our makeup first, then our clothes, just like men shave."

The boy looked at the old woman in the mirror. He rubbed cream around the corners of his eyes. "This is a finishing touch," he said. "If I did it first, how could it be a finishing touch?"

"This is not a day for you to go to a wedding," the old woman said.

The boy closed his eyes. He raised both hands to his face and began to rub the cream into his eyelids. He did this slowly. He took a long time with it and was nearly finished before he gave the old woman an answer. "They'll have champagne," he said.

"We have champagne here," the grandmother said.

"Not on ice," the boy said, still with his eyes closed. "Mother drank it all last night."

"She wanted to get them *down*," the grandmother said, disgusted.

The grandmother meant the boy's pills. The pills the mother had taken had belonged to the boy. The boy's pills were medicine; he took them every day because he had to. "It makes sense," the boy said. "You think it's going to be your last taste on earth, you want some sparkle." He opened his eyes; the old woman was looking at him in the mirror. He said, "You want effervescence."

The old woman smoked.

He said, "In your last taste on earth you want a lively pétillement."

"What's that?" the grandmother asked.

"Wine-talk for sparkle," the boy said. "Time to flick an ash, Angel Pie."

The grandmother said, "You're right. You *should* look better."

The boy rubbed vitamin E lightly over his lips. He said, "I find more and more as I get older that nothing is the end of the world."

"You find wrong," the grandmother said.

The boy could not drive. From his mother's desk, he made the first of three calls to taxi companies. When he was in a hurry, when he was not, it was his practice to call three taxi companies and to take whichever cab came first. The old woman always said that she was the one who had to stay behind to hear it when the late taxis came and the drivers blasted their horns down on the street.

"Someday they will all catch on to you," the old woman said. She had wheeled herself across the room, to the mother's dressing table. "Then, of course, you know what will happen, don't you? They will all stop coming, and the day will come when not one taxi cab company in this town will come to this house, and how are you going to like that?"

The boy was on hold. He took up the envelope that the grandmother had used for ashes and emptied it into the ashtray by the telephone. He took up the drink that she had left on the desk and tried a short taste. The drink was a bullshot. If it had not been a bullshot in the garden, it was a bullshot now.

He took a longer taste.

"Then what are we going to do?" the grandmother said. She was selecting lipsticks from a drawer in the mother's dressing table, testing colors on the back of her hand. "What are we going to do when, because of you, we can't get one cab in this entire city to come to this house?"

The boy looked across the room and said, "We'll call an ambulance. When we can't get a taxi, we can always call an ambulance."

The old woman selected compacts, eye shadows, blushers. In rows, she arranged her choices on the glass table top. She dropped the others back in the drawer, making clatter. She did not look up from the table.

"How about some lipstick?" she said. "You want some lipstick for your finishing touch?"

The boy drained the bullshot.

Still not looking up, the old woman said, "You can fix that for me. You can go downstairs and fix that drink for me, please."

The boy sucked on ice. When he spoke again it was not to the grandmother. With ice in his mouth, he gave the address of the house. He called the second taxi number and was giving the address again when the old woman wheeled herself into the mother's walk-in closet. Over the wheelchair's electric whine, the old woman shouted, "Fix it." Over her shout, the boy spelled the name of the street.

The grandmother came out, folding a nightgown into a shopping bag. The boy saw that it was a bag from a discount furrier. Dialing his third call, he made a face he did not know he was making. He watched the old woman wheel herself back to the dressing table and sweep the rows of makeup into the bag.

"This is for you to take to your mother," the grandmother said. "She is going to need these things."

Again on hold, the boy kept looking at the shopping bag.

"She will feel better when she looks better," the old woman said.

The boy looked around his mother's room. He looked at the bed that he had made in the middle of the night and at places around the room where the old woman had wheeled herself, reaching down to gather his mother's clothes from the floor. Together, after the mother had been taken from the house, the boy and the grandmother had cleaned the mother's room. They had stayed up through the night to do it.

"Do you think so?" he asked. "Do you think a nightgown and some makeup will help?"

The old woman picked up a hairbrush and a hand mirror, a matching silver set. They were the last items on the dressing table. She added them to everything else in the discount furrier bag and ran her hand over the dressing table's bare glass top.

She said, "Take them anyway."

The boy looked at the discount furrier bag. "*I* will feel better," he said, "if you put those things in some other bag. We must have a bag from someplace else."

The grandmother gave the boy a blank look that did not stay blank. "Go fix that drink," she said.

"Get me a bag from someplace else," the boy said.

That night, outside the large dining room window, the unlit garden was not dark. Light from upstairs, from the grandmother's room, shone down on the rising steam. The boy sat in his mother's chair, looking out, drinking champagne that he had put on ice before he left the house. He had chilled two bottles to help him sleep when he came back from the hospital and the wedding, to help put him out at the end of the day. Now he was making do with one bottle, the one that the old woman had not taken up to her room to drink with her massage.

He had not really counted on finding both bottles.

Every night a man came to the house to massage the old woman, while she watched the day's financial news. Every night, lying on a surgical table, she cried out, and the boy could never tell if it was her flesh or her finances that were killing her.

Tonight, the old woman's cries traveled down the stairs. They were not for pain or money. The old woman was calling down for the boy to come up.

When he had opened the bottle for himself, out of habit, he had put two more on ice. The habit was left over from his father, who, years ago, had told him that one must always have two of everything. Having two of a thing at all times, his father had told him, was the one way to be certain you will have it, at least one of it, when the time comes that you need it.

His father once had told him about two brothers, one of whom had been infertile. The brother who was fertile donated a testicle, and one year after the transplant both brothers, for the first time, became fathers. His father had said that nature itself is overcautious and abundant.

His father had said this more than once.

The boy looked out into the garden and thought there should be two gardens, two pools. And in a sense, there were. In a sense, he had two gardens, two pools, if he counted the pool and garden at his father's house. His father had said a man must have two houses, one to live in, one in reserve, the second one for when the first one burns, or when anything else that can happen to it, happens. The second house, the house in reserve, should be ready, his father had said, supplied with everything that the first house had had.

When his father moved out, there had been another house for him to go to, ready for him.

His father's point, as the boy had made it out, was that there are times when only excess is efficient, when nothing less makes sense. The boy touched his face and wished that he had ordered two jars of the anti-aging cream. He did not believe that his mother's vitamin E cream helped. But there was always the other side—if he had sent away for two jars, then his mother would have just had twice as much to steal; she just would have looked twice as young when she swallowed his pills.

When the boy had stolen a bottle of champagne from his father's reception, he had stolen two.

In the pool at his father's house, the water was kept cold to invigorate the blood.

Opening the chilled bottle was the first thing the boy had done when he came back from his father's reception. Chilling the two that he had stolen was the second. And after he had looked out into the garden for a while, before he answered his grandmother's calls, he went to the panel in the pool house that controlled the garden and the pool. He switched on all the lights that were set into the ground, under the jade trees, which came to muted life within the fog of the steam. He switched on every light in the garden, then switched off all the heat in the pool, and began to count the time that the steam would take to stop.

When the boy came upstairs, his grandmother was screaming at the man who was massaging her. She was undressed, covered by a sheet, smoking. The large man wore white trousers and a white sweatshirt with its sleeves cut off at the shoulders. Inside the sweatshirt his chest moved in time with his hands.

The boy was still dressed for his father's wedding. He stood in the doorway and looked in, unseen. He sipped from his wineglass and divided the man into two halves of white. The man's top half gripped and pounded at the old woman through the sheet, his bottom half shifted its weight from one large leg to the other.

They were very large legs.

The man pressed down upon the old woman. Now and then he raised his hands from her back to clear away her smoke.

The old woman was looking at the television. It was not tuned to financial news. A black-and-white movie was on, grainy-looking, with the sound turned low. The boy waited for the old woman to scream again at the man. When she did, he said from the doorway, "Mother thanks you for the makeup."

The old woman and the masseur both looked toward the door. The old woman could only turn her head. Pressing into the old woman, the masseur nodded at the boy.

The boy nodded back. "Hello, Hector," he said.

"I'm Victor," the man said.

The boy gave his face a slap. "Of course, you are," he said. He put his hand in his trouser pocket and slouched in the doorway, elaborately.

"How was she?" the grandmother asked.

"Did you change your name?" the boy asked the man.

"How did she look?" the grandmother asked.

"Like she needed makeup," the boy said. "Victor, tell me the truth, weren't you Hector once?"

The grandmother said, "Flirt with Victor on your own time."

The boy came into the room. He went to a table by the grandmother's bed and filled his glass from the bottle that was set on it, set in a bucket of ice. He looked across the room at the television.

"No market news?" the boy asked.

"It's the weekend," the grandmother said. "In case you haven't noticed, it has been the weekend for two days. Nothing happens on weekends. Be a boy and fill my glass."

The boy came across the room with the bottle. "She may not be coming home soon," he said. "When I was there she was waiting for a doctor to come look at her eyes."

"What's wrong with her eyes?" the grandmother asked.

"It's the lids," the boy said. "She says she hates them. She says she's been hating them for a while."

"What do her lids have to do with anything?" the grandmother asked.

"She thinks they droop," the boy said. "She wants to get them done."

"What do you mean *done*?" the grandmother said.

The man gripped at the grandmother's ribs. "He means lifted, don't you?"

"Victor, please," the old woman moaned. "Of course, he means lifted. *Done* always means *lifted* when you're talking about eyes. What I want to know is what does she think she's thinking, talking about getting her eyelids done at a time like this."

The boy said, "Actually, Victor, yes, I do mean lifted. My mother means lifted. She thinks now's a good time to get her eyelids lifted, since she's already in the hospital. Victor, would you mind terribly if I called you Hector?"

The man broke from his work to look up at the boy. "You can call me anything you want," he said.

"What does she think she can possibly be thinking?" the old woman said. "Where's my wine?"

The boy filled the grandmother's glass. He sat in a chair beside her. "When you think about it, Angel Pie, it's not a bad idea. I mean, as Mother's ideas go, a lift at this point is not entirely without merit."

The grandmother reached for her wine. "It's true," she said, "her lids *do* droop."

"Not really much," he boy said.

"Enough," the old woman said.

The boy said, "This is better champagne than they had at the wedding."

"Oh," the old woman said, "let's don't dwell on the wedding."

The boy squinted at the television. "Who's that woman?" he asked.

"What's wrong with *your* eyes?" the grandmother asked. "Why are you squinting like that?"

"They're burned," the boy answered. "That can happen when you swim in boiling water."

The man pressed down on the old woman. "I keep telling you, you keep that pool too hot," he told her. "If it steams, it's too hot, slows down circulation. Don't I keep telling you that?"

The man pushed smoke away from his face.

"Yes, Victor, you keep telling me," the old woman said. "But I like to look outside my window every morning and see that steam. I like to look down at that steam coming up and know every day that the water is hotter than the air, even if it doesn't need to be, and even if it shouldn't be. Every day that steam tells me that I've lived a long life and can afford to waste fuel. And that's not because I've been lucky, Victor. It's because I've been smart."

The man pressed down on the old woman's shoulder, and she screamed.

The boy moved closer to the television. "Who is this woman in the movie?" he asked.

The old woman said, "It's Loretta Young."

The man did not look up from his hands. He said, "It's Irene Dunne."

"Hector, I think you're right," the boy said. "I think Irene Dunne is who it is." He took a sip. "Is this the one where they're getting a divorce, and Irene Dunne keeps playing records all the time and thinks about Cary Grant and how happy they used to be, except they couldn't have children, so they adopt one, and it dies?"

The man blew at the old woman's smoke. "This is the one where they have an earthquake in Japan," he said. "They just had it."

"It's the same movie then," the boy said excitedly. "The one where she plays the records all the time has an earthquake in it somewhere. Except I think it's China, Hector. She'll start playing the records any minute."

The boy filled his glass.

"Give me some," the old woman said.

The boy emptied the bottle into the grandmother's glass.

"There's another bottle," the grandmother said. "I did leave you one bottle."

"Thank you," the boy said. "I drank it."

"*All* of it?" the grandmother shrieked. "You mean this is *it*? You mean this is all there *is*?"

"It would be," the boy said. "But it's not. I stole a bottle from the wedding."

The grandmother reached down and touched the boy's knee. "Good for you," she said.

The boy watched the screen and saw a record spinning on an old Victrola. The actress lowered the needle. The boy could not hear the music, but he imagined it to be the kind that, years ago, must have coaxed audiences in theaters to cry.

"Look, Hector," the boy said, "she's playing our record."

The man looked up just as the spinning record on screen dissolved to an image, people in a room.

"It's Japan," he said.

Before he went downstairs for more wine the boy told his grandmother about his mother.

"Actually, she didn't look as bad as she could have," he said. "Have you ever thought about doing it?"

For a moment, the old woman studied her glass. "This should have more fizz," she said. "I did a long time ago, but at my age what would be the point? When you're old as I am, the scars take forever to heal. And if I had my face lifted, what would I do with the *rest* of my body?"

The boy closed his eyes—the slow first half of a long unfinished blink. He had meant to ask her about what his mother had done, not what she was thinking about doing. "You'll like Daddy's champagne," he said. "Daddy's champagne is nothing *but* fizz."

The boy turned his face toward the man and opened his eyes, finishing the blink. "Hector, will you join us? Will you have some wine?"

The man looked up from the grandmother's back. He looked up from the sheet and up from his hands. He looked at the boy and did not answer.

"Go ahead, Victor," the old woman said.

The man nodded at the boy. "What about you?" he asked the boy. "Would you ever do it?"

The boy considered. "I might do it in small doses," he said, "a bit at a time, so no one could tell. I would not do it all at once."

"What would be the point of that?" the old woman asked. "The whole point is so people *can* tell."

The boy looked up at the man and saw that the man was looking at him.

"You'll do it when the time comes," the old woman said.

The boy did not say to his grandmother that there are people who do not do things every time the time comes. He was looking at the man when he said, "After I bring up the wine, I'm going to get out of these clothes and go for a swim."

The old woman said, "You know, you really don't look so bad in that getup."

"But I've had it on all day."

He left the room. On the stairs he stopped where he could see down the entire length of the house, through the dining room window and out into the garden. The light was on the jade trees. They cast blurred forms on the white umbrellas that were set into bleached-wood tables along the far side of the pool. He stood on the stairs looking out through the steam and remembered that his father had stopped him once from swallowing a jade leaf, reaching in with his hand to take it from his mouth. When he had asked his father then if jade trees can kill, his father had answered that one leaf cannot, but that you can get too much of anything. Even water, his father had told him, has some poison in it and will kill you if you drink enough to let its poison work.

The boy looked down, out into the garden. There was still too much steam, but from where he stood it looked already as though there might be less of it. He was still on the stairs when he heard his grandmother quietly telling the man that when he was finished with his work, if he wanted, he was welcome to a swim.

AYOR

• DAVID LEAVITT •

THE SUMMER I turned nineteen I took a short, sad, circular trip to the Great Smoky Mountain National Park, in Tennessee, with a friend I was in love with, or would have been in love with, had I known more about him or about myself. His name was Craig Rosen, and he lived down the hall from me freshman year in college. When he suggested taking the trip as a way of passing the interval between the end of school and the beginning of our summer jobs, I said yes in a second. Craig was good-looking, dark-haired and dark-eyed, and I desperately wanted to see him naked. I didn't know much about him except that he was an Economics major, and sang in the glee club, and spent most of his time with a fellow glee-clubber, a thin-mouthed Japanese girl named Barbara Love. Nevertheless I had certain suspicions, not to mention a rabid eagerness to be seduced which, in the end, was never satisfied. For five nights Craig and I shared a bed in that curry-smelling motel in Gatlinburg, and for five nights we never touched each other—a fact which, in all the years since, we have not talked about once. There is a code which applies here, I think, having to do with friendship and sex and their exclusivity, a code at least as mysterious and hermetic as the code of the *Spartacus Guide* which led us through Europe a few summers later. But that is jumping ahead of things.

We were, then, nineteen, East Coast college boys, Jews, homosexuals (though this we hadn't admitted). Gatlinburg, Tennessee, on the fringe of the park, with its sticky candy shops, its Born Again bookstores and hillbilly hayrides, may seem an unlikely place for us to have confronted (as we never did, it turned out) or shared secret sexuality. But I had grown up in amusement parks, glorying in the smell of diesel fuel and cotton candy, in roller coasters, in the wildness of rides which whirled at high speeds, round and round. I had had my first inkling of erotic feeling on those rides, when I was eleven, when the heavy artificial wind of a machine called a Lobster pushed my best friend Eric's body into mine, so that I couldn't breathe. Gatlinburg, with Craig, was full of that same erotic heat, that camaraderie of boys which seems always on the verge of dissolving into lust. Like children released from the better advice of our parents, we ate only the junk food which was on sale everywhere in the town—candied apples, wheels of fried dough swirling in vats of grease, gargantuan hamburgers and cheeseburgers. Craig shaved in his underwear, like a man in a television commercial, something I imagined to be a gesture of sexual display. Soon, I hoped, his eyes would meet mine, he would turn away from the mirror in the bathroom, his face still half-covered with shaving cream, and begin walking toward me. But it never happened. Why? I wondered each night, curled into my half of the bedsheets, far away from Craig. It would have been so easy for him to have done me that favor, I thought, and liberated me from my crabbed, frightened little body. And though I have come up, over the years, with many elaborate psychological explanations for why Craig and I didn't sleep together in Gatlinburg, only recently have I been able to admit the simple truth: we didn't sleep together because Craig didn't want to; to put it flatly, he wasn't in the least attracted to my body. I did not know it yet, but even at nineteen he had already had hundreds of men, including a famous porn star. Sex—for me a quaking, romantic, nearly unimaginable dream—

was for him an athletic exercise in alleviating boredom. It was—and this, I think, is the key—a way of determining self-worth; he wanted only the most beautiful, most perfect men not in order to possess them, but because their interest in him, their lust for him, confirmed that he was part of their elite. It was a matter of class, pure and simple; like his father before him, he wanted into a country club. And though it probably gratified him, on some mean level, to see his preening self reflected in my burning eyes in the bathroom mirror, sleeping with me not only wouldn't have gained him any points, it probably would have lost him some.

So why did Craig want me to come to Tennessee in the first place? It occurs to me now that my very lack of sexual appeal might have made me appealing to Craig in other ways, that week we spent together. I think I offered him a kind of escape, a safety hatch through which he could flee a life which, as I would later learn, was beginning to consist of little other than showers at the gym, circle jerks in Central Park, afternoons at the glory holes near Times Square. Perhaps he craved my innocence; perhaps he envisioned a wholesome, rejuvenating week in the wildnerness; perhaps he was recovering from some casually transmitted disease. I don't know because, as I said, Craig and I have never discussed that week in Gatlinburg, and I doubt we ever will.

When we arrived at the Great Smoky Mountain National Park, the first thing we did was go to the ranger station to plan our trip. We were going to do a six-day circle of the Park, long-planned by Craig, hiking seventy-five miles of forested mountain, much of it along the famous Appalachian Trail. The ranger girl chewed gum as she drew us a map. When she explained that we would probably be four days without human contact, four days in the depths of the park, more than a day's hike away from civilization, we looked at each other. Perhaps, in all this organizing, we simply hadn't thought enough about the realities of camping out for so long. What if something went wrong? What if a bear attacked us? Six days, alone, sleeping

outdoors, the weather unpredictable—the prospect was terrifying to us.

So instead of risking the dangers of the forest, we "camped
out" in a motel in Gatlinburg which was operated by a family
of Sikhs. The proprietress painted a dot on her forehead each
morning which by nighttime, when we saw her drift by in her
mass of sari, was beginning to stream out like a black-rayed
sun. She and her family lived in a group of rooms behind the
desk from which a strong odor of cumin emanated, wafting
down the linoleum hallways, inhabiting our room like an in-
cense. There was only one bed. We lay far apart, on either side
of it, Craig in his skimpy underpants, me in pajamas. I tried to
engage him in the closest thing I could muster to sexy talk; I
asked him why he preferred Jockeys to boxers. He said he liked
the "tighter feel," whatever that means. Then he fell asleep.

For lunch, out of guilt, we sat at a picnic site and ate the
dehydrated spaghetti and meat balls and chicken à la king I had
been so eager to taste ever since we had bought them in that
camping store on Park Row. Afterwards—having made our
perfunctory stab at the park—we headed back into town, to
wander the shopping malls of Gatlinburg, ride the funicular,
play at the hillbilly miniature golf courses. Craig had never said
anything explicit to me about his sexual life, though he was
always mentioning his ex-girlfriend in Connecticut. Eager for
signs, evidence, some sort of recognition, I tried to give off
feeble signals of my own—that is, I glanced at him needfully,
and sat with him, smiling like an indulgent mother, while he
ate the fried dough he so loved. None of these techniques
worked. As I have witnessed a hundred times over the years
we've known each other, Craig is not in the least impressed by
romantic mooning; in fact, it rather disgusts him. If he spared
me his contempt, that week in Gatlinburg, it was probably
only because he didn't recognize how far gone I was into
fantasy.

The fourth day, having done everything else, we went to the
Ripley's Believe-It-or-Not Museum. It didn't seem like much of
a place at first. In the window a mock witch's den was set up,

with a wax witch, a little cauldron, many elaborate rugs, a crystal ball. I was looking in the window rather disinterestedly when I heard a voice say, "Hey, you!" I looked around, behind me, but there was no one. "You," the voice said, "in the green shirt. I'm in here." I looked in the window, and saw the face of a pale girl reflected in the crystal ball. "I'm the genie of the Crystal," she said, with a strong Southern accent, "and I want to tell you what a great time you'll have here in the Gatlinburg Ripley's Believe-It-or-Not Museum."

"What the hell is that?" Craig said.

"And you too, in the red shirt, with the dark hair and pretty eyes," said the Genie of the Crystal. "Y'all can have a wonderful time here in the Gatlinburg Ripley's Believe-It-or-Not Museum, so why not come on in?"

Craig and I looked at each other. "Can she see us?" I asked.

"Sure I can," said the Genie of the Crystal, "just like you can see me. So why don't you come on in? A couple of cute guys like you could have lots of fun."

She was flirting with us—or rather, flirting with Craig. I imagined her in her little room in the back, looking at us on a television screen like the ones in the corners in drugstores, noticing Craig. Even through two layers of glass and several TVs, it was obvious where her eyes were focused.

"What happens inside?" I asked.

The Genie of the Crystal laughed. "You get to see all the attractions," she said, and smiling some more at Craig, added, "like me."

Craig smiled thinly. "Do you want to go in?" I said. "I think it might be fun."

He tried for anger. "Look," he said, "I didn't come camping for a week to spend all my time in stupid museums like this." But I persisted. "Come on, Craig," I said. "When are we ever going to have the chance again?" The Genie's flirtation titillated me, as if she and I were conspirators in Craig's seduction. "Listen to your friend, Craig," she said. "Don't you want to see the inside of my lamp?"

Craig looked for a moment through the window, at the

crystal ball. He sighed loudly. "All right," he said finally, making it clear he was doing me a big favor.

"Good," I said.

We paid our three seventy-five each and slipped through the turnstile, where a comforting sign which could only have existed in Tennessee assured us, "This is not a scary museum." For an hour we wandered among stuffed six-toed cats and immense toothpick mansions. We looked at pictures of a family of giants, listened to a tape recording of twins who had invented their own language. But the Genie of the Crystal really had been only doing her job; she was nowhere to be found.

"Did y'all have a good time?" she asked us afterwards, all mock-innocence, and we glared at her. Then a family—grandparents, parents, a blur of children—was crowding around the window, pushing us out of the Genie's view and mind. "What's that?" a little girl asked.

"I'm the Genie of the Crystal, honey," said the Genie of the Crystal.

The little girl started to cry.

"Don't be scared," the Genie said. "I'm your friend. And y'all can have a wonderful time here at the Gatlinburg Ripley's Believe-It-or-Not Museum."

Now—as Craig would say—"Time Warp." Five years passed. I was still a sexual innocent, compared to Craig, but I believed genuinely that I was making up for lack of experience with density of experience. Not Craig. Fear of AIDS had not compelled him to limit his activities, only to reduce their scope. He had as much sex as ever, but it was "safe sex," the rules outlined clearly from the beginning: no kissing, no fluid exchange, no collusion of mucus membrane areas. I don't think it was really much of a sacrifice for him; he claimed to have always liked it best that way anyway, watching someone watch him make love to himself.

We were both living in New York, that summer, just out of college. I had a stupid job at a bookstore, and Craig had an impressive job at a law firm which allowed him to make his own hours. Since I didn't have that many other friends in the city, I found myself becoming quite dependent on Craig—as a teacher, a tour guide, a mentor. We would go out to coffee shops together, in the afternoons, and he would tell me about having sex with soap in the West Side Y showers, and then about how he had developed bad sores between his legs from having sex with soap in the West Side Y showers. He described to me in detail the bizarre sexual practice of "felching," and what Quell was. I memorized these words, imagining they would be as important in my life as they appeared to be in his. At night, when we went to bars together, vain Craig refused to wear his glasses, and insisted I act as his seeing-eye dog. "That guy over there," he'd say. "Is he cute? Is he looking at me?" I'd tell him faithfully, though often our opinions differed. Always the tourist, I went home from these nocturnal expeditions alone, and woke up to Craig's phone call the next morning, describing the night's experience, usually bad. He was living with his parents, and had an immense collection of pornography which he stashed right under their noses, which he liked to trade from and bargain with, like a child with baseball cards. He claimed he could always tell how much hair a man had on his ass by looking at his wrists. And once, when we were in the Park, he led me on a circuitous route through bushes where men stood leaning against trees, caressing the prominent erections outlined in their pockets, and I burst out laughing. "Shut up," he whispered, grabbing my arm and dragging me away, back onto one of the Park's main avenues. "How could you do that? How could you embarrass me like that?"—as if I'd told a dirty joke to his grandmother. I kept laughing. I don't know why I was laughing—what I'd seen in the bushes hadn't struck me as particularly funny—but somehow I couldn't get hold of myself. The laughter controlled me, like hiccups, and would not abate, the same way a sly smile sometimes crept across my face just after I'd heard a piece of terrible news. It was as if a demon were shifting circuits inside my brain to turn Craig against me.

In the end, when I finally stopped laughing, I apologized to Craig. I did not after all want to offend him. I needed Craig a lot that summer because I felt safe doing things with him that I would never dare do by myself. When I entered the bars and pornographic bookstores alone, they were full of threats, and the biggest threat was that I might become, like Craig, their denizen. I could feel that urge in myself—it would be so easy to slip through the turnstile into the Adonis Theatre, as Craig often did, and once there, do what was beckoned of you, in the dark. With Craig I was protected. I could live vicariously. I was never tempted, because no man, seeing me and Craig together, would even notice me. He was dazzling in his dark, Semitic handsomeness, the perfect Jewish lawyer every mother wants her girl to marry. Neat tufts of hair poked out of his shirt collar. He was everyone's freshman year roommate, the president of the debate society, your sister's sexy boyfriend. I used his attractiveness as a shield; in its shadow I was invisible, and could watch, fascinated, as men approached him, as he absorbed all the damage that might be inflicted in those late-night places. It was Craig who got crabs, amoebas, warts. I always ended up at home—alone, but unscathed. Safe.

Craig's appeal, in truth, is limited. What long-term boyfriends he has managed to keep more than a week have emerged from extended relationships with him itchy and unsatisfied, for no matter how irresistible the prospect of a night with Craig, there is not much to warm up to in the thought of a life with him. This is, perhaps, his greatest tragedy, for when he does fall in love, it is with an intensity and fervor unlike any I've ever seen. So used is he to sexual control that, robbed of it, he becomes a madman, furious in his jealousy, pathetic in his adoration. If Craig loves a man, the man must be a God. It is a condition of his ego. I remember Sam, the blond architect he saw for a month, and finally scared out of New York with his loud worship; and Willie, the downtown artist, whose ripe body odor Craig found ambrosial, and spoke about with everyone, until Willie found out and got so embarrassed he refused to even speak to Craig. After his lovers broke up with him,

Craig was bitter, churlish, stingy. His contempt was loud and cruel, and usually directed toward those men who made the mistake of trying to court him in conventional ways—that is, with phone calls, letters, (God forbid) love poems. I remember one poor man who approached him on a Friday night at Boy Bar, an elementary schoolteacher who wanted to make him dinner. "I'm a competent cook," he kept saying, pleadingly. I think he only really meant that—that he wanted to cook him dinner. He just kept talking, telling everything to Craig, who never said a word, never even looked at him. And I thought, as I often thought when I was with him, how glad I was to be Craig's friend, because it meant I was spared the indignity of being his suitor.

At the end of the summer I quit my job at the bookstore and started business school—a mistake, I realize now, calculated primarily to please my father. It did not go well, but I passed most of my courses, and my parents, for my birthday, gave me what I'd been begging them for—a round-trip ticket to Paris, where I'd spent the spring semester of my junior year in college, and where I'd felt happier, I believed, than anywhere else I'd ever lived. When the ticket arrived, it was sealed in a red gift envelope bearing the airline's name, and there was wrapped around it a wildflower-patterned note from my mother on which she'd written a poem to me: "You've worked hard all year/to make your career/but now the term's done/so go have some fun! XXX, Mom." She fully believed, of course, that I was going to be coming back from Paris, that I was going to return to business school, and I wasn't about to tell her otherwise. Not that I had alternative plans. I had simply decided, in my own mind, that I wasn't going to come back. My life in New York was starting to repulse me, and I had to get away from it, from the endless repetition of my nights with Craig, or rather, the endless repetition of Craig's nights, the ragged edges of which I clung to. Perhaps I was also beginning to want things Craig would never have been able to get for himself, much less for me: a lover, nights watching television in bed instead of in bars. And I knew I wouldn't be able to free myself from my dependency on Craig unless I got far, far away from him.

In Paris, I lived in a beautiful apartment that belonged to an Italian woman, a friend of my parents—a sleek, modern studio in a crumbling fifteenth-century building near the Pompidou Center, in the Marais. *Marais* means swamp, and riding to the airport on the JFK Express I looked out the window at the bayou-like hinterlands of Queens; a muddy delta of broken-down houses, their little jetties thrust out into the sludge. It was a depressing view, and it didn't bode well for the summer. But the Marais turned out to be no swamp; it was an ancient neighborhood of tiny cobblestone streets, too narrow for most cars, in which art galleries and fancy bookstores, like newly planted exotic flowers, were just beginning to bloom. There were chickens and urinating children in the courtyard, sawdust on the uneven steps. Most of my neighbors were stooped old women who eyed me suspiciously, muttering *"L'Italienne"* to one another under their breath. Their rooms were as squalid as the courtyard; they shared squat toilets in the hall. I suspect they resented *"L'Italienne"* not because she was young and chic and was part of a growing movement to gentrify their neighborhood, but because she had her own fancy bathroom and water heater. I myself had never met *L'Italienne*, my patroness, so kindly allowing me to live rent free in her pied-à-terre, though she made her presence and personality known to me in the form of little notes stuck all over the apartment, instructing me how to turn on the water, which drawers to use, how to light the stove, not to mention the many notes that said, "Privé," or "Personal Drawer—Do Not Touch." I never did.

June afternoons in Paris are melancholic. Craig, who was himself going to be spending the summer Eurailing his way through Spain and Italy and Greece, had encouraged me to buy the *Spartacus Guide* for gay men before I left, and according to its instructions, I walked up and down the Tuileries each night at dusk, astonished at how many men there were there, some shirtless, others dressed head to toe in leather, lounging on benches, or leaning against the Orangerie, or staring dissolutely at the Seine. The *Spartacus Guide* really was, as it claimed, a world unto itself. Its entire middle was composed of advertisements from various pedophiliac presses for novels, short story collections, diatribes and defenses of the "boy-loving man" and "man-loving boy." When you looked up a bar, or a bathhouse, or an "outdoor cruising area" in the *Spartacus Guide*, you would get an entry something like this: B D LX M OG AYOR. You would then look in the key at the front of the book for a translation. "B" meant bar, "D" dancing, "LX" lesbians excluded, all the way down to "AYOR"—"At Your Own Risk." This last abbreviation appealed to me especially because I read it as a word—"ayor." "Ayor," I'd say to myself, walking up and down the length of the dusky Tuileries. I loved the sound of it, the way it rolled off my tongue into definitiveness. It was like a signal, a code of unwelcome, the opposite of "ahoy." "Ayor." Stay away. There are dangers here.

Because I was a good boy, I avoided the places that were labeled "AYOR." I only went to *Le Broad*, the big disco which the guide gave four stars, and described as "certainly the classiest and best-run gay establishment in Paris." It was a giant, cavernous place, with elaborate underground catacombs, dark links of rooms where who knows what happened, where I might have ventured with Craig, but never alone. Instead, I stayed on the dance floor, where, as it was perfectly acceptable to do so in Paris, I often danced by myself, for hours, caught up in the frenzy of music and movement, swept to my feet by the moment. The biggest song that summer was a ridiculous, campy concoction by Eartha Kitt, called "I Love Men," though she sang it, "I Love-Ah Men-Ah."

In the end, they always resist-ah
And pretend you didn't exist-ah
But my friend, somehow they persist-ah
And remain at the top of my list-ah . . .

I remember how the French men—so exotic-looking to me, with their thick syrupy smell of *parfum* and cigarettes, their shirts open to the waist, their dark skin, thin lips, huge black eyes—tried so hard to sing along with Eartha Kitt, though they didn't understand anything she was saying. Drunk and in love with themselves, they howled animalistically some rough approximation of the song. They made out in pairs and trios on the fringes of the dance floor. They were joyous in their collectivity. And why not? *Le SIDA* hadn't caught up with them yet. It was the first time in my life and the only place in the world where I have ever been able to imagine sex with a man without feeling fear or guilt or boredom. Instead, I imagined the prospect of adventure, celebration. I could taste it on my lips.

I met Laurent the second night I went to that disco. A fight had broken out somewhere across the dance floor, and the ripples of movement threw us literally into each other's arms. Laughing, we just stayed there. It was a glorious, easy meeting. Laurent was twenty, a literature student at Nanterre, son of an Italian mother and a French father, and the birth date carved on the gold chain around his neck was a lie. "Why?" I asked him that night, while we lay naked and sweating in my big bed, in the heat of the night, and I, at least, in the heat of love. He explained that his mother was already two months pregnant when she married his father, and they had had to lie to the Italian relatives about the birthday to avoid a *scandale*. He didn't mind because it meant he had two birthdays a year—one in France and another, two months later, in Italy. Except that he rarely saw the Italian relatives. His father, whom he hated, who drove a silver *Bay-Em-Double-vay*, had left his mother for her cousin. His mother had not been the same since; he had had to move home with her, to take care of her. He also had to babysit his own *petite cousine*, Marianne, every morning at nine, and therefore couldn't spend the night. (This seemed to be the ultimate, consequential point of the saga.) I said that was fine. I was ready to agree to just about anything.

From the moment I let Laurent out the door, in the early hours of the morning, I was jubilant with love for him—for his long, dark eyelashes, his slightly contemptuous mouth, his odd insistence on wearing only white socks. ("*Non, ce n'est pas les Français,*" he explained when I asked him, "*c'est seulement moi.*") Like most Europeans, he was uncircumcised—the only uncircumcised lover I have ever had. That small flap of skin, long removed from me in some deeply historical bris, was the embodiment of our difference. It fascinated me, and my fascination chafed poor Laurent, who couldn't understand what the big deal was—I, the American, was the one who was altered, *pas normal*, after all. I pulled at it, played with it, curious and delighted, until he made me stop. "*Tu me fais mal,*" he protested. Craig's eyes would have lit up.

But Craig was nowhere near, and I was in a limited way happy. My love affair with Laurent was simple and regular, a series of afternoons, one blending into the other. Around eleven-thirty in the morning, after finishing with *la petite Marianne*, he would arrive at my apartment, and I would feed him lunch. Then we would make love perfunctorily, for an hour or so. Then we would take a walk to his car, and he would drive me for a while through the suburbs of Paris—Choisy-le-Roi, Vincennes, Clamart, Pantin. He classified these suburbs as either *pas beau*, *beau* or *joli*, adjectives that seemed to have more to do with class than aesthetics. I was inept at understanding the distinction. "*Neuilly est joli, n'est-ce pas?*" I'd ask him, as we drove down tree-lined avenues, past big, imposing houses. "*Non, c'est beau.*" "*Clamart, c'est aussi beau, n'est-ce pas?*" "*Non, c'est joli.*" Eventually I'd give up, and Laurent, frustrated by my intransigence, would drop me off at my apartment before going off to his job. All night he sold Walkmen in a Parisian *drugstore*, a giant, futuristic shopping mall of red Formica and chrome which featured at its heart a seventy-foot wall on which sixty-four televisions played rock videos simultaneously. This huge and garish place is the sentimental center of my memories of that summer, for I used to go there often in the evenings to visit Laurent, unable to resist his company, though I feared he might grow tired of me. Then I'd stand under the light of the videos, pretending not to know him, while he explained to someone the advantages of Aiwa over Sony. When he wasn't

with a customer, we'd talk, or (more aptly), he'd play with one
of the little credit-card sized calculators he had in his display
case, and I'd stare at him. But I couldn't stay at the drugstore
forever. After twenty minutes or so, fearful of rousing the
suspicions of the ash-blond woman who was in charge of Laurent,
I'd bid him adieu, and he'd wink at me before returning to his
work. That wink meant everything to me. It meant my life.
Powered by it, I might walk for miles afterwards down the Rue
de Rivoli, along the Seine, across the brilliant bridges to the
Latin Quarter, filled in summer with joyous young Americans
singing in the streets, eating take-out couscous, smiling and
laughing just to be there. Often friends from college were
among their number. We'd wave across the street as casually as
if we were seeing each other in New York. It astonishes me to
think how many miles I must have charted that summer, zigzagging aimlessly across the Parisian night for love of Laurent.
It was almost enough, walking like that, wanting him. That
wink was almost enough.

Laurent had only been to America once, when he was fourteen. His parents had sent him to New York, where he was to
meet an aunt who lived in Washington, but the aunt's son was
in a car accident and she couldn't come. For a week he had
stayed alone at the Waldorf-Astoria, a little French boy who
didn't speak English, instructed by his mother to avoid at all
costs the subways, the streets, the world. These days, when
the meanderings of my life take me to the giant, glittering
lobby of the Waldorf-Astoria, I sometimes think I see him, in
his French schoolboy's suit, hiding behind a giant ficus, or
cautiously fingering magazines in the gift shop. I think I see
him running down the halls, or pacing the confines of his
four-walled room, or sitting on the big bed, entranced by the
babbling cartoon creatures inhabiting his television.

Craig is by nature a suburbanite. He grew up in Westport,
Connecticut, where his father is a prominent dermatologist and
the first Jew ever admitted to the country club. One evening in
college he embarrassed me by getting into a long argument with

a girl from Mt. Kisco on the ridiculous subject of which was a better suburb—Mt. Kisco or Westport. On the way back to our dorm, I berated him. "Jesus, Craig," I said, "I can't believe you'd stoop so low as to argue about a subject as ridiculous as who grew up in a better suburb." But he didn't care. "She's crazy," he insisted, "Mt. Kisco doesn't compare to Westport. I'm not arguing about it because I have a stake in it, only because it's true. Westport is much nicer—the houses are much farther apart, and the people, they're just classier, better-looking and with higher-up positions. Mt. Kisco's where you go on the way to Westport."

Suburbs mattered to Craig. He apparently saw no implicit contradiction in their mattering to him at the same moment that he was, say, being given a blowjob by a medical student in one of the infamous library men's rooms, or offering me a list of call numbers that would point to the library's hidden stashes of pornography. But Craig has never been given much to introspection. He is blessed by a remarkable clarity of vision which allows him to see through the levels, the aboves and belows, which plague the rest of us. There are no contradictions in his world; nothing is profane, but then again, nothing is sacred.

He was in Europe, that same summer as me, on his parents' money, on a last big bash before law school. In Paris I'd get postcards from Ibiza, from Barcelona, where he'd had his passport stolen, from Florence (this one showing a close-up of the *David*'s genitalia), and he would talk about Nils, Rutger, and especially Nino, whom he'd met in the men's room at the train station. I enjoyed his postcards. They provided a much-needed connection with my old life, my pre-Paris self. Things were not going well with Laurent, who, it had only taken me a few days to learn, lived in a state of continuous and deep depression. He would arrive afternoons in my apartment, silent, and land in the armchair, where for hours, his eyes lowered, he would read the Tintin books I kept around to improve my French, and sometimes watch "Les Quatres Fantastiques" on television. The candy-colored, cartoon adventures of Tintin, androgynous boy reporter, kept him busy until it was nearly time for him to go to work, at which point I would nudge my way into his lap and say, "*Qu'est-ce que c'est?*" I want to help you. But all he would tell me was that he was depressed because he was losing his car. His aunt, who owned it, was taking it back, and now he would have to ride the train in to work every day, and take a cab back late at night. I suggested he might stay with me, and he shook his head. "*La petite Marianne,*" he reminded me. Of course. *La petite Marianne.*

I think now that in continually begging Laurent to tell me what was worrying him, it was I who pushed him away. My assumption that "talking about it" or "opening up" was the only way for him to feel better was very American, and probably misguided. And of course, my motives were not, as I imagined, entirely unselfish, for at the heart of all that badgering was a deep fear that he did not love me, and that that was why he held back from me, refused to tell me what was wrong. Now, I look back on Laurent's life in those days, and I see he probably wasn't hiding things from me. He probably really was depressed because he was losing his car, though that was only the tip of the iceberg. His fragile mother depended on him totally, his father was nowhere to be seen, his future, as a literature student at a second-rate university, was not rosy. It is quite possible, I see now, that in his sadness it was comforting for him simply to be in my presence, my warm apartment on a late afternoon, reading Tintin books, drinking tea. But I wasn't content to offer him just that. I wanted him to notice me. I wanted to be his cure. I wish I'd known that then; I might not have driven him off.

In any case, I was very happy when Craig finally came to visit, that summer, because it meant I would have something to occupy my time other than my worrisome thoughts about Laurent. It was late July by then, and the prospect of August, when Paris empties itself of its native population and becomes a desiccated land of closed shops, wandered by aimless foreigners, was almost sufficiently unappealing to send me back to business school. In ten days Laurent would quit his job and take off to the seaside with his mother. There was no mention of my possibly going with him, though I would have gladly done so, and could imagine with relish staying by myself in a little pension near the big, elegant hotel where Laurent and his mother went every year, going for tea and sitting near them on the outdoor promenade, watching them, waiting for Laurent's wink. There would be secret rendezvous, long walks on beaches— but it was all a dream. Laurent would have been furious if I'd shown up.

And so I was happily looking forward to Craig, to the stories I knew he'd tell, the sexual exploits he'd so willingly narrate, and in such great detail. I met his train at the Gare de Lyon. There he was, on schedule, in Alpine shorts and Harvard T-shirt, the big ubiquitous backpack stooping him over. We embraced, and took the metro back to my apartment. He looked tired, thin. He had lost his travelers' checks in Milan, he explained, had had his wallet stolen in Venice. He had also wasted a lot of money renting double rooms at exorbitant prices just for himself, and was worried that his parents wouldn't agree to wire him more. I tried to sympathize, but it seemed somehow fitting that he should now be suffering the consequences of his irresponsibility. Stingy with anyone else, he was rapacious in spending his parents' money on himself—a trait I had observed often in firstborn sons of Jewish families. (I myself was the second-born son, and live frugally to this day.)

We went out, that night, for dinner, to a Vietnamese restaurant I liked and ate in often, and Craig started to tell me about his trip—the beaches at Ibiza, the bars in Amsterdam. "It's been fun," he concluded. "Everything's been pretty good, except this one bad thing happened."

"What was that?" I asked.

"Well, I was raped in Madrid."

Delicately he wrapped a spring roll in a sprig of mint and popped it in his mouth.

"What?" I said.

"Just what I told you. I was raped in Madrid."

I put down my fork. "Craig," I said. "Come on. What do you mean, 'raped'?"

"Forcibly taken. Fucked against my will. What better definition do you want?"

He took a swig of water.

I sat back in my chair. As often happens to me when I'm struck speechless, a lewd, involuntary smile pulled apart my lips. I tried to suppress it.

"How did it happen?" I asked, as casually as I could.

"The usual way," he said, and laughed. "I was walking down the street, cruising a little bit, and this guy said '*Hola*' to me. He was cute, young. I said '*Hola*' back. Well, to make a long story short, we ended up back at his apartment. He spoke a little English, and he explained to me that he was in a big hurry. Then there was a knock on the door and this other guy walked in. They talked very quickly in Spanish, and he told me to get undressed. I didn't much want to do it anymore, but I took off my clothes—"

"Why?" I interrupted.

He shrugged. "Once you've gone that far it's hard not to," he said. "Anyway, as far as I could gather, he and his friend were arguing over whether the friend would have sex with us or just watch. After a while I stopped trying to understand and just sat down on the bed. It didn't take me too long to figure out the guy was married and that was why he was in such a hurry. I could tell from all the woman's things around the apartment.

"Anyway, they finally decided the friend would just watch. The first guy—the one who said '*Hola*'—saw I was naked and he took off his clothes and then—well, I tried to explain I only did certain things, 'safe sex' and all—but he didn't listen to me. He just jumped me. He was very strong, and the worst thing was, he really smelled. He hadn't washed for a long time, he was really disgusting." Craig leaned closer to me. "You know," he said, "that I don't get fucked. I don't like it and I won't do it. And I kept trying to tell him this, but he just wouldn't listen to me. I don't think he meant to force me. I think he just thought I was playing games and that I was really enjoying it. I mean, he didn't hit me or anything, though he held my wrists behind my back for a while. But then he stopped."

He ate another spring roll, and called the waiter over to ask for chopsticks. There were no tears in his eyes; no change was visible in his face. A deep horror welled in me, stronger than anything I'd ever felt with Craig, so strong I just wanted to laugh, the same way I'd laughed that afternoon in Central Park, when he showed me the secret places where men meet other men.

"Are you okay?" I asked instead, mustering a sudden, surprising self-control. "Do you need to see a doctor?"

He shrugged. "I'm just mad because he came in my ass even though I asked him not to," Craig said. "Who knows what he might have been carrying? Also, it hurt. But I didn't bleed or anything. I didn't come, of course, and he couldn't have cared less, which really pissed me off. He finished, told me to get dressed fast. I guess he was worried his wife would come home."

I looked at the table, and Craig served himself more food.

"I think if that happened to me I'd have to kill myself," I said quietly.

"I don't see why you're making such a big deal out of it," Craig said. "I mean, it didn't hurt *that* much or anything. Anyway, it was just once."

I pushed back my chair, stretched out my legs. I had no idea what to say next. "Aren't you going to eat any more?" Craig asked, and I nodded no, I had lost my appetite.

"Well, I'm going to finish these noodles," he said, and scooped some onto his plate. I watched him eat. I wanted to know if he was really feeling nothing, as he claimed. But his face was impassive, unreadable. Clearly he was not going to let me know.

Afterwards, we walked along the mossy sidewalks of the Seine—"good cruising," the *Spartacus Guide* had advised us, but "very AYOR"—and Craig told me about Nils, Rutger, Nino, etc. I, in turn, told him about Laurent. He was mostly interested in the matter of his foreskin. When I started discussing our problems—Laurent's depression, my fear that he was pulling away from me—Craig grew distant, hardly seemed to be listening to me. "Uh-huh," he'd say, in response to every phrase I'd offer, and look away, or over his shoulder, until finally I gave up.

We crossed the Ile de la Cité, and Craig asked about going to a bar, but I told him I was too tired, and he admitted he probably was as well. He hadn't gotten a couchette on the train up here, and the passport control people had woken him up six or seven times during the night.

Back at my apartment, we undressed together. (Since Laurent, I had lost my modesty.) I watched as Craig, like any good first son, carefully folded his shirt and balled his socks before climbing into the makeshift bed I had created for him on my floor. These old habits, taught long ago by his mother, were second nature to him, which I found touching. I looked at him in the bed. He had lost weight, and a spray of fine red pimples covered his back.

Raped. I can hardly say that word. Besides Craig, the only person I know who was raped was a friend in my dorm in college named Sandra. After it happened, I avoided her for weeks. I imagined, stupidly, that simply because I was male, I'd remind her of what she'd gone through, make her break down, melt, weep. But finally she cornered me one afternoon in the library. "Stop avoiding me," she said. "Just because I was raped doesn't mean I'm made out of glass." And it was true. It was always Sandra who brought up the fact of the rape—often in front of strangers. "I was raped," she'd say, as if to get the facts out of the way, as if saying it like that—casually, without preparation—helped to alleviate the terror, gave her strength. Craig had told me with a similar studied casualness. And yet I suspect his motive was not so much to console himself, as to do some sort of penance; I suspect he genuinely believed that he had been asking for it, and that he deserved it, deserved whatever he got.

Perhaps I am wrong to use the word "underside" when I describe the world Craig led me through that first summer in New York, perhaps wrong in assuming that for Craig, it has been a matter of surfaces and depths, hells and heavens. For

me, yes. But for him, I think, there really wasn't much of a
distance to travel between the Westport of his childhood and
the dark places he seemed to end up in, guide or no guide, in
whatever city he visited. Wallets, travelers' checks, your life:
these were just the risks he took. I lived in two worlds; I came
in and out of the underside as I pleased, with Craig to protect
me. I could not say it was my fault that he was raped. But I
realized, that night, that on some level I had been encouraging
him to live in the world's danger zones, its "ayor" zones, for
years now, to satisfy my own curiosity, my own lust. And I
wondered: how much had I contributed to Craig's apparent
downfall? To what extent had I, in living through him, made
him, molded him into some person I secretly, fearfully longed
to be?

He lay on my floor, gently snoring. He always slept gently.
But I had no desire to embrace him or to try to save him. He
seemed, somehow, ruined to me, beyond hope. He had lost all
allure. It is cruel to record now, but the truth was, I hoped he'd
be gone by morning.

The next afternoon, we had lunch with Laurent. Because
Craig spoke no French and Laurent spoke no English, there
was not much conversation. I translated, remedially, between
them. Craig did not seem very impressed by Laurent, which
disappointed me, and Laurent did not seem very impressed by
Craig, which pleased me.

Afterwards, Laurent and I drove Craig to the Gare du Nord,
where he was catching a train to Munich. He had relatives there
whom he hoped would give him money to spend at least a few
weeks in Germany. For a couple of minutes, through me, he
and Laurent discussed whether or not he should go to see
Dachau. Laurent had found it very moving, he said. But Craig's
only response was, "Uh-huh."

Then we were saying good-bye, and then he was gone, lost
in the depths of the Gare.

On the way back to my apartment I told Laurent about
Craig's rape. His eyes bulged in surprise. "*Ton ami*," he said,

when I had finished the story, "*sa vie est tragique.*" I was glad, somehow, that the rape meant something to Laurent, and for a moment, in spite of all our problems, I wanted to embrace him, to celebrate the fact of all we had escaped, all we hadn't suffered. But my French wasn't good enough to convey what I wanted to convey. And Laurent was depressed.

He dropped me off at my apartment, continued on to work. I couldn't bear the thought of sitting alone indoors, so I took a walk over to the Rue St. Denis and Les Halles. The shops had just reopened for the afternoon, and the streets were full of people—giggly Americans and Germans, trios of teenaged boys.

I sat down in a café and tried to stare at the men in the streets. I wondered what it must have been like, that "*Hola,*" whispered on a busy Madrid sidewalk, that face turning toward him. Was the face clear, vivid in its intent? I think not. I think it was probably as vague and convex as the face of the Genie of the Crystal in Gatlinburg. Then, too, it was the surprise of recognition, the surprise of being noticed; it will do it every time. The Genie of the Crystal, she, too, had wanted Craig, and even then I had urged him on, thinking myself safe in his shadow.

I drank a cup of coffee, then another. I stared unceasingly at men in the street, men in the café, sometimes getting cracked smiles in response. But in truth, as Craig has endlessly told me, I simply do not have the patience for cruising. Finally I paid my bill, and then I heard the churchbells of Notre-Dame strike seven. Only five days left in July. Soon it would be time to head up to Montmartre, to the drugstore, where Laurent, like it or not, was going to get my company.

I GO BACK TO THE MAIS OUI

• JAMES McCOURT •

WHEN THE OLDSMOBILE convertible Jackson Pollock was driving hit the tree—

I call myself Delancey. (And why not?) "It's a Lazy Afternoon" was my song.

When the 1950 Oldsmobile convertible Jackson Pollock was driving in East Hampton on the night of August 11, 1956 hit the tree on Fireplace Road and flipped over, Jackson Pollock was sent "planing" into the air, some distance into the woods in Springs. His head hit the trunk of an oak ten feet up from the ground level, and that killed him instantly. When, after some time, a policeman and a neighbor from Springs came upon him, "He looked like an old dead tree lying in the brush."

We went to Greece last summer—Sicily and Greece, Phil and I—for old times' sake. Phil got to cry a lot in Sicily, looking out the windows of trains crawling along slower than the milk train out of East Hampton and standing for intervals of untold length in stations like Caltanissetta and Enna and Castelvetrano and Trapani, looking out over landscapes (to me reminiscent of Arizona, New Mexico, Nevada, and Southern California) he only dimly remembered from childhood, telling me we should have come in spring to see it all green; looking out at families he kept swearing all closely resembled his: whole families that came down to the stations to see one member off—off maybe as far as Palermo, or off to Rome, or Florence or Milan. (Phil said most Sicilians had never left their towns, that they were like the Bonackers in East Hampton's Springs, who had never been up island to New York and never would go. I asked what was he talking about? What about immigration, the Mafia, *foccaccerias*, Bellini? He said, "Shut up, you know what I mean." So I shut up. I knew what he meant; he was just wrong.)

Meanwhile, I've got the radio on, turned to the usual respectable call letters—wishing I could listen again to one program of *The Mysterious Traveler* instead of yet another quality evening on *Carnegie Hall Presents*, or wishing crazily that Carnegie Hall would present the Judy concert. (We've got the record, of course—I'm *on* it, out of my mind—but we never play it. I'd like to be taken by surprise, but *they* won't play it, not in my lifetime.) So, anyway, I'm listening, when over the track of a decent enough rendition of the *Appassionata*, this voice informs the listener that, "This music is not being played by a professional musician." It is being played by one Doctor Something-Slithery-or-Other *Dove*. (Not as in "*Dove Sono*"; as in the soap, as in the Holy Ghost.) Doctor Dove is a pianist whose talent is evident, I am informed; also a sculptor whose work has been recognized, and the director of Flashbacks, the institute for cosmetic reparation staffed by artists. I am invited to ask myself this question: Do I honestly want to keep looking the way I look, and *wondering*—

Click.

This line of attack is new to me from this station. I am myself, so far as the upkeep of the face and form is concerned, as it happens, a devout adherent to the Dolores Del Rio method: long, unhurried excursions in the Land of Nod, *wo die Zitronen blühn*. (Dolores, they say, went abroad for up to sixteen hours at a stretch, under a blanket of dried fruit. I can make do with eleven under Scandia duck down, but no matter; I feel myself taking a nervous turn for the worse.) The gall of them. What would Beethoven say?

Did Jackson Pollock, an artist whose work was at last and is for all time recognized, ever think along the cosmetic reparation lines? Or did his spouse? Not according to the snapshots of him and her we keep in an honored place in the living room. I have just been sitting reading in the new oral biography of the great martyr of modern art and former friend of the head of this household (who is not represented in the said work, by his own choice), and have been amused by one thing: Willem de Kooning's sputtering indignation in insisting that not for one minute of his life could Jackson Pollock have been considered a faggot. (I like Willem de Kooning. Once I spent an afternoon in his studio, blitzed by the work, and afterwards, in withdrawal, was admiring a collection of pre-Columbian sculpture distributed in the conversation pit of the living room. "Do you like it? It's my vife's. I dunno vat any of it is, but it's all *autentic*.") Amused because I think that, as specimens, both Pollock and de Kooning were what the Bonackers call "finest kind," and that they knew it. Angels with dirty faces; rough trade *rêve bateaux*, Satans in stained slacks; two big bad boys (despite Bill's size). They were *not* nice in the '50s, especially not to faggots. But I don't like thinking about that time too much, great as it was—*and we knew it*. All that sorrow in all that sunlight; express.

How far we've come from the river. Kyle, Mitch, Mary Lee, Delancey.

"Yes, yes," the Bonackers say. Jackson Pollock and Brando, Rock Hudson and Jimmy Dean. "Bent Shoulders" cologne. Then time goes by, and you say, "Fuck art, let's dance." The cha-cha, the way they danced it at the *Mais Oui*. And always, the Madison.

What I want to see more than anything is that pornography of Tchelitchew's. I want somebody to get it out of the Kinsey archives and make a book out of it, a book I can put right next to *L'Amour Bleu* and my glorious still-frame enlargements from the great Joe Gage trilogy, *Kansas City Trucking Company*, *El Paso Wrecking Corporation*, and *L.A. Tool and Die*. How I loved the Joe Gage aesthetic, and now it too is blasted.

Sister, I'm a child in the world who *does* still cry for the moon (even having had the stars, many of them, yes, yes).

I was brought up in a sharp school. So it turns out life isn't *anything* like I thought it would be.

I ordered from Wok Around the Clock one portion of cold noodles and sesame sauce and one portion of Szechuan ginger shrimp (no MSG). I got two tea bags, and *three* fortune cookies, but Phil repeated he isn't in the mood for anything until later. (Subtle.) In each of the first two fortune cookies there were two identical fortunes, two on yellow paper slips and two on cream white. On the cream white from cookie A: "Pass now, the risk is too great." I've never had such a fortune from a cookie in my life. Never mind. In the yellow, from cookie B: "Ignore previous fortunes." Sufficient unto the day. I wake up pure.

"When you wake up in the morning and you don't know what you want, ask an ad?" Remember that? I just woke up from a nap, turned on the radio again, and got an ad for *Je reviens*. How far from the river—whichever—in Manhattan. And let's not forget Monty and Marilyn either.

This girl—you heard me, I met her on the Old Met Line—asked me to take her to an important prom. I didn't rent anything; Phil got me the full dress regalia. (I remember I asked him, "Is this *off* anybody—anybody you used to know, up till last week?") It was beautiful, '40s. I still wear it, to those summer musicales on Long Island's glittering South Fork at which my Versace combinations might be considered too emphatic. The affair was at the Statler, in the ballroom with the big eagle over the bandstand. I danced the cha-cha and the Peabody with her. She was wearing *Je reviens*—a lot of it. I remember the Peabody especially, because it was the first time I'd ever had the chance to lead in it. (Not that I wasn't butch; I was butch, if it matters. Phil always told me I was a real butch entertainer. Only that he always led in the Peabody.) We went to the Copa after, got our pictures taken and put on matchbooks, and then to Reuben's, where we ate eggs Benedict and poured the Hennessey from the hip flask into the coffee. (That was the kind of thing you did.) Then over to the Plaza sidewalk to take a ride through the Park in a hansom. She slapped on more *Je reviens*. We didn't do *anything*. (I was not about to have those beads rattled on The Line is what I told myself, and anyway she seemed to like me, as we used to say in those days, for myself.) When we got back to the Plaza, I asked the driver could he drive us from there to the Met by way of Seventh Avenue and Broadway—the Mawrdew Czgowchwz route. It was very early on a Saturday in June, but of course we knew that they would all be there: the ballet line for the Bolshoi (the one the '50s goon flagwavers picketed). They were sleeping overnight. "As long as it's down Broadway, right down the middle," the hansom cabbie insisted. "I used to drive a crosstown bus. You wanna know why I stopped? The two rivers." So we got our tickets to Ulanova's last *Giselle*, and we stayed friends. I used to put on *Je reviens* from time to time. I'd waltz through Macy's on the way up to The Line and spritz it on from the samplers. It used to make Phil crazy in the dark standing room (only). Later, when we got rich and joined the Club (faggot central) in the Grand Tier—but that's another story.

This remembering performance is a relatively new thing. I thought it was all chalk dust rotting away in the vacated play schoolroom of the mind, with a very short half-life. But it's like it's gone up some flue instead, like snow up my fragile nostrils used to in the '70s, and is a kind of sky writing on my cerebellum's dome. Or something that figurative. I was sitting here, where I am now, in bed, having decided to switch to something very *now*, listening to Voltron Toilet, and wondering when the old wop is going to come in to rest from his heroic labors: recording the early '60s Sunday-night Judy show reruns, while (because of some strange propensity he has for spiritual balancing acts) watching the rerun of that terrible tribute to Maria

(Callas) that features about eleven minutes of herself and eleven hours of all the self-promoting foghorns who claim they ever crossed her path, physically, mentally, or spiritually. When is he going to click all that off and come in here to this tastefully appointed, mirrored boudoir and jump on my bones. When, *à propos* unearthing the past and what-not, I started in on a piece in the one magazine I read about this absolutely forgotten figure of the '50s Abstract Expressionist revolution and Vanity Fair by the name of Shapinsky. Shapinsky had been discovered in an East Side walkup over a Japanese restaurant by a diminutive, irreproachable zealot hailing from the Indian subcontinent; has been pitched to and caught by some ga-ga gallery retailers in London's Mayfair, and is going to wind up after all that—and some all that: everything but the bloodhounds—a generation after the death of Jackson Pollock, a rich man. Not as rich as de Kooning (and does de Kooning remember? Does de Kooning care? The best guess is that de Kooning is, as Ralph would say, "uhmbothered"), but a rich man. This is what is known as redress. What would *I* do by way of redress? Tear out Lincoln Center and reopen the *Mais Oui*? I might.

From Sicily to Brindisi to Athens, to Iraklion to Santorini to Naxos; back to Athens, through Yugoslavia to Venice. In two weeks. In Knossos, I found the entrance to the Labyrinth in the Queen's toilet, just behind the throne, but we didn't go down. (I *dreamed* I did, but that's also another story.) The *it*, the *what happened*, happened on Naxos, birthplace of Dionysius (my patron deity, according to the old publicity), Ariadne's way station.

We'd run into Kiki and Clio Fragosiki (a.k.a.—can-we-talk?—"Fafner" and "Fasolt"), having dinner on Santorini in a place called The Kastro, overlooking the harbor that is the remains of the volcanic crater from the eruption of whenever forever ago that raised the great wave that destroyed Knossos, and decided to sail with them to Naxos, on an ordinary tourist boat, with the people. Attention: The trip was horrifying. Kiki kept saying over and over that something must have happened suddenly;

but Clio, grim, but resolutely candid, kept correcting her. "Bullshit, Ki! You talk as if you don't know why *we* got out—and it wasn't sudden. And why we almost certainly will *never* come back. It's *over, very* over." After a seven-hour sail—the watchword was agony—we chugged into Naxos harbor. Leaning overdeck, Kiki went into a kind of forced rapture, remembering the concert Mawrdew Czgowchwz gave there in another lifetime, when she stood in the portal of the Temple of Apollo and sang "*Es gibt ein Reich*" to a regatta of the advanced elect. "Don't go looking for *her* in these parts either," Clio snapped. "After they disposed of what was left of Maria in these troubled waters, and the currents carried it back to Colchis, Czgowchwz realized what was over in the way of an era, too."

Es gibt ein Reich wo alles rein ist; er hat auch eine Namen; Totenreich. You'll notice, I said to myself, that the one M.C. wasn't part of the famous tribute to the other M.C. either, close as they'd been. (And we were *there*.)

Whatever kept Ariadne on Naxos was not what kept us. We were anxious to get up to Mykonos and over to Delos to spend a day in the last divine place in Hellas, but the wind came up—the one they call "*Melteme*," not the one they call "Mareye-ah," (remember, that John Raitt used to sing on *Your Show of Shows?*)—and held us there for three days until a boat big enough to make the voyage docked. On the afternoon of the third day, leaving the women behind among the bronzed German nudists in their cunning thatched-hut Tahiti colony at the beach along the strait facing Paros, we took a bus ride in search of something I'd seen listed in the guidebook, called the *kouros* of Melanes.

Kouros means boy—as in the Dioscouri, the two boys, the twins Castor and Pollux who stand together in the National Museum in Athens balls-ass naked in Parian marble, much with the arm of the one thrown over the shoulder of the other, who is holding inverted the ritual torch, which signifies that he will die, abandoning the other, while Demeter, isn't it?, one-third scale and off to the side, looks askance. The Dioscouri are too painful to look at, even in the mind's gay eye. The faggot's impossible dream has always been the same: the double, the complementary other (who is in fact the same, only more so); the one that comes into view getting away—remember the Madison? (No, I have no regrets to speak of, and yes, I love Phil, the insatiable old goat. After all, "only through the embrace of Pan, whose hairy thighs rub us raw even as they bring us ecstasy, can we learn to be fully alive." I said the Dioscouri were the faggot's dream. Dream lover, put your arms around you. Next.)

The *kouros* of Melanes is a giant stone boy, one of those that were attached to Apollonic temple precincts in the archaic period. (I'm remembering from a book I found once left behind on the ballet line.) The *kouros* I like best in the National Museum has his pubic hair sculpted into a seven-sided polygon comprising three triangles surmounting a trapezoid—the upper section, in other words, of a five-pointed star, so that it sits like a kind of party hat on top of the things themselves, the things we love, the things of life. Whereas, the Melanes *kouros* was abandoned, left unfinished. One day in the middle of whenever, obviously either an earth tremor or word of the landing of hostile forces in the harbor—something at any rate of greater consequence than a rustic panic or a long lunch hour—interrupted the work on this great stone boy, and either then or some time later he fell over backward, his right leg snapped off just above the knee, and there he's lain for 2,600 years. (If you fell over at the *Mais Oui*—from too many stingers or too much heart—the queens would cha-cha right over your body, but somebody would always check your breathing, anyway. You had the feeling that even if Saint Theresa wasn't interested, somebody was. Somebody would pick you up and take you home. Never your twin, never your opposite number, but somebody with a story; somebody who'd make breakfast. Somebody, with any luck, from the East Side. You remember when *nobody* lived on the West Side? "Except to do what I did last night, I never *go* to the West Side," the East Side breakfast cook would declare. "All those people pretending to be poor!")

*　　*　　*

Phil once told Jackson Pollard that if he would go back to an earlier style ("Just something *negotiable*, Jack"), he, Phil, could probably see to it that the resulting canvases were hung in some of the better Italian restaurants in Greenwich Village. Instead of which, Jackson continued painting atomic fission. Phil said, "O.K., I'll shut up and buy some." (Phil picked up on three right things in the '50s, besides me: Pollock, IBM, and Tiffany glass. Consequently, we are now what you would call comfortable.)

To find the *kouros*, you take the bus to Melanes and walk out of the town over a kilometer or more or rocky fields until the path ends at the base of a high hill, then turn left and climb over the stone walls until you find the sacred grove. An old Naxian woman sits at the edge of it in a rustic hut, selling ice cream. The easier way is to follow the main traffic road around the town and look for the sign that says KOUROS. This we found only on the way back, however (Cycladic Greeks being profoundly committed to withholding information), having failed to negotiate a return trip on the French-speaking bus tour back to the port, and having been mercifully picked up and driven there by a nice man from Piraeus—*the* town in Greece, absolutely—who was on vacation with his Naxos-born wife, but just then alone in the car, cruising (we decided not. Just a nice Greek. Goes to show you. The driver's name was Kalegeropoulos. "That was Maria Callas's name!" "Yes, it's the same." "What do you know," said Phil. The conversation went nowhere, but Mr. Kalegeropoulos certainly was a nice Greek).

Phil took my picture sitting on the *kouros*'s chest. Poor gigantic, broken abandoned boy: features worn smooth by centuries of wind and rain. What significance! What I did last summer in Greece: I had a religious experience on Naxos to beat any Dolores could ever have had in her sleep under that blanket of dried apricots. (Or, as has been said better, in a similar connection, "*Du musst dein Leben ändern.*" Ain't it the truth? Only how?)

I have always been particularly interested in Jackson Pollock's stone dowsing abilities. Apparently they, the stones, spoke to him from beneath the surface of the earth. He'd hear them, have them dug up, and relate to them thereafter. I think of it in connection with remembering.

Which reminds me of the time O'Maurigan insisted on dragging me to the MOMA party in honor of Douglas Sirk, and introducing me to the great man. I opened my mouth, and out came, "I'm so happy to meet you, Mr. Sirk. *Written on the Wind* changed my life." His eyes brightened. "Oh, how?" I found myself telling him: Mary Lee, looking across the river. . . . "Oh, yes, of course."

I met Phil not at the *Mais Oui*, but at the Cherry Lane. He sometimes tries to correct me, saying it was the Modern, but I remember that summer almost night by night, and it was the Cherry Lane. Phil gets confused because he remembers Trenchy being the mainstay at the Modern, but Trenchy left the Modern early that summer and went down to the Cherry Lane. We danced, Phil and I, which makes me absolutely certain, because there was no dance floor at the Modern. (Phil says there was no dance floor at the Floradora out in Jackson Heights either, but they all danced, which is what got the boys in blue so hot and bothered over at the 110th. But I remember it was the Cherry Lane; trust me.) We danced to the Everly Brothers' "All I Have to Do Is Dream" and "Maybe Tomorrow." Somebody sang "The Man That Got Away" along with Judy. Just another night in '50s gay New York. We did it on the way home— that's something else I remember—in the back of a deserted loading platform on Washington Street. Then we stopped off at Vinnie's Clam bar. We sat up drinking espresso with anisette at Phil's place on Mott Street, watching *June Bride* on the *Late, Late Show*, and when Robert Montgomery says to Davis, "I'm gay, I'm lovable, and I've got nice teeth—what more do you want?" I turned to Phil, smiled that crazy smile of the clown that used to advertise Tilyou's Playland in Rockaway Park, and said to him, "So?" He said, "So I'm takin' you away from Rockaway, away from Riis Park, away from Jones Beach, *and* away from Cherry Grove."

Typical Phil, that remark. His point was that, although I never went near Jones Beach in the daytime (none of us did, not even to investigate the notorious "Gay 1." Who had that kind of cab fare?), I *was* seeing a lot of that particular stretch of sand dune off the South Shore in the evenings. What had happened was that I fell—fell hard—for a gypsy in *A Night in Venice*. That was in July. By the Labor Day weekend, many performances of *A Night in Venice* later (which, incredibly, Phil started driving me out to, night after night), I was spending my last few days in Cherry Grove for twenty-nine years. It was there, away from him—but I'll confess hearing his lyrical *promessa* to take me the next summer to the real Venice—that I decided on him (Phil). I got the name "Gay Dawn" that weekend. (That was the level of wit at Duffy's in the Grove in the middle '50s.) It used to make me frantic sometimes to hear about the ascendancy of the Pines—which hardly *existed* then—in the '60s. There I was, an idle prisoner of love in uneventful Sagaponack (admittedly having seen the real Venice, and a lot more); but I know now, absolutely, that I wouldn't have made it, by way of the Grove, to Stonewall.

Stonewall. I've always thought it was ironic about Stonewall. I used to say the "*Mais Oui*" riots or the "Cherry Lane" riots or even the "Floradora" riots would have called out a classier crowd, if you're going to go in for the founding sisters performance. But I guess I'm prejudiced, maybe only because I was there *at* the Stonewall—which, let's face it, was a dump. (So what? So was the Bastille, right?)

I don't know why I went there that night, instead of home to our luxurious air-conditioned floor-through on Mott Street to pack for the country, except that I was wrecked, I admit it. It certainly was not to look at the go-go dancers. It was hot and I was wrecked. I was also a platinum blond that summer, and frankly, insecure as to my motives; but the big news of course and the big "reason" was that Judy was, finally, dead. I'd been up to Campbell's to see the remains of her—one dope-dead doll, lying there like the last lost illusion—and instead of getting on the late Montauk train, as I'd promised Phil over the phone from the Plaza, I swerved out the back door and over to the chic little baths with the imbedded-at-all-hours orgy parlor with the jalousies that looked down on West 58th Street; left there rather more stained than consoled, and went down to Kelly's on 45th Street to have a few beers. What I must have had in mind was some kind of sentimental tour of '50s doorways, but the next thing I remember is coming to, screwed onto the top of a stool at the Stonewall, looking alternately up into the glass eyes of a champagne-blond go-go boy and down into the crystal matrix of a stinger.

I saw the amphetamine-crazed drag queen throw the cocktail in the officer's unready face. I heard her scream over the dystonic strains of 1969, *"That's for Judy!!!"*

And, as Bridey says to the judge in the immortal pee-in-the-pot urinalysis story, that's when the fight started. Or, as Miss Charity would declare, "That's the 'T' on *that*, dihr." I got out of there and into a gay cab up the Avenue of the Americas to the heart of the former Tenderloin District. There have always been crises in my life—at least my life between my leaving of a certain institution upstate I may talk about later and the padlocking of the parks and stews in these plague years—in which the *only* comfort was the comfort of immersion in Everard's glamorous and refreshing bathing pool (No Diving), and there I fled at the hour of decision on that Friday night, until it was time to catch that milk train to Bridgehampton. Poor Judy. You know, at the end they were throwing dinner rolls at her, the Brits, when she sang at the Talk of the Town on Leicester Square. (It's nice to believe, but hard to be sure, that New Yorkers wouldn't have thrown something—like empty amyl nitrite vials, for instance—at her at, say, The Continental, had she made it back stateside that summer to sing, then die. I would like to hear the Carnegie recording again largely because I can pinpoint the *groove* in which the engineers bleeped out Hank's voice as he stampeded down the middle aisle screaming *"Juuuuuudy—sit on my faaace!!!"* (This is one of the many true-life details you won't be seeing in the—can you believe it—Stanley Donen musical—musical!—of Judy's life. And what are they going to call it? *If Love Were All*?)

So, am I going to call this Doctor Dove about a face lift?

I just got two fortunes in the third cookie. "A new opportunity will soon come your way," and, "You are heading for a land of sunshine and fun."

Wo die Zitronen blühn. Where the *kouroi* are all in perfect Joe Gage condition. Where I will station myself in repose under a raintree, signing autographs, prohibiting photographs, permitting certain delicate liberties to be taken with my person, *gratis*, and repeat and repeat in all ears, "I go back to the *Mais Oui*."

"Penny candy, candy for a penny. I ask for more than a penny now; I've grown very wise you see. . . ." Name the show; name the performer; next contestant.

After forty hours eating salami and drinking Zeus water on the Beograd cannonball, we got to Venice, now as then (that summer after the first, betrothal summer) my favorite ride in Europe. We always stay at the same hotel, the Fenice/degli Artisti. It rained, which was divine. Venice in the rain is only to be surpassed by Venice in the snow. After I'd done my adornment scenes at Versace, we went and ate at "our little *trattoria*," in back of the Teatro Fenice. There is a picture on the wall of the rear *salone* there of us from the '50s, taken at a party we gave for Vanna Sprezza—remember her? She was the daughter of Phil's mother's cousin. The party was given after the gala world premiere of Trovaso Corradi's *Livia Serpieri*, written for Vanna on commission from some Pacelli *pastificcio* and co-starring the then reigning Adonis of the Italian lyric stage, Giuseppe di Stefano ("Pippo"). It was a smash hit. I still play the Cetra recording, and think of Vanna, who lives these days in Taormina, up in the back. (We don't look her up anymore; there was an altercation.) Both M.C. and M.' C.' (as we used to write them then) were there—in fact, they came together, without husbands. That was either just before or just after Morgana Neri died; I can't remember which, only that Pippo told the funniest Neri stories anybody ever heard (in the

Sicilian, naturally). The composer, the oldest living *verista*, conducted. Sets and costumes—never mind.

I just came across some thrilling words of wisdom in a book of literary criticism, of which I buy a great deal at the Strand Book Store, and read while listening to selections on this serious music station, to calm my nerves (after, for example, a session with Voltron Toilet). "The past's unchallengeable facts account as much as the present's uncontrollable accidents for the tragedies of human fortune. Faith in the fixed idols of anteriority, whether personal or social, serves as well as the ruins of past authority and times to disorder the conduct of present life."

I ought to pay more attention to directions like these. I mean, so I go back to the *Mais Oui*. Big hairy deal. Phil goes back to Spivvy's Roof, and beyond; do you hear him walking around New York talking about it, or singing "Why Don't You . . ." at parties?

I've been thinking about that last time in Venice, though, because we had to get up early the other morning to go up to the boat house in Central Park, because old (and I mean *old*) Lila Aron, a former benefactress of Phil's mother, was having the genuine Venetian gondola she's giving to the city launched and floated out past the deconstructed Bethesda esplanade and around the Ramble promontory, featuring two, both genuine, Venetian *gondolieri* (talk about disordering the conduct of present life and the repose of a citizen with a piece of private theater). There we stood on a chilly morning, a handful of us, while "The Dogaressa" (Phil's expression) cackled over her *gondolieri* to her gay heart's content, twigging their dreamy nonchalance. (Each obviously possessed his own open-return ticket, Alitalia, to the Pearl of the Adriatic.) Of course the eerie little matinee had to remind me of what else but the Mawrdew Czgowchwz regatta, and of all the radiance of those times, time out of mind, but also, more so, of the O'Maurigan play *Panache*, in which, if anybody remembers anything in this age of information exchange, they may care to remember that I was a big hit in the juvenile lead, opposite the young Kaye Wayfaring. Well, you know how it is with a play: You never remember a line of your own. But I remember every syllable of that crazed old fairy Dixwell's monologue about Venice that was directed at me to this day, and it came to me like a funeral oration that morning, because, well, I suppose the ceremony of the gondola was to me a little, as the French say, *funeste*. Anyway, that speech was the gay hit aria of the play, and more veterans of domestic wars than can ever have heard it spoken during the brief run of *Panache* have asked me about it over the years at parties. For a while it was all you heard talked about—after the vogue for the anthill-crucifixion passage from *The Cocktail Party* had passed.

There is situate somewhere in the divine
Municipality of Venice—serene
Republic that was before Napoleon,
Like so much else upon which more depends—
In a backwater, uncharted, an island:
Sant'Ariano. No *vaporetto* stays
To discharge *passagieri.* Never ask where
Of a Venetian the boat . . . never suggest
A gondolier . . . for on said isle lie rotting
The bare bones of those poor souls who have not shot
More or less straight to heaven by the octaves
Of their superintended demises, nor
On the anniversaries, until the years collect
And leases lapse on their snug graves in the bone-
Yard of the divine serene that was before
Napoleon, like so much else—the Vatican's
Most recent discretionary directive
Indicating, though not stipulating, thus:
That diocesan procedure ought, as in
All negotiation since Napoleon,
Stay flexible. Avoiding the radical
Boue of contemporary transalpine death

Theology, endorsing the opinion
That only the bones of the souls in Purgatory
May be presumed to have "lasted" in their graves.
The bones of the damned dissolve into the soot
That blackens maggots in their evolution
Into dungflies, whereas souls in Paradise
Leave bones behind that *crystallize* overnight
Into a kind of marzipan, collected
And stored in the vaults of the *Basilica*
Di San Marco. (Marzipan to be dispensed
To those tots who have taken First Communion
Without incident of gagging.) Now about
That legendary sacrilege committed
One night in *Carnevale* in the serene
Before Napoleon, and recreated
At the Venice Film Festival in the year—
You remember: the notorious *Pranzo*
Dei Morti held on *Sant'Ariano:*
The supper at which dessert was said to have
Been *zabaglione,* with slices of that same
Marzipan—"Oh, my *God!*" screamed the New Yorkress
Overhearing the whole story at Harry's
American Bar. "That's *disgusting!* That makes
The *flesh* crawl right off my *bones!*" Like so much else
In backwaters, uncharted, never ask where. . . .

I sat there at lunch at Cipriani's in the Sherry Netherland,
after the gondola mass, eating *zabaglione* for dessert, and remembering that monologue again, word for word. Some people
can't forget the Gettysburg Address, or the letter Violetta
Valery gets from Giorgio Germont and reads in the last act of
La Traviata ("Teneste la promessa . . .").

You may remember that in *Key Largo,* for which the divine
Claire Trevor won the Academy Award as Best Supporting
Actress (and let's face this: with few, very few nods to the big
girls, this has been *the* fabulous gay category over the years
since its inception), that Gay Dawn's real name was Maggie

Mooney. Many people think, or used to think, that I got called Gay Dawn not just as a joke on Phil and his supposed (or much exaggerated) Cosa Nostra connections, but because my real name was Mooney. My real name, although Irish, wasn't, and isn't, Mooney. I knew and was beholden, however, to a Maggie, or rather a Marge, Mooney, and I always think of her in connection with Venice because she put me in a motion picture there one summer, and then died the next.

The whole thing came about in this way. Years before, I had been sent from Delancey Street "up the river," as the little old New York guttersnipes like me used to say, to a New York Archdiocesan correctional facility—a reform school—called Lincoln Hall. The fact is I got turned around there, through the efforts of a very kind and saintly monsignor called Gregory Mooney, whose sister was this enormous woman with three chins, right out of Dickens, whose occupation it was to engineer little musical vaudeville shows in grammar schools in the archdiocese. She came to Lincoln Hall and made me a star at eleven, singing "America, I Love You." More than eleven years later, some time after Lincoln Hall (and after the *Mais Oui* and *Panache*), I was walking across the Piazza di San Marco, and there coming out of Florian's, as large as life in the Italian manner, was Miss Margaret Mooney. "I'm here making a picture," she said. "I'd heard you'd gone into the profession, and from the look of you, you might be just right for the regatta scene we're getting ready to shoot. Come with me." That's how I got into—I can't even tell you what they finally called it, but Princess Saroya and Richard Harris (remember them?) were the stars. It's never, so far as I know, been screened here, but Miss Mooney and I did make the *Sunday News* picture centerfold. M.M. (or should I maybe say M.' M.'?) was playing a sort of Elsa Maxwell American party beast, and she sailed down the Grand Canal in a great draped gondola, and I sailed right down with her, as a Pierrot, without whiteface. I got a lot of offers from that appearance, which I turned down, but everybody asked me what I was doing, or *thinking about* in that sequence, because my face read deep mystery. (A similar question, you may recall, was once asked of Miss Garbo.) Well, what I was doing, since I had no character, no direction, no script, was: I was rolling that O'Maurigan *Panache* monologue in a slow crawl across my brain pan, and *seeing* Sant'Ariano and the supper party on it—although I must tell you I have never felt the slightest inclination to inquire as to the authenticity or whereabouts of that darkly fabled venue, as often as I've been to Venice. (For one thing, Phil. . . .)

Miss Mooney died the very next summer, as I've said, in Venice, but they shipped the body home, and I went to the funeral. I was by then, and resolutely, no longer in the profession. I remember thinking for a minute while shaking hands with Monsignor Greg that maybe I should go and work with the kids who came from where I had been, but the Holy Ghost, that dove, sort of let me know that that wasn't my line of work, either. I haven't been back to church.

Phil says what I ought to do is write a book. I said, "Sure, you'll get it printed and make sure it gets stocked by all the better Italian restaurants in the *city* now, right?" He says I ought to tell my story; he says he's sure it means something. He says I should write about it all, since when. I said, "Who's going to look after you after I start writing books and going on talk shows and end up going back into the profession as an attitude faggot?" "I could look after myself." "You could look after yourself. You could eat *scungils*, but you don't."

"Well, you ought to think about it, anyway."

"Should I put in what you heard Judy say to Diane deVoors that time?"

Phil really adored Judy. I guess I did, too. I must have; I was always there. This one time, just before she went onstage, she was looking from the wings over the house as it filled up, and she turned to Diane deVoors and said, "Why do I get all the cripples?" So, she was in that kind of mood, the poor woman, with God knows what variety of shit rocketing through her wounded veins. Do I have to repeat the story? Yes.

*   *   *

Many years ago now, in the infirmary at Lincoln Hall, I woke from what was billed as rheumatic fever, but was really a nervous breakdown—my first and last—hearing children's voices, alternately crying and calling like newsboys, "Read it and weep! Read it and weep!" The monitors had taken the letter away, and not a word was ever said about it. "What we were doing *was* wrong, no matter how it felt, no matter what you told me. Father says it was a question of honor. I must trust he won't tell anyone . . . but I know if we start again. . . ." You got it? Good. *My* confessor, grab this, had gone on about Saint Augustine and God's love and the illusory grandeur of the self. (I'd actually *said*, "I don't know why I'm telling you all this; I don't believe in hell, or in heaven, or in anything.") The illusory grandeur of the self! You ready? "Fuck you, Saint Augustine!" I cried. I had sung "America, I Love You," and brought down the house. I had almost sung "I love you" to another human being (*all right*, a guy, a fabulous, spectacular animal male). And there's one thing I'm glad of to this day and will be until I die, and that's that I had no mother to run to and babble at. Phil knows the right thing to do: He pats me on the head; we fuck. That's all I want; I've never wanted anything else. That is my absolution. (Which reminds me of something else I've heard of, but have never seen, in Venice: a very ancient Clorox-blond who supposedly tramps the Lido in August, every August, wearing *short pants* and a *sailor top*, looking for absolution, in *German*, from strangers, for a *sin he cannot reveal*.) (Italics mine.)

So, I should go on television in the mornings? Should I be the day keeper and diviner invoking the midmost seers, as it were, of the gone gay life? Should I rattle my beads like corn kernels or coral seeds in lots of four in front of the burnt offerings? Should I call upon Miss Desiree, *La Reine Voltige*; upon Diane deVoors; upon Miss Charity; upon the Good Witch of the South to take me back to—
The Maria program is ending. I hear her through the wall growling over Tito Gobbi's mortal coil, "*E avanti a lui tremava tutta Roma!*" She will leave the candles burning, drop the

WHY PEOPLE GET CANCER

• ANDERSON FERRELL •

I WANT TO TELL you the foolishness some people have when it comes to their own souls. Foolishness is all I know to call it. Right there in the *Bible* it says, "the wages of sin is Death," so if you're staring your own death full in the face, it's a deadly foolishness looks like to me. There she lay up there in that hospital, her lungs ate up with cancer, not knowing, or knowing and saying no to knowing. We come to give her the strength and the hope, but they turned us out.

At the time I thought, Well, maybe she don't even know we're here. You see, I was sure they had her drugged and all. Maybe she's just too sick for any knowing. I only talked to that friend of her son's, and he wasn't even in the family. What right did he have to speak for her or her son? That boy struck me funny right then and there. It turned out she knew plenty and then some, but I'm getting ahead of myself.

See, the reason I tell you this story in the first place is because it just shows so plain the way of Satan. How he'll spit in your face, and you'll just lick it off, make you walk right through a cow pasture and see nothing but the clover, give you nothing but misery and then let you stand there and thank him for it. I believe I can show you that right clear.

You see, saving souls is the main business of Christians. Well, Satan can make that business mighty hard, especially if that soul just don't want to be saved. It's hard to do, and you can't take the blame for that. But I'm going to make that clearer plus a few other things.

We, Earnest Sauls and me, were making our rounds of the hospital last Wednesday. Earnest and me were both saved on the same night, two years ago at a prayer meeting held by Reverend Pate, and from that time on, we've used our Wednesday lunch hours to help ease the suffering of others. We bring them the Lord's Word and a prayer and try to show them that it is Satan's work that has made them sick and not the Lord's. You'd be surprised how many times I hear people next to death, blaming the Lord for putting them there. Now Death is Satan's Saturday night good-time girl, and people have got to be shown that if they want to blame somebody they had better have a look in the mirror and blame who's looking back. They let Satan know they were interested, same as if you'd tell a friend you were looking for a live one. Well, Satan fixed them up with Lady Death, and up there in that cancer ward, she's got on her red high-heels, and she is open for business. But when they find out she don't come cheap, they start blaming the Lord for the shape they're in. You've heard people do it, I know: "If there was a God in Heaven, this wouldn't happen to me," "How can a just, loving God let folks suffer?" "If God's all powerful, how come he don't stop this or that?" On and on and on, I tell you, I've heard them all.

Now if it's two people that knows about blaming the Lord, it's me and Earnest. And, if it's two people that knows how the Lord works in ways you wouldn't think He would, it's me and Earnest. Of course, Satan can work in right many different ways too. He was doing a pretty slick job up there with Mrs. Eagles. That's her name, Mrs. Eagles. By the time I got there, He had put so much between her and salvation I was starting to wonder if the battle wasn't done lost. Satan don't just deal directly with the person involved, you see. He covers all the bases. He knows how to use your loved ones to get to you.

That was plain and clear what was going on over there with Mrs. Eagles. Satan's got a strangle hold on that friend of her son's, and the friend's a big influence on the boy. The only other link is the pure and natural feelings between a mother and her son. See how it works? But I really want to tell you about how the Lord works.

Before Earnest and me were saved, we lived for the Devil as hard as anybody ever has, drunk most of the time, a pint of Rebel Yell every other night, Wild Turkey if we could steal some mag wheels or chrome fender skirts. I could tell a lie long as from here to Biloxi, and about twice a week, Earnest would have to knock his way and mine too out of some scrap I'd get us into. Earnest Sauls is the best friend I got in this world, and back then he was the friend to have too. He's six foot one and weighs one ninety, and it's all power. Back then, no man wanted to meet up with Earnest in a dark alley. The ladies was a different thing. All that power's behind the Lord now, of course.

Now the one thing I never did, and I don't think Earnest did neither, not that he didn't get plenty of chances, was cheat on my wife. See, we were two sorry husbands of two of the best, Christ-lovingest girls in the community, and all that hell-raising would have gone on like it was going on if it hadn't been for our girls. They hung on when many a wife would have quit. But me and Earnest didn't know what we had. Finally my wife laid down the law. "It's me or the Devil," she said. "You got one week." Earnest said his wife told him just about the same thing. That was a Friday night. Me and Earnest didn't pay them one bit of mind. We went out and got drunk that very night. I saw Earnest more than my loving girl that week, but it wasn't nothing new about that. Anybody that didn't know better would have thought something funny about me and Earnest back then.

Now that's just a joke. But that son of Mrs. Eagles' and his friend, that is no kind of joke at all. There's nothing funny about that. It would be real easy to have a laugh about that and go on about your business. Some would say, what the heck, each to his own, and they're not hurting nobody. Well, the Lord don't see it that way. And they were hurting one in particular real bad. You'll see.

Now it was Saturday night, a week and a day after my wife had said what she did that I came home and found a note from her which said, "I can't have you and Jesus, and I'd rather have Jesus." Have you ever heard it put better? She's written some poems that Reverend Pate has read up in front of everybody in church. I can think of one mother's son that needs to hear an either-or something like that one.

Earnest moved in after my wife left me, and the place wasn't fit for white folks by the end of the day. Of course that was how we liked it, and it was a fine old time there for a while. Earnest is the kind of buddy you can just be with. You don't have to all the time talk junk about getting women with Earnest. A buddy like that is easy to live with. We had some laughs, and Earnest can still make me laugh. He didn't lose his funny nature when he got saved. It's a friendship we got that has held up to all kinds of tests. But that fellow and Mrs. Eagles' son, people like that just make it hard for you to have a friend. I can't laugh about them.

What is funny is how I talked against the Lord. Thought I was smarter than He is. I'd get drunk and think I was smart. Say things like "Religion has broke up many a home." It had broke up mine, hadn't it? Or, "More harm has been done in the name of Christ than in the name of the Devil," or the worst one, "It don't matter whether you are a Christian or not, long as you got a good heart, and don't hurt nobody." The Devil talking. "How long shall I bear with this evil congregation which murmur against me." Those are the Lord's words, and I can tell you the answer. Not long. The Lord got to work on me right quick. I started getting lonely. Missed my sweet girl, I reckon. I just got lower and lower. And I got something else, a funny feeling, like when you're kiting down the highway doing eighty in a fifty-five, and out of the corner of your eye you see that old blue light start to flashing through a clump of bushes at the bottom of a hill. It's just too late to slow down by then. That kind of feeling. It's funny, I didn't have no kind of interest in the good-time girls. Reverend Pate says that was just the Lord's way of wearing me down.

So then it was just me and Earnest, no sweet girls, no good-time girls even. Just me and Earnest, and I'll tell you right now Earnest just don't cut it that way. I hope you're getting used to my sense of humor. I tell you, it got so bad that one night Earnest and me waited outside the church in hopes of seeing our sweet girls. Now that was something to laugh at. There we were, like two old yard dogs, in the very place our sugars had tried to get us for years. You might not see nothing in that, but I see the Lord's hands in it. And I won't ever forget that it was Earnest that got me to go down there in the first place.

The girls came up directly and said the only way they'd even talk to us was if we'd go to the prayer meeting with them. We would have done anything by that time. We hadn't had nothing but canned stuff to eat since they left, and we were both going broke buying clean underwear. Nothing looks worse than a man in a laundromat.

Well, in we went, and to get to the point, God worked a miracle. That evening Reverend Pate preached a soul saver if I've ever heard one. I was ransomed from sin by the grace that makes you whole. Earnest gave his heart to Jesus too. Me and my sweet girl held hands in the pew.

All that was two years ago, and anybody around here can tell you I'm a happily married man now. Earnest too. But that's not the story I want to tell. That is just to point out to you that it was Satan and not the Lord that was the cause of my troubles. You see, the Lord is the answer not the question. I didn't get straight until the Lord took something away from me, until he worked through my sweet girl and through Earnest, through the people close to me. All that blaming the Lord made the crooked and evil seem more like the way to go. Out of my loss,

I was saved. It's these fine points that separate us *Bible*-believing Christians from the Methodists.

From the time it hit me, I wanted to show it to people. I started to search my heart to find a way. I asked myself, who are the ones more than likely to be mad about their situation and blame the Lord? Who would have the hardest time seeing the connection between their own lack of faith and their troubles? And just like Christ ministered to the lepers and all, I decided it was my mission to try and show this fine point of Christianity to the ones that needed to learn about it the quickest. The Lord showed me that my duty, as a Christian, lay in the cancer ward over there at Memorial. There is where I could make the biggest splash for Christ. I told Earnest about my plans, and you know what he said? He said with his muscle and my looks working for the Lord, it wouldn't be a sinner up there in Memorial inside of two weeks. Getting saved just made Earnest more fun.

We prayed about it with Reverend Pate, and with his blessing, we have taken our lunch hour every Wednesday to bring the Lord's Word, a prayer, and maybe a little hope to these poor dying men and women. And praise God, I know He will bless Earnest and me for it. Our reward will be great in Heaven, because I don't have to tell you this kind of work can get you down, down here on Earth.

But listen to me. There's Satan again, making me bellyache about doing the Lord's work. You just have to take His precious name and go about your business with a smile and a cheerful countenance, like the *Bible* says. And it helps to have a buddy like Earnest Sauls.

Anyway, we were making our rounds last Wednesday like always. We were both in a happy mood, praising the Lord and feeling like we were doing big things for Him. Earnest is real good with the sick ones. They see him bust through the door with that big old grin on his face and looking like he could take on the Army, and it's like they kind of soak up some of that power. One old fellow we had been visiting regular since we started our work had made the choice to accept Jesus Christ as his Personal Saviour. I don't have to tell you, it's times like that, makes it worth the effort for us. That man has gone on now, but it gives me a good feeling knowing that we got to him in time. Like I said, we're doing big things for Christ.

Now the next one on the list that day was Mrs. Eagles, room four twenty-four. We had run out of the pamphlets that we give, both "The Choice Is Yours" and "Whole Again." One of the nurses had wanted what we had on us, so I sent Earnest back out to my Barracuda to get some more. Well, wait a minute. I mean I asked Ernest to go get some more. You don't send Earnest Sauls nowhere he don't want to go. I gave him my keys and told him it was a case of each of the pamphlets in the boot. He said he hoped nobody he knew saw him with his hind end stuck out the trunk of a Plymouth. Earnest is a Ford man.

Now I want to tell you, that was one bad off lady. I am here to tell you she didn't look like she weighed more than a minute, and what they were pumping in her and out of her, I couldn't tell you. That woman had tubes everywhere they could find to stick one. And I got more hair on my head than she had, so you can see how bad off she was with that. But you can't look surprised when you're doing this kind of witnessing. You just keep a loving smile on your face and trust the Lord to help you do and say the right thing.

"Mrs. Eagles," I said, "how are you getting along today?"

She didn't say a word to me, just kind of groaned and stared at me with them eyes. They looked like somebody had beat her up, them eyes. Every breath that come out of her went, "Huh?" in her eyes, like somebody was asking her what she had said. Every breath was a question. You got to understand how bad off she was, because that just makes what come after harder to believe. I asked her if she belonged to any church and she swallowed real hard like she was trying to get down a pine cone.

"Presbyterian," she finally said, so low that if she hadn't been sick I'd have thought she was ashamed of it.

Now all this time I was wondering if it was any use. I figured she'd just had one of them treatments and was on some high-powered painkillers. You see, they have got to make these choices theirselves. It's too late if you try when they're half dead like the Catholics do. Well, I jumped in anyway.

"Mrs. Eagles," I said, "I want to tell you about Jesus Christ and his healing powers and how Him and us can whip Satan to win back your health." Good old Earnest come back with the literature, and I was sure glad to see him. He had both cases of pamphlets under one arm like they weren't nothing. I asked him and Mrs. Eagles if we could have a word of prayer. I prayed what I always pray for these poor folks, that the Lord will show me the way and make my words and actions what He'd have them to be. Mrs. Eagles was choking and gagging all this time, so I don't know if she heard a word of the prayer. After I finished praying, she leaned over the edge of the bed and coughed up something. After that, she eased off a little and looked towards me and smiled real weak and watery, a real loving smile just the same.

Well, I thought the Lord was working overtime that day. I thought it was going fine. Then I heard this Yankee voice behind me, and I wish I could say it just like it sounded.

"May I help you?" it said. I turned around and laid eyes on them two for the first time. Well, my first thinking was how nice they looked. They were dressed up, ties and everything. I figured they might be brothers. They looked as normal as any two men I have ever seen, equal to and better than some in my own church. I was ready to like both of them. You just would not have thought it was a thing in the world wrong with neither one of them. Now it's a hard lesson in that for you.

"May I help you," he says again and looks at me like I had just come from a hog fight. I didn't bother telling him that I got two used car lots, and Earnest holds a Seven-Eleven franchise. And think about that question he asked me. May I help you? Who could have helped who?

I said hey and told him who I was, introduced Earnest, and said we were from Calvary Church of God. I stuck out my hand. He shook it, and my hand smelled right frenchy the rest of that day. I told him we just wanted to have a word of prayer and a talk with Mrs. Eagles. I told him it wouldn't take but a minute or two. Earnest, I thank the Lord for him every day, jumps right in there.

"Ya'll boys ain't from around here, are you?" asks Earnest.

"No," says the friend. "We just arrived this morning from New York," didn't come from New York, you see, "arrived," thank you very much, "and would like to be alone with Mrs. Eagles." Then he gives Earnest a look that I believe was more than friendly.

Now right along about here I started thinking something wasn't exactly right, but I just laid it off to them being Yankees. Later on it hit me. All this time the son wasn't saying a word. I felt kind of sorry for him because you could tell it hurt him to see his mama like she was. He'd look at me and then his mama, and I thought he was going to bust. I believe if it had just been me and him he might have been glad I was there.

Oh, but that other one, he was real busy taking care of everybody. He looks me right in the eye, talks to me like he's talking to a colored man. Something in that one's eyes could just pin you down.

"As you can see, Mrs. Eagles is a very sick lady," he says. Now hadn't I been able to see that myself? "Her own minister has been around this morning and read Scriptures," I wish you could have heard the way he said Scriptures, and I can just hear the lukewarm prayer that Presbyterian slobbered over her. "We would really appreciate it if you would leave us alone."

Well, I thought to myself, it's in the *Bible*, "the fools despise wisdom and instruction."

Now right here is where a lot of people would have given up. But, I looked over at Earnest and saw him look at that one and then look back at me like as to say, "Well you know you can go one better than that," and I thought, this one is for you, bud. I mean there was Earnest, just as strong and good and trusting as they come, and there was that one looking back at Earnest, so I told that one I'd be glad to go, but I was going to leave a pamphlet with Mrs. Eagles, and I said he ought to have a look at it, too. I gave him "The Choice Is Yours." He took it from me, but he didn't look at it long enough to read the title and said for me to take it back.

I was about to get down to some serious soul-saving, but Mrs. Eagles started choking and gagging worse than ever, and the doctors and nurses come running, and we all had to leave.

Earnest and me started on down the hall to finish off our visiting, but Earnest had got real quiet. Before we come to the next one on the list, Earnest turned to me, and don't think nothing funny till I finish telling you this. He looked me full in the face, and it was like he was staring at the sunset.

"I'm mighty proud to be doing this for you," he said, and put his hand on my shoulder. The power in that hand on my shoulder, well, it must be something like that when the Lord lays His hands on you. I said yeah, that we'd been through it, hadn't we, and we went on in Mr. Raymond Bests' room, cancer in the throat.

When we come out of Mr. Bests' room we saw them two in the hall outside Mrs. Eagles' room. The doctors must have left them with real bad news because the son was leaned up against the wall with his head hung down, and he was crying. The other one was standing in front of him just talking, I thought. Then right there in front of me and Earnest, who thinks everybody is by and large good, that friend picked up Mrs. Eagles' son's chin in the tips of his fingers and kissed him full on the mouth. Well, right then the truth hit me for sure.

"Earnest, take a look and see Satan working full tilt," I said.

Earnest turned three colors of white and headed for the elevator. Something filled me up. The Lord's anger flew in me and give me strength then and there, and I knew I had to reach Mrs. Eagles one way or the other. You might say the Lord was testing me to see if I was the Christian I claimed to be. I took Earnest on home because seeing them two finished him off for that day. Sometimes Earnest just can't believe the world. I can. I knew this one was up to me alone.

I couldn't sleep that night without them two filling my dreams. I dreamed it was me in the bed with lung cancer, instead of Mrs. Eagles. I was tied down with tubes on my arms and legs and was being fed with a tube down my throat, and them two were out in the hall trying to decide whether to take all the tubes away or not.

The thought of Mrs. Eagles' last days being watched over by them sons of Satan was more than I wanted on my conscience.

I spoke to Reverend Pate about all this, and him and me decided that the Lord had laid this one on me for a reason. We prayed, and Reverend Pate gave me a little book that dealt straight out with Mrs. Eagles' problem.

Well, last Friday I got off work early, threw that book and my Bible in the front seat of my Barracuda and headed out for the hospital.

When I went into Mrs. Eagles' room, I saw just how far Satan will go. She was sitting up in the bed and looked like a May morning, color back in her cheeks, and her eyes looked like they knew what they were seeing. Somebody had tied a pretty kerchief on her head. Just like a different woman from that Wednesday before.

And whose work was all this? Sure not the Lord's. Now a week before that woman couldn't raise her head off the pillow, but she had them two there beside her keeping the Word of God well away. Satan wanted to make sure she kept on being looked after by his own. He's the one to give the credit for the improvement. Are you getting clearer on how he works now?

She looked up at me, and I could see she remembered me from the last time. I jumped right in before she could say a word.

"Mrs. Eagles," I said, "you were right bad off when I come by the last time, but I wanted to come back and give you this little book. It's called *Satan's Handmaidens*, and it's about people like your son and his friend and the Lord's view of their sin. I believe if you read this and pray on it, you'll see what's the very reason you're sick in the first place. I believe, like I believe in the Lord, that your health problems are God's way of punishing you and your family. With the Lord's help, you can beat Satan and turn your health around, permanent."

She took that little book out of my hand and stared at it, didn't open it, just stared at the cover, like not really seeing it, you know. She looked up at me after a minute, and great big tears come up in her eyes and didn't fall, you know, just filled up her eyes and kind of floated there. She looked at the book and didn't look at it, looked at me but wasn't seeing me. Then she did see me all of a sudden. Her tears come down like I never seen anybody's, and I believe it was right at that moment she was saved. Yes, I've seen this thing many a time and know it when I see it.

"Oh God, Mister. Do you know what to do? What can I do? What can I do to make it right?"

"Home free!" I says to myself. Then, I bore down. "Pray to the Lord God your Savior, Mrs. Eagles. Pray to Him who gave you life. Let the Lord have it. Give Him your son; give Him your cancer. Give it all to the Lord Great God Jehovah."

"Pray for me. You pray for me," she said and grabbed hold to both of my hands so tight and held on and wouldn't let go, like I was in this world, and she was slipping into the next, and the only thing between her and Satan was me. I was the only thing. So I held on, and I prayed.

"Lord, You have seen the suffering of Mrs. Eagles. Lord, You have heard her cries of pain. You have watched her nights of torment and sorrow. Lord, You have known Mrs. Eagles' burden of sickness, the sickness in her, and You have known a bigger sickness, a sickness of sin in her son. Lord, Mrs. Eagles is calling out to You now. She knows her part in this, Lord, and knows her punishment was just. But Lord, she's ready to turn all that around, Lord. She's ready for You to take over her life, Lord. She's ready to give her life over and let You use it. Use her life, Lord. Use her life to save her son. Get to her through her suffering, Lord. Get to her son through her life, Lord, and when that's done, give her life back to her whole and new. When she takes out that cancer in her son, You take the

one in her, Lord. She knows You can do it, Lord. She belongs
to You. In Jesus's name I pray and believe. Amen."

We both sat there for a minute and didn't say a word. I felt
like I had run a race. She looked tired, too.

"Amen," she says. "But, God, I've got to tell you. My chest
is killing me."

I said, "Mrs. Eagles, that's just Satan closing up shop."

"You are the first one that could do something," she says.

Now what happened with me and Mrs. Eagles just shows
you. Satan is working in this world. But we got to work harder
than him. That's all the Lord asks of you. I saw in the *Daily
Times* this morning where Mrs. Eagles passed away. She didn't
never see that boy again, I don't imagine, but she died a
Christian. You might think that's it, that Satan has quit on this
one. Well, I know better, and the Lord hasn't let her off yet. I
know where the funeral is. Her son wouldn't stay away from
his own mama's funeral, would he? Earnest says he wants to go
with me for the boy. You got to stay one step ahead of Satan all
the time, you see. You just got to.

NOBODY'S CHILD

• DAVID GROFF •

PAUL LIKED ANNIE because she was so annoying. The night Jeremy was born, over eight years ago, Annie's husband Ted was away in Miami and Annie had gone into labor on the East 77th Street subway platform. She had insisted on waiting for the next train. Paul had to prod her forcibly up the stairs and into a taxi. Just as they pulled up to St. Vincent's, her water broke; once she caught her breath, Annie squealed with delight at Paul's wet gabardine pants. In the four years since Annie's divorce, she saw Paul or phoned him nearly every day. Often Annie would surprise him late at night by ringing his doorbell, with or without Jeremy beside her, full of indignation or joy over a man, a movie, or a taxi driver. Against his better judgment Paul had found he was as comfortable with Annie as he could be with anyone. She had lost weight recently and had just cut her curly hair so that it barely grazed her shoulders.

Tonight she was, as usual, disgusted with him. "Paul, without a doubt the stupidest thing you've ever done was to dump Everett. In the last ten years you've had more boys than I've had menstrual cramps, and the only one who wasn't a loser was Everett. If there were a law against being an asshole you'd be serving a life sentence."

Paul looked around to see if anyone had overheard her, but the coffee shop was nearly empty: Three tables away a man held his infant son in his lap, feeding him a bottle and reading the *Wall Street Journal*. "Everett is ordinary, sweetheart," Paul said, without moving his teeth. "He's a bartender. He sniffles. How can you take out a mortgage with a man who sniffles? How can you love somebody with a wet mustache?"

Sometimes Paul could deflect Annie's pastoral letter by being funny. Annie did not laugh. She pressed her tea bag into her spoon and watched it drip into her cup. "Did you listen to him?"

"Of course I listened to him."

"That night at dinner you sat there and tore up matchbooks and looked like you wanted to vaporize him," Annie said. "Is that how you listen?"

"Well if the guy had said anything interesting beyond the wholesale price of Miller Lite—"

"You ought to get him some nose spray and invite him to the ballet. He seemed so sturdy."

"How's Jeremy?"

"Don't change the subject. Jeremy hates Cub Scouts. He's started throwing up whenever Ted comes over to take him out."

"The boy has taste," Paul said, lighting one of Annie's cigarettes.

"You ought to come over and read to him. Jeremy likes you. And if you're not serious with Everett"—Paul could hear one of Annie's ideas rearing its head—"you ought to take out a personal ad." Annie stared directly at him, appraising. "Thoughtful, balding, dissolute librarian, 34, seeks true love, no strings. I'll screen out the disco bunnies and the leather queens. Why was it exactly that you dumped Everett?"

"Jesus, Annie, we had five dates! What are you, the Justice Department? Why must you make a Broadway musical out of my personal life? I'm perfectly capable . . . I can run my own romances, thank you."

"Yeah, like the romance with the guy from the Five Towns

who had four daughters and a wife and a grandson? You ran *that* superbly."

Paul stubbed out his cigarette. "That was six years ago. I was young then."

"Or the kid who was kept by the psychiatrist on 72nd Street? *That* was January!"

"Well at least I didn't sleep with a stewardess in my wife's own apartment, like adorable Ted." Paul knew that comment would close this portion of the conversation.

Annie cocked her head and looked at him through only one eye. She took a deep, tragic breath. "Well, okay, if you're going to be neurotic about it." Grandly she pulled her cigarettes off the table, shrugged her purse onto her shoulder, straightened her bra strap, and stood up. "I know when my good advice isn't wanted." She swept out of the coffee shop, all flounced skirt, purse, and wild hair. Even after ten years Paul could never quite tell when she was kidding.

Annie called him at work two days later, which meant that all was forgiven or forgotten. Paul disliked it when she phoned the library because she could talk and do her ad layouts at the same time, but Paul needed absolute silence.

"Paul, I went to the doctor today."

"What did he say?"

"*She.*"

"What did *she* say?"

"Can you come over tonight? I'll make some macaroni and cheese."

The weather had suddenly turned hot and even the clean streets of the East Seventies seemed soft and gritty. Jeremy opened the apartment door and broke into a smile. Paul looked past him to where Annie sat smoking by the window overlooking the airshaft. A single beam of late-afternoon sunlight fell across her neck and down one arm; she looked like a Rossetti model, Paul thought, with that halo of frizzy hair. The studio was crowded with furniture: Jeremy's bed, which doubled as a sofa, covered by an orange patchwork quilt; a drafting table; three red hooked rugs; and two overstuffed chairs Annie had dragged from a dumpster over at Sloan-Kettering. Annie slept in an alcove between the kitchen and the bathroom. On a bureau with its bottom drawer missing sat Jeremy's model airplanes, painted red and green, mottled with glue. Paul always felt at once oppressed and excited when he visited Annie. Her life here was so dense.

"Jeremy, my boy, how goes it?"

"Hi, Paul," he said shyly.

Jeremy was not an appealing child. There was something misshapen about him, as if he still suffered from his struggle out of the birth canal. The boy's hair was dull brown, spikey, and his face was long and pointed at the chin, like an old man's. Over the past few months Paul had observed Jeremy's teeth grow in dramatically crooked; they rested on his lower lip in a rabbity way, so that he always appeared on the verge of tears. Sometimes, when Jeremy giggled, Paul could see the shadow of Ted's good looks cross the boy's face. But most of the time Jeremy made him slightly ill.

"How's school?" Paul asked, watching Annie. She lit another cigarette and gazed into the airshaft.

"School's out."

"Oh."

"But Mom has me in the day camp. Wait, I made you something." Jeremy ran into Annie's bedroom and seconds later reappeared, holding something made of brown cardboard and lots of tape, with a sticky star of glitter and glue on one side.

"You made this?" Paul turned it over in his hands.

"Uh-huh. It took two days. Keep it," Jeremy said, "and use it."

"What do I use it for?"

Jeremy looked confused. "It's a wallet. See? You put your credit cards in this slot and your money goes back here. But don't use it in the rain. It's just cardboard."

"Well, thanks, pilot. That's a nice gift." Paul patted the boy's shoulder.

"I'm making Mom a potholder," Jeremy whispered.

"Jere?" Annie said. "I need to talk to your friend for a while. Could you go play in the hall?"

"Okay." Jeremy picked up one of his planes. Paul could hear how sticky it was.

"And don't push the elevator buttons!" Annie shouted as he shut the door. She turned to Paul. "So did you call Everett?"

"Annie my sweet, no matter how much you badger me, I'm not going to call dear old Everett. He and I are not a marriage made in heaven. I saw the man only four times, and besides, I am emotionally espoused to a woman who lives beyond her means on the Upper East Side, a sixties holdover named Annie Kolwicki."

"I just thought he was gentle," Annie said. "He could have been good for you. I think you could do him justice if you tried."

"What did the doctor say?"

"What I mean is, it's time you found a nice boy and settled down."

"You sound like your mother. Why did you go to the doctor?"

Annie sighed. She leaned over and put out her cigarette. "I have another lump in my right breast."

"But you've had them before. Cysts." Paul looked over her body. It seemed the same to him: heavy and fertile, restless but solid.

"This one's big. The doctor wants me to go to St. Vincent's for a biopsy on Sunday."

They could hear Jeremy making airplane noises in the hall. "Have you told him?" Paul asked.

"Tonight. I'll have him stay with my mother. He'll probably come back sixty percent polyester."

The apartment was murderously hot; Paul was sweating into the sleeves of his silk sports coat and Annie was sweating too. He looked at her closely, focusing on the strip of white scalp at the part in her hair, and sat down beside her. "Lots of women get this. It's not going to be a big deal," he said "And it's treatable. And I love you."

"I just hate it when everything gets so complicated."

"So do I."

After dinner Paul thanked Jeremy for the wallet, kissed Annie hard and told her to call him in the morning, and then took a cab to his favorite bar in the Village, the Alibi. The red track lights and cinnamon-colored walls gave everyone a ruddy, unnaturally youthful glow that Paul very much appreciated. And the place was blessedly cool. He ordered a scotch, bought cigarettes—it seemed necessary to smoke in a place like this—and went to stand beside one of the video screens.

After three gulps of his drink he shut his eyes and saw Annie's face, and Jeremy's, the identical beads of perspiration that had dampened Annie's bangs and made Jeremy shine like a fish. He ought to buy them gifts, he thought, maybe a robe for Annie and a ready-made plane for Jeremy. No, something impractical and bizarre for Annie, like a black lace bra. Embarrassment swept over him; not a bra. He opened his eyes, shook his head free, and straightened his spine as he looked at the other men.

It was a challenge here, or at Everett's bar down the street, to capture anyone's gaze. Paul took Jeremy's cardboard wallet from his briefcase and began examining it. By the end of his drink he noticed a gray-haired man in a business suit start to smile at him.

His name was Matthew. "I like your wallet," Matthew said. His eyes were green. So was his tie.

"The son of one of my friends made it for me in day care. I'm not supposed to carry it in the rain." Paul smiled.

Matthew smiled. "My daughter used to make me things like that. Potholders, pencil boxes, a shaving kit."

Matthew had three daughters, Alice, aged fourteen, and twins who were ten. He had been divorced eight years ago, moved to New York from Louisville, and now worked for a law firm specializing in real estate. He had just come from the gym.

Paul seldom took anyone back to his own apartment. He liked finding out about someone by looking at his books and albums. They took the Fourteenth Street subway line across town to Matthew's place—which was a mistake, since Paul despised subways, but Matthew was oddly insistent. His apartment was large and expensive. Paul was appalled at how the place was furnished—in heavy, dark Biedermeier with silk flowers everywhere in little silver or cut-glass vases. A polar bear fur covered the bed.

Their sex was not especially successful, although it was rule-book safe. Matthew kept on talking: about his apartment, his job, and Paul's skin, which he said was lovely and reminded him of his last lover's skin. His last lover had just moved in with a younger man. To keep Matthew quiet, Paul had to kiss him. But Matthew did have an elegant chest, with thick gray hair. Afterward, they exchanged phone numbers, and Paul took a cab home. As he paid the driver, two things occurred to him: first, that Annie would not approve of Matthew or his polar bear or his preoccupation with his former lover; and second, that curiosity, just as much as lust, had made him go home with Matthew. He had mostly wanted to see him naked. These days, that seemed mostly what he wanted. To see a man naked, and to be held by him.

"I've fallen in love with Doctor DeWitt," Annie had announced the night before the biopsy. The surgeon had colored slightly and smiled at Paul as he left the room. He was obviously gay; his mustache had given him away. Annie had never been good at separating gays from straights, which had led to more than one annoyed late-night phone call.

Doctor DeWitt's biopsy on Monday showed that the lump was malignant, and the breast and lymph nodes were removed. Annie hadn't wanted Paul or Jeremy to visit her after the operation. "I look like the fall of Saigon," she said over the phone.

Now Annie was lying on Jeremy's bed, the orange quilt pulled up to her chin. Her face was ashen and her hair was unwashed, pulled back harshly from her forehead. For the first time she looked older than Paul did. "How are you feeling?"

he asked. He had a hard time meeting her eyes. Somehow she made the room close and completely stationary, just by lying there.

"Still stunned. Listen, Jeremy's coming back today with my mother. I couldn't stand to let her have him anymore. Ted's going to take him tomorrow through Friday night, but he's got a stewardess to seduce over the weekend, and I need to know if you can do something with him on Saturday. Otherwise, he'll go stir-crazy."

"Sure. There's a new drag show at the Garterbelt. How's Doctor DeWitt?"

"Gay."

Paul heard a key in the lock, and Annie's mother appeared, holding Jeremy by the hand.

"A party!" Annie cried. "The wicked witch of the west and my favorite munchkin!" With her left arm she pulled herself up and Paul saw the flat padded bandage beneath her nightgown.

"Annie dear, all this company at once . . . hello, Paul," Mrs. Kolwicki said, dismally. She put down her purse and let go of Jeremy. Her hair was a new shade of red that made Paul squint with dismay.

Jeremy looked quickly at his mother and then turned around. "Hi, Paul," he said, half-smiling up at him.

"Hey, pilot. How was New Jersey?"

"He was an angel," Mrs. Kolwicki said to Annie. "I just wish he would play outside more. He needs more sun—he's a ghost. How are you feeling? You look better than I expected."

"I'm just ducky. Come here, you beautiful boy, and give your sick old mom a kiss."

Jeremy went over and touched his teeth to his mother's eyebrow. Paul saw the boy's eyes drop to the strip of bandage taped to the hollow of her neck. Jeremy whitened. Annie held him by the shoulders and looked into his face, as if to make sure he was still the same boy. Jeremy's jaw jutted out a little; he stepped back out of her arms.

"You shouldn't leave the door open like this," Paul heard a voice say. "I could be anybody." Ted stood just inside the apartment, carrying a leather briefcase and looking blonder than Paul remembered. He strode over to Annie, bent to kiss her on the lips, and then stood up straight, looking her over.

"Go on," Annie said. "Try to think of something appropriate to say."

"How are you feeling?"

"Everybody asks me that. You never were very original, Ted. I'm fine, considering I'm an instant Amazon."

Ted smiled his trademark smile, which had nothing to do with his eyes; they remained as wary as Jeremy's. Ted was a series of well-ordered motors, Paul thought, like the engines of the jets he sold; he seemed like a plane that had touched down briefly between destinations. Ted swept Jeremy up in his big hands, holding the boy under his armpits until Jeremy looked him straight in the eye. The boy's sneakers kicked feebly. "How's my big guy?"

"Fine."

"Good." He put him down. "You're heavier. We're going to have a good time this week." He faced Paul, and his mouth got serious. "Hi, trooper. I can't tell you how grateful I am that you've been here for Annie. How have you been holding up? How's tricks?"

Annie snickered. Ted had left her four years ago, explaining himself in a note Annie and Paul had found taped to the TV screen when they came back from a movie. "Mostly good," Paul said. "How was Florida?"

"Dallas. It was good. Annie, I'm sorry, I'm really sorry, but it turns out I'm flying out Thursday, so I'll have to give you Jeremy a day early."

"Are you flying Trixie or Wendy?"

"You never quit, do you?"

Mrs. Kolwicki had been looking in the refrigerator. "Jeremy's going to be hungry, so I'm heading out to that grocery." She looked at Ted nervously. "I hope you'll stay for dinner, Ted."

"Thanks, Tanya, but I just don't think I can."

Mrs. Kolwicki seemed disappointed. She picked up her purse and opened it. "I got this from Beverly Novak," she said to

Annie, pulling out something that looked like the Land's End catalog. She looked at Ted. "Prosthesis," she whispered.

With one quick motion Annie pushed the catalog off the bed. Paul watched her face bunch up. "I'm not going to get one."

"What?"

"I'm not going to get one!"

"Annie—" Ted began.

"Jeremy, go out in the hall and shut the door."

When she heard the door slam, Annie opened her eyes. "I am not going to spend the rest of my life strapped to a piece of plastic. It may be right for some women but it's not right for me. It's silly and it's demeaning and I'm *not* going to do it."

"We don't have to talk about it now," Ted said.

"We don't have to talk about it *ever*! Why don't you all get out and let me alone for a while?"

"I will *never* understand how you think," Mrs. Kolwicki muttered. She straightened her blouse, swept up her purse, and opened the door.

Ted kissed Annie's forehead. "I'll call you tonight, muffin."

"I'm leaving too," Paul said once Ted shut the door. "I'll come back when that creep isn't here."

"Ted's not so bad. He's just an irresponsible stud. It's my mother that drives me crazy." Annie watched herself finger the quilt. "What do you think? Should I get a tit?"

"It's too soon to think about that."

Annie looked up at him sharply. Her eyes narrowed. "You prick," she said, with real anger.

Paul kissed her and started for the door.

"Paul."

"Yes?"

"Why the fuck haven't you seen Everett? He's a nice boy and you're just being a stubborn goddamn prima donna asshole. As per usual." Annie slid further under the covers, pushing her lower lip out in a pout that made her look like a nastier version of Jeremy. "I want you to call him tonight. Don't come back here until you've called him. If you don't call him you're as much of a mule as Ted."

Paul's chest tightened. "Relax, get some sleep. I'll call you tomorrow."

"It's the least you could do."

Paul shut the door behind him, hard.

Jeremy sat cross-legged in the hall, lining up Popsicle sticks in some intricate pattern. He had taken off his shirt and looked like a miniature Gandhi. "Hi, Paul," he said, brightening. He stood up.

"Hello, Jeremy."

"Mom said over the phone you're taking me on Saturday."

"Right."

"I'm always glad to see you," Jeremy said formally. He looked down at his sneakers. One was untied. Paul pressed the elevator button.

"Paul?"

"Yes."

"Is my mother going to die?"

"No, of course not." Paul pressed the button again.

"Paul, can I ask you something?"

"What?"

"Will you kiss me?"

Paul turned and looked down at the boy. Jeremy was smiling hopefully, his upper teeth resting on his lower lip. Paul thought of Annie inside, her right arm motionless on the quilt. He took a deep breath. "Sure, Jeremy."

He bent over and kissed the boy's warm forehead. Jeremy's smile widened.

"Mom said you liked to kiss boys."

Paul's knees went weak. "Go inside and wait for your grandmother." The elevator door opened and he stepped inside. "And, Jeremy?"

"Yes, Paul?"

"Tell your mother she was wrong."

Jeremy's smile vanished and the door shut.

Matthew called that night and Paul told him he had a lover he hadn't mentioned. Annie called Paul at work the next morning to ask if he had called Everett; when Paul said no, she hung up.

When he appeared at her door on Saturday morning to pick up Jeremy, she was only a little more pleasant. "I itch," she said. With her right arm in a sling she was standing at the sink repotting an aloe plant. Soil was spilled over the counter in little mounds. Her mother sat on Jeremy's bed, filling out a lottery ticket. Mrs. Kolwicki told him that Jeremy had spent Wednesday evening with Ted at Kennedy Airport. After eating two hot dogs he had thrown up on Ted's shoes. Ted had not been pleased. "Don't feed him anything fatty," she warned.

Jeremy wouldn't say more than a syllable to Paul. They went to Central Park, to the zoo, but it was closed for renovation. The two of them looked at the empty cages for a while and then walked up to the giant mushroom where Alice romped in bronze with her Wonderland friends. Jeremy stared at them gravely, as if the figures could suddenly, unpleasantly, come to life. At the edge of the Park they watched a juggler handle three burning torches, swinging them above his head and between his legs. Paul was annoyed that anyone would do something so foolhardy, even for money. Once the juggler dropped a torch at his feet but in one graceful motion swept it up and stepped on a firey leaf. Jeremy shivered and turned to grin at Paul, but caught himself. When the juggler took his bows, the boy squirmed to the front of the crowd and solemnly knelt to place a quarter in the man's suitcase. The juggler winked at him and Jeremy smiled back, his eyes alight and his teeth exposed.

By noon Paul's feet ached. It was deadly hot. They bought hamburgers and soft pretzels in the park and Jeremy threw up with conviction on Paul's shoulder bag.

Paul brought him a ready-made model airplane at F.A.O. Schwarz. He tried telling Jeremy some of the cleaner Bette Midler jokes he knew, but Jeremy only listened. At dinnertime they walked glumly back uptown; Jeremy held the plane listlessly by one wing.

"And how are my two big boys?" Annie asked as she opened the door.

Paul and Jeremy looked at each other silently.

"Everett," Annie murmured sweetly as she kissed Paul good night. She had made him stay for take-out Chinese and chatted constantly through dinner, as if by shepherding her son through a Saturday Paul had performed his penance for ignoring her advice. Mrs. Kolwicki conspicuously regarded the evening news. Annie, in spite of her animation, looked desperately tired. She ate nothing. Paul had never noticed her cheekbones before, or the lines that came down from her ears to the first line in her neck. He would have to get used to the new way she carried herself, with her chest thrust out on the right side, as if balance were something she had to think about now. Over the past weeks Paul had become more practiced at watching faces and bodies: He could estimate now how all of them—Annie, Ted, Everett, Paul himself—would look in twenty years.

That night in his apartment in Chelsea, Paul put the Doors on the stereo and looked at himself in the mirror. Pouring himself a scotch, he wondered about Matthew's daughters— what they looked like, what they thought of their father and his silk flowers. He thought about Everett. He had seen Everett the week before, leaving the bar he owned on Greenwich Avenue; he had recognized Everett's shoulders and remembered the freckles on his back. Everett had a salt-and-ginger mustache that Paul had liked. He considered calling Everett, but decided not to. Too much time had gone by. It wasn't often, though, in these last few years, that he had dated someone nine times.

The summer was the hottest Paul could remember. The streets seemed to glow with perspiration and the Puerto Rican construction workers walked shirtless down Fifth Avenue past Paul's library window.

Mrs. Kolwicki had gone back to Keansburg, New Jersey, and now took the bus up only on weekends. Annie had gone back to work part-time, belligerently wearing her silk blouse without a bra. "This way they won't have to strain their eyes," she said. In early August Ted announced he was taking a job in

San Diego; he wanted Jeremy to visit for Labor Day, if he could get the boy a free flight.

During the last week in August Paul flew up to a resort near Bar Harbor and met two men. One turned out to have a lover in the next room: "We took separate rooms so we could have our own adventures," Paul was told. He went sailing with a physician named Michael who was fifty, trim, and weatherbeaten. Michael had invited him to fly out to Lansing for Thanksgiving.

The day after Paul got back, Annie invited him over. When she opened the door, Paul saw Jeremy playing with the airplane from F.A.O. Schwarz. Jeremy put it down guiltily.

"Coffee?" Annie asked. "Or Valium?"

"Scotch, please." Paul took off his jacket, poured them both drinks, and sat down on Jeremy's bed while Annie took off her sandals and put on the ruby-colored ballet slippers Paul had given her that spring. He reached over and turned on the air conditioner.

"Jeremy—" Annie said.

"I know. Go play in the hall."

Annie laughed. She closed the door behind him and locked it; with her back pressed against the jamb, she grinned at Paul. "At last, I've got you alone, you beautiful man."

"Are you going to ravish me?"

"You bet. How was your trip? Are you married now?"

"No, but I had a good time."

"What a shame." Annie picked up her drink and sat down on the bed. "It's recurred in the scar."

She lit a cigarette, handed it to Paul, and lit another for herself. "What now?" Paul asked, finally.

"Chemotherapy. I found out last week while you were away. The worst part so far is that my armpit hair has fallen out. It had just been growing in again. Plus, I want to throw up all the time, like Jeremy."

Paul felt his hands start to shake. The air conditioner blew against his ear.

"So what do you think?"

He made himself look into Annie's eyes. "What can I do for you?"

"Be friendly, let me cry on your shoulder once in a while."

"Let's eat out—just you and me."

"I'm not hungry. And what about Jeremy?"

"We should do *something* tonight."

They were quiet for a while. Annie stubbed out her cigarette and took the butt from Paul's hand. "You know, lots of young people die all the time—wars, floods, famine, AIDS. You could die, too."

"That's silly." Paul stood up.

"Of course you could. You're as mortal as the rest of us."

"I mean you shouldn't think like that."

"Sooner or later I'll shuffle out. And I want to talk to you about Jeremy."

"We should all go to a movie."

"I want you to take Jeremy."

Paul went cold.

"In the event of my death, I want you to be Jeremy's legal guardian. I'm going to write it into my will tomorrow."

"Annie, I don't think—"

"No, we can't talk about it later. You always avoid things." Annie's mouth was tight.

"But Ted," Paul said feebly. "Or your mother." He felt himself sink into a chair. A picture flashed into his mind of Annie's apartment empty of its rugs and plants—and of endless days in Central Park with Jeremy's hot hand limp in his.

"My mother's a fool. She's old, she wants to move to Florida, she watches too much television. Jeremy cries before she comes to visit. I don't want Ted to have him. And Ted doesn't want him."

"Annie—"

"I don't think you like Jeremy very much."

"Of course I do."

"He's a very difficult boy to love. He's ugly. He picks his nose. I'm not even sure he's smart, although he may be. He's been through a lot. Ted never wanted him; I think he would have preferred a dog."

"But Jeremy won't even talk to me!"

"I mentioned this to Ted before he left for San Diego," Annie continued. She poured herself another drink. "I've never seen such relief on a grown man's face. I'll get him to give you child support, in return for visitation rights, and I've got a college fund for Jeremy. Now I still have to talk to my mother. She'll bitch and moan and complain about you, but she'll be putty in our hands."

"Annie, *no!*"

Paul felt his sweat trickle into his mouth.

"No what?" Annie said.

"No you're not going to die."

"You mean, no you don't want Jeremy."

"Annie, I'm a certified all-American homosexual. I'm nobody's father—I sleep around, I've got a small apartment. Jesus Christ, I have friends who wear dresses!"

"As far as the apartment is concerned, you should move in here so Jeremy can stay as P.S. 31—and if Jeremy is going to wear dresses, he's going to wear dresses. You're a good man. You can be dippy sometimes, and I'm not sure you know what you want your life to be, but you're basically a good man. Jeremy loves you."

Paul stared at his knuckles; they were the color of paste. "I don't love Jeremy."

"You will, after a while. He grows on you, like athlete's foot. Besides, you need him. He'll do you good, loosen you up. He'll keep you out of the bars. You're too old for that anyway." She stood up. "So will you take Jeremy? I know this is all sort of sudden—"

"No!" Paul banged his drink down on the table. "No, you're not going to die, and no I'm not going to take Jeremy!" He walked dizzily toward Annie. The room seemed smaller, all color.

"Damn it, Paul, do you think I want to? Do you think—"

"Put him up for adoption."

Annie gasped.

"Put him up for adoption. Get Ted to surrender custody and talk to an agency. He'll get a good home, with plenty of money and freedom, two parents. He's white—"

Annie began to cry in thick sobs that exploded from her chest. She sat on Jeremy's bed and pushed her hair into her face.

"Annie."

"Get out."

Paul touched her hair and she pulled away. "Get out."

Taking his jacket, he walked like a drunk man to the door, but it wouldn't open at first; he panicked and fumbled for the lock. As soon as the door shut behind him he started to cry. He felt the hiccup in his shoulders and he could barely see.

Jeremy didn't hear him. He had his arms outstretched and he was making airplane noises, swooping toward the elevator door and swerving up and out just in time to avoid crashing his head against the wall. His lips sputtered. Sweat glistened on the back of his neck and his hair was wet. With his knees bent, he started to dive toward the ground and then, seeing Paul, he stopped sharply, almost losing his balance, but not quite.

"You're crying."

"Uh-huh."

"What's wrong?" Jeremy looked suspicious then curious.

"Nothing."

"Liar." Jeremy hesitated a second, cocked his head, and then took Paul's hand. "Sit down," he said, pointing to the cigarette urn. Paul sank down on top of it. Jeremy was blurry before him, but Paul could see that the boy was smiling his little rabbity smile, the smile he had given to the juggler. "Now tell me," Jeremy said. "What's wrong?"

ONCE IN SYRACUSE

• DAVID BRENDAN HOPES •

I WENT SLINKING nights to Clinton Station, singing to the warped tracks, "Like a Rolling Stone," to make myself feel cold and forlorn. I took my leisure when the downtown stores closed and the down-eyed walkers emerged and the nighthawks set to hunting around the sky-high neon. I flattened against walls at the purr of the approaching police car. I joined dazed souls wandering between Clinton and the Park, seeking nothing in particular, seeking anything misplaced or forgotten in the frowsy dark. I learned which mean drunk to steer clear of. I learned which alley was safe, which back door left open. If I had known what I wanted I might have known where to look. But I walked, night after night. I lounged on glassy walls, poked into grates, nosed the trash of courtyards, listened at cracked windows, prowled parks and streetglared plazas, through radical night.

Cops must have thought I was hustler long before I was. I don't know what the hustlers thought at first, but they saw me watch them. I learned their feint-dance to the tentative car doors. I learned their slouch and swagger, how they machoed protectively when the streets were empty and they were thrown back lonely on each other. I learned the moves. I was good, and when it was for real the cops never saw me. Cars stopped. *Need a ride?* I'd shrug, look bored, get in. They drove for a while, feeling me out to see if I were a cop or a crazy, and I them. They stopped in the shadow of a building, or in an open parking lot where you could see trouble coming a long way. Touch me. Suck and nuzzle, I kicking the floor and arching my back against the seat. They took me to the Baths over Dunkin' Donuts. Dark and stench, men supine in tiny rooms, waiting, the dim light turning flesh to wax and corpse. They'd lay me down. Crushed, smothered, wanting more. I heard a voice groaning in the salt and heat, and it was mine. At morning, light lay on Warren Street, pristine, accusative. You'd look both ways at the door to make sure nobody would see you leaving.

I had a girl friend then. She didn't ask what I was doing because she knew. Her marvelous self-confidence would not permit even a moment's jealousy. It was something I had to get out of my system. She was certain that when I had sampled it all I would see what was better and return to her, so lovely. In a perfect world she would have been right.

I knew the major cruise bar long before I dared to enter. Yet could one simply walk in? Was there a membership ritual? A card? A password? Once admitted, what did you say? I practiced "gin and tonic" in the shadow of the Dunkin' Donuts until it had an easy, familiar ring. I would say "gin and tonic." Just here for a drink. They might think I had come by accident. If it were horrible I would turn and go. If it were horrible enough perhaps it would shock me normal. I might have deliberated forever if it hadn't been for the cop cars passing, slower each time they cruised my corner and saw I hadn't moved, if it hadn't been for the whores asking every five minutes, each time with greater vehemence, if I didn't need a date. I filled my lungs, ran Warren Street, let that mysterious door click shut behind me.

Men danced on an elevated platform caught in a crossfire of strobes. The air was hot and tinctured with a clash of colognes and piss and old beer. A bartender in beard and pearls asked

me what my pleasure was, and, although I don't remember
uttering a syllable, a gin and tonic wafted through the smoke
into my hands. The tonic gleamed with black light. My shirt
was a purple conflagration. I had never seen that before, and I
took it for a baroque and peacock omen. The bartender put his
mouth to my ear and said, "This one's on us, honey. Relax and
enjoy. We are fam-i-lee."

I relaxed and enjoyed.

In succeeding months I ran at rolling boil. I was consuming
fire. In one week I slept alone one night and in ten other weeks
not at all. I stopped keeping track. I would leave one asleep in
his bed and crawl out into the wee-hours streets cruising for
another. Usually I made them take me to their place, but if that
were impossible and the weather was not right for the bushes of
Thornden Hill, I brought them home humping and groaning in
my room until the spent sleep of morning.

I saw in the bar mirrors that I was golden. Men said, "There's
nobody in the bar like you," and I believed them. I perched on
my stool, legs spread, looking bored and sexy, waiting. And I
met August.

I have given up trying to imagine what August thought first
seeing me. In memory what I thought at that instant was
beautiful! What I tasted was longing. What I saw was a face
thin and angular, the effect refinement rather than emaciation.
It tapered severely toward the mouth, its one weak feature.
High Inca cheekbones. Skin coppery under curled hair that
seemed sometimes silvery, sometimes jet black. The blue eyes
shown huge and luminous, their blueness the more striking for
being housed in that Minoan face. A scar like a tiny lightning
bolt divided the right eyebrow. Around him stirred a scent of
spice. Without realizing what I did, I leaned in to smell the
spice. He touched my face to welcome me.

Never had I felt more beautiful. We met at the theater bar
when he was starring in a bad production of a bad Albee,
without distinction other than the melancholy grace with which
he moved amid the disaster. His social smile altered to surprise,
then delight, then a multivalent seductiveness calculated to

suggest at once the Marlboro Man and the coquette. His facility of expression confused me. Such openness could belong either to a whore or a naif. Of course it was a performance, but anyone who has ever performed knows that to "perform" at moments of high emotion does not necessarily imply insincerity, but the desire that appearance might duplicate passion. I stared. He stared back. He looked like a man turning a diamond over in his hand before naming a price.

August asked the barmaid for a pen. He wrote a note on a cocktail napkin. He folded, gave it to me, telling me not to open it until he was gone.

When he had swept through the door I opened it. It read just, *Midnight*. I knew where. Of all the assignation bars along Warren Street, to only one would you be drawn by the single word *midnight* on a cocktail napkin.

As I hustled to the Bunkhouse I checked my look in the back store window. I was all right. I was golden. The whores knew me by then and let me know with their eyes whether the streets were safe. Andi swayed on her stilettos in the flower dress that meated her bones. She lifted her eyes up and to her right. *OK, CD. Copless. Sultry. Can't talk now, risk losing the john in the red Camaro. Everything copasetic.*

I pushed back the Bunkhouse door, let it swing shut in a slow arc. The visible thing inside was August, a pale flame, imperial, drawing light from around and concentrating it in himself, bent over a sparkling drink at the bar. He was dressed all in white. Maybe there were other colors, but I saw only the white of August in the dark of everything. His belt studded with polished metal glinted like mirrors in the barlight. I felt myself breathing hard, as though I had run a long way. A man stood beside him, with his hand looped in the mirror belt. But August was not looking at him. August was looking at me.

I strutted to his side. I lifted my hand to touch him. His escort's hand met mine midair. He moved to stand between August and me. He said, "Can I help you?"

"Yes," I said, "you can get out of my way."

Maybe it was August's dancing on the strobe-lit disco floor, shifting and weaving with black-lit tonic in his hand, the gas-blue whiteness of his shirt. Maybe it was the fire when we danced that first or any time, when in the world there were two dancers, dark wings of sweat across our backs, angels stigmataed by sweat and liquor in the smoky light. There was nobody like us. Maybe I loved him for the eyes that hooked us from the shadows when we danced, eyes that loved and wanted us as daily men are never loved and wanted. We were antelope and crane, steel gear, white silk. We stole something from the night beyond the room, something from the real stars the bar light mocked. The Dance came in, drumming through our feet as the disco one/two thumped out against the trash street. Had it been just love I could have ridden it better, survived unscathed as I had survived before, or at worst wept bitterly with my knuckles in my teeth a night or two and been at peace. But he was not another pick-up, not another man. He was the first Lover. Whatever man he was already counted less, was already forgotten.

August's escort laughed. He stopped laughing when August pushed past him into my embrace. I saw the man's face twist with loss. I wanted to touch him. I wanted to say I was sorry, but I wasn't; I was exultant; I was sick to my guts with exultation and triumph and fear. August breathed to me, "Let's dance," and we danced, hard, hot, so the men backed against the wall clapping rhythmically, shouting Go! into the smoky strobes. When we were done, we turned our backs like gods done with god-ing for the night.

August waved down a cab on Warren Street and took me to his apartment. I remember shying from him, because of the driver, but the driver was his regular and had seen everything, and August's tongue moved on my neck. I wrestled him to the floor just inside his vestibule, unable to wait, unable to get close enough no matter how I gathered him in. August laughed, high and clear. I've always hated screamers, but I heard myself screaming. His blue eyes floated over mine, sweat bright on his face in the candlelight, the black hair curled with damp on the back of his neck. A cloud of spice. I ground him into the sheet

with my chest, unable to get close enough. He laughed, pulling, holding, of whatever I gave him wanting more. By the
candle my skin was snow on his honey, ivory against gold. I
couldn't believe two men could be so beautiful.

We heard the commotion at the front door. We ignored it
until the knocking shifted from the front to the glass doors onto
the patio. There was a thud, then the high sparkle of glass
shattering. I rushed out, naked, and saw the man from the bar,
the man who had laughed with his hand in August's belt.

"No," he said, looking around me to find August. He held
out his hands, a gesture of supplication. Blood rilled onto the
floor. Blood pooled in the crooks of his arms, glittering here
and there with bits of glass. I walked forward to help him. He
swung at me, his fist only half closed, because of the glass.
Blood curved from his arms across me like a red sash as he
swung. He said "No," again, stumbling as he saw the blood,
the shock glazing his eyes. I said, "Let me help you."

He swung again, weakly, the blood-swath dropping on the
rug at his feet. I was afraid he was dying. I jumped, hit him
twice. He slumped to the floor.

August stood at the end of the hall with a blanket gathered in
front of himself. It was too dark to see the expression on his
face. I was angry because he stood there while I fought his
fight, but angry too as if I had seen in his indifference to the
cut man the end of us.

Goddammit, I said.

August dropped the blanket and picked up the phone. The
cut man was nearly unconscious, but he reached out and touched
August's ankle as he dialed. I would have hated had August
pulled away, and he didn't. The man's voice grew strange. I
thought he was dying.

August misdialed twice before he finally snapped on the
light. Wind blew through the shattered patio door, billowing
the curtain over red splatters on the rug and wall. I vised the
man's upper arms, trying to staunch the blood. I was drenched
with it, and an observer would not know who was the wounded
one. One arm seemed to be clotting all right, so I freed one

hand to pick the larger slivers of glass out, as each time he moved they dug in deeper. August brought towels and bed-clothes to press on the wounds, then dressed and went to wait out front for the ambulance. My feet and knees opened on the glass, and the man and I bled together into the rug. When they arrived, the medics appeared not to notice I was stark naked. Curious lights burned in neighboring apartments by then, and whatever watchers there were saw me hold the door for the stretcher, bloody and bare to the starlight.

August wore a speckle of blood across his chest from one of the man's swings. I stood scarlet from breast-bone down. We stepped into the shower. Ruby water whirled for a moment at our ankles. All the towels were soaked with blood, so we dried each other with the bathroom curtains.

We returned to the rumpled bed, took up where we left off. During a lull I said, "Who was he?"

"Who?"

"That guy."

Silence in darkness for a moment. August said he didn't know his name. He began to laugh.

Some nights are for dancing. I wear what I can sweat in without looking too gross: red T-shirt, denims, leather flight jacket against the chill, and because it makes me feel tough and sexy. I go out singing. I turn my collar to the night. Leather. A bulwark.

I love love, the heat, the hunt, the rough-and-tumble. I smile at anyone who smiles at me. Strangers offer me money. No one knows if I am a hustler or not, not the cops, not even August sometimes, I am so full of love. Some nights I am so beautiful you have to be drunk to talk to me. But I am furthermore in *love*, a thing altogether different and better. It is like a fruit both bitter and sweet, so you can't tell whether you like it, but you keep biting, harder, deeper. August likes when I am in heat. All homage and seduction returns to him at last, whom alone I love.

Thursday nights at the Bunkhouse: hotter than other week

nights, mellower than weekends when the queens and hustlers and golden-agers totter in to try their luck. Sometimes it's harsh and sour, the queens in the blacklight spitting "girl" this and "Mary" that until the soul goes to sleep. Sometimes fights break out, the opposites so drunk they don't know where they've been hit, nor by whom. They flail in the dim, connecting, striking wild, in fury whipping short bright knives from their boots. But mostly, it's glad and innocent. Men sit with their elbows on the bar, laughing. Whores come off Warren Street to warm up or throw the cops from the scent. Glum machos yearn in the corners, pin-ball lights glinting from their studs.

I come early to talk with my friends. I keep my back to the door so August can make an entrance. I know when he enters from the hiss of welcome ascending from the queens. They adored him first, look on me with a sense of bemusement, like court ladies thrown over for a goatherd. I pretend to notice nothing. I don't turn to the door. I move my finger along the mist of my glass. August makes his way toward me. The crowd parts, closes back. He presses his chest against my back.

August wears costumes sometimes, bringing it off even at the borders of absurdity. Tonight it's Gucci cowboy: high boots, stetson, silk shirt ruffled and open Byronically to his waist. *CD* he says. I turn and kiss him. He's been drinking. I like the smell of beer on his breath; it's sexy. I've nagged him out of the habit of street make-up, but tonight a dab of mascara around his eyes has smeared in sweat or tears. The cloudy dark makes his eyes supernaturally bright in the bar light, makes his body seem spent and haggard in comparison. I suppose that's sexy to me too. Once again it is the first night. Always. I hold him and the room is reduced to two. If I were a metaphysical poet I would tie us in a true love's-knot; I'd refine us to an alloy, electrum, gold and silver, the incorruptible and the precious corruption. I'd sing of a Silver Age, whose only grief is time.

*   *   *

August feared me sometimes. I was violent. I was more than I appeared to be. The gentlemen he was used to went gently behind their magnificent and magnifying exteriors. He lacked the talent to be either steadfast or cruel. He lacked the power to either lose or to seize control. Those powers in me dismayed him. I took the power and used it, always thinking it was what he wanted. My greatest power over him I didn't understand then, but exercised nevertheless: the power of my uncertainty, that looked to the world like indifference. Did we argue? I would win by turning away. I could seduce him with a change of stance at the bar rail, he followed me with blazing eyes. I hurt him, used him, worked his terror of the clock. He could have used a hundred weapons against me had he ever tried. I would have shown him what they were. I would have put them in his hand.

If I had my way it would still be Thursday night, I tilting my head back from his chest to see his eyes glitter in the dark, hand intertwined with hand so I did not know which was mine, before a word was said between us, all the world balanced between one delight and the thousand uncertainties. They say Eden fades. I say it is stolen.

He says "Dance?" and we trot to the floor. We circle, getting used to the music, deciding how our bodies move tonight. The jock sees me and through the seamless shimmer of disco blasts old-time thunder-rock, green, salty, a beat like the falling of an ace. I kick the floor so you can hear it over the music. THUM-pa THUM-pa. When we get cooking the other dancers stop, draw to the sides, cheer in rhythm *go go go*, shaking their fists at the ceiling. The medallion, the moon of silver leaps on his chest. I close my eyes to dance. He scans the room, to watch them watching. You watch him dance but it's me you want to dance with. Together we are a unity, a sphere, a diamond rough and brilliant in the bar light. Nobody is like us.

I come with August tugging my arm, pulling me back toward the bar. We glitter with sweat, August's black hair plastered to his temples. I jam my fingers into what I hope is my glass for an ice cube. August moves against me, heat at the places where we touch. And there I stand, sucking ice, thinking how beautiful I am, we are, probing the room to see if there is anybody like us, and there isn't. I could turn where I stand and kiss the hollow of his throat and that would be the end of wanting.

One of the queens puts the moves on me. I play macho monosyllable, because they love that. August hears every word. The queen says how handsome I am, what a dancer. She leans in on her spikes and hisses, "But get rid of that one, sweetie. We're, how do you say?, over the hill. I mean, can we talk? We're talking *Medicare*." She holds her rhinestones to her mouth as though astonished by her own boldness. I laugh, thinking August will think it's funny too. But he shakes behind his luminous eyes. August admits to ten years older than I. I think it's more, but it has never mattered. I see, for the first time, horror in a human face. I say,

"Look, don't take that old queen seriously."

"Why not?" my love answers. "You do."

I sprint home. I pretend to be angry, but the stars are broad as platters, the nighthawks airy above the roofs, and I run in exultation. I hear his voice behind me, calling my name. I run on, knowing he can never catch me.

Each time it was I who turned my back, maybe expecting him to, maybe wanting to strike first. I said, "Leave me in peace," wanting not peace but a sweeter turmoil.

And tonight I sit home saying Christ forgive me over and over, not knowing where August is, nor how to say it to him.

I ask August what it was like to love me. He says, "Like metal, somehow, beaten at a forge and drawn out."

"Gold?"

"No, silver, something corruptible. An age of silver."

I thought time would pass quickly to lovers, but our days were heavy—golden I said, though he would not—slow, endless. Good endless, light folding into light until you wondered how you had acquired such a store of grace. I ask him again at the end of the day, "How does it feel to love me?" I want to know. He says, "Weariness, CD, it makes me weary. Let's go to sleep."

"That's worse than the age of silver."

August says nothing. I vow to stay awake to watch him sleep, but I sleep first, he holding me from behind, his face buried in the back of my head so he may read my dream.

August says he knew me from before, at the bars or someplace, but I don't think so. Neither of us possesses the gift of unobtrusiveness. But I know what he means. Life seems filled with him in retrospect.

I am walking at sea's edge. There's a man in the water, bent, looking at something in the wavelets at his feet. I approach. He welcomes me with his hand briefly on the back of my neck. He puts his fingers to his lips in a hush gesture and points to the water. There are miraculous white birds no bigger than my hand. They nest underwater, breathing that green like fish. I have never seen such birds again, but the man is August.

I am very small and lost in a sea of grass. If I were six inches taller perhaps I could see over. The grass is beautiful, silvery green, but I am not in the mood to adore it. I want to cry, but as that seems purposeless, I walk forward, parting the silver barrier with my hands. Over the familiar meadow smell I catch a different scent, perfume, exotic, like a broken spice tree. I follow it. I come to an open space in the grass, a circle trampled down by dancing. I see the dancer. He is very beautiful. He motions me to come dance with him. I enter a cloud of spice.

A midnight Dancer, a wild god, dances through my corner of the forest. I want to go with him. I say, "Wait, I cannot find my friend. I can't find August." The god laughs and dances on. I have time to join or time to wait. I must decide.

The man who crashed through August's door sits beside me in the Bunkhouse. He's healed, but for scars like whip marks on his arms and under his right ear. I think there is going to be a scene, but he doesn't recognize me.

"August has a lover," he says.

"Do I know August?" I reply, overdoing it.

He shrugs. My experiences are immaterial. He has a story to tell. "A hustler," he says. "His new lover is a hustler. Somebody said anyway."

"What's he like?"

"Mean. You know. He cut me like this."

I nodded. Oh, I knew. The man drank a little of his drink, then moved down a few stools and said to his new neighbor, "August has a lover."

I ask myself, "What do I need from August?" The answer is, nothing. It is the answer I want. How wonderful it is to love for nothing at all. I would tell August, but I cannot say it right, cannot say it so he would think it a triumph rather than a concession.

Warren Street welcomed us with open arms. When we walked into the Bunkerhouse the disc jockey put on a foot-stomping country rock that he knew I favored. Even if we were tired or not in the mood, we'd dance a little, like visiting royalty honoring a local custom, the men shouting *go go go*, fists raised in the air. At Ryan's the jock slipped on the satiny disco that made August shine. At Cissy's, where there was no dancing and one went to talk, they brought my vodka tonic and August his almondy concoction without being asked. At Cissy's we sat in a booth with a green flowered glass shade over the light. That was courageous of August, for green was his worst color.

August has begun to call me College Boy. I retaliate with "Gramps," but my heart isn't in it. Each time one of his old friends calls him "girl" or "she" I feel my hand clench under the table.

Some lovers speak of identity so great that they know what the other will say or do, know his mood and desires as though one mind drove all their limbs. Not so for August and CD. We are a far country. We are perpetual surprise, confusion, exhaustion. Night after night I touch his skin, bury my face in the black-silver of his hair, kiss the body as it sleeps. Along its shoulders, throat, wherever I can go without jostling its sleep. And still I do not understand. I wake to find August's eyes staring into mine, rapt and uncomprehending, steady as a cat's. We follow each other to a dead bright end. We hurt and enflame each other. It is always the first night.

I watch one of my school friends as we shoot baskets in the gym. He looks goofy and happy in his New York State Fair T-shirt, sweat plastering hair to his forehead. Not pretty like the boys at the bar, I guess. He'll be bald before he's thirty. A little gut, although only someone like me would notice. When he passes the reflecting windows of the press box he doesn't look to see himself, the way I would, the way we all do. He doesn't care. Everybody he wants to love him already does. He sees me watching him and shouts, "Heads up," bulleting the ball to me as though that's what I wanted. I feel the sting on my hands. I launch into the air too far from the basket, hot-dogging to keep my thoughts going for a second, to compare his simplicity, his wholeness, his sweet unconsciousness to August and to me. We come off second best.

The ball drops through the hoop without touching anything. He whallops my back and whoops *Goddam*.

I realized at that instant that if I did not love August I wouldn't like him very much. The thought horrifies me; like adultery, but without even the candor of a deed. My friend beat me by seven baskets and told me to get my mind on my game. But I ran downtown to buy August a gift, to make up for the horror of an abandonment he never knew he had undergone.

To give it, I invited him formally to supper at Phoebe's Garden Cafe, where the waiters wear tight green T-shirts and know the dirt. At Phoebe's you sit in a glass terrace and watch the Genesee Street derelicts puke into the gutter. You peer at fellow diners around palms, and cheekboney women sailing in from the theater in their opals. Phoebe's was already a conces-sion on my part, for the worst of August's old coterie haunted it, smoking clove cigarettes and dishing in their sibilants so the sound from their tables was an everlasting low hiss. August warned the queens who fluttered over to dish that I would not be in the mood, his mouth pressed to their ears as though I were a child so easily to be patronized. Like a great lady holding court, I would think with momentary revulsion. August never sent them away, never stopped them when they called me she or Arty—Arty being R. T., which meant "rough trade"—but nodded at their advice and complaint like a prince at the counsel of courtiers he knows to be at once monsters and necessities. If I didn't love him, would I like him? High faggotry was ever in him a potential, and that was repellent to me. Perhaps part of my love was the belief that I could keep him from that, that I could keep him a man. I felt the gift in my pocket. It would be atonement.

August can't resist a little dishing with the theater wardrobe mistress. He pats my hand and says, "You don't mind." That one time I don't. While he's gone I set a package beside his water glass. It's a silver medallion on a silver chain. Silver, his corruptible metal. I had it inscribed and wrapped in a sea-blue box. When he returns, the blue box waits.

He isn't sure what to do. "CD," he says. "Should I open it?"

"Sure."

He unwraps. I don't know why I haven't done this before, his face shines so with expectancy and surprise. He lifts out the medallion, the silver glittering on the tablecloth.

"It's in Latin," he says.

"Yes."

He leans over so I can put the chain around his neck. "It's beautiful, CD. I'll never take it off."

I'm glad he chose to let the inscription go untranslated. It's not something to be spoken over Cointreau and amaretto cookies. Silver, corruptible, but rub it in a thousand years. It shines again. I'll know him. I'll whisper the words and we'll wake. The inscription is what God said to Saint Teresa as He stabbed her over and over with the barb of His love. He said, *Nisi coelum creassem ob te solam crearem.* "If I hadn't already created heaven, I would create it for you alone."

LIFE SUCKS, OR ERNEST HEMINGWAY NEVER SLEPT HERE

• TIM BARRUS •

Time is dead as long as it is being clicked off by little wheels; only when the clock stops does time come to life. — William Faulkner, *The Sound and the Fury*

ERNEST HEMINGWAY LIVED directly across the street from my island house. If I look out my front window, I can see the inevitable line of polyestered festive souls—tourists—waiting their turn for the guided tour of Hemingway's old digs. The tour costs three bucks. The inside of Ernest Hemingway's house is fascinating because what it gives you is a glimpse of what existed inside Ernest Hemingway's semi-manic more than slightly remorseful head. Literary necrophilia. Hemingway had a thing for felines, and the neighborhood still crawls with the arrogant descendants of the alley cats Hemingway brought here years ago. At last count the Hemingway house itself had over ninety cats. For an island only twelve city blocks long ninety felines in any one place is ninety too many.

The tourists with their festive Japanese cameras all get to walk past Ernest Hemingway's festive typewriter. It is to my knowledge the only typewriter in history to have sprouted a rude patch of literary pubic hair.

Hemingway himself avoids the crowds. He never did like much fuss unless the fuss was somehow related to his patrician-sized ego. I see him regularly, he comes over. We drink cheap warm island rum at my kitchen table (which sightly tilts so we keep porno magazines under the leg so the rum doesn't spill) and we discuss (bitch about) the ins and outs of how much better the olden days were as opposed to the ins and outs of today.

The olden days were better something considerable. In the olden days island time was dead and Hemingway lived here. Today, island time is like time anywhere. It has a post-modern tendency to breath down our necks, and Ernest Hemingway blew his bloody brains out in Idaho. Hemingway thinks the fishing here has gone to shit and then some. It simply ain't what it used to be.

Hemingway would kick the polyester-clad tourists out of his house if he could. But ghosts have an obligation to remain somewhat demure. Particularly the literary ghosts. Key West has more than its share of them. On the block where I live we have no less than seven (usually sober) Pulitzer prize winners. In time they will all turn into necro-literary ghosts as it is difficult to keep a good writer down. Or sober. Writers are stubborn and they refuse to die. Key West has more writers and more ghosts and more stubbornness than Ernest Hemingway had cats.

Hemingway reads all of my manuscripts before I send them out. He is usually somewhat less than encouraging.

"This manuscript sucks a big fat one," is a par-for-the-course comment. "The manuscripts were better in the olden days."

"Do you always sit around other people's kitchens, drinking other people's liquor," I asked him, "reading other people's manuscripts? I thought that you were a novelist?"

"I am a novelist," he replied. "Sitting around other people's kitchens, drinking other people's liquor, reading other people's manuscripts is what novelists do. And then we go fishing although the fishing has gone to shit if you ask me."

I didn't want to move to Key West. I am not the literary type although I do enjoy fishing. And I had no fucking idea who the hell Ernest Hemingway was until I moved here. It wasn't my idea to move to an island in the middle of nowhere. My lover, Lucas, made me do it. I am not really a fun-in-the-sun role model. I look silly poolside. I was forced into moving here. It's easy to blame my lover for everything. Everything. It's all his fault. My lover was one of those men looking for . . . something. I don't know what Lucas was looking for. (It was not Ernest Hemingway.) My lover isn't a man of many words. I'm the wordy one. Those were the olden days. And in the olden days my lover was looking for a refuge because everyone was looking for a refuge. Mostly from life. It's what my generation became known for. It's what we did. Some of us did it better than others; some of us are still doing it. In the South refuge is a concept related to home; a Southerner cannot be lost anywhere in the South because he is in the South. He is home.

We were not lost. We simply weren't where we wanted to be, not that we had any idea whatsofuckingever about where we wanted to be. We wanted to "experiment." The word got thrown around a lot and got more positive press than it either warranted or deserved. People from the South do not experiment. There are no experiments worth any sort of significant change in the moral order of the Southern universe. At the time we went to places like Taos, Haight-Ashbury, Aspen, Woodstock, and the Boston Common. You had to be there. None of these places were in the South. We were all looking for some kind of refuge from reality, and if we couldn't find one that suited us, we frequently built our own. From scratch, from the ground up.

Lucas and I came to Key West a zillion years ago because at the time it was a refuge from things like an unpopular war you didn't want to fight in but you fought in it anyway. Key West made some kind of sick Southern sense. Most of the people who lived there seemed to have served in Nam in one capacity or another. And it was okay to throw up your guts rotdrunk and Southern stupid on a hot night in the middle of Duval Street. No one minded.

You had a real hard time shaking off having lost in Nam. You weren't supposed to have lost. Certainly, Ernest Hemingway would not have lost. Hemingway had big balls. And big cats. He was a man in an age when men were men, and men did not lose. You wanted to forget. We were men who had learned that sometimes it's enough to simply forget and . . . survive. To have come out of something that had been really crazy with your Southern humanity intact even if your Southern sanity wasn't . . . intact. You were alive. Slightly gaga but alive. It was something. And this was a festive place, an island where it was okay to simply make it from one day to the next. Being alive and forgetting was enough. Key West for us at the time was a place removed from the realities of ex-wars, ex-wives, ex-lovers, ex-writers, Jesus, New York City parking tickets we had no intention of paying, and telephone answering machines. Hello, I'm not here right now. I'm out praying for Jesus . . .

Key West was a place in the sun where we could forget about the oriental adolescents we had murdered. Key West was a place where we could wipe the stench of rotting meatsmell, the odor of human ears strung in a fishline necklace—erased—from our Southern consciousness. Key West was a place where we could wash our brains with soap and disinfect the image of our buddies putting grenades into fifteen-year-old Vietcong assholes— pull the pin. Clean up the mess.

The Rock was a place we could embrace because when we moved here we were embraced, we were not merely accommodated. Key West was a place that had nurtured the likes of Ernest Hemingway. Maybe we could somehow become writers, not that we had any notion about what becoming a writer would mean. You learned how to kick newspaper vending machines in order to get your grubby hands on some coffee change. You ate something called food on Mondays, Wednesdays, and Saturdays. On Sundays, Tuesdays, and Thursdays you fasted. On Fridays you drank. Rum mainly. Key West was a place where we could gulp down neurological Ex-Lax. Everyone had his own internal versions of fantasy. Key West was a place where I could shit out the diarrhea of death from what was left of my constipated Southern soul.

Lucas was a Yankee.

This was the edge of sunset, the edge of the earth, and this was where we were either going to fall off the edge or totally disintegrate into starless indigo bits and pieces. To us at the time—eons ago—The Rock was more or less a psychological cave, an aberration, a malignant phenomenon where we could confront the fact that we were irrevocably where we were because we had chosen to live there. Key West was madness come home.

My lover and I moved here, to this island place, in the middle of the hottest September in the history of mankind. And then some. It was hot something considerable. It was so hot the bottoms of my cheap tennis shoes dissolved when I walked on Key West blacktop. It was so hot all the Island mongrel dogs turned into melted porch pup. Mainly. It was so hot the dogs refused to fuck in the alleys thus cutting down on our diet of evening entertainment. We'd been living in the back of our pickup truck in a migrant campground on one of the less chic outer keys, a bluecollar fishing stink of a place called Stock Island, where they really know h-o-w to drink. There are a lot of ex-Navy people on Stock Island.

Lucas and I were trying to decide if we really wanted to live here. Or maybe we'd bit off more than we could Jesus chew. Again. This time. We spent nights drinking rum, stretched out in the back of the truck, reading the accumulated works of Ernest Hemingway. We smoked joints the size of Cucamonga, hallucinated on mescaline, and fished because food stamps were insulting. It was a time when we took most everything, particularly ourselves, much too seriously. And if we believed in anything, in the only constant reality that our small universe could grasp, we at least knew that the sun also rises. It did it pretty near every Jesus day.

Somehow it all seemed appropriate. The tropical stars were awesome. "If we win here," Hemingway once wrote, "we will win everywhere. The world is a fine place and worth fighting for and I hate very much to leave it." We knew in our emotional exhaustion who the bell tolled for, but we could not hear the bell. All we could hear was the crying sound of the vagabond sea.

It was the hottest summer in the history of the universe. It was so hot we always seemed to soak our bed in some kind of a psychotic sweat. It was Saigon hot. If I woke up screaming from my meemee dreams, my lover was always there to hold me. To tell me that it was okay. You're in Key West, now. And when he screamed at night in the Southern heat from his own version of the meemee dreamboogies, I'd be there to hold him. We were men, and somewhere along the line we had learned that simply because we were men it didn't mean we would never need to be held.

That was the summer we needed to be held. We wanted to be wanted. But our ex-wars, our ex-wives, and our ex-lovers didn't want to want us. Much less hold us. Hello, we're all not here right now. But if you need us, leave a message at the beep. Jesus loves you.

So somehow Lucas and I ended up in Key West with our accumulated junk, our fallingapart Jesus shit pickup, Ernest Hemingway, and each other, because we wanted us. We were all we had. Was this a refuge or was this a refuge? This was a refuge. No one we met here owned a telephone answering machine. My lover found an apartment we could (barely) afford. We moved in.

The rain reminded us of Vietnam. It still does.

Our place came with Hemingway's cats. The cats are still here. They think they own the place. I also think they own the place. We gave them cute names because we were broke and tired and filled with a numbed despair that eluded us. We could not fathom it, and we needed to give the cats cute names. Angel Bananas is my favorite. He's sort of small for a tom. Although Angel Bananas is totally fearless. A lot more fearless than I am or ever will be. He's a tiger. At night he climbs on our bed and eats the lizards he brings to us. Angel Bananas is Jesus arrogant. We push him off the bed and yell but yelling at

Angel Bananas does no damn good. He eats most of the lizards but he always leaves the heads. Lizard heads do not appeal to him.

He's Southern.

Angel Bananas basically comes and goes as he pleases. I ought to have him fixed. Every time a publisher sends me a check for a piece I've totally forgotten about having written—surprise—I swear to Angel Bananas that this time he's going to the vet's to be fixed. And then I find myself in one of those cutie-pie chacha designer grocery stores we have on the island, now, buying a bottle of very nice delicious French wine. Because I deserve it and the check was an unexpected treat and nice wine is no damn good for me (mainly) and Angel Bananas still has his tiger gonads.

For the life of me I cannot pinpoint the exact date that all the telephone answering machines first started coming into town. There is now an army of them. I have my suspicions as to WHO the little busybody WAS who snuck the first telephone answering machine into Key West. There ought to be a law. I blame my ex-wife. It's convenient. I blame her for everything. Everything. It's all her fault. It was right about the time that she arrived for a little visit that people started buying telephone answering machines. Hello, I'm not here right now. I'm visiting my ex-husband in Key West. My ex-husband is a fag. If you can believe it. Edward Albee was right; some things are, indeed, too much. Just ask Jesus.

She wanted to know if I was really gay as opposed to only partially perhaps just maybe a little bit temporarily Southern gay, and why had I moved here, and why didn't I have a telephone answering machine, and did I want the kids for the summer? My ex-wife is an inveterate liar—it is a skill that comes naturally. She was born corrupt. I love her. I try not to. I try NOT to love that woman that beautiful bitch with tits the size of Texas. She drives me to madness but there it is. I hate her. Yes, I wanted the kids for the summer. But when I got them she did not want me to have them although she wanted me to have them. At least for the summer.

Or something.

My ex-wife's desire to be as independent as possible, a woman of the world, conflicted with her desire to be a mother. The battle still rages. Ernest Hemingway says things used to be less complicated. The world used to be a somewhat slow and simple place. Men were men and women (even women with Texas tits, and Hemingway says all the women had Texas tits in the old days) knew their place in the social scheme of things.

Angel Bananas ate a dead lizard (he left the head) on my ex-wife's bed which was really the living room couch. My ex-wife was less than amused. In the olden days Key West used to be this island place where no one (no one I knew) had a telephone much less a telephone answering machine. And everyone let their kids run loose. If you wanted to talk to someone you went over to their house. And you talked. Maybe you had a margarita sitting in the swing on the front porch. Margaritas for Jesus. And then you talked some more. Maybe you had ten margaritas for Jesus. Maybe you passed out on their floor. No one cared. No one gave a damn Jesus shit. Now on the streets of Key West I invariably meet the people I left New York to avoid. Most of them are Yankee writers with ex-wives and word processors. Most of this scum owes the City of New York a ton of money in unpaid parking tickets. Neither the writers nor their ex-wives nor their word processors nor their parking tickets have any business whatsoever running around the South loose. All of these things, these people, are in dire need of close supervision.

Most of the porch swings here have rusted. Key West has joined the rest of civilization. Today you need a machine that can call someone else's machine and leave a message. Jesus loves everyone. Today, even in a place as removed as Key West, you need kids who are capable of understanding the social complexities of something as emotionally knotted as the AIDS crisis. If your adolescent doesn't understand AIDS, we will all end up with uninformed teenagers hot between their sweaty little fuck-me legs who will almost certainly confront having the disease itself.

I make my teenage son carry around rubbers. I demand this from him. There is no room for compromise. I roll with the punches. Occasionally the punches roll with me. And occasionally I roll a joint to roll with the punches when the punches knock the wind out of me. When my son goes out at night I sound like an old nagging maid. Be back by midnight. Do you have your rubbers?

You never know when it might rain.

Angel Bananas thinks Key West has become too much like the rest of the universe. Angel Bananas likes for me to read to him at night. It soothes his weary spirit. I'd read to my kids at night but my kids complain that they are too big for it. My daughter now wears eye shadow and people who wear eye shadow are not people who have bedtime stories read to them. So I read to my cat. He's partial to Samuel Clemens. My cat cannot stand Earnest Hemingway.

The last few words of Mark Twain's *The Adventures of Huckleberry Finn* go like this: ". . . so there ain't nothing more to write about, and I am rotten glad of it, because if I'd a knowed what a trouble it was to make a book I wouldn't a tackled it and ain't a-going to no more. But I reckon I got to light out for the Territory ahead of the rest, because Aunt Sally she's going to adopt me and sivilize me and I can't stand it. I been there before." Angel Bananas objects to civilization and ex-wives on mere principle.

My ex-wife does not understand AIDS, Mark Twain, cats, daughters who wear eye shadow, or teenage sons with their pockets full of rubbers. After my kids visit me she makes them wash their hands. With soap. My ex-wife likes the new about-to-be-very-pink Holiday Inn which is, of course, rising like a glorious phoenix from the ashes of what was once Key West downtown decay. Angel Bananas has nothing against Holiday Inns although too much of the color pink in any one place gives him severe migraines. Angel Bananas even stayed in a Holiday Inn once in Boston where he was smuggled under wraps into the room. Angel Bananas didn't think too much of Boston. There were very few lizards to eat there.

My ex-wife is waiting for them to finish the pink Holiday
Inn so she can stay there when she visits me because pink
Holiday Inns do now allow cats who enjoy eating lizards on the
beds. They are unwelcome. Pink Holiday Inns do not have
AIDS because pink Holiday Inns use Lysol. Or something.
What was once some kind of unexplainable enigmatic island
refuge from the realities of wars and pinkness and goodness and
Holiday Inns and rules and Lysol is now a place that virtually
seethes with ex-wives, ex-lovers, pinkness, and parking tickets.
Southern writers and semi-Southern writers, here, are now a
dime a dozen, and we now have more Holiday Inns and fruit-
flavored prophylactics than you can shake a leg at.

In the Key West I once knew time was timeless. The pink-
ness was rationed. There were no telephone answering machines and Jesus was reserved strictly for Sunday morning
excess. This was a place full of men who in many ways were
warriors, the kind of men who cannot deny this part of who
they are. When I think of Lucas I think of a warrior, only
Lucas is a warrior who now works quietly with wood. Lucas
makes things because making things, wood things in his work-
room, defines the new Lucas, the gentle Lucas. I blame him for
everything but mostly I blame him for letting Key West slip
through our fingers.

My kids came to visit me in the summer, here, and they
turned deeply Caribbean brown. They came from San Francisco, life with their urban mother fast, furious, frenetic, and
they slowed. They gave up their nervousness, trading it in for
sunsets. Time stopped and came to life. Evenings were ice
cream at strange laid-back places with strange Cuban names
like La Bodega and sunset was whenever sunset was. This
summer I am informed by my children that sunset is . . . set. It
has an exact time established by someone with a Jesus clicker.
Sunset takes place precisely at somethingorother. There is a
schedule and schedules must be followed. I no longer go to
sunset. Let's face it. Sunset here is now something of a middle
class zoo complete with Coney Island plastic cups for the
tourist-liquor. In the olden days Ernest Hemingway and I

preferred our sunset refreshment straight from the bottle. Key West will never be the same.

"Life sucks," Hemingway said.

"Life sucks," I repeated. There are times when it is simply wise not to argue with a literary ghost. Ernest Hemingway's eyes flashed shit-hot fire with an inner anger as dry-iced as the Arctic Sea on a clear bluecold day at breathless noon. Angel Bananas jumped up onto the old man's lap and purred. "He wants my rum, you know. Once a Southern drunk always a Southern drunk. Some things never change. He's never asked for milk."

My kids and Angel Bananas keep telling me to stop bitching about change. Change, they tell me, is inevitable. Key West is no longer such a great place for my kids during our summers. The island is no longer a state of mind. It has become a public relations advertising illusion. Another gimmick. The telephone answering machines have won. Hemingway has gone fishing. Forever. And he vows that he will return only when hell itself freezes over. This past summer my children left this place as frenetic as they had arrived. I can see it in their hush baby eyes.

You have to be their dad to see it. Or their cat. Now, even their kisses are furtive. It's not that I resent change. What I resent is that as time keeps getting clicked off by all the little wheels that have invaded my home, I have less and less to give to my children. To my lover. To the people who Jesus count. To the people who will hold me when I need to be held. The clock doesn't stop here anymore. It just keeps on ticking. Time is money. Or time is how much time you've got left. Time here is like time everywhere else. Time is a series of cost-efficient Jesus units being clicked off by little people with little wheels that make a lot of nervous racket. And unless you can grab ahold of time and make her do your bidding you fail at life as we know it. What was once so special about this Hemingway-esque place was that so many of us, here, had failed at something somewhere else. Something considerable. But here it didn't matter. We stopped the clock and we survived for as long as we survived because surviving was enough. It was an art. I have failed and failed and failed at, oh, so many many things. Just ask Angel Bananas. We frequently drink margaritas for Jesus together with Ernest Hemingway at the kitchen table until the cows come home. Hemingway does not believe in Jesus.

Hemingway is a Yankee.

Angel Bananas would be a writer if he could. Unfortunately, he is a Key West feline. He will never win the Pulitzer Prize and I am rotten glad of it. I'm the failure in the family. A bum. Bill Faulkner used to call it white trash. The only really special thing I had was that I lived where I lived. My citified kids were, oh, so very impressed with the slowness that once existed here on the street—languidly—like those melted porch pups that first hot summer ages ago. Time became real. Island slowness was molasses Southern thick and magic. Island nights were bibleblack and jasmine sweetness filled the air. This summer my kids got on an Eastern Airlines WhisperJet at the Key West International airport for their ride back to their mother who lives in San Francisco where time is money and there's never enough of it to spend with the kids these days. Time flew off like a WhisperJet and time does not travel tourist.

Our island never used to have WhisperJets. They didn't come here. And then our airport expanded—it was good for the economy. It became an "international" airport and now even the house of Ernest Hemingway shakes like it has the running Jesus shits whenever the jets scream by overhead. I stood there and watched the thing roar off. It could have been Chicago. It could have been LaGuardia. It smelled like Ton Son Nhut. Being in Key West didn't mean anything more than Jesus loves you and Jesus loves only Jesus. We kissed and we all cried and my kids got onto a jet, the belly of the aluminum beast, whooosh they were gone. I'm not home right now. If you'd like to leave a message, leave your name and number at the sound of the goddamn beep. I shall miss Key West. I shall think about it often. But I, too, am gone. In many respects I've been gone for a long time.

My lover now thinks I'm crazy. I have never denied it. There are a hundred thousand editors out there in the real world who will spit-and-swear on the Holy Bible to testify to it. Angel Bananas knows of my insanity. So does my ex-wife. It's her fault. Miraculously enough, it is my children who believe in me. I could fail at everything. I could promise to go to Disney World (Angel Bananas LOVES Disney World) and then not go because I was too hungover to drive to Orlando. But my children would still believe in me. Here and now it is really all that I have. Their baby faith.

And all I really now have to offer them in return for their faith is my fanaticism, my courage about making if from one day into the next, my scars, my horrible ability to love them, to bleed with them, and all too often I'm bleeding all over them. It was my children who insisted that the time had come—for me—to leave Key West. Before they left at the end of our last island summer we sat around and discussed the things we would remember about this place.

This is the place where many of my friends are dying. Not gracefully. None of them are going gently into that good night. There is, oh, so very much justified rage. Many are already dead. It is so hard. Watching them go. I will cry and hug them when I leave them but leave them I must. We will all promise to write. These will be lies. Convenient lies. Nevertheless, these will be lies. They will die and I will not be there for them when they die. Someone else will have to hold them. I am too dry and too cried out to hold any more of them when they die in this island place.

This is the place where my lover, Lucas, has no idea (until he reads this) that I used to go into straight bars in order to talk to straight men when men in gay bars would not talk to me. Sometimes I just needed someone to talk to me. This is the place where I got to stir up dirt and trouble in the gay community (writers are scum) because the gay community here is so very comfortable. And well off. And complacent. And confused. And hurting. And haughty. And apathetic to an extreme. And scared. And sadly oftentimes horribly addicted to the cheap cocaine that is now this island's smuggled lifeblood. "I can't stop shaking. I've got the shakes," my friend Brian would say. Light a cigarette. Brian, Angel Bananas, Ernest Hemingway, and I used to gather around the kitchen table regularly to discuss the fact that Brian had been shaking for as long as any of us could remember, and Angel Bananas said that Hemingway could remember back to Jesus. Brian was my friend—another NamVet. Although I find it difficult to be around other NamVets, Brian was still my friend.

"He's had the cocaine shakes for as long as I can remember," Hemingway said. "In the old days we drank smuggled gin and gin could give you the gin shakes and the gin blossoms. Damn Jesus shit. The Rock has gone to the dogs if you ask me." We all felt a certain amount of honest sympathy for Brian, his shakes, and his anal warts. Angel Bananas said that Jesus had anal warts, too, although Ernest Hemingway mainly denied it.

When AIDS first became the nightmare that it has become, it was assumed in Key West that the island and its moral universe would be spared such awesome tragedy. After all, this was rightly paradise and such a thing could never happen here. Sweet Jesus, don't tell the tourists. Not only did it happen here, but it happened with a stunning vengeance. Something considerable. Jesus loves you. Where festive renovation was once the hope of Key West, many of those original Southern boy-renovators are no longer with us.

"I was going to paint the house this year," Brian would tell us. Brian had been talking about possibly painting his raggedy house for as many summers as any of us could remember. "But what with these shakes and anal warts and all . . ." Brian never did paint that raggedy house. He died and it sucked a big fat one losing Brian and his shakes. Visions have been buried. Visions have been replaced with Holiday Inns. Where so many gays in places like San Francisco and New York take for granted the fact that their communities have support systems, and a shared sense of identity, we in Key West have none of these things. These idealistic traits have eluded us in this place.

This is still very much the South. The traditions are deeply rooted. The Ku Klux Klan is alive, and well, and living—it thrives—here. "Weirdo alert," Lucas would whisper to me late at night when we were living in the back of the truck on Stock Island. Sometimes the Klan boys would put on their Jesus robes and engage in what could only be described as a drunken brawl on the beach complete with hate, torches in the night, and enough white Woolworth sheets to fill an entire linen department. Lucas and I did not venture (except to pee and you tended to pee fast) from the truck, our refuge, when these Southern extravaganzas took place. "More weirdos than weirdos in a weirdo tree," Lucas would say, although he tended to say it awesome quietly.

Gay folks in Key West are well-aware of who hates them. To their credit, Key West gays are capable of raising hundreds of thousands of local dollars for national AIDS organizations. It is possible to remain Jesus anonymous with this kind of thing. As well it should be. But dime one for locals stricken with the disease has yet to be seen. There is no support. There is no such thing as welfare. There are no resource centers in this part of the planet. Local indigents are literally buried at night, under cover of darkness so no one can see how it's done, at county expense in plastic garbage bags in unmarked graves.

Brian was put in a garbage bag, buried as if he were a untouchable criminal, and none of us ever knew if he ever really did get over the cocaine shakes.

The Key West graveyard has run out of room for the indigents. The moon in the graveyard shines soft like the incandescent light from my first lover's eyes. There is literally nowhere else to bury the dead, here. If Key West has become less of a good place to do our living in, it has also become less of a good place to do our dying in.

"We have rules, you know, what with burying the indigents," the manager of the graveyard tried explaining to me. "I can't tell you . . ." He paused. "I'm not supposed to tell anyone where we bury them or when we do it. Those are the rules, boy. I'm sorry. But if you happened to be here maybe tonight around midnight you might see us burying your friend, although I have to tell you upfront that it won't be a pretty sight." That night I silently watched them bury Brian in his garbage bag in the rainsoaked Southern ground. I told myself that I wouldn't cry. I was from the South and people from the South do not cry at the sight of either death or alienation. We are death; we are alienation. I did not want to cry. I choked it back. And then the dam just damn Jesus broke.

Perhaps it is not at all ironic that in an island place where gays are an important part of the social fabric those very gays are absolutely terrified into the center of their Southern souls to publicly display something as insignificant as a picnic on Gay Pride day, a date that is totally and utterly ignored in Key West. It doesn't happen. Where dollars and drugs and property have been so very easy for so many of my friends to grasp, here, their humanity, their courage, and the bonds which bind them have been an altogether different proposition.

Now that many of them are dying, they are beginning to find the strength to assert their courage. Yet most struggles in this place remain inner struggles because outer struggles—at least in the South—imply nothing less than civil war.

"The problem with most Yankees," Angel Bananas said recently, "is that they think too damn much." You have to be from the South to understand that the South has never really given up fighting the Civil War. Somewhere in the bones of every Southerner who is really a Southerner lives the hope and the knowledge that the South will rise again. And if it doesn't rise again the least it can do is hang onto its intransigent traditions. Gracefully. The social influences that affect those gays with AIDS in this place are far removed from the social influences that affect gays in Manhattan and San Francisco. Key West's outer skin makes her look like any other whore. But she is a Southern whore. There is a difference. Those gay Southerners with this particular disease are alone in ways that a gay man from the North could never in a million years understand.

For a long time Brian lived in his car (after he lost his raggedy unpainted house) which he parked permanently (the tires went flat) alongside a deserted canal on a sparsely populated key just to the east of Stock Island simply because there was nowhere else for him to go until he moved in with me, Lucas, Angel Bananas, my two kids, and then he died. It left my kids stunned and breathless. After the ambulance took his body away I found a copy of *The Sun Also Rises* under Brian's pillow. The sun does it every Jesus day. Before he moved in to die, Brian and I ate mushrooms one late afternoon and watched the canal his car was parked beside float and ease its deep cool current into the sea, which mesmerized us with whispered sorcery.

"See how the water flows so smoothly," Brian observed. "I want to merge with the universe smoothly. Like indigo dust." Brian did not want to go in a garbage bag.

In a way it is good that Tennessee died before Key West really started going down the tubes. This is the place where Thomas Lanier Williams and I used to walk along the beach at sunrise and laugh about nothing of significance whatsoever. The milk train doesn't stop here anymore. Maybe it never did. Key West is no longer timeless. This is the place where a Miami paper I wrote for fired my ass. They canned me because I screamed bloody murder about the lack of pay. The pay got a lot worse. This is the place where the rent went up. And up. And up again. I used to live next door to black folks from the Bahamas. The smell of deep fried conch used to linger in the air till midnight. The black folks are gone. A movie star bought the house, fixed it up, sold it. And left. I don't know who lives there, now. This is the place where cute little trains of tourists taking pretty pictures pass by my house and wave. Only occasionally do I give them the Jesus finger. This is the place where I played basketball with black kids with laughter, with sweat, with muscle. This is the place where so many times I came face-to-face with my own typically Southern sense of Southern hypocrisy something considerable.

This is the place where I caught midnight fish in midnight canals, and if I fell in, at least it'd sober me up and then some. This is the place where my neighbors would give me big fat juicy grouper and red snapper and stone crab from their week-end catch. Brian and I would boil the stone crab over an open fire down by the canal where I never got used to the fact that Brian was living. Such as living was, and living could still be rich. Warts or no warts. "Angel Bananas likes lobster," Brian would say and then he'd feed the feline big fat sweet globs of luxurious Florida lobster.

This is the place where my kids and I sold all of the furniture in the house in a yard sale in order to buy one week's worth of groceries. There was nothing genteel about our poverty. This is the place where I danced in the pouring rain down the middle of the street because I had been published. This is the place where I learned the difference between being published and being paid for being published. This is the place where my daughter learned how to swim and how to apply eye shadow. This is the place that I leave. I leave it with sadness, gladness, a certain amount of relief, and the clock still . . . ticking.

I have such a love–hate relationship with this island. Pink-ness and goodness give my cat severe migraines. I'm gone. I want to go to New Mexico and visit my father who still swears by mountain fishing. I hear that the fishing is also good in Alaska. They have yet to define sunset in Alaska. I want to spend some time in Mexico. I want to run along the beach in Mazatlán. I want to go to Paris and see a friend of mine who is a hooker. A woman who is not too unlike this place: made-up, rouged over, full of contradictions, ironies, making it one min-ute, and dying the next. I want to fuck this town and leave it. Slam, bam, thank you, ma'am. It is now only a so-so fuck.

This is the place where when it got really tight with money I used to sell my ass to tourists who were on the island for only a short while—maybe just for a quick tennis weekend—and they wanted some island buck to fuck with and I could fit the bill. Sometimes the wife would watch. Sometimes the man would watch. I never did play any tennis. Lucas never knew and it occasionally could put groceries on our table which was no mean accomplishment. Usually it'd be with a straight man, invariably they all had families—somewhere—and the Marriott got used to seeing me come and go. And sometimes if the man was nice I might let him play, although I had to often close my eyes and pretend that it was Lucas. And now I am leaving even gentle Lucas who says that he's not moving around with me another time anymore not ever again nada. Lucas sees me as being more difficult than I really am. I blame him for everything.

It was a pretty stupid thing to do, whoring, but we needed the money. People who only managed to survive are no longer tolerated, here. The bars get crowded with strangers who stare. Kindness here has been overglamorized, overindulged, and obsessively overrated. The hotels are too damn pink. And everyone swears by their telephone answering machines. Jesus loves you. My lover, Lucas, says he'll meet me there: wherever. Wherever I end up. Perhaps when he can get a day off. Someday.

Mainly, Lucas sees me as being Jesus shiftless, Jesus unrooted, and Jesus Southern. Jesus was better in the old days. Lucas says he's staying right smack where he is and he's not inclined to discuss it further because he's not moving no matter what I say and he gets mad just thinking about me trying to talk him out of what he's already settled on in his Yankee mind. "I'm not moving off to Jesus anywhere just because you've got a scratch in your ass to move us all over again because either they're kicking us out or you're over it and can't stay put any more than a Tom can keep his dick out of a pussy cat's pussy." Lucas ain't coming. For company I'm taking my truck and Angel Bananas. It's about time that cat had an adventure or two. We will go around Orlando. We'll find someplace where time has stopped. Where time lives. Where Ernest Hemingway never slept. Where the time you have left is the time you have left. Where it's what you do with what you have that counts versus how much you have left of it. Where there are no little people with little clickers clicking—time is money. Where the sun sets whenever the sun damn well feels like it.

I am still looking for whatever it is I have always been looking for.

My cat and I will read Henry James, Thorton Wilder, Henri de Montherlant, Tolstoy, and Melville to one another. None of

RED LEAVES

• MELVIN DIXON •

YOU CAN'T WALK on 12th Street no more on account of the leaves covering the ground. Even in Abingdon Square just this side of Key Foods where only two or three maples give shade there are leaves everywhere, and when I walk outside I step on them. Some stick to my heels and scratch against the ground in a hurt voice. When it rains the leaves turn to mush and dirty my sneaks—not Adidas, but cheaper ones just as good. Even inside houses and buildings you got leaves brought in by all kinds of people. It's October, the season of yellow, copper, gray, and red, real red. The leaves are cut-off hands curling up like fists. If they grab for my sneaks, I just walk faster and harder to get them off. Like that faggot reaching for me out of the dirt and shedding red like some gray bone tree. You know the trees I'm talking about. You've seen them faggots. They all over this city like flies on shit. You hear the scratchy tumble of red leaves everywhere until someone rakes the place clean. Don't let nobody tell you that leaves don't talk. They pile up on you like something or someone is gonna burn.

The funny thing is whether it happened like you remember it happening or if your head changes it all, gets the people and action messed around. I'd talk to the other fellas, but they'd think I was trying to punk out, see, and make like it was more than it was. Simple. We was getting back at him for trying to come on to me. You know, like I was some goddamn bitch. He probably wanted all of us, not just me, although we got him really scared by then, turning pale and twitching his eyes like he couldn't believe it was really happening to him out there alone at 4:30 in the morning in October in 1975. Wasn't he smiling at us? I remember his lips curling up, then down, his mouth moving like he was eating up the beer stink and smoke until he gagged. He acted weak, hungry, drugged up worse than the rest of us, but almost like getting fucked in the ass was an end to it. The hunger, I mean. I could tell he was hungry. We all could.

That night wasn't the first time I seen him. In fact, I seen him several times and knew where he lived. Sometimes I seen him go toward the docks and meat-packing houses. Why? Drinks, maybe. There are a few bars around there, where I've never been. He could have been one of the guys, you know, going after a six-pack at the corner grocery. He wore track sneaks—real Adidas—and jeans and a plaid flannel shirt opened from the neck on down. That day you could feel the season change right in the air, so I thought it funny seeing the open V of his chest like that. The morning chill had cooled off what was left of Indian summer, but it was too early for leather jackets and thick collars. I thought he was one of the guys 'cause he didn't swish like them over at Sheridan Square that got makeup on or their hair too neatly trimmed around the neck. This guy walked like a regular fella. Someone you'd want to talk to, chase pussy with, or get shit-faced on Budweiser together like we do most nights. Yeah, I seen him. Lots of times. Sometimes he didn't even know I was seeing him. Not until the day I was gonna meet Cuddles after his job when he actually come up close to me. It was near Cuddles' meat-packing house up by the docks and burned out piers where Little West 12th Street runs into traffic on the downtown detour from the closed up West Side Highway.

He was just walking and I was walking. I looked at him. He

looked at me. I didn't mean nothing by looking at him close like that, face-to-face. He didn't *look* like no faggot. So I nodded "Hey, man," and kept on walking. I mean, I wanted to be civil and shit. He might be able to lay you on to some drugs. But I said what I said, and he nodded and both of us went our separate ways. Easy, see. But damn, man, no sooner do I reach the door to Cuddles' job where he's supposed to be waiting but ain't, than I turn around to see that guy looking at me. He was watching my ass. Checking me out like you check out a bitch. Like he wanted something from me. Needed it. Scheming how he was gonna get it. But he didn't make no moves. Cuddles finally came outside and slapped me on the shoulder. I turned around and the guy was gone. Good thing, too. With Cuddles I forgot about him 'cause we was gonna get Maxie and Lou and ride around. I didn't give a fuck about that guy looking at me. Before joining the others, Cuddles and me had a beer where they don't check IDs. A little pre-drink drink. Get ready for the night. We always had good times. We tight, Cuddles and me.

Cuddles' father makes him work after school. Trade school. My old man died too soon to make me do nothing. Half the time I live in the streets. I should quit school, get a full-time job. Get the cash Cuddles has most times—where I got to ask my Moms to spot me some coins, mostly for cigarettes. Don't need no subway fare. Just jump the turnstile soon as the train screeches in. I do the best I can. Cuddles is the one in the money. Ain't tight-assed about it either, which is why we hang together. I like him better than Maxie or Lou, but I can't tell them that, not even Cuddles 'cause he'll start calling me names and picking on me 'cause I'm only fifteen and he's older. Just a little older.

"Two drafts, what d'ya say?" I tell him.

"Just what I need. Throat's tight as a damn drum."

"Mine's like a hose, man. Only it's empty."

"What's eating you? I been working all day."

"Shit, man, this dude, you know, like the rest of them in the

Village. Always coming on to you, checking you out like you some bitch."

"They think it's their turf, Lonny. We just tourists, you know."

"Yeah. Faggots is everywhere."

"You ain't got nothing to worry about, long as they keep a distance."

"But this dude act like he wanted it and could get it."

"He say anything to you, man."

"Naw, he just kept looking."

"He touch you, Lonny? He touch you?"

"Why you wanna know?" I say, but nothing else, just set my jaw tight so he'd know not to fuck with me. You can never tell about Cuddles. Always fucking with somebody.

"Drink up, Lonny. The guys gonna be mad cause we got a headstart." Cuddles slaps me on the shoulder and ruffles my stringy hair.

I'm grinning now, feeling stupid, too.

"I know what you need, man," he says. "Let's get the rest of the guys and blow outta here."

I don't say nothing more to Cuddles and just "Hey, man" to Maxie and Lou waiting for us at the cycle garage in Chelsea. Lou has his machine up on the racks and comes toward us wiping the grease off his hands. Maxie sits on a locked bike and leans forward and back like he's speeding down I-95 and going into a long S-curve. He thinks he's in some kind of pro race, but ain't none of us old enough for the big time yet. Some places you got to be eighteen.

I'm just a year away from quitting school if I want. Maxie is out of school already, but he don't have a job. Maybe 'cause his round pink face is full of acne. Cuddles is blond and older than me by a couple of months. He's funny, and you never know if he's gonna turn on you, especially if he can act big around Lou and Maxie. Lou is eighteen and works at the cycle garage where we hang out. I usually get Cuddles after his job 'cause he's near where I live. We walk the rest of the way. Sometimes Cuddles has his moped and we ride over. Junior cycle, we call it. Wish

I had one. Once I stole a ten-speed and spray-painted it over. I rode around, got Cuddles, and we rode double, Cuddles peddling and me on the seat, my hair blowing into spikes behind me and me holding Cuddles at the waist with my feet spread out from the double chain and derailer. He told me not to hold on so tight. Lou laughed his nuts off at us riding up to the garage on a stupid bike like that. He called us silly shitheads. I didn't care since he's mostly friendly with Maxie and thinks we just punks anyway. That's when Cuddles tries to act tough. But when I told Lou how I stopped this kid in the park on the East Side, took the silver ten-speed right from under his ass, raced downtown and spray-pained it red, he looked at me weird like he didn't think I had the balls to do that on the East Side. "You a mean dude," he said. And I said, "Naw, just regular white trash." I grinned all over myself and slapped his palm. Slapped Cuddles on the palm too.

This time walking up on the guys already at the garage and with me feeling the slow buzz of brew on a warm day, I don't say much to Lou or to Maxie 'cause Cuddles is already talking big and laughing. Then I get the drift of some shit that really puts me out. "Man, what Lonny needs is some pussy," Cuddles is saying. "He ain't had none in so long he's watching the boys on Christopher Street." And Cuddles laughs, poking me in the side like I'm supposed to laugh too. But I'm hot in the face, red all over, itching to dance on somebody. But shit, Cuddles is my man, or supposed to be. He can turn on you and get Maxie and Lou on his side. Now they're all laughing.

"No shit. You mean Lonny's sneaking after some faggot pussy?" says Lou.

"Maybe Lonny just getting tired of the front door," says Maxie. "He wants to come round the back."

"Can't get it open no more, huh, Lonny?" says Lou.

They make me feel like shit. I probably look like shit too. Damn Cuddles, I could kill him. Punch them all out. Why he had to goof on me like that when I was enjoying my buzz. When these guys start loudmouthing, no telling what they gonna do. "Naw, man," I tell them, "The only thing I do with a back door is shut it with my fist."

"You into fist-fucking!" Maxie screams. I don't even know what he's talking about. Then he balls up his greasy hands and starts waving all in my face like I'm gonna stand there and take it.

My hands get tight, maybe tighter than his. What I got to lose? "Yeah—and if you don't watch out, I'm gonna fist fuck yo face."

"Whoaaa," Maxie hollers, pretending to fall down, his mouth and eyes shoot open.

"Whoaa," says Cuddles, slippery as spit.

Then Lou goes, "Aw, man, we just messing with you. We know you cool."

"Yeah, he cool," says Maxie. "When you got a shitty dick, you gotta keep cool, and clean."

That's when I pull him off a that locked bike where he thinks he's king or something. Get him down tight between my legs, face red, and I'm about to beat his pink acne head to a pulp when Cuddles and Lou pull me back by the hair. I'd lose anyway. Maybe Cuddles and Lou know something I don't know.

"Cut the shit, man."

"Yeah, cut it."

I let him up. Maxie brushes himself off real calm like it was nothing but a punk getting out of hand. Being naughty. Shit. I push him away. "Next time you wanna give some lip," I'm saying. And I grab my cock in a mound, point it at him. "Wrap your lips around *this*."

"Whew," says Lou. "You don't need no taste that bad."

"Let's get the fuck out of this garage," says Cuddles. "Who's buying this time?"

We head for Key Foods and load up on two sixes. We get our regular bench in Abingdon Square which tries hard to be a park with a little grass and dirt, but it's mostly concrete benches and jungle gyms. We sit and sip and sit and sip. Can't wait for night to come, and I'm still trying to be cool.

It ain't always bad, drinking with the guys. About what I dig most these days, biding time till I can quit school. Be out on my own. More time to hang out. We get so plastered sometimes that night comes up on us with a scare and you wonder where the day went. Night is all right by me in the summer, but in October, man, you see things start dying all over the place. Not just red leaves circling down from the trees, but the cold whooshing in, cleaning the air of summer dog shit and roach spray. I can tell it's gonna be an early winter. Long one too. Sooner than anyone expected, October came in like an old lady screaming burglary or rape.

On the concrete bench next to me Lou says beer and night get him horny. His eyes snap at any piece of ass walking by. "Not any piece," he says all loud and blustery. "Just the ass that squats to pee." He starts stroking himself and gets up, saying he got to have some woman, and beer sprays from his mouth. Maxie says he needs some woman too. They say "woman" cause they won't get anything calling it pussy. Cuddles stands next to Lou holding him up then pushing him aside. "Forget about the woman," Cuddles says. "I just want some snatch." He poses like a hero out of some spy flick or war movie. I listen to them laughing and cackling but I don't say nothing about women or anything else.

"Listen, if we all put our money together—"

"What money," I say. "I just blew what I had on the beer."

"See, I told you he was small," says Maxie.

"Shit."

Cuddles says he got ten dollars left. "And I got ten," says Lou. "Twenty's enough."

"Ain't a bitch in town for that amount," I say. Nobody answers. Every time we start cutting up on beer or herb or cycling around, somebody gets horny and we end up talking about bitches and chasing leg.

"Drink up," Cuddles tells me.

"Let's blow back to the garage," says Lou. "Then the road to heaven."

We split up, riding double.

"Hey, Lonny," Maxie goes. "Don't hold so tight."

"Sorry."

I feel bad not having any money, but that's all right with the guys. We don't go to a house or a place with rooms. We ride uptown, along Broadway, near 79th Street where Cadillac headlights dim and slow to a cruising speed. Ten blocks further you see the bitches in miniskirts, all legs and face and not much chest, which is fine with me. Maxie pulls to a curb where Lou and Cuddles are leering at somebody. I stay at the bike while Maxie walks over to them. Suddenly she's laughing out loud like they was the funniest thing she ever seen. She waves her hand away and goes back to her pose in the door of a bakery closed for the night. Maxie goes ahead a half block further and approaches another and another one until he comes running back to me.

"Any go?" Lou asks for all of us. Me included.

"Yeah, some bitch around the corner at Ninety-first. You guys down?"

"Yeah," Cuddles says and looks at me. I say yeah too.

We go on up to 91st Street and turn in between Broadway and Amsterdam. We stop at the first abandoned building, which is really near Columbus. The woman—I'll say woman too this time—has dyed blond hair that looks like straw under the street lamp. She pulls at her skirt and pops gum in her mouth. "Hurry up now," she says. "I ain't got all night. For this little shit money, I'm doing you a favor. Be glad I got the real money early. Roscoe be on my ass if he finds out. Be on all your asses, too."

She enters the dim hallway and Maxie and Lou follow her up to the first floor. I wait with Cuddles against the parked cycles. They are gone only about five minutes when she comes out again. "Anybody got a jacket? It's damn cold in there."

Cuddles hands over his jacket. Up close now I see she's not much older than me, maybe younger. I wonder why she's doing this. I want to say something to her but I don't. Besides, what can I say? I'm here. Cuddles winks at me and points to her swaying ass as she goes back inside. We wait.

When our turn comes Maxie and Lou watch the bikes. Cuddles goes first. He doesn't take off his pants all the way, just unzips his fly and plows in. He's fast. Faster than I'll ever be. Maybe. It's already my turn. Her face turns up to me from the floor, her eyes tiny like they're holding something in. "What's the matter? You scared?"

I don't say anything. I make my eyes tiny, like hers.

"If you don't come on, you lose. Ain't no discounts, now." And she laughs. Cuddles laughs, too. I climb on top, my clothes tight at the waist.

I feel around her titties and she turns her tiny eyes away from me, arching her back. "Stop fumbling with my chest. Ain't nothing there." I want to say I like it like that, but I don't say nothing. This close I can see her teeth ain't clean.

Cuddles moves toward the door, keeping a lookout. I try to say something but she starts moving her hips around and my dick pops out of my pants. The tightness is gone. I'm all in her now and working, watching her face, her head shaded by the denim jacket and her tiny eyes doing nothing like she's the middle of a sunflower or a wheel of cloth spinning now until her eyes open up on me doing what I'm doing.

Cuddles comes over and just stands there like I'm taking too much time. Shit, he got his. I'm getting mine. He watches me. I try to say something, anything. His eyes hold me. Her eyes pinch tiny again and I feel the pull way down between my legs. I get it in my throat and say, "You see me, Cuddles." And he says, "Yeah, man." The girl breathes deeply, but she don't say nothing. It's just me and Cuddles. Me and him with words. "You see me getting this pussy?"

"Yeah, I see you, man."

"I'm getting it. I'm getting it, Cuddles." And my head goes light all of a sudden as if a weight was easing off me and going her way, maybe his. My hands grip the ends of the jacket like they're the spokes of a wheel turning me. My head circles faster than my body or her head below mine as I push my face against the cloth and away from her tiny eyes and straw hair. I feel Cuddles' eyes on me again, then her eyes on me. The smell of denim and armpits makes me tingle all over and tingle again until my whole body heaves and pulls. The jacket lets go the smell of grease and body all in my face and I can't do nothing but let go myself. The bitch had nothing to do with it. Riding on empty, I ease up. She smooths her skirt back into place. I don't say nothing and she don't say nothing. We walk outside.

Maxie hands her the twenty dollars. She looks like she could cast a spell. "You better be glad Roscoe ain't around. He'd be on all your asses for this lousy twenty bucks."

We rev up for the ride downtown. Cuddles brushes off his jacket and climbs behind Lou at the handlebars. "I was just shiting you, Lonny, about that faggot stuff. You cool, man. I seen you. You cool."

"I know," I tell him. "I know I'm cool." I slap him on the back. I climb up on Maxie's bike. I ain't grabbing tight this time. In a minute we're gone.

Like I keep telling you. October is a bitch, a mean red bitch. And you still don't believe me. Shit, you got the red leaves, you got early nightfall and twisted chilly mornings freezing you back into bed. You got people in scarves and caps tilted to the side like Hollywood detectives. You got October. What more do you want? You want red leaves clogging the sewers? You want legs and arms splayed out like tree limbs after a storm? You really don't believe in fall, huh, or how people can change too, just as fast. You want all this? Then you're no better than that faggot who wanted me.

He said his name was Metro. Just like that, he said it, out of the blue. So I said, "Yeah." Nothing more. The way he looked at me I could tell he was thinking he'd seen me around and knew I'd seen him around, too, and after saying hello just once he could come up to me a week later and tell me his funny name.

I was on my way to meet Cuddles who had the smoke this time. I had my mind on herb and didn't really see him until he was close enough to speak. "Metro," he said. I thought he was asking for directions. But he stuck out his hand cause it wasn't a place he was telling me, it was his name. I felt a load on me from the moment he spoke. All I said was "yeah." He didn't take the hint. He waited for more. Maybe he was thinking the cat got my tongue and he wanted it. I looked closer. He was about my height and build. Had wavy hair, not stringy like mine. He looked like any regular guy, except he spoke first in a drawl straight out of *Gone with the Wind*, then changed back to a normal voice. He said again his name was Metro. What could I do? He waited until I told him my name, but I never did. I finally said. "You know what you are?"

"Metro."

"Shit, man. You better get out of my face." And I left him standing there at the corner of West 12th and Bank looking like he just lost some money or came home to find his apartment broken into and his stereo and favorite records gone. With the wind. How do I know he even had a stereo? I don't know. He never invited me in to smoke dope or listen to records. Which is the only reason anyone would go with him. With a name like Metro what would you expect?

I didn't expect nothing at all. The third time I seen him walking into the corner building, I knew he lived there. I wasn't meeting Cuddles this time. I didn't know why I was even in the neighborhood. You get used to meeting friends in the late afternoon and it gets to be routine. Metro was dressed in a suit, no jeans, no flannel plaid, no white undershirt poking from inside the open collar. He looked like one of those Wall Street businessmen, he looked so square, so regular. He might have been somebody's husband or somebody's father even though he wasn't *that* old. You should know about fathers. They're the most important people to a kid trying to be a man, when everyone is out to get you or fix you into a can or a crate going six feet down.

My father built things. He was a carpenter mainly. He'd build things, take things apart and build them again. But he was also an electrician, a house painter, a wallpaper hanger, a welder, a car mechanic, a plumber. All for money and for fixing up other people's houses. He could fix anything. A regular jack-of-all-trades, a handyman. I remember he used to make toys for us at Christmas because he couldn't buy any. We was living in the Bronx then and my father would load up his beat-up station wagon every morning and go off on the jobs people called him for. He owned his business. He *was* his own business. That's what Moms said to write in the blank beside "father's occupation" on school registration forms every September, "self-employed." I didn't even know what it meant, because my father never talked to us. He didn't tell us about who we were. I mean, as a family. And since I didn't know who I was aside from nothing or no one, I thought I could be anybody I damn well pleased.

"You ain't never had a chance, did you?" Moms said once.

"What you talking about? I'm anybody I'm strong enough to be."

"And mean enough," she said, shaking her head like she did when my father died. He worked all the time and kept his feelings locked inside until his heart burst open. The fucking load he must have been carrying. Shit, I could have carried some of that load.

"You ain't never had a chance," Moms said again.

"I make my own chances. I'm self-employed."

Naw, Metro couldn't have been anybody's husband or father. You could tell by the way he walked and, if you listened close enough, by the way he talked. But he had what you call opportunities. Maybe if you don't ever have kids you can build things for yourself. Do things. He just made the mistake of wanting to do me.

"You can come up to visit sometime, you know. Now that you know where I live."

"You mean me?"

"Sure. What's your name?"

"Lonny."

"I'm Metro."

"You told me before. Remember?"

"Yes. I thought you didn't remember. You didn't say anything."

"I didn't know what to say. Besides, where'd you get a name like that?"

"You'll see."

"Listen, man, you trying to get wise or something?"

"Let's be friends, Lonny."

"I got to go now."

"Some other time, then?"

"Sure, man, sure."

"Call me Metro. I like that."

"Sure."

I got away and ran all the way to Cuddles' place. He wasn't even expecting me. But I was there just the same, leaning against the corner beam of the loading platform. It was about five feet off the ground so that the packing trucks could be loaded from the level of the storage and work areas. I could have been holding up the very corner of the building myself or at least the sign saying Holsworth Meat and Poultry Packing, where you could actually see the sides of beef, the blood and fat making the loading platform floor slippery and the whole place smell like rotten armpits.

Maybe it was the heat. Or just me, hot with my tangled nerves sizzling electric. All from talking with that guy Metro and running breakneck speed to Cuddles' job like it was the only safe place. I was hot standing there thinking about Metro and hating myself for letting him talk like that to me. Shit, he talked like he knew who I was or who I could be. Like he could actually see into my corduroy jacket, his eyes like fingers in my clothes and touching me. You ever get that feeling talking to someone? Shit. I hated him for thinking he knew who I was and could come on to me like I was some bitch. He didn't know who he was messing with. Sure, I told him my name. We was just talking. Wouldn't you talk before you realized his eyes were fingers crawling all over you? I know you would, mostly because you'd think a guy wouldn't do that to another guy. Later, you'd swear he touched you. Wouldn't you? You'd think that talking was all right. It was only some words between you, not hands. You'd think that as long as he didn't touch you it would be all right to speak. Long as neither of you was touching. It don't mean that you're one of them, just cause you say "Lonny," like I did. We was only talking, man. But when you realized his eyes were fingers taking hold, you'd hate him even more for pulling it off, undressing you right there with his eyes and laughing at your naked ass or shriveled-up cock. You'd be mad enough to kill him.

"You lying," Cuddles says when I tell him. "You lying, man."

"Naw, I ain't."

"Shit, man. Wait till I see Maxie and Lou."

"What for?"

"We oughta kick his ass."

"Look, Cuddles. Maybe we can just forget it, huh?"

"Naw, man. You one of us. What happens to you, happens to us. You forgetting the pledge."

"What pledge?" I ask after him, and he's dancing on the same short circuit I'm on.

When we catch up with Maxie and Lou it's Cuddles doing the talking. "Man, we should celebrate," he yells, looking me over.

"Celebrate what?" I ask.

"Losing your cherry to a faggot, what else?" he says.

My face burns. "He didn't touch me, man."

"Aw, Lonny, we know you got a little bit," says Maxie, grinning.

"Don't start no shit," says Lou.

"Maybe that's what I'm smelling," says Cuddles, moving up then back from me and flailing his arms like he's brushing me off.

"You mean the shit on *your* breath," I say, stepping up to him.

And Maxie jumps up, saying "Whoa," and Lou goes "Whoa," and I go "Whoa."

Cuddles backs off. "I'll fix your ass," he says. "Fix it real good."

"Aw, man, we been low too long now, let's ride high," says Maxie.

"Beer and smoke?" I ask.

"Yeah."

"Let's ride and fuck the night," adds Lou. He revs up the cycle with Cuddles holding tighter to him than I ever held. At the first red light Cuddles turns to me saying he'll fix me real good. I tell him where to put that shit.

Around midnight after five trips to Burger King for fries and hot apple pies to ease the munchies, we get back to the garage in Chelsea. I am high, yeah, I admit it. Feeling good. We stop cutting up with each other and just enjoy being so bloated we can barely move. We keep talking shit, though, like it is all we can say. But I still feel funny about Metro earlier in the afternoon. Then a numbing tingle comes through my face like I'm getting high all over again or just burning slowly inside.

Then I feel light again as if something is about to happen to ease the beer and marijuana out of me on a cool streak and I'd lift off the garage floor, lift up from the street and concrete and glide out to 12th Street and Bleecker again, then to West 4th where I'd be sure to see him and we'd talk. Just talk. Maybe this time I would get to hear his stereo. Maybe he likes the same music I do. Maybe he really is like me or Maxie or Cuddles or Lou, just a little haywire. But we leave the garage again and move in a group throguh the meat-packing section of lower West 12th and up toward Bleecker where men walk alone or in twos passing us. Lou scowls. Cuddles sets his shoulders broad. We're a solid block and tough. Them faggots is just maggots on rotting meat. They move away from us and off the sidewalk quick. Lou and Cuddles laugh, and I hardly know their voices. When I laugh too, just to be laughing, the chuckle comes out of some gray pit inside me and the voice isn't mine, honest. The shit you can carry just waiting for a time like this to stink.

Some guy up ahead is selling loose joints for a dollar. "All our joints loose," says Maxie, laughing and trying to unzip his pants. When we come up to him Maxie asks, "Got fifteen?"

"We'll get blasted to hell," I say. But no one answers. They all look like they know something I don't know.

Maxie asks for change of a twenty. I see Cuddles and Lou sneak in close, so I move in close. The guy fumbles around his pockets and gives me the joints to hold. As soon as he brings out a wad of bills it's a flurry of green and fists. Cuddles first, then Maxie, Lou and me pounding hard on the upbeat.

"That's all the money I got," the guy whines. Cuddles pushes him away from us. The flash of metal makes the kid back right into Lou who feels his ass. Cuddles gets a feel, too. His face goes red and his voice quivers, "Leave me alone. You got what you wanted."

"You oughta be glad we don't make you suck us off," Lou says, pushing him away. "Now get the fuck outta here."

The kid disappears down a side street. We count the new joints and money and move in close ranks like an army of our own, the baddest white boys out that night. Everyone else moves off the sidewalk as we approach, some we even push deliberately into the street just close enough to a car to scare them clean out of their designer jeans and alligator shirts. The funniest shit is that some of them have on combat jackets and here we are doing the combat. We blow some of the cash at the liquor store off Sheridan Square.

On a vacant stoop near West 4th Street, we finish off the beer and the joints and divide up the rest of the money. Everything is sweet now. Sure we have our fights and fun and great highs. So what if they don't last long.

Sure as shit and just as loud as the beer and smoke would let him, Cuddles goes, "Lonny, man, how's Beatrice these days?"

"Don't be bringing my Moms into your shit."

"Keep it clean, guys," says Maxie.

"I was trying to keep it clean," Cuddles starts. "But the bitch had her period right when I was fucking her."

In a second I'm on him with fists and feet. He deserves no better. "We dancing this one, asshole."

"Yo, man, cool it," say Lou. He and Maxie pull me off Cuddles, but not until I land some good ones. Cuddles is too high to fight good. I could be faster myself, but what the hell.

"Aw, man," Cuddles says, rolling to his side, sliding down the concrete stairs away from me. "I just wondered if she knew about your boyfriend. You know, the one you said lived around here."

"Whoaa," says Maxie. "Lonnie getting faggot pussy again? Keeping it all to himself?"

"It ain't true, man," I say.

"What ain't true?"

"This guy just told me his name, that's all. I didn't say anything else. Nothing."

"Why he tell you his name then?"

"Cause he wanted to, that's why. You jealous, Cuddles?"

"Shit, man."

"He wanted to do something, I guess," I say.

"Of course he wanted to," says Maxie.

"He was trying to rap to me," I say, but I'm talking too much and can't stop. "Like I was some bitch."

"He touch you, man? He touch you?" Maxie asks.

"Shit," says Cuddles. "Faggots everywhere."

"I ain't no faggot," I say.

"He touch you, man?" asks Maxie.

"Like you touched that reefer kid back there?"

"That's different, Lonny. We was on top."

"Shit," says Cuddles. "Pass me another joint."

"Me, too."

"Pass Lonny another joint. He cool."

"Thanks."

Hours pass. Or minutes that seem like hours. The streets are suddenly quiet and so are we. But in the kind of quiet sneaking up and banging like a fist on your face that makes you think something's about to happen and no laughing or getting high can stop it. What you do won't be all that strange, either, more like something you always thought about doing but never did. I hate that feeling. It makes me think that something's burning in me that I don't know about. And I've got to let it out or choke on the fumes.

Cuddles is the first to see him strolling down the street. He nudges me and Maxie. Maxie nudges Lou, who's half asleep and stroking himself hard again.

"Aw shit." My voice gives it away.

"That's him, ain't it?" asks Cuddles. "That's Lonny's faggot, ain't it?"

"I didn't say that," I say, but it's too late.

"He the one touch you?" ask Maxie.

"That's the one," says Cuddles.

"How do you know?"

"*You* told me," Cuddles says, but his voice also tells me something I can't get a hold of. They ease into the street and wait. I join just to be joining them. Metro approaches dizzily, either drunk or high or plain out of it, but not as bad as the rest of us. Cuddles speaks up like he has it all worked out in his head.

"Hey, baby," he goes, in a slippery, chilly voice.

"Huh?" says Metro.

"Hey subway, baby," Cuddles goes again.

"The A train, right? I just took the A train," says Metro.

"We got another train for you, baby. A nice, easy ride."

I can't believe what Cuddles is saying. I try to hide my surprise by not looking at Metro, but they both scare me like I've never been scared before. It's something I can't get hold of, or stop.

"Metro. Why do they call me Metro?" he goes, talking to himself all out of his head now. Does he even see these guys, hear them?

"Hey, baby," says Lou, getting close to him.

I stay where I am near the concrete steps.

"Ooh, baby," says Maxie, joining in.

"They call me the underground man," says Metro, his words slurring. "You wanna know why? I'll tell you why." His eyes dart to all of us, locking us in a space he carries inside for someone to fill. Then he sees me for the first time. He stops, jaws open, eyes wide. "Is that you, Lonny?"

I say nothing. The guys are quiet too.

"You wanna know why, Lonny? Cause I get down under. Underground. Metro. Get it?" Then he laughs a high, faggoty laugh. And I don't know him anymore. He suddenly stops. No one else is laughing. He feels something's wrong. He looks straight at me, then at the others now tight around him.

"Lonny, what's going on? Who are these guys?"

Cuddles touches him, his hand gliding down Metro's open shirt. Metro's eyes get round.

"Lonny, I don't know these guys."

"That's all right," says Maxie. "We're Lonny's friends. Ain't that right, Lonny?"

I say nothing. Lou kicks me square in the shins. "Yeah," I say. "Yeah." But nothing more.

"And when Lonny tells us you go under, man, you give it up nice and easy, don't you?" says Cuddles.

Metro reaches into his pockets and pulls out a raggedy leather wallet. "I don't have much money." He shows the wallet around so we see the single ten spot inside. "That's all there is. You want it? It's all I have."

"No, baby," says Cuddles. "Keep your money. Right, fellas?"

"Right."

Metro looks worried. "My watch? I don't have anything else. Nothing, honest. You can check if you want."

"We don't want your watch," says Lou. His hand falls to Metro's ass, feeling it. Then to the front, gathering Metro's balls into a hump, and slowly, ever so slowly releasing them.

"Lonny says you been after him."

"After him? I don't understand. What are they saying, Lonny?"

I don't say nothing, but I want to say something. When I step closer, I feel metal pointing in my side, a blade tearing my shirt. Cold on my skin.

"Yeah," I say. "You been after me."

Cuddles steps up. "You wanted to suck his cock? Take it up the ass?"

"Hold it, Cuddles," I say.

"Naw, you hold it," says Maxie. "You could be like that too, for all we know. Ain't that right fellas?"

"Shit, man. You tell him, Cuddles. Tell him he's crazy to think that. You seen me with that girl."

"Naw, man. *You* show us," Cuddles says.

They hustle me and Metro to an alley near an abandoned building. Maxie and Lou hold Metro by the armpits. Cuddles twists my arm behind my back and from his open breath I know he's grinning ear to ear. "Aw, man," he whispers to me. "We just having fun. Gonna shake him up a little."

"What about me?"

Cuddles says nothing more. He looks at the others.

Maxie pushes Metro to the ground. The alley carries his voice. "You wanted to suck him, huh? Well, suck him."

Cuddles unzips my pants.

"I didn't touch you, Lonny. I never touched you."

"You lying, subway man," says Cuddles.

"Ask him," says Metro. "Did I touch you, Lonny? Ever? You can tell them. Please, Lonny. I never touched you."

All eyes are on me now, and even in the dark I can see the glimmer of Metro's eyes looking up from the ground. From the sound of his voice I can tell he's about to cry. Suddenly, the click of knives: Lou's and Maxie's. Metro faces away from them and can't see. I see them, but I say nothing. Cuddles twists my arm further. The pain grabs my voice. His blade against my skin. "I told you I'd get back at you, shithead."

Pain all in me. Metro jerks forward. "Ouch," he feels the blade, too. Then Metro's mouth in my pants. Lips cold on my cock. Then warmer. Smoother. Teeth, saliva, gums. I can't say anything, even if I want to.

It don't take me long. I open my eyes. Metro's head is still pumping at my limp cock, but his pants are down in the back and Lou is fucking him. Lou gets up quickly, zips up his pants. Maxie moves to take his place. I move out of Metro's mouth, open in a frown this time or a soundless cry. Maxie wets his cock and sticks it in. Cuddles pumps Metro's face where I was.

Metro gags. Cuddles slaps his head back to his cock and I hear another slap. This one against Metro's ass and Lou and Maxie slap his ass while Maxie fucks him. Lou has the knife at Metro's back and hips. He traces the shape of his body with the blade. Metro winces. "Keep still, you bastard. Keep still," Lou says.

I try to make it to the street, but Cuddles yanks me back. He hands me a knife and I hold it, looking meaner than I am. "You ain't ever had a chance," I'm thinking and realizing it's for Metro, not for me. Cuddles finishes and pulls out of Metro's dripping mouth. His fist lands against Metro's jaw, slamming it shut. I hear the crack of bone and a weak cry. The next thing I know Maxie, still pumping Metro's ass and slapping the cheeks with the blade broadside, draws blood, and once he finishes he shoots the blade in, gets up quickly, pulling the knife after him. Lou's hand follows. Then a flash of metal and fists.

"Shit, man. Hold it," I yell. "I thought we was only gonna fuck him. What the hell you guys doing?"

"Fucking him good," says Lou.

"Stop. For God's sake, stop."

But they don't stop.

"Oh my God. Oh my fucking God." It's all I can say, damn it. And I hear my name.

"Lonny?"

"Oh my God."

"Lonny?" Metro's voice is weak, his words slurring on wet red leaves. "Help me."

Lou and Maxie jump together. "Let's get the fuck outta here."

"Yeah," says Cuddles. He kicks Metro back to the ground where his arms and legs spread like the gray limbs of a tree.

"Oh my fucking God." I keep saying it, crying it. But it's too late. The guys scatter into the street like roaches surprised by a light. Running. They're running. I look back at Metro and he rolls toward me. His still eyes cut me like a blade. "Never touched you," the eyes say. "Never touched you."

I hold my breath until my ears start to pound. I hold my head. I run, stop, run again. The knife drops somewhere. I run again. Don't know where the fuck I'm going, just getting the hell out of there. Don't see anybody on the street and not for the rest of the night. Not Lou, not Cuddles. Not anybody else at all.

October is red, man. Mean and red. Nobody came back there but me, see. And Metro was gone by then. Somebody had raked the leaves into a clean pile. I ran through it and scattered the leaves again. Once you get leaves and shit sticking on you, you can never get them off. And when you start hearing the scratchy hurt voices coming from them, the red leaves I mean, not patches of skin or a body cut with knives, or a palm of broken fingers, you'll start talking back, like I do. You stop hanging out at the meat-packing warehouses on lower West 12th or walk the loading platforms mushy with animal fat and slime where your sneaks slip—not Adidas, but cheaper ones just as good.

When I found Cuddles and told him about the talking red leaves, he said to get the fuck away from him, stop coming around if I was gonna talk crazy and dance out of fear like a punk. But I wasn't dancing. My feet was trying to hold steady on the loading platform but my sneaks wouldn't let me. You ever hear the scratchy voices of leaves? You ever try to hold steady on slippery ground?

Like I was telling you and telling Cuddles, after Maxie and Lou cut us loose and before Cuddles cut me loose. Mine wasn't the only hand on his ass or on his face that night. Metro tried to make me. He wanted it that way. They all do. Man, October is a mean, red bitch. I know. But what if it ain't the only bitch? What if you could answer the leaves and tell them to stop falling 'cause winter is here now. It's cold, getting colder. Aw shit, man, trees don't talk.

They had the body marked out in chalk on the ground behind some blue sawhorses saying, "Police Line Do Not Cross." It was right where we left him. I saw it glowing. "Here's Metro," I told myself. Here's anybody, even me. A chalk outline and nothing inside. A fat white line of head, arms, body, and legs. A body curled into a heap to hold itself. Like the shape of a fallen leaf or a dead bird, something dropped out of the sky or from a man's stretched out hand. It was amazing. But it was also the figure of somebody. A man. Any man. So I walked around the outline, seeing it from different angles. How funny to see something that fixed, protected from people or from falling leaves or from the slimy drippings from sides of beef. The outline wasn't Metro. It was somebody like me.

Once I saw the chalk figure I couldn't get enough of it. I kept coming back and walking slower and slower around it, measuring how far it was from the police barricade and from where I stood looking down at it, sprawled where we left him. But I figured out a way to keep looking at it and not step in the garbage scattered nearby. You know, leaves, rags, torn newspapers, bits of dog hair, blood maybe, and lots more leaves. I went three steps this way and three steps that way, keeping the chalk outline in sight and missing the garbage and dog shit. One two three, one two three. Up two three, down two three. Then I saw one of the neighbors watching from a window and I cut out of there. But I knew by then how to keep the chalk outline of a man and not fall like a leaf.

That night I came back. The chalk shape was glowing brighter under the street lights like crushed jewels. I took off my shirt and pants and didn't even feel cold. I crossed the barricade and sat inside the chalk. The glow was on me now. It was me. I lay down in the shape of the dead man, fitting my head, arms, and legs in place. I was warm all over.

The police came and got me up. Their voices were soft and mine was soft. They pulled a white jacket over me like some old lady's shawl. I shrugged a little to get it off, but my arms wouldn't move. When I looked for my hands, I couldn't find them. The police didn't ask many questions, and I didn't say nothing the whole time. Besides, there was no red leaves inside the chalk, not a single one. At the precinct a doctor talked to me real quiet like and said the leaves would go away forever if I told him everything that happened to the dead man and to me. But they didn't call him Metro, they called him some other

MAGIC

• GARY GLICKMAN •

TWENTY YEARS AGO this place was called the artists' beach. Artists did come, perhaps to paint the wide strip of white sand submitting to the waves sometimes gratefully, sometimes unwillingly, steeply, violently, or else to catch the blue sweep of the Gulf Stream, or else the more subtle wilderness of the dune grass where no mansions were. The town was still a frontier then, as far out as possible from the city, just about, before falling off the island into the sea. And the beach was as far as possible outside the town, between villages, so that what went on here, that is, who sat down with, or even lay down with whom on the sand, was not so well overseen as further in, beneath the eyes of high society and local prudery. Thirty years ago Communists took sun and refuge here with other blacklisted sympathizers; homosexuals, surely, and any of the men with long hair or strange grooming back then—a beard, maybe a beret—who would have been stared if not hounded off the other beaches. Forty years ago there were submarine patrols, local volunteers too old for combat who walked the beaches twice a day, dawn and dusk, for any sign of a German invasion. Fifty years ago, and further back for as long as the country can remember—more than three hundred years, ac-

cording to the locals, the Daytons, the Conklins, the Milfords—
the old volunteers were young men with their fathers and
grandfathers, hauling whales out of the surf, summer and winter year after year, to be cut up alive into meat. In bad years
there were beach pirates, stoking up fires, hoping a ship would
mistake the signal and founder in the shallows, although none
of the old families will point a finger. That whole time there
were slave traders as well, also unmentioned now, and otherwise only the occasional Acabonack wandering out from his
woodland camp, gathering shells and hunting deer.

This midnight the cars are as plentiful as during the day,
though toward sunset the lot empties out, only retired couples
and people with dogs stopping a while to watch the stone blue
of the sky sink down into dusk. Now, though, after dark, it is
crowded again, as every weekend, with fancy cars from the
city: Mercedes, BMWs, Alfa Romeos, as well as the more local
wheels—pickups and jeeps and vans with dark glass. At this
hour none of the adamant signs are respected: no parking here,
no dogs, no picnics, no fires. Policemen leave the place alone,
at night at least. The few who do come, come as men, for
relief, for company. With the night and the dark ocean so close
in this town, loneliness seems always only a few breaths away,
even now in high summer as if, like the moist fog rolling in
over the fields, lighted by the moon sometimes or by headlights, it could swallow a person up, even safe in his car, could
obscure him and blind him just long enough to be fatal.

Voyeurism aside, we have come to walk the dog. It is late
enough to be an adventure, but in town the sidewalk is still
crowded with teenagers crowding around the movie theater and
the ice-cream store, both of them already closed. Even the
bookstore has finally closed, although in the light of its window
brightly dressed weekenders still stroll up and down with their
spouses and even toddlers asleep in strollers, most of them just
off the late bus, unwilling yet to go home and concede an end
to Friday night. For quiet, and also for enough dark to see the
stars, the beach is the only place.

Knowing the answer I ask, "Why are we here?"—as if asking might keep the answer away, or change it.

"Who's that?" he says.

"What do you mean, 'who's that?' Can't you see me in the dark?"

"Have a sense of humor," he says. "I was just kidding. Of course I can see you. Even if I can't I still know it's you."

"How?"

"By your insecurity. Relax, will you? No one's going to jump out and grab you."

"But what are we doing here?"

"You know," he says. "Same as all these guys."

"No," I tell him, "I don't want that. I don't even think we should be walking the dog here. You know it's just an excuse. Look at her, she's scared of all the silent men. They make me nervous too. What are they doing?"

"Same as us. Looking at the stars. Looking for their fathers."

"What are you talking about?"

"What you always talk about. You'll see."

"No I won't. I feel uncomfortable here."

"No you don't. It's only that your eyes haven't adjusted. You've been here before plenty, admit it."

"But that was during the day. During the day it's a beach."

"It's exactly the same now. The people are the same. The cars are the same. The ocean is the same, so black and nervous. Even the dunes are in exactly the same place. Look, I left my sandals here, and here they are!"

There are sounds of moaning, very much like wind, and then a few whispers. We are not making people comfortable. They walk away.

"Sounds different, though," I say.

"Well," he says, "you can hear things better at night."

There is more moaning, definitely not wind.

"Do you think he's all right?"

And then a deep sigh, too close to mistake for anything but pleasure.

"Yeah, I think he's fine. Let's go see."

"No," I say, "you go. I don't think I'm ready yet."

"Are you sure you're all right alone?"

"I'm not alone," I tell him. "I have the dog. Don't do anything I wouldn't do."

"That's generous of you."

"I'm concerned," I say. "For your health."

"What should I do if I see your father?"

"Do what I would do. Bend over."

"You sure you wouldn't be jealous?"

"Look," I say. "Just tell him it's for me."

"I'm sure he'll love that."

"I'm sure you will too."

We kiss, lightly, and separate.

It's true, my father might be here. Some of the men on the beach look like him. Once, I was running here with the dog, a guy followed me in a Jaguar just like my father's. He had the same black beard, too, and the same eyes, heavy lids, like Nixon's. They always seemed to be closed from smiling, but after a while you know better. There he was just like my father, and I was—evidently—just his type. He followed me here, it was just sunset, and I thought, well, maybe he's my type too; why is this so exciting, otherwise? The guy wasn't handsome, I could see that even from across the road. If he wants me so much, I thought, he can't be such a catch—so much am I my father's son, unloved once, maybe, forever now unwilling to accept love. Still, I was willing to try, until he got out of his car, a dumpy, unhappy man, leering with disbelief. I unleashed the dog and ran away toward the water.

When I look for my father—look for him, that is, not here but with my mind's eye, rummaging among the old scenes and inscribed moments from the past: rocking on his lap until I fell asleep, for example, the old rocking chair squeaking gently each time he leaned back, thinking up the next line in his song—I am swept along, further and further from any time I can remember well, impatient and unsettling as a quick wind pushing in from an open window. I still see him, occasionally, for dinners across a restaurant table, or for a brief moment outside

a graduation, a wedding, a funeral. He was there at home, I
know, until age thirteen (my first and almost last wet dream
that year—desire right away reached out with my hand to
fulfill itself). But his business meetings had gotten later and
later, his meals, breakfast and dinner anyway, were brought to
him in the bedroom by my mother, who apologized to us with
her eyes as she disappeared across the house with his tray,
leaving us to our supper watching "*Star Trek*," if my brother
was home, and something animated and inane, if my sister,
whose chair was closest to the television, had her way. The day
my father left, calling me from touch football a moment to his
vast green Cadillac, he was already long gone. "I'm going away
for a few days," he said, and I nodded and shrugged as if I
believed him, just to let him get away smoothly, he had left so
long before. "A few days," was our secret code, his and mine,
whether or not my mother and the rest of the world had
understood. To make this parting easier, and all of his goings
and comings and absences even right there among us, he had
been preparing us, in happy moments as well as in trouble, to
disregard him, to contradict our perceptions and feel their
opposites: to see him when he wasn't there, to ignore him when
he was, to hear the truth when he spoke something else, and to
listen in his silence for the answers we needed. He did not eat
with us but his place at the table was set; when he did appear it
was behind a wall of the newspaper, flimsy and translucent,
but which we dared not assault either with our hands or our
voices. When he held my hand, as we walked along the street
or drove somewhere in the car, he would squeeze it sometimes,
returning my squeeze, but soon I would have squeezed too
often, asked that way once too much for his response, and then
his return squeeze would be dramatic, suddenly demonstrative,
but also false, because it signaled his escape, his fingers wrig-
gling quickly from my grasp, lightly scratching my palm, perhaps to fool my hand with affection.

When he scratched my back, rocking there in the chair until
I could fall asleep, his fingers like an unsettled animal would
lightly brush my skin, his thoughts and desires somewhere else,

sleeping perhaps, the rounded, manicured nails never too sharp or too deep, though sometimes his attention would leave entirely and if I did not wake him his hand, skipping back again and again like a song trapped in a broken record, would grate deeper and deeper into irritation. If some curve or patch of skin, however, needed him intensely, some itch gaping to be scratched, I might lightly moan or arch my back as his fingers trailed by accidently—never tell him outright, though, never correct or direct him there, because once he was awakened, that playful animal brushing against me would be gone, and his hand, too quick and hard now, though still warm and polished and powerful, would return from its small and innocent dream self, an untamed creature suddenly impatient, trapped beneath the cotton of my shirt, anxious to wriggle out and be free.

Once when he came home there seemed to be a sheep or a lamb bleating inside his coat. He shrugged at our surprise, said he couldn't hear it. "Yes!" we said, "there it is again!" As he turned upstairs the sheep bleated again, and we chased after him, squealing already with the knowledge that somewhere, sometime soon he would divulge his wonderful secret. Together with us he looked under the pillows in his bedroom (where we had heard the sheep again), we looked among the tasseled shoes and dark suits in his closet, where the animal seemed to have fled, we gave up during dinner and then heard it outside, when he had stepped out to the door to look there. Even when finally, before we went to bed, he took out that small box which if you turned it upside down would bleat like a sheep (and another time it would moo like a cow, and once it laughed hysterically within its velvet pouch—a laughing box, he called it), our delight was not diminished but neither, entirely, was our confusion. That box was too small to contain all his mystery. Along with us he had looked for those creatures and now, even when the answer had been revealed and was shown to be simple, the mystery remained: something we had searched for with him, that together, the next day or the next, we still might find.

There were jokes, there were sight gags, there were long

stories about people who never existed, which would end at last with either a funny answer or else an outrageous impossibility—shoes and sneakers grew from trees until they were the right size; snow snakes would reach up from the snow to bite our sleds as we raced headlong down the hill—at which point one of us would have to complain away our excitement and disbelief. Then he would smile, preserving the pleasure of his silence as we clung to him, climbed all over him, clamoring still to get inside somehow, inside his knowledge, inside his head, his embrace, all the time begging for the truth.

But that was what he could not give; my father would not tell us the truth, much as he liked to teach us, much as he liked to show that behind every mispoken sentence of ours he knew the grammar, behind every equation he knew the math; indeed behind every game he played, checkers and hangman and tic-tac-toe, secretly he knew all the answers. "Brothers and sisters," he would say, looking up from his newspaper to see if we were still waiting for his attention. We stopped our arguments, put down our forks and our glasses, ready for this familiar riddle we could never solve, and waited for him to continue. "Brothers and sisters, I have none," he would say, smiling at his own conundrum. "But that man's father"—and he would point across the table, close but not exactly to where I was sitting—"that man's father, is my father's son. Now who is that man?"

In North Jersey, where we lived among my mother's family—cousins everywhere down the block, doors opening all over town like secret clubs—the neighborhoods were still called by the names of the farms they had displaced—Butterworth Fields, Linsley Acres, Franklin Orchard. The hills swelled up intimately to contain them, giving over, on their far sides, to farms as yet unsubsumed, open country of old orchards and wild meadows not yet plowed under into highways and condominiums. The road to where my father's family still lived wound along those hills through farmlands and orchards toward the flat, sandy south of the state, finally cutting a straight ribbon through the low forest of the Pine Barrens, which at that time separated Philadelphia from Atlantic City. There were untill-able marshes, dense, half brown but still thriving stands of pine and scrub oak, and dark, uncharted canals winding toward the sea, small rivers visible sometimes, unexpectedly, always surprisingly, from the road as the car sped through. Each time, I always promised myself, I would ask my father to stop there with me someday in the future, when we could camp out in the Pine Barrens together, and paddle quietly along those secret canals.

When we sped past, however, we were always late, my father driving quickly and nervously toward his family home, resentful usually because my mother had taken too much time dressing us, cleaning us, reminding us to go to the bathroom, spreading, cutting and wrapping sandwiches for the two-hour trip, packing our clothes, her clothes and my father's clothes, and finally standing beside the dog until he too had relieved himself. I never found the right moment to ask my father, he never got the idea himself to take me camping in that place, and now the marsh has been drained, the trees uprooted, and the canals, if they still flow along somewhere, must run beneath concrete and macadam, unknown and unperceived by the children of modern neighborhoods.

Every year, for the Fourth of July, we hurried south, already late for the family picnic, which had grown to such proportions that all over the state even the family of family was invited, expected to come, missed and cajoled later if one year they were absent, and when present were seated by intricate priorities at metal tables unfolded in the large mown field behind the house. All my father's family came, rich cousins from Philadelphia, poor cousins from Atlantic City, unrelated people from as far south as Maryland. From the North, where the accents tilted toward New York rather than Philadelphia, there was only us—my mother's family. Her parents came as well, and her brother and sister too packed up their own families for the morning's drive; "a long way to go for a hot dog," my brother complained, and every year we quoted him. There is still no easy way to get there, although now that old road, patched and potholed and transforming for a stoplight or two into small-town main streets, has been cut up by the highways, shadowed by overpasses and stripped of its scenery. By Madison, the town just beyond our own, bananas had emerged from my mother's bag; by Princeton there were no more peanut butter and jelly sandwiches left, and by New Brunswick we were racing toward the nearest gas station, my mother, in her modest whisper, urging my father's weight on the pedal. When eventually we emerged from the Pine Barrens, there were peach orchards, scrubby blueberry farms, wild azalea hedges, and we knew we were close. "When will we get there?" one of us always asked, not from petulance or impatience, but for the half-desired frustration elicited by my father's annual response: "Just as soon as we finish this poem. But you can't interrupt me." And he would clear his throat several times before beginning:

Jack in the beanstalk, itty-bitty boo,
I love Mommy, Daddy, Grandma, Grandpa,
Grandma, Grandpa, Aunt Debbie, Uncle Marty . . .

and the list would continue, including our fish, our hamsters, and the iguana my father had been hand-feeding for years with mealworms, until one of us in the back would say, "Come on, Dad!" Then he would say we had interrupted, and we had to start all over, waiting a second time while again he cleared his throat. Finally, however, despite the whining and some real tears of frustration, old trees began to shade the road, reaching out from either side until they had closed the gap of summer sky, a rich canopy of moving green enclosing us, welcoming us into town. There, each time, with a final, satisfied, attentuated cadence, my father always just finished his list of the people we loved.

Somewhere in this town, I always knew, I would find him. He had grown up here, had fished and boated and planted gardens with his own father, had urinated in a patch of poison ivy and, to the howling delight of his family, had infected his penis. He had been a schoolboy here; had spoken his bar-mitzvah portion across the street in the synagogue his parents had built for the town's few Jews; had kissed someone for the first time, no doubt; had studied, applied to the state university, and before leaving home seen his brother come back from the war missing two limbs—in a basket, the story went; it was that that killed the grandparents. I had never fished or boated or planted gardens with my father, but I watched him as he did these things alone, sometimes with us in attendance: cast into the surf with his heavy rod, the tip bending from the weight of squid and clam chunks, or plastic lures; hunt under rocks and logs and among muddy stream bottoms for salamanders and crayfish, or net tadpoles from the banks of a pond; pull up crabs from their trap at the bottom of a bay, leaning out over his reflection on the jumping surface of the water. I escaped once from a baseball game to come to him in his garden, just visible through the school fence at the end of the field. He did not look up from his planting, but neither did he quite ask me to leave, go back to the game, or continue home where I would be welcome. Silently he dusted his tomatoes, harvested his beans, pulled up a stone from the soft earth. Silently and alone he fed his iguana; trained the dog; identified constellations from a circular map of the sky.

Still I knew the stories; my mother had told them, instilling us as best she could with a sense of his past, his personality, all that he must have possessed but could not share. By the time he was born his brothers had grown up; alone, he learned to catch frogs and keep rabbits, not to make up plays or argue the score of ballgames. He made up stories, but they were told to his dog, hunting woodchucks in the field. At his college play, when The Shadow was finally unmasked onstage, he appeared at an open window in a second Shadow costume, mystifying the audience, infuriating the cast. "Why?" we asked, delighted by his lonesome perversity, but he only shrugged, suppressing a smile.

With him our questions went unanswered, until they were

redirected to my mother. The imbalance was not in the least stable; naturally our curiosity drifted north, to where we ourselves were born and lived, where we saw every day the characters from my mother's stories, if not in person then in the persons of their old houses, their old streets, or their children, grown up by that time with children of their own. And my mother had frustrations of her own; "Why does red mean stop, Dad?" I asked one day from the backseat, when both of them were sitting there, staring ahead. After a moment, in which there was no answer, I asked again. "Dad, why does red mean stop?" I thought he would make up an answer, a fantasy law of nature, or else chuckle deeply and slowly without turning around, saying as he often did, without explanation, "Only the Shadow knows!" But the next pause was as empty as the first, if denser with refusal. "Mom," I asked, addressing her then instead, "Why does red mean stop?"

"Ask your father!" she shouted, her face, as she turned around, by then red as the light. To this day that question remains unanswered.

But as the car neared my father's childhood home, he was full of information, turning around often while he drove to see our faces, pointing out the farm where he had learned to drive a tractor, the lake where he had fished and hunted turtles with his father, and where even still there were bicycle boats to rent which his father, he said, had invented, for the use of the County Park. It was a wonderful but natural thing, that one's grandfather had invented something so widespread and famous as bicycle boats. Perhaps he really did invent them, as he sat on the high stool in his basement workshop, hiding from his wife's card parties. Even today I am proud when I see a bicycle boat anywhere at all: on the lake at Como, at Lugano, in California, even in a picture of a great lake in Japan. Maybe this pride is deep and instinctual, wiser in fact than my more modest skepticism; maybe, in his way, loving what was necessary if not real, recreating by need and desire what was not available, my father was telling us the truth after all.

"Hey."

"Who's that?"

"Not that again."

"Where have you been?" I ask him, just to hear it.

"Just looking around," he says. "I think I saw your father. What are you doing?"

"Just thinking about some things."

"Does it matter if no one's listening?"

"Someone was."

"But you didn't know that."

I tell him, going too far, "I had my suspicions."

"What's that supposed to mean?"

"Nothing. I'm just saying things. I'm lonely."

"I'm here with you now."

"How do I know when you'll go off again?"

"Well," he says—and I should appreciate the truth—"I don't know that you can. But I'm here now. Isn't that enough? How come you won't answer? Come on, I want to hear more. Is that what you love about me, that I'm like your father?"

"You're nothing like my father," I tell him, realizing already I am wrong.

"But you wish I was."

"Maybe. No, you're not at all. That's why I love you."

"No," he says, "I think I am. There's something you want from us both."

"What's that?"

"Well," he says, putting his arm around me in a strange way, affected, comfortless. "That's what I want to find out. That's why I was looking for him too. Your father."

"You mean that guy in the car? Let's go look at the stars."

"I am looking," he says.

"No, I mean, really look at them. Tonight they're amazing."

"I guess they just look like stars to me. You always want me to see something I can't."

"You can. You won't."

"No, I'm sorry. I don't think I can."

"Ah ha! You see," I tell him. "You're nothing like him."

"I don't know," he says. "You might be surprised."

"What's that supposed to mean?"

All of a sudden he is serious, and shakes my hand as if that will help me understand. "Maybe you want what you can't have," he says. "From both of us. Don't you see what I mean?"

I do not see.

"What happened after you got there? To the picnic."

"Oh, that!" I say, quickly returning to what's safe. As if time could go sideways, filling out always with alternatives instead of falling so swiftly down. "That's where he disappears. The whole thing, really, is looking for him."

"Go on."

"Well, then you take the dog," I tell him, handing her over. "That way I know you'll stay."

"I'm just going over there a minute. I'll be right back."

He says he'll be back, but everyone thinks that. It makes going away easier, pretending every kiss is not the last kiss, that every desperate caress and kindness, as usual, will be returned again and again, uncountable. I don't know for sure. We do need to stretch away sometimes, I've felt it myself, stretch and stretch until the fibers of our love strain into visibility, and we can feel secure again, give ourselves up to it, exercized, satisfied and peaceful. But it's dangerous. The roots can pull up, and then you're holding on to nothing, held back by nothing, still reaching toward some stiff breeze that's as flippant as any, up close. Love can't show itself, all flaccid and tangled. There seems, in fact, no connection, a kite flopping on the beach far away; and new roots take hold unexpectedly. The old thing, too long in the sand, rots.

Rushed as we always were during our trip, there was never a rush once we had arrived. Inside the house was calm as if hardly anyone at all lived there, in its dark cool rooms, its silent hallways and wide creaking stairs. It might have been a mansion. Set just off the road behind a stand of old oaks, the front steps swept grandly up to a plantation veranda, transformed, by the time we ever saw it, into real rooms, with a desk, an

Oriental rug, and a light that turned itself on at dusk, or when we made a shadow over it with our hands. My father would disappear with the luggage and the dog, my mother would continue in to find my grandparents, expecting us to follow, while we ourselves ran from treasured object to treasured object, forgetting to follow, forgetting even to notice our parents had gone. Instead there was a lava lamp, which boiled and then blossomed with orange wax; there was a telephone with a lighted dial on the bottom; a dancing ballerina trapped, with music, in a bottle; cigarette lighters of heavy golden metal in the shape of boats and dragons; and windows around three sides, louvers with gray metal handles which opened unexpected panels of glass all up and down the wall, so that even inside that room the world outside seemed very close.

Downstairs was large and elegant, a world where adults were well dressed and quietly reading that attracted us very little with its crystal chandeliers, its thick Oriental rugs, its little tables too small to rely on in any way, except to hold the undiminishing plates of taffy and smokey candies wrapped in wax paper. Upstairs, however, high up beyond the wide but steep staircase that creaked too much ever to allow an escape, a part of my father still seemed to live, that part of him which I could never see and never know: his young self, perhaps, but also the person, young or old, who was scared sometimes, and excited, and happy, who collected stamps and studied for tests and looked in the mirror, hoping the future would be wonderful. There were three bedrooms for three sons, and although which of them lived where once upon a time was always ambiguous—they seemed to have moved around—one of the rooms was called my father's, and it was there we slept, my brother and I. On his desk were still the tools from his childhood, old fountain pens and blotters and a crystal inkwell, painted postcards, an ivory letter opener and a green cloisonné lamp with a matching jar, where all the foreign stamps he had saved were still stuffed and unsorted, stamps from his brothers in the war, all around the Pacific and in Europe. The front bedrooms were bigger, looking onto the street and the traffic, but this small back bedroom for the youngest son looked onto trees and a grape arbor and the old field where his rabbit hutch still tottered on three rotting legs. It was here he had dreamed—of being a man, we thought, of having sons like us, of the bogeymen that might any minute come through the window, moaning in the wind, or when an airplane droned across the sky—and so we loved to be left there at night, waiting for those same dreams to come to us.

Where is he in this house, this memory of a house, already burned to the ground and replaced? At seven I sat at his desk trying to conjure him up, rolling the blotter pad again and again over papers by then twenty years dry. I sorted the stamps before stuffing them back in their jar. I tried to smell, in the old woolen blankets and cotton sheets and cedar drawers of his dresser, the child he had been, before the man he became wrapped a cloak around himself and disappeared. He had been, as a child, a magician. Once I found his magic bag in a chest in the attic, deep folds of crimson velvet, along with a dried-out violin from the days when my uncle still had both his arms. The magic bag that was my father's made things disappear, silk handkerchiefs, watches, combs, a little red ball, or even a flower. Long after I had found it and he'd shown me how to use it, twisting the handle subtly while distracting people's attention, he took it along to a birthday party. He had bought his friend a cheap, garish tie, and for a joke took it back a moment, cut it up, to everyone's horror, into little bits, and dropped it into the bag where it should have transformed, come back together, or else disappeared entirely. When he dumped it out again the tie was still cut up. This was the joke. A good tie, a silk tie in conservative colors, was still wrapped up in his pocket. But although some of his friends laughed, not all of them laughed. This was the same year he left us.

The first man I loved was a lawyer like my father, a curly-haired, handsome thirty year old at a time when for me thirty was still far away. He turned me over in the dark and without a word, showed me silently what he wanted, as if the admission would be fatal to speak, shameful at least, to himself anyway; as if, having desired him, I had already given up any further right to shape or share in the event. You want it, his silent rhythm and stony face seemed always to be saying, you got it. And his sweaty defeat as well, rolling off me afterwards with his back to me at once: you wanted it, shameless member of a shameful tribe, you got it. One thing he did say was that he did it with boys to get back at his own father. I returned the favor only once, and he lay there mute, motionless, buttocks clenched but guiltily willing, indeed needing someone to reciprocate at last in vengeance and in love. When I left him, to go home to college and the rest of my life, he cried. "How can you do this to me?" he asked, helping me to pack my suitcase. "Do what?" I asked him back, and through his tears he said, "Make a person love you, and then disappear."

Once, at a ballet opening where Jackie Onassis had brushed past me on her way to her box, we sat, by pure chance, just across the balcony from my father and his wife of that time. He sat in the last box, we sat nearby at the balcony corner, and until the intermission we kept staring back and forth into our similar eyes, smiling, unbelieving. There was my father, there was his son who looked like him, arm inextricably close however to another strong arm, irrefutably a man's. What did my friend's strength make me seem, I wondered, submitting to him even just by being smaller; what, to my father, did this very manly-looking man make me, since I loved him? And what, finally, would my father say, when eventually we found each other between acts, now that he had seen the flesh I loved, the eyes and lips and fingers and muscles that were not his, that loved me?

This is a strange summer here. All up and down the coast the dolphins are dying. Every day scientists come to wrap up a new corpse and haul it away in the back of a truck, while people in bathing suits stand around shaking their heads, mourning because dolphins have always been a sign of hope, and never cease with that sentient smile even when they are dead.

South of the city, in New Jersey, the tides have washed up wave after wave of pure garbage, ruining most of the beaches. There was sewage in the water, and medical refuse, old hypodermic needles and bloody bandages and, evidently, worse. A garbage ship could not find a place to dump, and wandered the Atlantic for a month before returning here to burn its cargo. And just down the beach a huge old whale died in the surf, attracting thousands of sharks. They've buried it, and the beaches are open again, but the locals say it seeps out from the sand, what's left of a carcass, and you don't bury a whale onshore, and the sharks will be back.

On this beach, we have our own problems. Everyone you meet has probably slept with someone who slept with someone who slept with someone who died. And what do you do with that? You can close yourself up, choose stoic patience over intimacy and risk. How much is it worth to you? Or you can find yourself a love, and because life is dear, risk everything for that love, through hurt and perseverance and frustration, even when the breezes blow attractively elsewhere, anywhere but here. Or else, until that love comes, you can step out on this beach looking for it, waiting for it, hoping for it, trying to be prudent but knowing that everything going on here, all the connections and pleasures and meetings and excitement and disappointment are just a few swift steps anyway from that unknowable darkness already lapping into high tide.

"Hey there," someone says. "What're you doing?"

"Looking at the stars," I say.

"I'm looking at you."

I nod, and smile, keep looking at the stars. He comes closer to me, puts his hand against my cheek.

"How you doing, tonight?"

"Fine," I say.

He puts his arm around me, bites my ear and then wets it with his tongue. I am still standing, and if asked what I am doing, would still say looking at the stars. He is maybe fifty-five, my father's age, sufficiently handsome—at least at night—and confident with liquor. I let him almost kiss me, then pull away.

"You want to go back there?" he says, nodding toward the dunes.

I shake my head, but not emphatically enough, and he touches me until I touch him back. I can hear my dog nearby, the muted clanking of her tags. Of course I am being watched, that's why I'm doing it. This is where my love has been; where I am now. Whose fault has it been? Mine? His? We are swept away sometimes, together, powerless.

"I want to be with you. All night."

"I'm with a friend," I say.

"Can't you tell your friend to go home?"

"No, I promised him."

"You like this?"

"Yes."

"I know you like this. I like this too. I could be with you all night, doing this."

He could, too, no doubt. But I am bored before we begin, because already I have been seen, this has been recorded between us, and I have reclaimed something, some pride perhaps, or perhaps now I have given it up. I have given something else up, too, larger, irretrievable, but don't yet know what, being so much in the middle all the time, so blinded by the wind of now, now, now. Soon it is finished, and I walk away, back toward my life, my love, and my dog.

"What were you doing?" he asks.

"Same as you," I say. A foolish retribution, I can see that already. A stupid way to say come back to me. But perhaps, given this, given his own insecurity, he will come back now. He calls me to him, my name a slight whine on his voice, perhaps a welcome beginning of regret. But all he asks is this:

"Why did you leave me with the dog?"

I wonder if I will ever hold him again? Out on the beach, where the stars light up the night sky but leave us in darkness, he is far away even so close to me, sitting just above the surf, the sand beneath us still warm from the day. How did we come to this? When did a few feet become so far, so impossible to traverse? We met as children, it seems now, conjured up and clinging to each other like gravity, a new home, a safe place we could finally trust because it would not crumble, or disappear. "I think," I said that first time—and his eyes, panicked, said Must you leave me? "I think," I continued, "we should see each other again. And again." Now we are looking at each other, and what do we see? Two bodies merely small and vulnerable beneath all this expanse, hardly home to each other, hardly salvation, but still despite everything we are here, and perhaps the small gesture may sufficiently imply the rest, cupped hands holding water enough to drink. I move closer, a foot or two. I want to say I hope the moon will rise, and show a path along the water, tempting but unreal. Will he know what I mean? Will he answer? Together still, at least until the tide comes in, we listen to the waves one more time, and say nothing.

I remember one day long ago at another beach, I was lying with my father under the umbrella, surrounded by the whole family and a beachful of other families. My arm was thrown over his chest, while with my head I nuzzled for a hollow space on his shoulder. Sometime then, as I struggled to find the right spot, I realized what he must be feeling, why he had stiffened suddenly, his body unaccommodating and comfortless; it was too late for this, now, he must have decided; our time was over; I was too big. To the world, and to him then as well, we were unbelievably two men lying there like that, suspicious, shame-less, shocking—no longer simply man and child, no more father and son.

"Where is he?" we asked, meaning our father, who had disappeared from his seat at the main table in the center of the field. Hamburgers and hot dogs were still sizzling on the grill, and an old uncle was speaking into the microphone. Still, from the children's table we had noticed him leave, and before long we had to run inside after him. Sarah, my grandmother's helper, was the only one we found. She shrugged in front of the sink, didn't answer for a while, and finally said, "In the basement, most likely," assuming probably we had meant our grandfather, who often disappeared down there. She could not understand him and had long ago stopped trying—with her he pretended he was deaf, ignoring questions, calls to dinner, phone calls in her presence, and after a while she must have believed him. We had often watched our grandfather there in the basement, sitting silently at his workbench among jars of nails and frightening saws and drills and coils of colorful wire, and everything from the house that had ever broken or rusted or come unglued: a cuckoo clock, the bird unwilling to come out; a silver pitcher without a handle; a picture frame with shattered glass. He had fled the picnic just before our father, as he had fled much of his married years, escaping the shame of not being loved. His wife tolerated him at best, though they never by that time voiced a quarrel. Her rich father was his boss, and the whole family, it seems, had been quickly unimpressed. A quiet man, a cheerful man with a round face and a mirthless grin, he had sat mostly silent through this family picnic as he did every meal, smiling when the sarcasms, even by his sons and wife, even in company, would imply his stupidity, his weakness, the embarrassment of his presence. Once, as a joke, his elder sons had stripped a turkey carcass of every scrap of meat, and for his dinner passed him only the dry pile of bones. He didn't look up from his plate, didn't look for ridicule or mocking or even more food, but in good faith merely set to work with his knife and fork, looking there still for sustenance.

We knew the basement, what it looked like, what the staircase looked like in the somber light of its one exposed, transparent bulb. But we could never remember where it began, where the door was that led down to that quiet world, where our father and his own father had evidently taken refuge. And Sarah had turned back to the sink, finished most definitely with our questions. We did remember, however, my father's constant answer whenever we asked him where the basement was. "Downstairs," he would say, pointing down. "You get there through here." He would lean over into a huge red Chinese vase standing against the wall, shiny and fragile and taller than either my brother or myself, on which fishermen had been enameled, casting their nets, and a small boat sailed along the horizon. We could only hold on to the white ceramic lip and stretch up to see the blackness contained inside that pot. The bottom was invisible to us, and so we believed my father somehow, although at its neck the vase was very narrow, and could not have held even a child in its wider but inaccessible belly. Still we knew that as children we could not understand everything, and because this was a mystery, and because we tried to peer down into it every time we passed it, hoping we had grown up enough finally to see, we never forgot. It was to this vase we wandered again now, knowing we still would not understand what my father had meant about getting to the basement this way, and that it was perhaps untrue, or half true, or true somehow only to him.

My brother, somewhat taller, leaned over, and called down "Hello in there! Anybody home?" We heard the hum of an echo, enough of an answer to continue. "Come back!" I yelled, not tall enough to shout into the vase; there was no echo. So I shouted again, this time jumping up for an instant above that ceramic mouth, as if it were a water fountain up there, and I might reach the spigot just long enough for a sip. This time my own high voice made the vase hum for a second with life. "Dad!" we yelled, taking turns jumping up, because by now the thing itself was a game, a pleasure between us, and whether or not we believed he would hear us, we could not stop. The vase began to rock, toward me when it was my turn, away from me when it was my brother's. "Dad!" during my brother's turn became suddenly "Don't!" but I was too excited by then to stop—he had let go and I would get two turns in a row. "Dad!" I yelled again, squealing by now with pleasure, and took my second turn before my brother could stop me. And as I yelled again, still trusting my weight against my brother's, the vase suddenly slipped across the smooth oak of the floor, fell down on top of me, and like the eggshell of a chick just hatched, cracked and shattered around me into pieces big and small, liberated but useless.

Later, when I was perhaps twelve instead of six, I had forgotten the beginning of this story, seeing our father leave the table, chasing after him inside, hunting for him, wondering where he had gone. I remembered only the shame, as I lay there, of the aftermath, the arrival first of my father and brother, and then other people, my mother and grandmother, who lifted me up but cried, and relatives who shook their heads in anger and regret, having hoped perhaps to inherit that perished vase someday themselves. I remembered most of all my father standing there, rubbing his own forehead, unaware that I had hurt myself, or that I'd been looking for him and now had found him, angry no doubt but also unwilling to admit, even through punishing me, that I was his. All he could say, grimacing and shaking his head, was "How?"

By twelve I understood and even accepted this contempt, which might have been undeserved, I considered, but at least kept us connected, his raised lip a real response to something about me, even something unknowable I could not yet see.

He embraced me only once. To assuage some trouble between my parents we had taken a family trip, and in a tourist shop there was a trinket I could not resist, though I knew it was too foolish a thing to ask for—a tiny moonshine jug with a kernel of corn inside. So I slipped it in my pocket, and my father, all the way down the aisle, must have seen me. Near the door he approached, smiling too widely, arms extended as though he wanted to hug me, but really he only wanted to catch me out. His embrace was too emphatic, too tight and exploratory, his hands reaching where they had never reached. In helpless agony I returned his caress, holding on, even knowing he would find on my person what he knew was there already, that guilt, and shame and love, though it was only the trinket he wanted.

Still, somehow, he had been the first to arrive after that crash in which I fell to the floor, hit my head and shattered that priceless vase. As soon as I fell, I remembered at once where the real door to the basement was, revealed clearly now by my brother's frantic steps afterwards against the wooden floors, through the hall, back into the kitchen, and into the dark pantry, where a door should not have been but was. Just across the wall I heard him open that door, race down the stairs, and suddenly stop. There was no conversation, no frantic report, even no movement that I could hear, and I could not imagine what my brother saw that made him suddenly stop, and not speak.

Now I can. My father's father is sitting on the high stool at his bench, pliers in hand, twisting wires round and round a nail. My own father sits on a bottom step silently watching him as long before he used to watch him, waiting for him to turn around and speak. My brother, halfway down, stops in his flight because neither the crash upstairs nor even the troubled pounding of his feet this close has distracted them, caused them even to look up, or turn, or speak, as if perhaps by concentrating harder, by not responding, by working just another minute they might still succeed at whatever invention it was, and for everything before them, broken, misused, or forgotten, it would not yet be too late.

THE BOYS IN THE BARS

• CHRISTOPHER DAVIS •

1

WHILE WE CLUSTERED around the end of the bar, behind us, in the light August dusk, a thin man was screaming in our direction from across the street. I could not hear what he was saying through the window but I could hear the melodic rising and falling of his voice, punctuated with an occasional sudden roar, and I turned to watch, missing, for a few moments, the conversation around me. The man wore a long wool coat that reached his ankles and as he screamed he clutched the sides of his coat tightly and bent toward us.

"After they come I throw them out," Peter said, and when I heard that I turned back.

"What, no orange juice?" another friend, Robert, asked.

"Orange juice, hell. Fuck 'em and throw 'em out!"

"In high school—" I started.

"Can you remember back *that* far?" Terry interrupted, but I ignored him.

"In high school we used to call that the four F's: Find 'em, Feel 'em, Fuck 'em and Forget 'em."

"Except in his case he finds them and they fuck him," Terry said.

"You've got that right!" someone else said.

"Why is it that because we're gay we have to talk about what we do in bed?" I asked. "You'd never talk to a straight man about the way he has sex with his wife."

"But *we're* not straight," Peter said. "That's the greatest thing about being gay: You don't have to be uptight about sex."

"Sex is the *only* thing about being gay," someone else said.

"You're right there," Peter said. "Like I said, after they come, throw them out!"

"You don't know a man until you know what he does in bed," Terry quoted.

"I can't wait to hear you when you finally find the man you love," I said to Peter.

"There goes Gene, The Romantic," someone said.

"Fuck love," Peter said. "Just give me a Puerto Rican boy with a huge cock."

I saw a flashing light from the side and turned back toward the windows. A police car slowed and then stopped by the man across the street, who screamed a single long note when he saw it. Two people in uniform, a man and a woman, got out and approached the man from either side. They left the lights on the car flashing and the mirrors inside the bar caught the lights and spun them around the room. The man still screamed, and he backed up against the iron fence that circled the park and then took off his coat and held it in front of himself as a shield. He wore a sleeveless T-shirt, and I could see that his arms were extremely thin.

"Why can't they shut off those fucking lights," Peter said.

No one answered him. We were all watching the scene outside. It was like watching pantomime because we could not hear the words.

"I'm going to walk around," Peter said, and he picked up his drink and went into the other room. There was a piano there, and he stood at the end of the keyboard and watched the pianist's hands.

An ambulance with its lights spinning came down Seventh Avenue and turned by the bar. It stopped facing the wrong way on the one-way street; the police car and the ambulance were head to head and both sets of lights flashed spasmodically. Traffic moved very slowly around the vehicles and there was a cacophony of horns. A crowd was gathering, attracted by the lights and the noise, and I asked the bartender to watch my drink and went outside.

"I'm going to kill you all!" the man was screaming. "All of you!"

The policeman and woman and the men who had come with the ambulance talked quietly to the man, but he screamed, "I'm going to give you all AIDS!" and he rushed at them, holding his coat like a matador's cape. There was a ripple of sound through the crowd when the man said "AIDS," and everyone, the men from the ambulance, the policeman and woman, and the crowd, moved back quickly. The policeman and woman drew out their clubs, and I did not want to watch but I did. The policewoman stood in front of the man and slowly slapped her club against her palm and then carefully walked around the man's side, and as she did the man turned with her until his back was away from the fence. Then the policeman handed his club to one of the ambulance men and jumped on the man from behind. The man screamed with rage and he twisted and tried to bite the policeman's hand, and when he did that the rest of them all jumped on him quickly, as if they were recovering a fumbled football. The man went down hard. He struggled on the ground and the policeman, a large, heavy man, lay flat on top of him and bent his arms back roughly until he could get his wrists into handcuffs. When the handcuffs were locked the man suddenly stopped struggling and went limp, and then he sobbed with great animal cries. The police officers pulled him to his feet. His forehead was bleeding and he shook his head, trying to keep the blood out of his eyes.

"Show's over, folks!" the policewoman yelled. "Let's move on now!"

The crowd started to break up. First the people on the outside started to move and then a few at the center turned and pushed their way to the outside, and I left also. I went back into the bar and picked up my drink and looked for my friends. They were all standing by the piano.

"Did you see what happened outside?" I asked.

"If you've seen one crazy you've seen them all," Terry said.

"Not quite. This one had AIDS. He said he wanted to spread it."

Peter's eyes followed an attractive young man who walked across the room. "Too young, no dick, and I don't like redheads," Peter said. He looked back at me. "That happened to someone I knew," he said. "He had AIDS and he went really crazy. He had to be put away."

"If that ever happens to me, I hope somebody shoots me," I said.

"It would be a pleasure," Peter told me.

As we spoke the disco downstairs started and Peter picked up his glass. "I'm going down for a while," he said, and he told me that he would see me later. My other friends went with him, and after they left I said hello to someone who had been sitting at the piano watching us.

"Sit," the guy said, patting the stool next to him, and I did.

A young man with dark, curly hair walked in from the bar. He wore a white tank top that showed his muscular arms and shoulders and that was tight around his small waist.

"Hi! My name's Rico," he said to us. He spoke with a heavy Spanish accent.

"Just Rico?" I said.

"Just Rico."

"Gene." I held out my hand. He did not take it but instead bent over and kissed my neck.

"Is he your boyfriend?" he asked me. The young man whom I had just met and I smiled at each other.

"No," I said.

"Do you have a boyfriend?"

"Yes," I said. I lied.

"I'm looking for someone," Rico said. "I want a *boyfriend*," he added, and he started to walk away.

"Wait!" I said. "Save my seat. I know just the person."

Rico sat on my stool with his back to the piano, watching the crowd, and I ran down the stairs to the disco. Peter was leaning against the bar watching a shirtless black man dancing with himself in a mirror on a square column.

"C'mon, I want you to meet somebody," I said.

"I'm busy."

"Forget him. I've got a live one for you—a Puerto Rican with a huge cock."

"This better be good," Peter said and he followed me, carrying his drink.

"Peter, this is Rico," I said upstairs. "Rico, Peter." Rico kissed Peter's neck and nuzzled him a little, and Peter lifted his eyebrows at me over Rico's head. The two of them stayed at the piano with me for a while and then moved to an empty corner of the room, and a few minutes later I watched them put down their glasses, still half-full, and push their way through the crowd to the door.

I said good-bye to the man at the piano and left then too. The doorman gave me a kiss, and I stood talking with him for a few minutes.

"I hear there was a nut case here earlier," he said.

"Yeah." I stood back to allow some people to pass between us. "He had AIDS," I said when the people were inside.

"I heard."

"It's sad," I said.

"It is sad. But if anybody's going to act like that, they should be locked up."

"He probably will be," I said, and I said good-bye and crossed the street. It was a warm night and the sidewalk was crowded. There was a brown stain on the concrete where the man's head had hit it, and when I stopped to look I was bumped from behind.

"What the fuck's wrong with you!" a man yelled at me, and he rushed on. I walked slowly down Christopher Street toward the river. A friend was sitting in the window of a bar and he motioned for me to come in, but I smiled and waved and shook my head no and walked on, enjoying the evening.

I saw Peter and the others the next day at cocktail hour, as I did almost every day. It was Monday and Peter was wearing a suit. I was wearing a T-shirt and blue jeans.

"So, you didn't go to work today?" he asked.

"I went in this morning, but my secretary was out sick so I said that I had a dentist's appointment and left at lunchtime."

"What'd you do?"

"Went to the pier, of course," I said.

"I'll bet all the beauties were out today," Peter said.

"They sure were. I'm going crazy with this look but don't touch business."

"I think you carry that to extremes," Terry said. "It isn't necessary to give up sex, you just have to be careful."

"That's the trouble. I can't be careful."

Another friend heard the end of the conversation. "You complaining again, Gene?" he said.

"I'm just getting tired of the old right hand," I said.

"Use your left," Peter said.

"Use both hands," someone said.

"He wishes," Peter said, and everyone laughed.

If they only knew, I thought. "How was Rico?" I asked.

"He was a ten," Peter said. "Puerto Rican, built, and with the biggest dick you have ever seen."

"I don't want to hear about it," I said.

"He has beautiful soft skin," Peter added.

"Did you let him spend the night?" someone asked.

"I did not," Peter said.

"If you're through with him, I'll take him," someone else said.

"I am not through with him," Peter said. "In fact, I'm meeting him tonight."

I hushed the crowd around us and raised my glass. "That's two nights with the same man, guys," I said. "Here's to a record!" I took a drink from my glass.

"Get over it," Peter said.

The next night was the first workday evening any of us could remember that Peter did not come in to the bar at all. He was always there by five-thirty, and often we all had dinner to-gether, but that night we waited for him until almost eight. "Well," I finally said, "I don't know where he is, but I'm hungry and I'm tired and I've got a busy day tomorrow. Who's going to dinner?" Some friends said that they had to leave, and one who had been cruising someone across the bar said he wanted to stay for a while, but three of us went up the street to a new restaurant and intimidated a straight waiter.

Peter did not come in the next night either, or the night after that, but when I arrived on Friday he was already there, surrounded by our friends. I ordered a drink and waited for a pause in the conversation.

"What happened to the Ten?" I asked.

"I let him stay for a couple of nights and then threw him out."

"At least he got orange juice," someone said.

"Yes, but I made *him* buy it," Peter said, and everyone laughed.

2

I spent the next three weeks in Los Angeles, and then a few days in Mexico. My firm was opening a small office in L.A., and I was asked to go out to help set it up and to work with the local client that was the major reason for the new office, and although I knew it would be exhausting I agreed to go. I spent several evenings in the bars there, and I made a few friends, but when most of the men I met realized that I was interested only in some temporary companionship and not in sex they drifted away. There were a couple of attractive young men who thought that I was good mate material, and they allowed me to buy them drinks and were broadly affectionate, but I did not encourage them. Occasionally I took a tanned, blond, surfer-type with muscles and dimples and high cheekbones to dinner, but it was always a commercial transaction: I received a few hours of companionship from someone who, if not the best conversationalist, was at least pleasing to look at, and they received a dinner. One of the dinner companions was friendlier than the others and I took him out several times but always refused his invitations to go home with him afterward. I assumed that he was looking for something more permanent than a few dinners and I knew I could not offer it, and one evening, when I was very tired and had drunk too much wine, after he asked me again to go home with him I told him what I thought were the precise responsibilities of each of us in the transaction we had entered into. I was startled when the young man started to cry and then threw his napkin onto his plate and shouted, "You're a cold son of a bitch!" and jumped up and ran out. After that I ate alone.

I arrived back in New York late one Saturday afternoon, and although I was very tired and knew I should rest I stopped at my apartment only long enough to leave my suitcase in the front hall. The friend who had been watering the plants and caring for the apartment had bundled the mail into neat packets and left it on a table by the door, but I opened none of it. I was in the bar within two hours of the time the plane touched the ground at LaGuardia and my friends and I were all happy to see each other.

"Well, hello stranger," one of them said, and another said, "What, no tan?"

"Where's Peter?" I asked.

"If you can answer that question, you win the prize," Terry said, and for the next few minutes I was told about Peter. He had not been in once while I had been away. People had left messages with his secretary, who had said that he was fine as far as she knew, and people had left messages on his answering machine, but Peter had not returned the calls and he had not responded to several written invitations to the kind of parties and dinners that he usually loved because, with his sharp tongue and vast knowledge of sexual trivia, he was usually the object of everyone's attention.

"Don't worry," I said, although I was worried. "He'll be around again," and someone added, "They always are," and the conversation moved on.

I went home early. I had been in the same clothes for more than twelve hours and I was exhausted and wanted to take a shower. Later, when I was comfortable again, I went through the mail while I listened to my messages. There were several calls from someone with whom I had once had a brief affair, and I called him back first.

"What's up?" I said.

"I need a date," he told me.

"I'm too tired. I just got in."

"Not for tonight. For tomorrow night."

I was silent.

"Someone gave me an invitation to the Saint. It's even free."

"Come on, Andy. You know I don't go there anymore."

"Please," Andy said. "I've never been and I don't want to go alone."

I remembered a time of long, drug-heavy nights when we would all dance until dawn, bathed in an atmosphere sharp with poppers and glowing with love, love for the music, love for ourselves, love for life, and then, sometimes, if we were still coordinated enough, we would go to the baths in a group. There, after an hour or two, and two or three men, we would drift to the snack bar and exchange stories over thick slices of chocolate cake and large paper cups of milk, and the thought of it all, now that several members of that group were dead, was not pleasant.

"I can't," I said.

"*Please*," Andy begged.

"I'm sorry, but no," I said.

"I won't go unless you do," Andy said.

"I'm sorry."

Andy was quiet. "Okay," he said after a few seconds, and then after a few seconds more, "How was California?"

We spoke for a while longer before saying good-bye, and then as I walked away from the phone I began to feel sorry that I had disappointed someone who had never disappointed me. "But that's life," I said to myself, and I called a local Mexican restaurant that delivered and started opening the mail. There was a familiar white envelope in one of the bundles, and it held an invitation to the same party that Andy had asked me to attend. I sat and remembered and heard the music and felt the smooth floor under my feet and saw the lights, and I thought about the times I had liked best, when the disc jockey would play long, sweet sets of music at the end of the evening and we would dance slowly, drugged and swaying with exhaustion, until it was time to go out into the morning.

I called Andy back and said that I would go.

"Great!" Andy said. "I'll stop over and pick you up at ten."

"Ten! For what?"

"The invitation says eleven," Andy told me.

"Midnight should be early enough," I said.

"Midnight! I won't get to meet anybody who's there for the party."

"You *can't* be serious," I said.

I had thoroughly changed my mind by the next evening, and as I walked toward the familiar door with Andy beside me I knew it was a mistake. I did not recognize any of the doormen and as I walked down the black hall I could feel the presence of friends with whom I had once danced through the night and into the morning and who now danced in a different universe, and when I walked out into the main room I thought I might cry but I fought the feeling back until it went away.

It was crowded. I did not recognize any of the bartenders either.

"Well, this is it," I said.

"It's like something out of *Satyricon*," Andy said.

"Petronius?"

"No, Fellini."

"Oh," I said.

"I want to dance," Andy said, so I led him up the stairs to that familiar place under the stars. It was filled with shirtless, sweaty bodies as if nothing had changed, and I observed that the bodies looked the same as they always had. Only the faces were different.

We danced. I danced mechanically, poorly. I did not like the

D.J.'s selections, or perhaps I just could not follow his thoughts. It was different without drugs. While Andy danced he stared at the other dancers or looked up at the lights. Someone bumped me from behind and I ignored it, but then it happened again, still with no apology, and I turned around.

"Hey man, remember me?" he said. It was Rico, the Ten, and Peter was with him. Their shirts were in their back pockets; Peter's was in his right, Rico's in his left.

"Peter! Where the fuck have you been!" I pulled him off the floor to the side. "Everyone at the bar is worried about you." Rico and Andy followed us, and we all sat on the risers. Rico held Peter with both arms and rested his head on Peter's shoulder.

Peter was embarrassed. "Rico likes me to stay home," he said.

"*Oh*," I said.

"That's right," Rico said. "I don't like that bar. I don't like to stand around and drink. I like to dance."

"Now come on," I said. "I met you there. Besides, you don't have to stand around and drink. You can dance there too."

"You met me when I was hunting, man," Rico said. He hugged Peter more tightly. "And I don't like to dance in a cellar."

We spoke for a few more minutes until the music changed and then Rico pulled Peter out onto the floor again. Peter looked back and waved, but soon they were indistinguishable from the other shirtless men.

I did not want to dance anymore, and I took Andy's hand. "Come on, I want to show you something," I said, and I led him out into the hall and up the tight-curving open metal staircase to the balcony above the dance floor. "We used to come up here for sex when we were tired of dancing," I said. "We'd be hot and sweaty and we'd come up here and find someone else who was hot and sweaty and we'd play for a half hour and then go back and dance. Sometimes we'd fall in love on the spot and we wouldn't want to take the time to go home, so we'd go to the baths up the street."

Andy said nothing and we leaned on the railing and looked out at the semitransparent dome over the dance floor. The strobes around the outside flashed in a jarring sequence and we could dimly see the dancers jerk and turn disjointedly. As we stood there, screams went up when a new song began to come in under the music. Once I would have known what it was and screamed too if I had been dancing, but now I did not recognize it and I was suddenly terribly sad.

"I'm getting out of here," I said. "But you stay."

"No," Andy said. "If you go, I'll go too."

"Suit yourself," I said, and I ran down the steps quickly and Andy followed. At the bottom, when we were walking toward the exit, someone called my name but I did not stop.

"Want to come home with me?" Andy asked while we were waiting for our coats.

"I don't think so," I said, although I would have liked to; it would have been nice to hold someone.

"Please."

"Lay off, Andy," I said.

"How about a drink someplace then?" he asked.

"Not tonight. I'm tired, and I'm going home and going to bed."

"I guess I will stay, then," Andy said. He was disappointed.

We said good-bye and Andy went back into the main room. Outside, a cab stopped to let passengers out and I held the door for them and then got in and after I gave the driver the address I laid my head back against the seat and closed my eyes.

3

It is a beautiful day for November, warm, like spring, and clean. In the afternoon I take my camera to the park along the river. The Hudson is smooth and still. Downriver, the sun is too bright to look at. Most of the leaves are gone from the trees; squirrels run and dig in them on the ground, making sudden rustling noises. Only the oaks still hold their orange-and-brown crowns, and I pull a leaf from one and examine it. It is smooth and flawless. I crush it and smell it and it smells like an autumn leaf: spicy. A man wearing black leather leans against a stone wall and looks down, and I come to the wall and lean against it and look down also. Another man sits below us on another wall at the bottom of a flight of stone steps. He is hugging his knees and looking out at the river; the back of his head is toward us. The man near me turns his head toward me and looks into my face and then deliberately looks down at my crotch and slowly back at my face. He smiles, and I look away at a shirtless runner, who passes close enough for me to smell the sweat. I want to reach out and touch him, but I do not. As I look back over the wall at the man below he turns to look up at us and I see that it is Peter, whom no one I know has seen since I saw him that night at the Saint a month ago.

"Peter," I yell, and I run down the steps, holding my camera tightly against my stomach so it does not slap. "Peter," I say again at the bottom, "are you all right? Everyone's worried about you."

"I'm fine," Peter says.

"So why the hell don't you answer your calls?"

"I just want to be left alone."

Peter turns back toward the river. The man above us moves away.

The last person who told me that he just wanted to be left alone died of AIDS four months later, and I sit beside Peter on the wall, which is cold to sit on although the air is warm.

"Are you sure you're okay? Physically, I mean."

"I'm sure, I'm sure," Peter says.

I look out at the river for a while and do not speak, and then I ask, "Why are you cruising the park?"

"This way you don't have to throw them out," Peter says. "I'm not really cruising," he adds after a few moments.

"What happened to Rico?"

Peter gets up and starts to climb the steps and I climb beside him.

"He left," Peter says.

"Just like that?"

"Just like that. One day I came home from work and everything of his was gone. There wasn't even a note."

"That's awful," I say. We reach the top of the steps and walk north. We do not speak. The runner who passed me earlier passes us going in the other direction and he smiles.

"Did you ever meet your fantasy man?" Peter asks after we have walked a little.

I go to the wall and lean on it, looking out across the river, and Peter comes and leans beside me. "Yes," I tell him. "Once. I was his too I guess."

"So what happened?"

"We lived together for a few months, but then we decided to separate before one of us got killed."

"You lost me," Peter says.

"I don't know which was hotter, the sex or the fights," I say.

"What did he look like?"

"You know me. He was the Nordic type."

"Probably not a brain in his head, either."

"Oh, there was," I say. "That was the problem."

Peter is quiet and I am too. We watch another runner pass, sleek and healthy. This one is wearing a T-shirt that says "Gay Pride Run."

"He's almost enough to get me running again," I say.

"Oh God," Peter says. "I loved him."

I cross myself. "I'm a witness to that statement," I say. "The last of the tough guys has fallen."

"You're a pretty cold fish yourself," Peter says, and I know that it is true, but I know why too.

"So what went wrong?" I ask.

"You were lucky," Peter says. "When you met your fantasy man you were his too." Peter's voice starts to break. "The trouble was, I wasn't Rico's," he says, and he sniffs and rubs his eyes and then his breath begins to come in gasps and I can see tears on his cheeks and then he starts to cry with loud sobs. I am embarrassed and I turn away but he grabs my wrist. "Don't go," he says through his tears, and I turn to him and first I take his hand and then I drop it and put my arms around him and hold him tightly. I cannot prevent tears from coming to my eyes.

Gradually our tears stop and we separate. We do not speak for a long time but we are comfortable with our silence and we leave the wall and walk slowly back in the direction from which we have come.

"You know," I say, "in the three years I've known you I think this is the first genuine, human moment we've ever had."

"So whose fault is that? You're the one who's become the great untouchable."

"I guess I have; I never used to be," I say, and again I think about why.

"I'm scared of dying," I say after a pause.

"Me too," Peter says.

"*You*? What happened to 'throw them out after they come'? I thought you were still working your way through every eligible man in New York."

"You don't believe everything I say, do you?" Peter says. He kicks at a leaf and misses it. "There's a lot of the world I haven't seen yet, like Patagonia and Pago Pago."

"Check," I say. I make a motion in the air with my finger as if I were making a mark on a blackboard.

We are near the wooded hill where men cruise in the summer, where on a warm evening you could once hear the sounds of sex and the scent of poppers drifted on the breeze.

"Hey," I say to Peter. "How about a picture?" I point to the hill. The leaves are off the trees and they form a thick cover on the ground.

"Here?" he says. He laughs.

"Sure. Why not?"

Peter climbs the hill and leans against a tree and looks down at me. His body is striped with shadows.

"This is going to be quite a basket shot," I say, and he pushes his crotch out toward me. I take several photographs from different angles and then, when I am finished and am climbing up to him, I see an empty brown popper bottle in the leaves. It has a red cap and I pick it up and hold it for Peter to see. He laughs and we kick aside the leaves and soon uncover another one, and then Peter finds a blue foil packet that had held a condom and he points it out with his foot.

"Rubbers in the park," he says. "It's a sign of the times."

I agree, it is a sign of the times, and I take Peter's hand and lead him down the hill and out into the bright sunlight, and I have to look away as I begin to tell him my terrible news.

ADULT ART

• ALLAN GURGANUS •

I've got an extra tenderness. It's not legal.

I SEE A TWELVE-YEAR-OLD boy steal a white Mercedes off the street. I'm sitting at my official desk (Superintendent of Schools), it's noon on a weekday and I watch this kid wiggle a coat hanger through one front window. Then he slips into the sedan, straight-wires its ignition, squalls off. Afterwards, I can't help wondering why I didn't phone the police. Or shout for our truant officer down the hall.

Next, a fifty-nine Dodge, black, mint condition, tries to parallel park in the Mercedes' spot (I'm not getting much paperwork done today). The driver is one of the worst drivers I've ever seen under the age of eighty. Three pedestrians take turns waving him in, guiding him back out. I step to my window and hear one person yell, "No, left, sharp *left*. Clown." Disgusted, a last helper leaves.

When the driver stands and stretches, he hasn't really parked his car, just stopped it. I've noticed him around town. About twenty-five, he's handsome, but in the most awkward possible way. His clothes match the old Dodge. His belt's pulled up too high. White socks are a mistake. I watch him comb his hair,

getting presentable for downtown. He whips out a handkerchief and stoops to buff his shoes. Many coins and pens spill
from a shirt pocket.

While he gathers these, a second boy (maybe a brother of the
Mercedes thief?) rushes to the Dodge's front, starts gouging
something serious across its hood. I knock on my second-story
window—nobody hears. The owner rises from shoe polishing,
sees what's happening, shouts. The vandal bolts. But instead of
chasing him, the driver touches bad scratches. He stands, patting them. I notice that the guy is talking to himself. He wets
one index fingertip, tries rubbing away scrawled letters. Sunlight catches spit. From my second-floor view, I can read the
word. It's an obscenity.

I turn away, lean back against a half-hot radiator. I admire
the portrait of my wife, my twin sons in Little League uniforms. On a far wall, art reproductions I change every month
or so. (I was an Art History major, believe it or not.) I want to
rush downstairs, comfort the owner of the car—say, maybe,
"Darn kids, nowadays." I don't dare.

They could arrest me for everything I like about myself.

At five sharp, gathering up valise and papers, I looked like a
regular citizen. Time to leave the office. Who should pass? The
owner of the hurt Dodge. His being in the Municipal Building
shocked me—as if I'd watched him on TV earlier. In my
doorway, I hesitated. He didn't notice me. He tripped. Over a
new two-inch ledge in the middle of the hall. Recovering, he
looked around, hoping nobody had seen. Then, content he was
alone, clutching a loaded shirt pocket, the guy bent, touched
the spot where the ledge had been. There was no ledge. Under
long fingers, just smoothness, linoleum. He rose. I stood close
enough to see, in his pocket, a plastic "caddy" you keep pens
in. It was white, a gift from "Wooten's Small Engines, New
and Like-New." Four old fountain pens were lined there, name-
brand articles. Puzzled at why he'd stumbled, the boy now
scratched the back of his head, made a face, "Gee, *that's* funny!"

An antiquated cartoon drawing would have shown a decent cheerful hick doing and saying exactly that. I was charmed.

I've got this added tenderness. I never talk about it. It only sneaks up on me every two or three years. It sounds strange but feels so natural. I know it'll get me into big trouble. I feel it for a certain kind of other man, see. For any guy who's even clumsier than me, than "I."

You have a different kind of tenderness for everybody you know. There's one sort for grandparents, say. But if you waltz into a singles' bar and use that type affection, you'll be considered pretty weird. When my sons hit pop flies, I get a strong wash of feeling—and yet, if I turned the same sweetness on my Board of Education, I'd soon find myself both fired and committed.

Then he saw me.

He smiled in a shy cramped way. Caught, he pointed to the spot that'd given him recent trouble, he said of himself, "Tripped." You know what I said? When I noticed—right then, this late—how kind-looking he was, I said, "Happens all the time. Me too." I pointed to my chest, another dated funny-paper gesture. "No reason," I shrugged. "You just *do*, you know. Most people, I guess."

Well, he liked that. He smiled. It gave me time to check out his starched shirt (white, buttoned to the collar, no tie). I studied his old-timey overly-wide belt, its thunderbird-design brass buckle. He wore black pants, plain as a waiter's, brown wingtips with a serious shine. He took in my business suit, my early signs of graying temples. Then he decided, guileless, that he needed some quick maintenance. As I watched, he flashed out a green comb and restyled his hair, three backward swipes, one per side, one on top. Done. The dark waves seemed either damp or oiled, suspended from a part that looked incredibly white—as if my secretary had just painted it there with her typing correction-fluid.

This boy had shipshape features—a Navy recruiting poster,

forty years past due. Some grandmother's favorite. Comb replaced, grinning, he lingered, pleased I'd acted nice about his ungainly little hop. "What say to a drink?" I asked. He smiled, nodded, followed me out. How simple, at times, life can be.

I'm remembering: During football practice in junior high gym, I heard a kid's arm break. He was this big blond guy, nice but out of it. He whimpered toward the bleachers and perched there, grinning, sweating. Our coach—twenty-one years old—heard the fracture too. He looked around: somebody should walk the hurt boy to our principal's office. Coach spied me, frowning, concerned. Coach decided that the game could do without me. I'd treat Angier right. (Angier was the kid—holding his arm, shivering.)

"Help him." Coach touched my shoulder. "Let him lean against you."

Angier nearly fainted halfway back to school. "Whoo," he had to slump onto someone's lawn, still grinning apologies. "It's okay," I said. "Take your time." I finally got him there. The principal's secretary complained—Coach should've brought Angier in himself. "The *young* teachers," she shook her head, phoning the rescue squad. It all seemed routine for her. I led Angier to a dark waiting room stacked with textbooks and charts about the human body. He sat, I stood before him holding his good hand, "You'll be fine. You'll see." His hair was slicked back, as after a swim. He was always slow in class—his father sold fancy blenders in supermarkets. Angier dressed neatly. Today he looked so white his every eyelash stood out separate. We could hear the siren. Glad, he squeezed my hand. Then Angier swooned back against the bench, panting, he said something hoarse. "What?" I leaned closer. "Thank you," he grinned, moaning. Next he craned up, kissed me square, wet, on the mouth. Then Angier fainted, fell sideways. Five days later, he was back at school sporting a cast that everybody popular got to sign. He nodded my way. He never asked me to scribble my name on his plaster. He seemed to have forgotten what'd happened. I remember.

*   *   *

As we left the office building, the Dodge owner explained he'd been delivering insurance papers that needed signing—flood coverage on his mother's country property. "You can never be too safe. That's Mother's motto." I asked if they lived in town; I was only trying to get him talking, relaxed. If I knew his family, I might have to change my plans.

"Mom died," he said, looking down. "A year come August. She left me everything. Sure burned my sisters up, I can tell you. But they're both in Florida. Where were *they* when she was so sick? She appreciated it. She said she'd remember me. And Mom did, too." Then he got quiet, maybe regretting how much he'd told.

We walked two blocks. Some people spoke to me, they gave my companion a mild look like they were thinking, What does Dave want with *him*?

He chose the bar. It was called "The Arms" but whatever word had been arched between the "The" and the "Arms"—six Old English golden letters—had been stolen; you could see where glue had held them to the bricks. He introduced himself by his first name: Barker. Palms flat on the bar, he ordered beers without asking. Then he turned to me, embarrassed. "Mind reader," I assured him, smiling and—for a second—cupped my hand over the bristled back of his, but quick. He didn't seem to notice or much mind.

My chair faced the street. His aimed my way, toward the bar's murky back. Bathrooms were marked "Kings" and "Queens." Some boy played a noisy video game that sounded like a jungle bird in electronic trouble.

Barker's head and shoulders were framed by a window. June baked each surface on the main street. Everything out there (passersby included) looked planned, shiny, and kind of ceramic. I couldn't see Barker's face that clearly. Sun turned his ears a healthy wax red. Sun enjoyed his cheekbones, found highlights waiting in the wavy old-fashioned hair I decided he must oil. Barker himself wasn't so beautiful, a knotty wiry kid—only his pale face was. It seemed an inheritance he hadn't noticed yet.

Barker sitting still was a Barker almost suave. He wasn't spilling anything (our beer hadn't been brought yet). The kid's face looked, back-lit, negotiable as gems. Everything he said to me was heartfelt. Talking about his mom had put him in a memory-lane kind of mood. "Yeah," he said. "When *I* was a kid . . . ," and he told me about a ditch that he and his sisters would wade in, building dams and making camps. Playing doctors. Then the city landfill chose the sight. No more ditch. Watching it bulldozed, the kids had cried, holding onto one another.

Our barman brought us a huge pitcher. I just sipped; Barker knocked four mugs back fast. Foam made half a white mustache over his sweet slack mouth; I didn't mention it. He said he was twenty-nine but still felt about twelve, except for winters. He said after his mother's death, he'd joined the Air Force but got booted out.

"What for?"

"Lack of dignity." He downed a fifth mug.

"You mean . . . 'lack of discipline'?"

He nodded. "What'd I say?" I told him.

" 'Dignity, discipline.' " He shrugged to show they meant the same thing. The sadder he seemed the better I liked it, the nicer Barker looked.

Women passing on the street (he couldn't see them) wore sundresses. How pretty their pastel straps, the freckled shoulders; some walked beside their teenaged sons; they looked good too. I saw folks I knew. Nobody'd think to check for me in here.

Only human, under the table, my knee touched Barker's, lingered a sec, shifted. He didn't flinch. He hadn't asked about my job or home life. I got the subject around to things erotic. With a guy as forthright as Barker, you didn't need posthypnotic suggestion to manage it. He'd told me where he lived. I asked, Wasn't that out by Adult Art Film and Book? "You go in there much?"

He gave me a mock-innocent look, touched a fingertip to his sternum, mouthed, "Who, me?" Then he scanned around to make sure nobody'd hear, "I guess it's me that keeps old Adult Art open. Don't tell, but I can't help it, I just love that stuff. You too?"

I nodded.

"What kind?"

I appeared bashful, one knuckle rerouting sweatbeads on my beer mug. "I like all types, I guess. You know, boy/girl, girl/girl, boy/boy, girl/dog, dog/dog." Barker laughed, shaking his fine head side to side. "Dog/dog," he repeated. "That's a good one. *Dog*/dog!"

He was not the most brilliantly intelligent person I'd ever met. I loved him for it.

We went in my car. I didn't care to chance his driving. Halfway to Adult Art, sirens and red lights swarmed behind my station wagon. "This is it," I thought. Then the white Mercedes (already mud-splattered, a fender dented, doing a hundred and ten in a thirty-five zone) screeched past. Both city patrol cars gave chase, having a fine time.

We parked around behind; there were twelve or fourteen vehicles jammed back of Adult Art's single Dumpster; seven phone-repair trucks had lined up like a fleet. Adult's front asphalt lot—plainly visible from U.S. 301 Business—provided room for forty cars but sat empty. This is a small town, Falls. Everybody sees everything, almost. So, when you *do* get away with something, you know it; it just means more. Some people will tell you Sin is old hat. Not for me. If, once it starts, it's not going to be naughty, then it's not worth wasting a whole afternoon to set up. Sin is bad. Sex is good. Sex is too good not to have a whole lot of bad in it. I say, Let's keep it a little smutty, you know?

Barker called the clerk by name. Barker charged two films—slightly discounted because they'd been used in the booths—those and about thirty bucks in magazines. No money changed hands; he had an account. The section marked "Literature" milled with phone linemen wearing their elaborate suspension belts. One man, his pelvis ajangle with wrenches and hooks, held up a picture book, called to friends, "Catch *her*, guys. She has got to be your foxiest fox so far." Under his heavy silver gear, I couldn't help but notice on this hearty husband and father, jammed up against workpants, the same old famous worldwide pet and problem poking.

I drove Barker to his place; he invited me in for a viewing. I'd hoped he would. "World premiere," he smiled—eyes alive as they hadn't been before. "First show on Lake Drive anyways."

The neighborhood—like Barker's looks—had been the rage forty years ago. I figured he must rent rooms in this big mullioned place, but he owned it. The foyer clock showed I might not make it home in time for supper. Lately I'd overused the excuse of working late; even as Superintendent of Schools there're limits on how much extra time you can devote to your job.

I didn't want to peeve a terrific wife.

I figured I'd have a good hour and a half; a lot can happen in an hour and a half. We were now safe inside a private place.

The house had been furnished expensively but some years back. Mission stuff. The Oriental rugs were coated with dust or fur; thick hair hid half their patterns. By accident, I kicked a chewed rubber mouse. The cat toy jingled under a couch, scaring me.

In Barker's kitchen, a Crockpot bubbled. Juice hissed out under a Pyrex lid that didn't quite fit. The room smelled of decent beef stew. His counter was layered with fast-food take-out cartons. From among this litter, in a clay pot, one beautiful amaryllis lily—orange, its mouth wider than the throat of a trombone, startled me. It reminded you of something from science fiction, straining—like one serious muscle—toward daylight.

In the dark adjacent room, Barker kept humming, knocking things over. I heard the clank of movie reels. "Didn't expect company, Dave," he called. "Just clear off a chair and make yourself at home. Momma was a cleaner-upper. Me . . . less. I don't *see* the junk till I get somebody to . . . till somebody drops over, you know?"

I grunted agreement, strolled into his pantry. Here were cans so old you could sell them for the labels. Here was a 1950s tin of vichyssoise I wouldn't have eaten at gunpoint. I slipped along the hall, wandered upstairs. An archive of *National Geographics* rose in yellow columns to the ceiling. "Dave?" he was hollering. "Just settle in or whatever. It'll only take a sec. See, they cut the leaders off both our movies. I'll just do a little splice. I'm fast, though."

"Great."

On the far wall of one large room (windows smothered by outside ivy) a calendar from 1959, compliments of a now-defunct savings and loan. Nearby, two Kotex cartons filled with excelsior, stuffed—I saw on closer inspection—with valu-able brown-and-white Wedgwood—place settings for forty maybe. He really should sell these—I was already mothering Barker. I'd tell him which local dealer would give top dollar.

In one corner, a hooked rug showed a Scottie terrier chasing one red ball downhill. I stepped on it, three hundred moths sputtered up—I backed off, arms flailing before me. Leaning in the doorway, waiting to be called downstairs for movie-time, still wearing my business clothes, I suddenly felt a bit uneasy, worried by a famous thought: What are you *doing* here, Dave?

Well: Barker brought me home with him, is what. And, as far back as my memory made it, I'd only wanted just such guys to ask me over. Only they held my interest, my full sympathy.

The kid with the bad posture but (for me) an excellent smile, the kid who kept pencils in a plastic see-through satchel that clamped into his looseleaf notebook. The boy whose mom—even when the guy'd turned fourteen—*made* him use his second-grade Roy Rogers/Dale Evans lunchbox showing them astride their horses, Trigger and Buttermilk. He was the kid other kids didn't bother mocking because—through twelve years of school-ing side-by-side—they'd never noticed him.

Of course I could tell, there were other boys, like me, studying the other boys. But they all looked toward the pink-and-blond Stephens and Andrews: big-jawed athletic office-holders, guys with shoulders like baby-couches, kids whose legs looked turned on lathes, solid newels—calves that summer sports stained mahogany brown, hair coiling over them, bleached by overly chlorinated pools and an admiring sun: yellow-white-gold. But while others' eyes stayed locked on them, I was off admiring finer qualities of some clubfooted George, a kindly bespectacled Theodore. I longed to stoop and tie their dragging shoestrings—ones unfastened so long that the plastic tips had worn to frayed cotton tufts. Math geniuses who forgot to zip up: I wanted to give them dating hints. I'd help them find the right barber. I dreamed of assisting their undressing—me, bathing them with stern brotherly care—me, putting them to bed (poor guys hadn't yet guessed that my interest went past buddy-hood). While they slept (I didn't want to cost them any shut-eye), I'd just reach under their covers (always blue) and find that—though the world considered these fellows minor minor—they oftentimes proved more major than the muscled boys who frolicked, unashamed, well-known, pink-and-white in gym showers.

What was I *do*ing here? (Well, my major was **Art** History.) I was busy being a collector, is what. And not just someone who can spot (in a museum with a guide to lead him) any old famous masterpiece. No, I was a detective off in the odd corner of a sidestreet thrift shop, I was uncovering (on sale for the price of the frame!) a little etching by Wyndham Lewis—futuristic dwarves, or a golden cow by Cuyp, or one of Vuillard's shut-tered parlors painted on a shirt cardboard.

Maybe this very collector's zeal had drawn me to Carol, had led me to fatherhood, to the underrated joys of community. See, I wanted everything—even to be legit. Nothing was so obvious or subtle that I wouldn't try it once. I prided myself on knowing what I liked and going—shameless—after it. Every-body notices grace. But appreciating perfect clumsiness, that required real skill.

"Won't be long now!" I heard Barker call.
"All *right*," I hollered, exactly as my sons would.

I eased into a messy office upstairs and, among framed
documents and pictures, recognized Barker's grandfather. He
looked just like Barker fattened up and given lessons. During
the fifties, the grandad served as mayor of our nearby capital
city. Back then, such collar-ad looks were still admired, voted
into office.

A framed news photo showed the mayor, hair oiled, present-
ing horse-topped trophies to young girls in jodhpurs. They
blinked up at him, four fans, giggling. Over the wide loud tie,
his grin showed an actor's worked-at innocence. He'd been a
decent mayor—fair to all, paving streets in the black district,
making parks of vacant lots. Good till he got nailed with his
hand in the till. Like Barker's, this was a face almost too pure
to trust. When you considered the eyes of young Barker
downstairs—it was like looking at a *National Geographic* close-up
of some exotic Asian deer—you could admire the image forever, it wouldn't notice or resist your admiration. It had the
static beauty of an angel. Designed. That unaffected and willing to serve. His character was like an angel's own—the perfect
gofer.

I heard Barker humming show tunes, knocking around ice
trays. I opened every door on this hall. Why not? The worse
the housekeeping got, the better I liked it. The tenderer I felt
about the guy downstairs. One room had seven floorlamps in
it, two standing, five resting on their sides—one plugged in.
Shades were snare-drum shaped, the delicate lining frayed and
split like fabric from old negligees.

I closed all doors. I heard him mixing drinks. I felt that buzz
and ringing you learn to recognize as the sweet warning sign of
a sure thing. Still, I have been wrong.

I checked my watch. "Ready," he called, "when you are." I
passed the bathroom. I bet Barker hadn't done a load of laundry since last March or April. A thigh-high pile made a moat

around the tub. I lifted some boxer shorts. (Boxers show low self-esteem, body wise; my kind of guy always wears them and assumes that every other man on earth wears boxers, too.) These particular shorts were pinstriped and had little red New York Yankee logos rashed everywhere. They sure needed some serious bleaching.

There he stood, grinning. He'd been busy stirring instant iced tea, two tall glasses with maps of Ohio stenciled on them. I didn't ask, Why Ohio? Barker seemed pleased, quicker-moving, the host. He'd rolled up sleeves, his skin as fine as sanded ashwood. The icebox freezer was a white glacier dangling roots like a molar's. From one tiny hole in it, Barker fished a gin bottle; he held the opened pint to one tea glass and smiled. "Suit you?"

"Gin and iced tea? Sure." Seducers/seducees must remain flexible.

"Say when, pal." I said so. Barker appeared full of antsy mischief.

For him, I saw, this was still his mother's house. With her dead, he could do as he liked; having an illicit guest here pleased him. Barker cultivated the place's warehouse look. He let cat hair coat his Mom's prized rugs; it felt daring to leave the stag-movie projector and screen set up in the den full-time— just to shock his Florida sisters.

I couldn't help myself. "Hey, buddy, where *is* this cat?" I nodded toward the hallway's gray fluffballs.

"Huh? Oh. There's six. Two mother ones and four kid ones. All supershy but each one's really different. Good company."

He carried our tea glasses on a deco chrome tray; the film-viewing room was just ten feet from the kitchen. Dark in here. Ivy vines eclipsed the sunset; leaf-green made our couch feel underwater. I slouched deep into his dated scalloped cushions.

Sipping, we leaned back. It seemed that we were waiting for a signal: Start. I didn't want to watch a movie. But, too, I did. I longed to hear this nice fellow tell me something, a story, anything, but I worried: talking could spoil whatever else might happen. I only half-knew what I hoped for. I felt scared Barker might not understand my particular kind of tenderness. Still, I was readier and readier to find out, to risk making a total fool of myself. Everything worthwhile requires that, right?

I needed to say something next.

"So," is what I said. "Tell me. So, tell me something . . . about yourself. Something I should know, Barker." And I added that, oh, I really appreciated his hospitality. It was nothing, he shrugged then pressed back. He made a throaty sound like a story starting. "Well. Something plain, Dave? Or something . . . kind of spicy?"

"Both," I said. Education does pay off. I know to at least ask for everything.

"Okay," his voice dipped half an octave. The idea of telling had relaxed Barker. I could see it. Listening to him relax relaxed me. "See, they sent my grandad to jail. *For* something. I won't say what. He did do it, still, we couldn't picture prison—for him. My mom and sisters were so ashamed that, at first, they wouldn't go out to see him. I wanted to. Nobody'd take me. I called up prison to ask about visiting hours. I made myself sound real deep, like a man, so they'd tell me. I was eleven. So when the prison guy gave me the times, he goes, 'Well, thank you for calling, ma'am.' I had to laugh.

"They'd put him in that state pen out on the highway, the work farm. It's halfway to Tarboro and I rode my bike clear out there. It was busy, a Saturday. I had to keep to the edge of the Interstate. Teenagers in two convertibles threw beer cans at me. Finally when I got to the prison, men said I couldn't come in, being a minor and all. Maybe they smelled the beer those hoods'd chucked at my back.

"I wondered what my grandad would do in the same spot (he'd been pretty well-known around here) and so I started mentioning my rights, *loud*. The men said 'okay, okay' and told me to pipe down. They let me in. He sat behind heavy-gauge chicken wire. He looked good, about the same. All the uniforms were gray but his was pressed and perfect on him—like he'd got to pick the color of everybody else's outfit. You couldn't even hold hands with him. Was like going to the zoo except it was your grandaddy. Right off, he thanks me for coming and he tells me where the key is hid. Key to a shack he owned at the backside of the fairgrounds. You know, out by the pine trees where kids go park at night and do you-know-what?

"He owned this cottage but, seeing as how he couldn't use it—for six to ten—he wanted me to hang out there. Grandad said I should use it whenever I needed to hide or slack off or anything. He said I could keep pets or have a Club, whatever I liked.

"He said there was one couch in it, plus a butane stove but no electric lights. The key stayed under three bricks in the weeds. He said, 'A boy needs a place to go.' I said Thanks. Then he asked about Mom and the others. I lied: how they were busy baking stuff to bring him, how they'd be out soon, a carful of pies. He made a face and asked which of my sisters had driven me here.

"I said, 'Biked it.' Well, he stared at me. 'Not nine miles and on a Saturday. No. I've earned this, but you shouldn't have to.' He started crying then. It was hard, with the wire between us. Then—you might not believe this, Dave, but a black guard comes over and says, 'No crying.' I didn't know they could do that—boss you like that—but in jail I guess they can do anything they please. Thing is, Grandad stopped. He told me, 'I'll make this up to you, Barker. Some of them say you're not exactly college material, Bark, but we know better. You're the best damn one. But, listen, hey, you walk that bike home, you hear me? Concentrate on what I'm saying. It'll be dark by the time you get back to town but it's worth it. Walk, hear me?' I said I would. I left and went outside. My bike was missing. I figured that some convict's kid had taken it. A poor kid deserved it more than me. Mom would buy me another one. I walked."

Barker sat still for a minute and a half. "What else?" I asked.

"You sure?" He turned my way. I nodded. He took a breath.

"Well, I hung out in my new cabin a lot. It was just two blocks from the busiest service station in town but it seemed way off by itself. Nobody used the fairgrounds except for October and the County Fair. You could smell pine straw. At night, cars parked for three and four hours. Up one pine tree, a bra was tied—real old and gray now—a joke to everybody but maybe the girl that'd lost it. Out there, pine straw was all litterbugged with used rubbers. I thought they were some kind of white snail or clam or something. I knew they were yucky, I just didn't know *how* they were yucky.

"I'd go into my house and I'd feel grown. I bought me some birds at the mall with my own money. Two finches. I'd always wanted some Oriental type of birds. I got our dead parakeet's cage, a white one, and I put them in there. They couldn't sing, they just looked good. One was red and the one was yellow, or one was yellow and one was red, I forget. I bought these seedballs and one pink plastic bird-type of toy they could peck at. After school, I'd go sit on my man-sized sofa, with my bird cage nearby, finches all nervous, hopping, constant, me reading my comics—I'd never felt so good, Dave. I knew why my grandad liked it there—no phones, nobody asking him for favors. He'd take long naps on the couch. He'd make himself a cup of tea. He probably paced around the three empty rooms—not empty really: full of cobwebs and these coils of wire.

"I called my finches Huey and Duey. I loved my Donald Duck comics. I kept all my funnybooks in alphabetical order in the closet across from my brown sofa. Well, I had everything I needed, a couch, comics, cups of hot tea. I hated tea but I made about five cups a day because Grandad had bought so many bags in advance and I did like holding a hot mug while I read. So one day I'm sitting there curled up with a new comic—comics are never as good the second time, you know everything that's next—so I'm sitting there happy and I hear my back door slam wide open, grownups.

"Pronto, I duck into my comics closet, yank the door shut except for just one crack. First I hoped it'd be Grandad and his bust-out gang from the state pen. I didn't believe it, just hoped, you know.

"In walks this young service station guy from our busy Sunoco place, corner of Sycamore and Bolton. I heard him say, 'Oh yeah, I use this place sometimes. Owner's away awhile.' The mechanic wore a khaki uniform that zipped up its front. 'Look, birds.' A woman's voice. He stared around. 'I guess somebody else is onto Bobby's hideaway. Don't sweat it.' He heaved right down onto my couch, onto my new comic, his legs apart. He stared—mean-looking—at somebody else in the room with us. Bobby had a reputation. He was about twenty-two, twice my age then—he seemed pretty old. Girls from my class used to hang around the Coke machine at Sunoco just so they could watch him, arm-deep up under motors. He'd scratch himself a lot. He had a *real* reputation. Bobby was a redhead almost a blonde. His cloth outfit had so much oil soaked in, it looked to be leather. All day he'd been in sunshine or up underneath leaky cars and his big round arms were brown and greasy like . . . cooked food. Well, he kicked off his left loafer. It hit my door and about gave me a heart attack. It did. Then he was flashing somebody a double-dare kind of look. Bobby yanked down his suit's big zipper maybe four inches, showing more tanned chest. The zipper made a chewing sound.

"I sat on the floor in the dark. My head tipped back against a hundred comics. I was gulping, all eyes, arms wrapped around my knees like going off the high dive in a cannonball.

"When the woman sat beside him—I couldn't believe this. You could of knocked me over with one of Huey or Duey's feathers. See, she was my best friend's momma. I decided, no, must be her identical twin sister (a bad one) visiting from out of town. This lady led Methodist Youth Choir. Don't laugh but—too—she'd been my Cub Scout den mother. She was about ten years older than Bobby—plump and prettyish but real real scared-looking.

"He says, 'So, you kind of interested in old Bobby, hunh? You sure been giving Bob some right serious looks for about a year now, ain't it? I was wondering how many lube jobs one Buick could take, lady.'

"She studies her handbag, says, 'Don't call me Lady. My name's Anne. Ann with an E.' She added this like to make fun of herself for being here. I wanted to help her. She kept extra still, knees together, holding onto her purse for dear life, not daring to look around. I heard my birds fluttering, worried. I thought: If Bobby opens this door, I am dead.

" 'Anne with an E, huh? An-nie? Like Li'l Orphan. Well, Sandy's here, Annie. Sandy's been wanting to get you off by yourself. You ready for your big red dog Sandy?'

" ' I didn't think you'd talk like that,' she said.

"I wanted to bust out of my comics closet and save her. One time on a Cub Scout field trip to New York City, the other boys laughed because I thought the Empire State Building was called something else. I said I couldn't wait to see the Entire State Building. Well, they sure ragged me. I tried and make them see how it *was* big and all. I tried to make them see the logic. She said she understood how I'd got that. She said it was right 'original.' We took the elevator. I tried to make up for it by eating nine hotdogs on a dare. Then I looked off the edge. That didn't help. I got super-sick, Dave. The other mothers said I'd brought it on myself. But she was so nice, she said that being sick was nobody's fault. Mrs. . . . . the lady, she wet her blue hankie at a water fountain and held it to my head and told me not to look. She got me a postcard so, when I got down to the ground, I could study what I'd almost seen. She acted so kind. Now, with her in trouble in my own shack, I felt like I should rescue her. She was saying, 'I don't know what I expected you to talk like, Bobby. But not like this, not cheap, please.'

"Then he grinned, he howled like a dog. She laughed anyway. Huey and Duey went wild in their cage. Bobby held both his hands limp in front of him and panted like a regular hound. Then he asked her to help him with his zipper. She wouldn't. Well then Bobby got mad, said, 'It's my lunch hour. You ain't a customer *here*, lady. It's your husband's silver/gray Electra parked out back. You brought me here. You've got yourself into this. You been giving me the look for about a year. I been a gentleman so far. Nobody's forcing you. It ain't an accident you're here with me. But, hey, you can leave. Get out. Go on.'

"She sighed but stayed put—sitting there like in a waiting room. Not looking, kneecaps locked together—handbag propped on her knees. Her fingers clutched that bag like her whole life was in it. 'Give me that,' he snatched the purse and, swatting her hands away, opened it. He prodded around, pulled out a tube of lipstick, said, 'Annie, sit still.' She did. She seemed as upset as she was interested. I told myself, She *could* leave. I stayed in the dark. So much was happening in a half-inch stripe of sunshine. The lady didn't move. Bobby put red on her mouth—past her mouth—too much of it. She said, 'Please, Bobby.' ' "Sandy," ' he told her. 'You Annie, me Sandy Dog. Annie Girl, Sandy Boy. Sandy show Annie.' He made low growling sounds. 'Please,' she tried but her mouth was stretched from how he kept painting it. 'I'm not sure,' the lady said. 'I wanted to know you better, yes. But now I don't feel . . . sure.' 'You will, Annie Mae. Open your little Orphan shirt.' She didn't understand him. ' "Blouse" then, fancy pants, open you "blouse," lady.' She did it but so slow. 'Well,' she said. 'I don't know about you, Bobby. I really don't.' But she took her shirt off anyhow.

"My den mother was shivering in a bra, arms crossed over her. First his black hands pushed each arm down, studying her. Then Bobby pulled at his zipper so his whole chest showed. He put the lipstick in her hand and showed her how to draw circles on the tops of his—you know, on his nipples. Then he took the tube and made X's over the dots she'd drawn. They both looked down at his chest. I didn't understand. It seemed like a kind of target practice. Next he snapped her bra up over her collarbones and he lipsticked hers. Next he threw the tube across the room against my door—but, since his shoe hit, this didn't surprise me so much. Bobby howled like a real dog. My poor finches were just chirping and flying against their cage, excited by animal noises. She was shaking her head, 'You'd think a person such as myself . . . I'm having serious second thoughts here, Robert, really . . . I'm just not too convinced . . . that . . . that we . . .'

"Then Bobby got up and stood in front of her, back to me. His hairdo was long on top, the way boys wore theirs then. He lashed it side to side, kept his hands—knuckles down—on his hips. Mrs. . . . the lady must have been helping him with the zipper. I heard it slide. I only guessed what they were starting to do. I'd been told about all this. But, too, I'd been told, say about the Eiffel Tower (we called it the Eye-ful). I no more expected to have this happening on my brown couch than I thought the Eye-ful would come in and then the Entire State Building would come in and they'd hop onto one another and start . . . rubbing . . . girders, or something.

"I wondered how Bobby had forced the lady to. I felt like I should holler, 'Methodist Youth Choir!' I'd remind her who she really was around town. But I knew it'd be way worse for her—getting caught. I had never given this adult stuff much thought before. I sure did now. (Since, I haven't thought about too much else for long.) Bobby made worse doggy yips. He was a genius at acting like a dog. I watched him get down on all fours in front of the lady—he snouted clear up under her skirt, his whole noggin under cloth. Bobby made rooting and barking noises—pig then dog, dog and pig mixed. It was funny but too scary to laugh at.

"He asked her to call him Big Sandy. She did. 'Big Sandy,' she said. Bobby explained he had something to tell his Orphan gal but only in dog talk. 'What?' she asked. He said it—part-talking part-gargling, his mouth all up under her white legs. She hooked one thigh over his shoulder. One of her shoes fell off. The other—when her toes curled up then let loose—would snap, snap, snap.

"I watched her eyes roll back then focus. She seemed to squint clear into my hiding place. She acted drowsy then completely scared awake—like at a horror movie in the worst part—then she'd doze off, then go dead, perk up overly alive, then half-dead, then eyes all out like being electrocuted. It was something. She was leader of the whole Methodist Youth Choir. Her voice got bossy and husky, a leader's voice. She went, 'This is wrong, Bobby. You're so low, Robert. You are a sick dog, we get in deep trouble, Momma's Sandy. Hungry Sandy, thirsty Sandy. Oh—not that, not there. Oh Jesus Sandy God. You won't tell. How *can* we. I've never. What are we *do*ing in this shack? Whose shack? We're just too . . . It's not me here. I'm not *like* this.'

"He tore off her panties and threw them at the bird cage. (Later I found silky britches on top of the cage, Huey and Duey going ga-ga, thinking it was a pink cloud from heaven.) I watched grownups do everything fast then easy, back to front, speeding up. They slowed down and seemed to be feeling sorry—but I figured this was just to make it all last longer. I never heard such human noises. Not out of people free from jail or the state nuthouse. I mean, I'd heard boys make car sounds, 'Uh-dunn. Uh-dunn.' But this was like Noah's ark or every zoo—out of two white people's mouths. Both mouths were lipsticked ear to ear. They didn't look nasty but pink as babies. It was wrestling. They never got all the way undressed—I saw things hooking them. Was like watching grownups playing, making stuff up the way kids'll say, 'You be this and I'll be that.' They seemed friskier and younger, nicer. I didn't know how to join in. If I'd opened my door and smiled, they would have perished and *then* broke my neck. I didn't join in but, Dave? I sure was dying to.

"By the end, her pale Sunday suit had black grease hand-prints on the bottom and up around her neck and shoulders. Wet places stained both people where babies get stained. They'd turned halfway back into babies. They fell against each other, huffing like they'd forgot how grownups sit up straight. I mashed one hand over my mouth to keep from crying or panting, laughing out loud. The more they acted like slobbery babies, the older I felt, watching.

"First she sobbed. He laughed and then she laughed at how she'd cried. She said, 'What's come over me, Sandy?'

" 'Sandy has,' he stroked her neck. 'And Annie's all over Sandy dog,' he showed her. He blew across her forehead, cooling her off.

"She made him promise not to tell. He said he wouldn't snitch if she'd meet him and his best buddy someplace else. 'Oh no. No way,' she pulled on her blouse and buttoned it. 'That wasn't part of our agreement, Robert.'

" 'Agreement? I like that. My lawyers didn't exactly talk to your lawyers about no agreement. Show me your contract, Annie with an E,' then he dives off the couch and is up under her skirt again. You could see that he liked it even better than the service station. She laughed, she pressed cloth down over his whole working head. Her legs went straight. She could hear him snuffling down up under there. Then Bobby hollered, he yodeled right up into Mrs. . . . up into the lady.

"They sort of made up.

"After adults finally limped from sight and even after car doors slammed, I waited—sure they'd come back. I finally sneaked over and picked up pants off my birds' roof. What a mess my couch was! I sat right down on such wet spots as they'd each left. The room smelled like nothing I'd ever smelled before. Too, it smelled like everything I'd ever smelled before but all in one room. Birds still went crazy from the zoo sounds and such tussling. In my own quiet way, Dave, I was going pretty crazy too.

"After that I saw Bobby at the station—him winking at everything that moved, making wet, sly clicking sounds with his mouth. Whenever I bent over to put air into my new bike's tires, I'd look anywhere except Bobby. But he noticed how nervous I acted and he got to teasing me. He'd sneak up behind and put the toe of his loafer against the seat of my jeans. Lord, I jumped. He liked that. He was some tease, that Bobby, flashing his hair around like Lash LaRue. He'd crouch over my Schwinn. The air nozzle in my hand would sound like it was eating the tire. Bobby'd say, real low and slimy, 'How you like your air—regular or hi-test, slick?' He'd made certain remarks. 'Cat got your tongue, Too-Pretty-By-Half?' He didn't know what I'd seen but he could smell me remembering it. I dreaded him. Of course, Dave, Sunoco was not the only station in town. I worried Bobby might force me into my house and down onto the couch. I thought, 'But he couldn't do anything to *me*. I'm only eleven. Plus I'm a boy.' But next, I made pictures in my head—and I knew better. There were ways, I bet . . .

"I stayed clear of the cabin. I didn't know why. I'd been stuck not nine feet from everything they did. I was scared of getting trapped again. Too, I wanted to just live in that closet, drink tea, eat M&M's, praying they'd come back. Was about six days later I remembered: my birds were alone in the shack. They needed water and feeding every other day. I'd let them down. I worried about finches, out there by their lonesomes. But pretty soon it'd been over a week, then days, twelve. The longer you stay away from certain things, the harder it is—breaking through to do them right. I told myself, 'Huey and Duey are total goners now.' I kept clear of finding them, stiff on the bottom of the cage. I had dreams.

"I saw my den mother uptown running a church bake sale to help hungry Koreans. She was ordering everybody around like she usually did, charming enough to get away with it. I thought I'd feel super-ashamed to ever see her again. Instead I rushed right up. I chatted too much—too loud. I wanted to show that I forgave her. Of course, she didn't know I'd seen her do all such stuff with Bobby. She just kept looking at me, part-gloating part-fretting. She handed me a raisin cupcake, free. We gave each other a long look. Partly, we smiled.

"After two and half weeks, I knew my finches were way past dead. I didn't understand why I'd done it. I'd been too lazy or spooked to bike out and do my duty. The house felt different. *I* belonged in prison—Finch Murderer. Finally I pedaled my bike in that direction. One day, you have to. The shack looked smaller, the paint peeled worse. I found the key under three bricks, unlocked, held my breath. I didn't hear one sound from the front room, no hop, no cheep. Their cage hung from a hook on the wall and, to see into it, I had to stand up on my couch. Millet seed ground between my barefeet and the cushions. Birds had pecked clear through the back of their plastic food dish. It'd been shoved from the inside out, it'd skidded to a far corner of the room. My finches had slipped out their dish's slot. Birds were gone—flown up a chimney or through one pane of busted windowglass. Maybe they'd waited a week. When I didn't show up and treat them right, birds broke out. They were now in pinewoods nearby. I wondered if they'd known all along that they could leave—if they'd only stayed because I fed them and was okay company.

"I pictured Huey and Duey in high pines, blinking. I worried what dull local sparrows would do to such bright birds, hotshots from the Mall pet store. Still, I decided that being free sure beat my finches' chances of hanging around here, starving.

"Talk about relief. I started coughing from it, I don't know why. Then I sat down on the couch and cried. I felt something slippery underneath me. I wore my khaki shorts, nothing else, it was late August. I stood and studied what'd been written on couch cushions in lipstick, all caked. Words were hard to read on nappy brown cloth. You could barely make out 'I will do what Bobby wants. What Sandy wants. Whatever Sandy needs worst. Whatever Bobby needs most. So help me Dog.'

"I thought of her. I wanted to fight for her but I knew that—strong as the lady was—she did pretty much what she liked. She wouldn't be needing me. I sat again. I pulled my shorts down. Then I felt cool stripes get printed over my brown legs and white butt. Lipstick, parts of red words stuck onto my skin—'Wi' from 'Will'—the whole word 'help.' I stretched out full-length. My birds didn't hop from perch to perch or nibble at their birdie toy. Just me now. My place felt still as any church. Something had changed. I touched myself and—for the first time—with my bottom all sweetened by lipstick—I got real results.

"Was right after this, I traded in my model cars, swapped every single comic for one magazine. It showed two sailors and twin sisters in a hotel, doing stuff. During the five last pictures, a dark bellboy joined in. Was then that my collection really started. . . . The End, I guess. The rest is just being an adult."

Barker sat quiet. I finally asked what'd happened to his grandfather. How about Bobby and the den mother?

"In jail. My grandad died. 'Of a broken heart,' Mom said. Bobby moved. He never was one to stay anyplace too long. One day he didn't show up at Sunoco and that was it. Mrs. . . . the lady, she's still right here in Falls, still a real leader. Not two days back, I ran into her at the mall, collecting canned goods to end World Hunger. We had a nice chat. Her son's a lawyer in Marietta, Georgia, now. She looks about the same, really—I love the way she looks, always have. Now when we talk, I can tell she's partly being nice to me because I never left town or went to college—and she secretly thinks I'm not too swift. But since I kept *her* secret, I feel like we're even. I just smile back. I figure, whatever makes people kind to you is fine. She can see there's something extra going on but she can't name it. It just makes her grin and want to give me little things. It's one of the ten trillion ways you can love somebody. We do, love each other. I'm sure. Nobody ever knew about Bobby. She got away with it. More power to her.

"She still leads the Youth Choir. Last year they won the Southeast Chorus prize—young people's division. They give concerts all over. Her husband loves her. She said winning the prize was the most fulfilling moment of her life. I wondered. I guess everybody does some one wild thing now and then. They should. It's what you'll have to coast on when you're old. You know?" I nodded. He sat here, still.

"Probably not much of a story," Barker shrugged. "But, back then it was sure something, to see all that right off the bat, your first time out. I remember being so shocked to know that—men want to. *And* women. I'd figured that only one person at a time would need it—and they'd have to knock down the other person and force them to, every time. But when I saw that, no, everybody wants to do it, and how there are no rules in it—I couldn't look straight at a grownup for days. I'd see that my

Mom's slacks had zippers in them, I'd nearabout die. I walked around town, hands stuffed deep in my pockets. My head was hanging and I acted like I was in mourning for something. But, hey, I was really just waking up. . . . What got me onto all *that*? You about ready for movie-time, Dave? Boy, I haven't talked so much in months. It's what you get for asking, I guess." He laughed.

I thanked Barker for his story. I told him it made sense to me.

"Well, thanks for saying so anyhow."

He started fidgeting with the projector. I watched. I knew him better now. I felt so much for him. I wanted to save him. I couldn't breathe correctly.

"Here goes," he toasted his newest film then snapped on the large and somehow sinister antique machine.

The movie showed a girl at home reading this illustrated manual, hand in dress, getting herself animated. She made a phone call; you saw the actor answering and, even in a silent film, even given this flimsy premise, you had to find his acting absolutely awful. Barker informed me it was a Swedish movie; they usually started with the girl phoning. "Sometimes it's one guy she calls, sometimes about six. But always the telephones. I don't know why. It's like they just *got* phones over there and are still proud of them, or something." I laughed. What a nice funny thing to say. By now, even the gin and iced tea (with lemon and sugar) tasted like a great idea.

He sat upright beside me. The projector made its placid motorboat racket. Our couch seemed a kind of quilted raft. Movie light was mostly pink; ivy-filtered sun to a thin green. Across Barker's neutral white shirt, these tints carried on a silent contest. One room away, the Crockpot leaked a bit, hissing. Hallways smelled of stew meat, the need for maid service—back-issues, laundry in arears—one young man's agreeable sweetish curried musk. From a corner of my vision, I felt somewhat observed. Cats' eyes. To heck with caution. Let them look!

Barker kept elbows propped on knees, tensed, staring up at

the screen, jaw gone slack. In profile against windows' leaf-spotted light, he appeared honest, boyish, wide-open. He unbuttoned his top collar button.

I heard cars pass, my fellow Rotarians, algebra teachers from my school system. Nobody would understand us being here, beginning to maybe do a thing like this. Even if I went public, dedicated a whole Board of Education meeting to the topic—after three hours of intelligent confession, with charts and flannel boards and movie projections—I knew that when lights snapped back on, I'd look around from face to face, I'd see they all still sat wondering your most basic question:

Why, Dave, why?

I no longer noticed what was happening on-screen. Barker's face, lit by rosy movie light, kept changing. It moved me so. One minute: drowsy courtesy, next a sharp manly smile. I set my glass down on a Florida-shaped coaster. Now, slow, I reached toward the back of his neck—extra-nervous, sure—but that's part of it, you know? My arm wobbled, fear of being really belted, blackmailed, worse. I chose to touch his dark hair, cool as metal.

"Come *on*," he huffed forward, clear of my hand. He kept gazing at the film, not me. Barker grumbled, "The guy she phoned, he hasn't even got to her *house* yet, man."

I saw he had a system. I figured I could wait to understand it.

I felt he was my decent kid brother. Our folks had died; I would help him even more now. We'd rent industrial-strength vacuum cleaners. We'd purge this mansion of dinge; yank down tattered maroon draperies; let daylight in. I pictured us, stripped to the waists, painting every upstairs room off-white, our shoulders flecked with droplets, the hair on our chests flecked with droplets.

I'd drive Barker and his Wedgwood to a place where I'm known, "Old Mall Antiques." I bet we'd get fifteen to nineteen hundred bucks, easily. Barker would act amazed. In front of the dealer, he'd say, "For *that* junk?" and, laughing, I'd have to shush him. With my encouragement, he'd spend some of the bonus on clothes. We'd donate three generations of *National Geographics* to a nearby orphanage—if there are any orphanages anymore and nearby. I'd scour Barker's kitchen, defrost the fridge. Slowly, he would find new shape and meaning in his days. He'd start reading again—nonporn, recent worthy hardbacks. We'd discuss these.

He'd turn up at Little League games, sitting off to one side. Sensing my gratitude at having him high in the bleachers, understand we couldn't speak. But whenever one of my sons did something at bat or out in centerfield, (a pop-up, a bodyblock of a line drive) I could feel Barker nodding approval as he perched there alone; I'd turn just long enough to see a young bachelor mumbling to himself, shaking his head Yes, glad for my boys.

After office hours, once a week, I'd drive over, knock, then walk right in, calling, "Barker? Me."

No answer. Maybe he's napping in a big simple upstairs room, one startling with fresh paint. Six cats stand guard around his bed, two old Persians and their offspring, less Persian, thinner, spottier. Four of them pad over and rub against my pant cuffs; by now they know me.

I settle on the edge of a single bed, I look down at him. Barker's dark hair has fallen against the pillow like an open wing. Bare chested, the texture of his poreless skin looks finer than the sheets. Under a blue blanket, he sleeps, exhausted from all the cleaning, from renewing his library card, from the fatigue of clothes-shopping. I look hard at him; I hear rush-hour traffic crest then pass its peak. Light in here gets ruddier A vein in his neck beats like a clock, only liquid.

I'm balanced at the pillow-end of someone's bed. I'm watching somebody's decent sleep. If the law considers this so wicked, then why does it feel like my only innocent activity? Barker wakes. The sun is setting. His face does five things at once: sees somebody here, gets scared, recognizes me, grins a good blurry grin, says just, "You."

*   *   *

(They don't want a person to be tender. They could lock me up for everything I love about myself, for everything I love.)

Here on the couch, Barker shifted, "Look *now*, Dave. Uh-oh, she hears him knocking. See her hop right up? Okay, walking to the door. It's him, all right. He's dressed for winter. That's because they're in Sweden, right, Dave?"

I agreed, with feeling. Then I noted Barker taking the pen caddy from his pocket, he placed it on the table before him. Next, with an ancient kind of patience, Barker's torso twisted inches toward me; he lifted my hand, pulled my whole arm up and around and held it—by the wrist—hovering in air before his frontside as if waiting for some cue. Then Barker, clutching the tender back part of my hand, sighed, "Um-kay. *Now* they're really starting to." And he lowered my whole willing palm—down, down onto it.

I touched something fully familiar to me, yet wholly new.

He bucked with that first famous jolt of human contact after too long, too long alone without. His spine slackened but the head that'd shivered to one side, righted itself, eager to keep the film in sight. I heard six cats go racing down long hallways, then come thumping back, relaxed enough to play, with me—a stranger—in their house. Praise.

Barker's voice, all gulpy, "I think . . . this movie's going to be a real good one, Dave. Right up on my Ten Favorites' list. And, you know? . . ." He *almost* ceased looking at the screen, he *nearly* turned his eyes my way instead. (The compliment stirred me.) "You know? You're a regular fellow, Dave. I feel like I can trust you. You seem like . . . one real nice guy."

Through my breathing, I could hear him, breathing, losing breath, breathing, losing breath.

"Thank you, Barker. Coming from you, that means a lot

Every true pleasure is a secret.

ABOUT THE AUTHORS

GEORGE STAMBOLIAN is the author of *Marcel Proust and the Creative Encounter* and *Male Fantasies/Gay Realities: Interviews with Ten Men*, and the editor of *Twentieth Century French Fiction*, *Homosexualities and French Literature* (with Elaine Marks), and *Men On Men: Best New Gay Fiction*. His interviews, essays, and fiction have appeared in *Christopher Street*, *The New York Native*, and *The Advocate*. He is Professor of French and Interdisciplinary Studies at Wellesley College and lives in Boston, New York City, and Amagansett, Long Island.

ALLEN BARNETT studied writing at Columbia University and is the recipient of a New York Foundation for the Arts Fellowship. His fiction, reviews, and essays have appeared in *Christopher Street*, *The New York Native*, *Poets and Writers Magazine*, and *The Advocate*. Born in Michigan, he lives in New York City, where he is working on a collection of fiction.

TIM BARRUS has published two novels, *My Brother, My Lover* and *Anywhere, Anywhere*, a volume of poetry, *Streets of Vision*, and a collection of stories, *Hot Acts*. His fiction and essays have appeared in a variety of magazines and newspapers, including *Drummer*, *Mandate*, *Christopher Street*, *The Sentinel*, *The Dallas*

Voice, and *The Miami Herald*. He recently completed two new novels, *Genocide, The Anthology* and *Sonic Darkness*, which will be published within the coming year, and is working on another novel, *To Indigo Dust*, which will develop his story, "Life Sucks." He has received a Ford Foundation Grant and lives in San Francisco and Pentwater, Michigan.

CHRISTOPHER COE is the author of a novel, *I Look Divine*, and his fiction and reviews have been published in *Story Quarterly*, *Harper's*, and *The San Francisco Chronicle*. He is currently completing a second novel and a collection of stories, *Rich People Having Fun*. He lives in Paris and New York City.

CHRISTOPHER DAVIS lives and works in Manhattan, and is the author of two novels, *Joseph and the Old Man* and *Valley of the Shadow*.

MELVIN DIXON teaches literature and creative writing at Queens College and the Graduate Center, CUNY. He is the author of a volume of poetry, *Change of Territory*, and a work of criticism, *Ride Out the Wilderness: Geography and Identity in Afro-American Literature*. His poetry and fiction have appeared in *The Southern Review* and in *In the Life: A Black Gay Anthology*. Recipient of a National Endowment for the Arts Fellowship, he divides his time between Provincetown, Massachusetts, and New York City, where he is working on a novel and a second volume of poetry.

DAVID B. FEINBERG's first novel, *Eighty-sixed*, will be published in early 1989. His fiction has appeared in *Mandate, Torso*, and *The James White Review*. A graduate of the Massachusetts Institute of Technology and New York University, he lives in New York City and is completing a collection of short stories.

ANDERSON FERRELL comes from North Carolina and was a dancer before turning to writing. He is the author of a novel, *Where She Was*, and his fiction has appeared in such periodicals as *The Mississippi Review* and *The Quarterly*. He has received a grant from the National Endowment for the Arts and now lives in New York City, where he is working on a second novel.

GARY GLICKMAN was born in Morristown, New Jersey, and lives in New York City and East Hampton, Long Island. He is the author of a novel, *Years from Now*, and the recipient of a New York State Council for the Arts Grant. His fiction has appeared in *Vanity Fair, The Mississippi Review*, and *The East Hampton Star*. He is currently at work on a novel about East Hampton.

DAVID GROFF is an editor at Crown Publishers and a graduate of the University of Iowa's Writers' Workshop in poetry. His poems have appeared in *The American Poetry Review, The Georgia Review, The Iowa Review, The Missouri Review, The Mississippi Review, The North American Review, Prairie Schooner*, and *Poetry Northwest*. He was a finalist in The Walt Whitman Poetry Competition and The National Poetry Series. A resident of New York City, he is completing a volume of poems, "Personal Land," and working on a series of short stories.

ALLAN GURGANUS teaches creative writing at Sarah Lawrence College and is a graduate of the University of Iowa's Writers' Workshop. He is the author of a novella, *Good Help*, a recently completed story collection, *White People*, which will include his story, "Adult Art," and a novel, *Oldest Living Confederate Widow Tells All*, which will be published in 1989. His fiction has appeared in *The New Yorker, The Atlantic Monthly, Harper's, The Paris Review, New American Review, Blueboy*, and *Antaeus*. He has received two grants from the National Endowment for the Arts, grants from the Ingram-Merrill Foundation and Wallace Stegner, and has been awarded two PEN Syndicated Fiction Prizes. He lives in Chapel Hill, North Carolina, and New York City.

DAVID BRENDAN HOPES holds a Ph.D. from Syracuse University and lives in Asheville, North Carolina. He has published a volume of poetry, *The Glacier's Daughters*, a play, *Timothy Liberty*, and a work of nonfiction, *A Sense of the Morning*. His poetry and fiction have appeared in *The New Yorker*, *The James White Review*, *The Arts Journal*, *The Literary Review*, *The Nashville Review*, *The Carolina Quarterly*, and *The Kansas Review*. He has received the Juniper Prize, the Saxifrage Prize, and the Southern Playwrights Prize. He has just completed a novel, *An Age of Silver*, and is working on a nonfiction book, *Men's Lives*.

ALBERT INNAURATO's plays include "Passione," "Ulysses in Traction," "Earthworms," "Wisdom Amok," "Gemini," "The Transfiguration of Benno Blimpie," and "Coming of Age in Soho." The last three were recently published in *Best Plays of Albert Innaurato* and six others have been collected in *Bizarre Behavior*. He has been awarded grants from the Guggenheim Foundation, the Rockefeller Foundation, the National Endowment for the Arts, and has received a Dramaturgue Award. He has directed several plays and has written on opera and the theater for *The New York Times*. He lives in New York City, where he is completing a novel, *Fatty's Revenge*.

DAVID LEAVITT is the author of a collection of stories, *Family Dancing*, and a novel, *The Lost Language of Cranes*. His fiction and essays have appeared in *The New Yorker*, *Esquire*, *Harper's*, *Vanity Fair*, *The New York Times Book Review*, *Christopher Street*, *The Village Voice*, *The Boston Review*, and *The Washington Post*. He has received a National Endowment for the Arts Fellowship and was a finalist for the National Book Critics Circle Award and the PEN/Faulkner Prize. He has just completed a novel to be published in the winter of 1988–89, and is working on a second collection of stories. He lives in East Hampton, Long Island, and New York City.

RICHARD MCCANN lives in Washington, D.C., and teaches creative writing at American University. He is the author of a volume of poetry, *Dream of the Traveler*, and the editor of *Landscape and Distance: Contemporary Poets from Virginia* (with

Margaret Gibson). His fiction and poetry have appeared in *The Atlantic Monthly*, *Esquire*, *Shenandoah*, and *The Virginia Quarterly Review*. He holds a Ph.D. from the University of Iowa, has received fellowships from the MacDowell Colony and the Corporation of Yaddo, and was a Fulbright Fellow at Göteborg University, Sweden. "My Mother's Clothes" is part of his first novel, which will be published soon.

JAMES MCCOURT has published two works of fiction, *Mawrdew Czgowchwz* and *Kaye Wayfaring in Avenged*. His stories have appeared in *The New Yorker*, *Grand Street*, *The Paris Review*, and *Christopher Street*. He is the recipient of an Ingram-Merrill Award and is completing a sequel to *Mawrdew Czgowchwz* entitled *Time Out of Mind*. He lives in New York City and Dublin.

JOSEPH PINTAURO is the author of two novels, *Cold Hands* and *State of Grace*, several volumes of poetry, and a collection of plays, *The Short Plays of Joe Pintauro*. His other plays include, "Snow Orchid," "Cacciatori," and "Wild Blue," and he is company playwright with the Circle Repertory Theater in New York. His fiction and essays have appeared in *Christopher Street* and *Chicago Magazine*. He lives in New York City and Sag Harbor, where he is working on a nonfiction novel, *Aquamarine*, and completing another novel that will develop the characters in "Jungle Dove."

JAMES PURDY's many novels include *Don't Call Me by My Right Name*, *Dream Palace*, *Color of Darkness*, *Malcolm*, *The Nephew*, *Eustace Chisholm and the Works*, *In a Shallow Grave*, *Narrow Rooms*, *On Glory's Course*, and *In the Hollow of His Hand*. He is also the author of volumes of poetry, *The Running Sun* and *Will Arrest the Bird that has No Light*, collections of plays, *Children is All*, *Proud Flesh*, *The Berry-Picker and Scrap of Paper*, and a collection of stories, *The Candles of Your Eyes*. His work has appeared in *Esquire*, *The New York Review*, *Mademoiselle*, and *Harper's*. A fellow of the National Academy of Arts and Letters, he lives in Brooklyn, New York, and is completing a novel, *Garments the Living Wear*.

LEV RAPHAEL is Assistant Professor of American Thought and Language at Michigan State University and the co-author of a work on psychology, *The Dynamics of Power*. His fiction and essays have appeared in such periodicals as *The James White Review*, *Mirage*, *The Evergreen Chronicles*, *Redbook*, *Commentary*, *Shmate*, and *Reform Judaism*. He is the recipient of a Harvey Swados Fiction Prize and *Amelia Magazine*'s Reed Smith Award, and is at work on a novel, *Where Is That Country*, which will expand his story in this collection. He lives in Okemos, Michigan.

PUBLICATIONS OF INTEREST

Fiction on gay subjects has appeared in several mainstream periodicals in recent years. The following is a selective list of journals and magazines that *regularly* publish gay fiction. Contributors should inform themselves of the editorial policy of each publication before submitting manuscripts.

ADVOCATE MEN. P. O. Box 4371, Los Angeles, CA 90078

AMETHYST: A JOURNAL FOR LESBIANS AND GAY MEN. Southeastern Arts, Media and Education Project, Inc., P.O. Box 54719, Atlanta, GA 30308

BGM (black gay men). The Blacklight Press, P.O. Box 9391, Washington, DC 20005

BLACK/OUT. National Coalition of Black Gays, P.O. Box 2490, Washington, DC 20013

CHRISTOPHER STREET. P.O. Box 1475, Church Street Station, New York, NY 10008

THE EVERGREEN CHRONICLES: A JOURNAL OF GAY AND LESBIAN WRITERS. P.O. Box 6260, Minnehaha Station, Minneapolis, MN 55406

FAG RAG. P.O. Box 331, Kenmore Station, Boston, MA 02215

THE JAMES WHITE REVIEW: A GAY MEN'S LITERARY QUARTERLY. P.O. Box 3356, Traffic Station, Minneapolis, MN 55403

MANDATE. Mavety Media Group, 462 Broadway, 4th floor, New York, NY 10013

MIRAGE. 1987 California Street #202, San Francisco, CA 94109

OTHER COUNTRIES (black gay men). P.O. Box 21176, Midtown Station, New York, NY 10129

OUT/LOOK: NATIONAL LESBIAN AND GAY QUARTERLY. P.O. Box 146430, San Francisco, CA 94114-6430

RFD: A COUNTRY JOURNAL FOR GAY MEN EVERYWHERE. Route 1, Box 127E, Bakersville, NC 28705

TORSO. Mavety Media Group, 462 Broadway, 4th floor, New York, NY 10013